W9-AZW-543

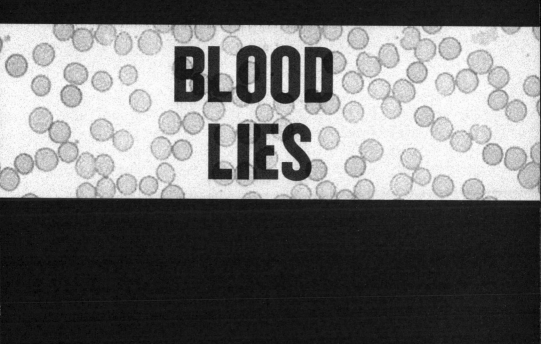

BLOOD
LIES

FORGE BOOKS BY DANIEL KALLA

Blood Lies
Pandemic
Rage Therapy
Resistance

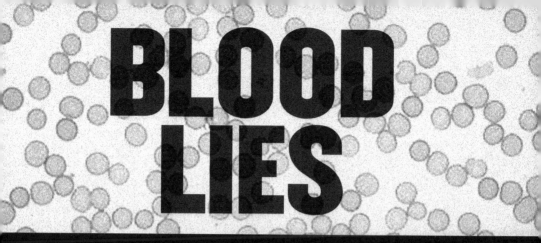

BLOOD LIES

DANIEL KALLA

A TOM DOHERTY ASSOCIATES BOOK

NEW YORK

BLOOD LIES

Copyright © 2007 by Daniel Kalla

A Forge Book
Published by Tom Doherty Associates, LLC
175 Fifth Avenue
New York, NY 10010

www.tor-forge.com

Forge® is a registered trademark of Tom Doherty Associates, LLC.

Library of Congress Cataloging-in-Publication Data

Kalla, Daniel.
    Blood lies / Daniel Kalla.—1st hardcover ed.
        p.   cm.
    "A Tom Doherty Associates book."
    ISBN-13: 978-0-7653-1832-9
    ISBN-10: 0-7653-1832-6
    1. Physicians—Fiction.   2. Twins—Fiction.   3. Seattle (Wash.)—Fiction.
    I. Title.

    PR9199.4.K34B56 2007
    813'.6—dc22

                                                    2007004340

First Edition: June 2007

Printed in the United States of America

0 9 8 7 6 5 4 3 2 1

To my brothers,
Tim and Tony

ACKNOWLEDGMENTS

As always, I am deeply indebted to the many friends and family members who encourage, support, and generally put up with my compulsion to write. I can't list everyone, but I have to mention a select few who have gone above and beyond the call, including Duncan Miller, Scott Lamont, Dave Allard, Brooke Wade, Jeff Petter, Nancy Stairs, Janine Mutch, Lisa and Rob King, Dee Dee and Kirk Hollohan, Beth Allard, Dal Schindell, Geoff Lyster, Theresa and Alec Walton, and Alisa Weyman.

I want to heap tons of credit on the wonderful Kit Schindell, a peerless freelance editor who reviews each manuscript chapter by chapter and draft by draft and guarantees that I get the most out of the story. Thanks, Kit.

I want to thank my agent, Henry Morrison, for his wisdom, advice, and long-term perspective. I am so grateful and proud to have found a home at Tor-Forge. Tom Doherty and Linda Quinton are publishers who bring a warm personal element to the business. Thanks, as well, to Patty Garcia, John Morrone, Elena Stokes, and Paul Stevens.

And, of course, I cannot praise enough my awesome editor and friend, Natalia Aponte, for her inspiration and collaboration. You're the tops, Natalia!

I would be nowhere without the support of my family. I want to acknowledge Mom and Dad, my brothers and their wives, my nieces, and my in-laws for their love and encouragement. And my wife, Cheryl, and my daughters, Ashley and Chelsea, constantly remind me of how complete my life is.

Finally, I want to thank you, the readers, who have taken a chance on my books and helped me to realize a dream.

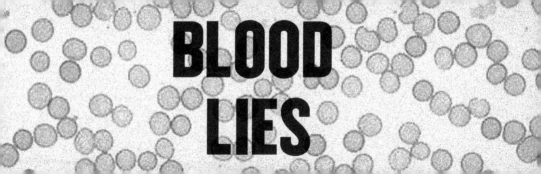

CHAPTER

1

The siren choked off in mid-wail. Within seconds, the flashing red light swept through the frosted glass of the ER's sliding door like a disco ball on overdrive.

I heaved a self-pitying sigh. Ten minutes before the end of a long night shift, I'd counted on an uneventful and punctual exit. Any chance for either vanished when the ambulance stretcher and two paramedics burst through the main Emergency Room doors.

"Which room?" the tall scraggy paramedic yelled as they careened past the triage desk.

"Trauma Two," the triage nurse called back.

I ran alongside the paramedics, but our pace wasn't fast enough to outrun the acrid smells of urine and vomit wafting up from the stretcher. A woman of indeterminate age lay on her side, twitching and thrashing. Without the restraining hand of the female paramedic she might have bucked off the stretcher. Legs and arms jerked in violent rhythm. Her chin slammed into her chest. A mess of long brown hair covered her face. Her T-shirt was spattered with vomit. A chain of drool connected the corner of her mouth to the sheets. An image of Linda Blair from *The Exorcist* flashed in my mind.

"What's the story?" I asked the baby-faced female paramedic running beside me.

"Seizing when we got to her. Found down at Cloud Nine." She

glanced at me, deciding I was old enough to require clarification. "It's an after-hours club."

"Thanks," I grunted. "What's she got on board?"

"Her sister says she dropped two tabs of Ecstasy about an hour before we got to her. First-time user. Otherwise the kid is healthy."

"Kid?"

"Fourteen years." She wiped her flushed brow with a palm. "Name's Lara Maxwell."

"How long has she been seizing?"

"Twenty minutes, give or take."

Way too long. Within half an hour of a continuous seizure, or status epilepticus, irreversible brain damage can occur. "What have you given her?" I asked.

"Nothing. We scooped and ran. Impossible to get an IV in her in the back of our rig." She flailed her own arms, as if the wildly twitching patient wasn't explanation enough.

We wheeled into Trauma Two, one of St. Jude's three identical resuscitation rooms. Nothing architecturally unique about this or any resuscitation bay I've ever seen; all are big bland rooms filled with medical supplies, lights, X-ray viewing boxes, and, at times like these, people. The place swarmed with them. Some moved with purpose, others—the usual array of wide-eyed students and ER lookie-loos (staff who find any excuse to turn up whenever something exciting rolls in)—just milled about.

Swaddling her in the ambulance stretcher's sheet, the two paramedics swung the patient over to the room's stretcher. Lara Maxwell was oblivious to her new surroundings; her arms and legs never missed a beat of their syncopated contraction.

Anne Bailey, arguably the poster girl for hardened frumpy ER nurses the world over, was the nurse in charge. She had no time for the bustling crowd. "If you don't serve a purpose, get out!" Anne shouted and, on cue, the room thinned. She turned to the other nurses. "Lucy, two IVs. Jan, get an oral airway into her. Tommy, you record, okay? And where are my vital signs?" Anne turned to me, her lower jaw working side to side as if chewing a gob-stopper. "What meds do you want us to give, Ben?" Despite her businesslike tone, her eyes clouded over with urgency.

Relieved as I was to see Anne in charge, the rare show of concern on her face concerned me. "Lorazepam 4 mg IV push, now," I said, referring to the Valium-like drug we use for seizures. "Full lab panel including calcium, magnesium, and phosphate. ECG. Chest X-ray. Blood gas. Urine drug screen ASAP, and—"

The nurse cut in from bedside. "Pulse is 140, pressure 260 on 140, respiratory rate of 28, and temperature of 38.4." There was a pause as she fiddled with the oxygen saturation probe that kept slipping off Lara's jerking finger. "Oxygen saturation is sitting at 88 percent."

Not a normal vital sign in the bunch. "Sugar?" I asked.

"Glucometer was normal at the scene," the scrawny paramedic piped up.

Damn! Gone was the most rectifiable cause for a seizure: low blood sugar.

I edged closer to my patient. The mingled odors of vomit and urine assaulted me, forcing me to breathe through my mouth. Lara's hair had fallen back from her face, and I could see beyond the strands of drool and blood. The flickering eyelids and gnashing jaw belonged to the face of a child, someone who had no business being near after-hours clubs and their inevitable cache of designer drugs. I felt familiar stirrings. *Fucking junk!* I wanted to shout.

I glanced at the clock. Five minutes since arrival, twenty-five minutes since onset, and the seizure showed no sign of lessening. The drool at her mouth had begun to bubble, and became a rich froth like an exploding soda pop can. As I reached for my stethoscope, my worry meter crept higher.

"Another four of lorazepam. And hang a Dilantin drip. Run in a gram over fifteen minutes," I said, calling for the heavy artillery of anti-seizure drugs. Pulling the stethoscope off my shoulders, I leaned over Lara's jerking form and raced through a head-to-toe physical exam. Filled with fluid, her lungs were all gurgles and wheezes. A bluish tinge enveloped her fingers and lips. I glanced at the monitor. Her oxygen saturation had dipped into the seventies—respiratory failure territory—and her blood pressure had risen even higher. "We have to stop this seizure. *Now!*" That meant medically paralyzing the young girl. I recited the drugs and sequence I wanted them given.

"Dr. Dafoe, you better look at this. . . ." Jan waved an ECG printout at me like it was a flag.

I studied the twelve squiggly lines, stunned by their implication. "A heart attack? *At fourteen*? She must have cocaine on board, too." I looked to the respiratory technician. "Everything ready?"

She nodded, and pointed shakily to the tray beside me.

"Okay, Anne, give her 100 of sux."

Anne stuck a syringe into one of the four IV lines leading into Lara's arms. She pushed on the plunger. Within seconds of administering the succinylcholine—a fast-acting drug that paralyzes muscles and renders patients into rag dolls—the twitching began to subside. Soon Lara lay still on the bed. As expected, she stopped breathing. What I didn't foresee (but should have) was the fountain of foam spewing from her mouth, as her lungs passively expelled their fluid contents.

I grabbed for the scythe-shaped laryngoscope. The knuckles of my left hand ached, and I glanced down at the source: the healing jagged gash from my bike chain that ran across my knuckles like a jailhouse tattoo. Ignoring the pain, I clicked open the laryngoscope's blade and eased it into Lara's mouth, pushing her tongue out of the way. To pass the endotracheal tube into her windpipe, I needed to see her vocal cords, but I couldn't visualize anything through the froth. I stuck a suction catheter in her mouth but it was as hopeless as trying to vacuum up water from a burst and still-spewing pipe. The monitor's alarm screamed, warning me what I already knew: Lara's oxygen level was dangerously low.

"Bag her!" I said to the respiratory technician who fumbled to cover Lara's mouth with the clear face mask and pump oxygen in with a balloon-shaped Ambu-Bag.

I turned to Anne. "I have to do this retrograde."

Anne's eyes betrayed her skepticism as she reached for the retrograde intubation kit. Her doubt was well founded, too. It was a technically challenging procedure at the best of times, and I was firmly perched on the "wing and a prayer" side of the statistical success curve.

I took a long deep breath and willed my hands to steady. I reached for the open tray Anne held out for me. Setting it on the bedside, I scoured through it until I found the syringe with the long ominous attached needle. I slid an index finger along Lara's soft damp neck until I felt it dip into the groove of her cricothyroid membrane.

The alarm throbbed in my ears.

With a slight tremor, I aimed the needle, directing it slightly upward for the skin over the cricothyroid membrane. I held my own breath as the needle pierced the skin. I felt a pop as I penetrated Lara's windpipe. Suddenly the tension on the syringe's plunger gave way, and air whooshed into its hub. I steadied the syringe and uncoupled it from the needle.

"Ben, her oxygen saturation is critical," Anne said calmly over the shrieking alarm.

"Noted," I grunted, as I reached for the soft metal guide-wire that looked like a loose coil of silver string. Steadying my hand, I threaded the guide-wire through the needle. "Stop bagging her," I said, needing a clearer view of her mouth.

Hesitantly, the respiratory tech pulled the mask off Lara's blue face.

I kept advancing the guide-wire through the needle until a glint of metal appeared through the froth of Lara's mouth. Then more wire poked out. My hand shot out to grab it. I nodded to Anne, and she handed me the clear endotracheal tube. I snaked the wire through the length of the tube. Then, using the wire as a guide, I threaded the tube into Lara's windpipe. Sighing with relief, I felt the welcome resistance of the cartilaginous tracheal rings as the tube bumped down the rest of her windpipe. The moment its tip reached her lungs, frothy white sputum erupted out of its end.

I grabbed the Ambu-Bag, attached it to the tube, and squeezed the balloon-like pump, meeting fierce resistance. My forearms ached as I fought to squeeze breath after breath of oxygen into Lara's waterlogged lungs. For a while, the abysmal oxygen reading held constant on the monitor, but slowly, almost reluctantly, it began to climb as pinkness crept back into her blue complexion. I passed the bag over to the respiratory tech, who pumped it feverishly. Lara's color steadily improved. Even the monitor took a much-needed break from its relentless screaming.

Tasting the sweat drip into my mouth, I wiped my brow and turned to Anne. "What's a child doing with this crap in her blood?" Though, of course, I knew as well as anybody.

"She were my daughter? I'd kill her soon as she gets out of the ICU." Anne's lips cracked slightly at the corners in what passed for her version of a smile. She nodded once at me. High praise indeed, coming from Anne.

At nine A.M., three hours past the scheduled end of my shift, I still sat charting in Trauma Room Two. Though she awaited an ICU bed, Lara Maxwell was out of the woods. Her lungs had dried out, and the heart damage appeared to have been reversed after the amphetamines and cocaine (their presence confirmed on the lab tests) had cleared from her system.

The nurse had stepped out to restock the carts, leaving me alone in the room with Lara. She lay peacefully on her back. Wires, IV lines, and tubes ran to and from her, but medical gadgetry aside, she now looked like a typical fourteen-year-old. Tall and gangly with budding breasts and a few scattered pimples, she teetered at that awkward stage between childhood and adulthood. But her high cheekbones and full lips guaranteed she was going to mature into a beauty, providing she survived adolescence.

As I documented Lara's rocky drug-induced ride along the brink of death, my frustration welled. Sleep deprived and adrenaline tanks empty, my temper control (shaky at the best of times) failed me. "Fourteen years old!" I snapped at the still-comatose teen. "What the hell were you doing at a rave, Lara?"

I dropped my pen and walked to her bedside. I glanced from the whirring, microwave-sized ventilator (that pumped oxygen in and out of her lungs) back to Lara. Staring at her naïve face, I suppressed the urge to shake her. "This the high you were looking for?" My voice rose. *"God damn it, Lara, what were you doing there?!?"*

I turned at the sound of the glass door sliding behind me. Anne stood at the doorway. She eyed me with an expression that questioned my sanity. Her left arm supported a waiflike girl, whose hair was dyed unnaturally red and whose legs swayed precariously.

"Lara?" The girl choked out the word before her voice dissolved into sobs. She scrambled to the opposite side of the bed, nearly yanking out two IVs and toppling the ventilator in the process. She grabbed Lara's flaccid hand and squeezed it with both of hers.

"Dr. Dafoe, this is Isabelle," Anne said. "Lara's older sister."

Isabelle gaped at me. With tears and mascara streaming down her cheeks, she could have passed for an underage drag queen. "Doctor . . . ," her voice wavered. "Will my sister be all right?"

I ignored her question. "You're the one who took Lara to that club?"

"It wasn't like that," she sobbed. "Lara wanted to come. I had no idea that—"

"How old are you?"

"Eighteen, but—"

"Not even legal yourself! What possessed you to take your little sister there?"

Isabelle held up her hands helplessly. "She kept pushing. She was desperate to get to a rave. If I went with her, I thought it would be safer . . ." She dissolved into tears again.

"Safer? *Safer?!?* She's your own flesh and blood. She just about died because of you. Your own sister!"

Isabelle's head dropped. She buried her face in her sister's gown. "I am so sorry . . ." Her muffled whimper was barely audible.

"Siblings look out for each other, don't they?" I said, but I wasn't talking about Isabelle or Lara anymore. I was remembering my own brother.

Anne had heard enough. She folded her arms over her chest and took two steps into the room. "You've made your point, Doctor."

I looked from Anne to Isabelle and then nodded slowly. When I spoke again, my voice was calm. "Lara is going to pull through, Isabelle. But it will take time."

Isabelle looked up at me and sniffed her relief.

"Where are your mom and dad?" I asked.

"They're in New York for the week." She dropped her head in her sister's gown again, and added in a hush, "They left me in charge . . . I was supposed to look after Lara."

I didn't comment. My fury had dissipated. Replaced by guilt. *Who am I, of all people, to criticize anyone for endangering their sibling?*

I reached across the bed and laid a hand on Isabelle's vibrating shoulder.

Tina, the young ditsy unit clerk, appeared behind Anne. "Phone call, Dr. D.," she chirped.

"I'm tied up, Tina," I said. "Can you take a message?"

"It's a policewoman. Made it sound kinda urgent."

Anne spoke up. "You go. I'll cover."

I walked over to the central nursing station. As soon as I picked up the receiver, Sergeant Helen Riddell boomed: "Benjamin! Hope I didn't catch you at a bad time? You weren't in the middle of pulling Christmas lights or a model airplane out of someone's rear end?" She laughed heartily. "People sit on the darnedest things, huh?"

"No," I sighed. "Just finished screaming at a comatose girl."

"A coma, huh? Well, I'm sure she had it coming." She chuckled again. "Doctors. You're all a mystery to me."

"What's up, Helen?"

"Oh, yeah," she said, as if she'd forgotten the purpose of her call. "We're at a murder scene. Wanted your help."

"A poisoning?"

"Who said anything about poisons?

"Why else would you call me?" As the toxicology consultant to the Seattle Police Department, I took calls only on poisonings.

"You know at least one of the victims."

"What?"

"In the bedroom, where we found both bodies, there's a photo of the female victim standing with an arm around you and your brother."

I was overcome by a sense of déjà vu. My mind flashed to Helen's call of two years earlier. The one regarding my twin brother, Aaron. I sat down in the chair by the desk. "Who?" I asked, but of course I already knew.

"Male victim not yet identified. His wallet is missing. But the woman? We're pretty sure her name is Emily Jane Kenmore."

I was quiet for a long time, and Helen respected my silence. I cleared my throat. "Why do you need me there?"

"For one, to confirm the woman's ID. Second, you might know our John Doe. And finally, to give us your medical opinion."

"My opinion?" I said in a monotone. "You'll get far more from the CSI team and the forensic pathologist."

"Ever since that hit TV series, those CSI guys are insufferable." Helen chuckled. "Besides, maybe you can add something. You see a lot of stabbings, don't you?"

"One or two."

"Can you drop by here on your way home? The address is—"

"I know the address."

After all, I had once lived there, too.

CHAPTER

2

Barring an alien abduction, I must have driven to Emily's condo myself. But after the shock of Helen's phone call and my busy night shift at the ER, I have no recollection of the trip. When I emerged from the fog, I stood at the doorstep of apartment 302, on the third and top floor of the Tudor-style building. The door was wide open. People in blue Windbreakers with the letters CSI emblazoned on the back bustled past while I stood motionless.

Two years earlier, I'd hurtled over yellow crime-scene tape in my rush to get to the trunk of the battered and burned BMW where my brother had lain. Even though his body had been moved to whereabouts unknown, the huge puddles of congealed blood left little doubt that he was dead. And that bloody trunk had opened a wound that had yet to heal.

This time, I felt no urgency. I stood for what seemed like ages at Emily's door, ostensibly to compose myself, but secretly knowing that my inertia was the only thing preventing what I was about to see from becoming my unpleasant reality. However, when the tall bulk of Helen Riddell appeared on the other side of the threshold, I knew the game was up. At nearly six feet and pushing two hundred pounds, Helen was tough to miss. Dressed in a loud green pantsuit, she greeted me with her trademark effusive smile that exposed the prominent gap between her two front teeth. "Hey, Benjamin, thanks for coming down." She held her big arms apart, as if she might hug me, but stopped a few feet short.

I nodded. "Hi, Helen."

"One of the CSI boys told me there was a guy hanging out by the door. He called you a statue." She laughed. "And unless my gay-dar is way out of whack, I don't think he meant it in a homoerotic way, neither."

I forced a smile and crossed the doorstep to join Helen in the spacious but dark living room.

Glancing around, I fought to hold back the flood of memories associated with the sight of Emily's framed black-and-white sketches and photos. But the scent of her Calvin Klein perfume and the wax of candles (which she burned to mask the smell of her cigarettes) broke past the mental barrier. An image of Emily—wrapped in nothing but a sheet as she stared down at me with that vaguely amused post-orgasmic glow—still burned in my brain.

Helen raised an eyebrow. "You spent some time here, huh?"

I nodded. She didn't press me for the details, and I didn't offer any.

"Think you'll be okay to see the bodies?" Helen chewed her lower lip and her gray eyes were drained of their usual jocularity. "Ought to warn you, Ben, it's not pretty."

I shrugged and began to move in the direction of the noise. After a couple of steps, Helen tugged at my shoulder. "You'll need these *dahling* accessories." She dangled a pair of latex gloves and plastic foot covers. As I was slipping into them, Helen asked, "Ben, you ever been to a murder scene before?"

I shook my head. I'd been a consultant for Helen and the Seattle Police Department for more than five years, working one or two cases a year and befriending Helen in the process. But despite all the poisonings I'd consulted on, I'd attended only a handful of the autopsies. There were no crime scenes to speak of. And the trunk of Aaron's car wasn't technically a murder scene without a body.

"Couple of pointers," Helen said. "Don't touch anything without checking with me. And don't step over the chalk lines or on any of the . . . you know . . . bloody spots. Believe me, you never met anyone as territorial as the CSI guys." She smiled. "They're worse than male wolves with very full bladders."

Helen's attempt to lighten the mood was wasted on me. My edginess spiraled with each step down the hallway.

We hadn't even passed the guest bedroom when I caught sight of the pair of shoes jutting out the doorway of Emily's bedroom. "That's our John Doe." Helen nodded at the legs in jeans and sneakers.

I took a breath and continued. Another few steps, and the bedroom opened up for me in graphic detail. In his late twenties, tall and muscular, the John Doe lay draped across the doorway. He stared wide-eyed at the ceiling, both blood-drenched hands clasping his neck, and his sculpted features cast in an expression of utter disbelief. The front of his pale blue shirt had blackened as had the beige carpet surrounding him. There were no visible slash marks on his face or chest, so I assumed all the blood came from his neck. And judging by the sheer volume of it, I determined that one or both of his carotid arteries must have been severed.

"Know him?" Helen asked.

"No." And I didn't. Not even his name. But I neglected to mention I'd once met him.

I scanned the rest of the bedroom. Complete shambles. A bomb could have done less damage. The bedcovers were shredded and strewn across the room. Emily's oak bureau, her prized family heirloom, was toppled on its side, the drawers scattered. Both nightstands were upended. The wall mirror lay facedown on the floor, bits of glinting glass encircling it like spectators at a car crash. Only one charcoal sketch managed to cling askew to the wall; the rest of the frames scattered the floor. But everything paled compared to the walls. Someone had unleashed a sprinkler of blood on them. Streaks and blotches spattered every surface. It dripped down from the upended furniture and soaked the carpet beneath. Even the ceiling was sprayed.

I still didn't see Emily.

Helen directed her gaze to the far side of the king-sized sleigh bed. Following her eyes, I sidestepped John Doe's sprawled form and walked along the foot of the bed.

I stopped cold on the other side. Nothing I'd seen so far prepared me for the sight of Emily Kenmore.

My legs weakened. The room whirled. I almost gagged. I'd never been as close to seeing hell.

I felt Helen's arm steady my right elbow. "C'mon, Ben. Let's get out of here."

I shook my head and gently pulled her hand away. "I'm okay," I lied, forcing my eyes to survey the carnage.

In a tank top and hip-hugger jeans, Emily sat on the floor propped against the side of the bed, her blue eyes staring at the radiator ahead. She was pale to the point of gray. Both arms hung limply at her side. A huge gash ran across her neck, exposing a flash of a bone and trachea through its ragged edges. But unlike the male victim, the wound wasn't isolated. She was slashed from head to toe. Her face had multiple nicks and lacerations. Her shirt was hacked in several places. I could see at least three stab wounds on her exposed abdomen; the one above her belly button was so long and deep that a loop of small intestine poked through it. Blood obscured the rose tattoo that I knew blossomed below her belly button.

I closed my eyes and breathed slowly. When I opened them, someone else had joined us. "Whoa, Ben, you don't look so hot. Need a seat?" he asked.

I turned to see Helen's partner, Detective Richard Sutcliffe. Dressed in a silky gray Italian sports coat with a shiny V-neck shirt and expensive-looking loafers, Rick's handsome smile, as always, smacked of insincerity. "I didn't think anything would faze a guy who works the ER."

Annoyance was just the tonic I needed. "We don't see that many murder victims in the ER," I said.

"Guess not." His smile didn't waver. "But lots of attempted murders. Not to mention the car smashups and all that."

I should have let it go, but walking away at the right time was never my strong suit. "Yeah, but most of my trauma patients haven't been mutilated and left for dead for twelve hours."

Rick shrugged. "The CSI boys figure closer to fourteen."

"Plus, I usually don't know the victim."

Unruffled, his smile grew wider. "Of course." He raised his left hand, which held a blood-spattered framed photo.

The snapshot captured happier days for all three of us. Emily, gorgeous in a red summer dress, held up a fruity drink and toasted the camera. Aaron and I each had an arm around her while we hoisted umbrella-clad cocktails of our own. We'd taken the carefree Hawaiian trip seven years earlier, but were it not for the photo, I would've questioned my presence; it seemed like one of those vague early-childhood memories that might have been just a remembered dream.

"That you on the right?" Rick pointed at Aaron.

My finger tapped the other side of the photo. "I'm the one with the beard."

"Identical twins! That must happen a lot." He paused. "I mean before your brother disappeared."

"You mean, before he died," I said.

"Yeah," Rick said. "Unofficially."

A CSI guy squeezed around Helen to get to the corner of the room, but not before flashing us an annoyed frown.

"Don't go getting your Windbreaker twisted in a knot. We're leaving soon," Helen said to him. Then she turned to me. "You seen enough?"

More than enough, but I found it hard to take my eyes off Emily. Despite the carnage, her eyes hadn't lost their enigmatic distant charm. As I turned and walked away from her for the last time, I felt a pang of loneliness.

I followed Helen and Rick into the living room. Standing by the door, we formed a triangle. Rick still held the holiday snapshot in his hand, but Helen began the interrogation. "Okay if we ask you about Emily?"

I nodded.

"How did you know her?"

"We met at a party about ten years back. Hit it off right away."

"Serious?" Helen asked.

"At times."

She arched an eyebrow.

"We were on-again, off-again for a few years," I said. "It ended for good about five years ago."

"On friendly terms?" Rick twirled the photo with a gloved hand.

I shrugged. "Civil enough."

Helen nodded. "Have you seen her much since?"

"Intermittently. Sometimes we'd go months without seeing each other." I stopped to swallow. "Other times we'd have more contact."

"She never married, right?" Rick asked.

I shook my head.

"Shacked up?"

I shrugged again. "Don't think so."

"Only ladies' stuff in the closets and bathroom." Helen thumbed back toward the bedroom. "You don't know if she was involved with our poor John Doe back there?"

"Not that I know of. But Emily always had a boyfriend on the go. Sometimes more than one." I caught a sly glance from Rick, but he didn't comment. "Emily and I ran with very different crowds. . . ."

"Meaning?" Helen encouraged me with her eyebrow again.

"Emily was an addict." I almost leaned back against the door, but thought better of it when I noticed one of the CSI guys eyeing me. "When I first met Emily, she drank too much and dabbled in coke. But she managed to sober up and stay dry for a few years." I rubbed my eyes, suddenly overwhelmed with fatigue from shock and my overnight ER shift. "Then she got more heavily into the drugs . . ."

Helen nodded empathetically. "The slippery slope, huh?"

"Yeah, Emily bounced from one crutch to another: coke, crystal meth, designer drugs . . . Didn't seem to matter." I looked down at the booties still covering my running shoes. "She tried. Christ, she tried! Detox, rehab, AA, you name it. She would stay clean for a month or two, but inevitably, she'd slip. The pull was too strong."

"What did Emily do for work?"

"She's—she was—an MBA. She worked in hotel management for a while. Then commercial real estate. Not lately, though. I'm not sure if she's even had steady work in the last year or two."

Helen's gaze circled the living room before resting back on me. She chewed her bottom lip again. "Ben, this place looks like it would cost something to maintain. And the drugs . . ."

"Emily always managed to find money," I said. "Her parents are well off. And I never knew her to date anyone without means, you know?"

Both Helen and Rick looked at me expectantly.

"Yeah, myself included."

"She was gorgeous, huh?" Helen squinted and her teeth dug into her lower lip to the point where I thought I might see blood. "A pretty woman supporting a hefty drug habit . . ."

"Are you suggesting Emily was a hooker?" I asked.

"Not a street worker," she said. "But high end. An escort."

I stared at her, unwilling to dignify her question with an answer, even though I knew it was reasonable to speculate.

"Okay. Is it possible she dabbled in the drug trade?"

"Anything's possible," I said. "But hooking, trafficking . . . I just can't picture it."

"When did you last see her, Ben?"

"A week ago."

"How was she?" Helen asked.

"Clean," I said. "Said she'd been off everything for over a month. This time, her words didn't ring as hollow to me as usual. Not that I ever trusted her on that front, but I kind of hoped this time . . ."

Helen ran a hand through her wild black curls. "She didn't mention any kind of trouble? Anyone she was concerned about?"

"She was as happy as I'd seen her in a long time. Like the old Emily . . . free of drugs."

Rick, who had stood suspiciously silent for the last few minutes, grinned again. "Never married or anything, right?"

My irritation rose again, but now it was accompanied by slight foreboding. "Why do you keep asking?"

Rather than answer, he turned and walked to the coffee table. Just before he reached it, I understood the reason for his smirk. He picked up a big glossy coffee-table book—a collection of baby names, complete with rundowns on their cultural derivations and cutesy baby photos. Up to that moment, I'd forgotten about the book.

Rick brought it over to where we stood. Wordlessly, he flipped it open. Inside the cover, the scrawled inscription read:

To my best friends, Emily and Benjamin,
    Congratulations on the engagement! Wishing you the happiest of lives together. Looking forward to all those beautiful nieces and nephews.
    Much love,
    Aaron

CHAPTER

3

I stumbled out of Emily's apartment in a state beyond exhaustion. I had no idea whether Helen or Rick had bought my explanation for glossing over my engagement to Emily. Nor did I care.

I needed a fix. Anything to settle my inner tumult. As soon as I parked the car, I changed and grabbed my helmet. Fifteen minutes later, I was pushing my mountain bike as hard as I could through the trails. Every stump, bump, and jump was a welcome distraction. The branch that nearly decapitated me brought the first smile to my face in hours. A mental train wreck, I should've known better than to hop on a mountain bike. But I needed the rush. No matter how steep or treacherous the hill, I couldn't ride fast enough.

Nothing worked. I couldn't shed the vision of Emily sitting lifeless against the same bed where we used to make love. And that damn engagement gift from my brother! I never even liked the book. I always associated it with the beginning of the end for Emily and me.

Six years earlier, twenty-eight years old and fresh out of ER residency, I was determined to knock down my debt load. I vacuumed up shifts no one else wanted, which meant I wound up working a lot of weekends and nights. I'd just finished one such brutal Friday-evening shift at St. Jude's. (An inner city hospital, St. Jude's is the Ellis Island of Seattle—welcoming, with varying degrees of enthusiasm, her poor, huddled masses of disenfranchised psychiatric patients and addicts.)

The downtown had been in a surly mood that Friday. Her denizens couldn't punch, club, stab, or shoot each other fast enough. But it didn't dampen my mood. Stitching up the slit that, thanks to a cheated hooker wielding a wine bottle, ran from ear to ear along the scalp of my final patient, I hummed loud enough that the old drunk warbled along with the tune.

At one A.M., I changed out of my scrubs, grabbed the bouquet of flowers (that had drawn so many friendly digs from the staff) from the bedpan-cum-vase in the staff lounge, and raced home to my new fiancée.

Hoping to rouse her from sleep—one of our favorite ways to initiate lovemaking—I was disappointed to hear noise coming from inside the apartment. I opened the front door to find a small party in the living room.

"Welcome home, bro!" Aaron rose from the chair and greeted me with a hug before heading into the kitchen.

"You didn't need to bring flowers," my cousin, Kyle Dafoe, called from the couch where he sat with an arm draped around his flavor-of-the month hard-bodied girlfriend. "Your presence alone is sunshine enough for me."

"I've got something other than flowers in mind for you," I said. "Something a lot heavier."

"Join the club." Kyle laughed. "Good to see you, Ben. Been way too long."

I followed Aaron into the kitchen. I stuffed the flowers into a vase.

"Beer?" Aaron asked from behind the open fridge door.

I nodded. "Where's Em?"

"Bathroom." Aaron handed me a cold bottle. "How was work?"

I took a long swig, savoring the cool sweetness. "Usual Friday-night crowd." I pointed to the counter, littered with empty beer bottles and a nearly drained twenty-six-ouncer of Johnnie Walker Red Label. "I'm surprised none of you ended up there."

I heard Emily's voice from behind me. "Honey, it's a celebration!" I smelled her perfume as her arms wrapped around my waist, hugging me from behind. "And you brought lilies! My favorite. God, you're sweet."

I spun to face her. I hadn't seen her in three days, and her cropped blond hair came as a surprise. I'd never seen her with short hair. It framed her sharp features, full lips, and blue eyes, somehow changing the accent on her face, making it rounder. Softer. Sexier, too. The haircut, the tank top showing off her rippled midriff, and our time apart melded into a dizzying aphrodisiac. I wished away the guests. I wanted to take her right there.

*Reading my face, she whispered one word—*Soon—*in my ear.*

"What are we celebrating?" I was concerned she might have told my cousin about our engagement.

She understood immediately. Not that, *she mouthed with a wink. "I heard from school today."*

"You heard!" I picked her up and spun her around. "And?"

Still in my arms, she kissed me full on the mouth. Her soft tongue slipped between my teeth, arousing me to the point that I ignored the faint taste of alcohol on her breath. She pulled her face back a few inches. "You just French-kissed an MBA," she said, beaming.

"Cheers!" Kyle called out from the sofa, and drained the last of the scotch from his glass tumbler. "Now it's official, Emily. You're way too good for him."

I laughed. "Kyle might have a point."

She cupped my face in her hands and kissed me on the nose. "I'll never be good enough." Her smile flickered. "I love you."

"An MBA, Em!" I kissed her on the lips again. "We're gonna be rich!"

"We'll see about that, tiger-boy." She jumped on me, almost knocking me into the fridge. Her lithe legs straddled my waist. The pressure of her pelvis against mine was deadly sexy. She whispered in my ear, "We've got to lose these guys. I can't wait much longer." Her tongue darted in and out of my ear.

"You're the one with the master's degree in ruthlessness." I laughed. "Cut the deadweight loose, while I go use the john."

Washing my hands at the bathroom sink, my smug smile stared back at me in the cabinet mirror. I couldn't fault myself too much for it. I was as happy as I could remember. Things had finally fallen in place for us.

Not for long.

Turning off the tap, I noticed the little red straw that had fallen behind the faucet. It looked as innocuous as a straw from a child's juice box, but I knew better. I stared at the nasty remnant for a long time. Snatching it up, I crumpled it into a twisted mess. Fucking junk! I stomped out of the bathroom, squeezing the straw in my fist until it stung.

When I got back to the living room, Aaron and Emily were sitting on the couch with their feet resting on the coffee table. Aaron was drinking a beer, Emily a mineral water. Kyle and his girlfriend were nowhere to be seen.

Emily thumbed at my brother. "He wouldn't leave."

Aaron shrugged. "Don't know what Kyle's rush was, either. It's early." He grinned. "And it's not even a school night for his girlfriend."

Emily patted the couch beside her, but I stood firm.

Aaron pulled out a wrapped package from behind his back. "Now that it's just us, no harm in celebrating your hush-hush engagement." He held out the gift, but I didn't move.

Emily took it out of it his hands. "You're too sweet!" She leaned over and kissed him on the cheek.

"What can I say?" Aaron shrugged. "Good-looking as he is, you picked the wrong brother."

"You wish." Emily tore open the package. Her forehead crinkled. Tears welled in her eyes. "Oh, Aaron . . ." She cradled the baby-name book in her hands, as if it were a baby.

Aaron gently reached into her hands and flipped the cover open to the page with his inscription. He tapped it. "No joke. I want to see some nieces and nephews. As in yesterday."

They both looked at me for a reaction, but I stood stone-faced.

Aaron grinned. "Too masculine for you, huh, Ben? Knew I should've got something else. A tea cozy, lace doilies, or maybe those little frilly—"

I held out my hand and opened my fist, revealing the bent straw. Aaron stopped in mid-joke. The room fell into cold silence. Emily looked away.

"That's mine," Aaron finally said.

I stared at Emily. "You promised, Em."

He stood up from the couch and stopped within arm's reach of me, blocking my path to her. "You hear me, Ben? I brought the coke. She didn't touch it."

I eyed him ferociously. "You and Kyle, and your goddamn drugs!" I was as close as I'd been since we were twelve to punching him. "You bring this crap over to our place? To Emily, when you know . . ." I shook my head in disgust. "You had no right."

"Are you listening, Ben?" His voice rose to match mine. "She didn't touch it."

"Don't play me for an idiot!" It was as if I was yelling at my own reflection in the mirror. "Look at her bloodshot eyes. The dilated pupils. If I checked her pulse and blood pressure, they'd be up, too! Shall we run a urine drug screen and make it official?"

"Stop being a doctor for two seconds," Aaron said. "You're just reading what you want—"

"It was a celebration," Emily said softly, cutting Aaron off in mid-defense.

I pushed Aaron aside. For a moment, he resisted and I thought we might end up in our first fistfight in sixteen years, but then he relented. He walked to the door. With his hand on the door handle, he turned back to us. He stood there for a long moment, as if he was about to say something, but he left without a word.

Emily sat on the couch, clutching the book in her hands and staring straight ahead. I walked over and sat beside her. Our bodies were inches apart, but the divide between us was expanding rapidly.

Emily cleared her throat. "It's not their fault."

"You don't pour gas on a wildfire."

"That's how you think of me?" She turned to me, genuine hurt in her eyes. "Totally out of control?"

I shook my head. "It's hard enough without them waving temptation right under your nose."

"Ben, it was just a couple lines of coke."

"And a couple of drinks, too."

"Can't you cut me a little slack?" she said. "Remember? We had my six-month cake last week."

"And now we're back to day zero."

"No." She took my hand in hers. "We're going to get married next month. Remember? This . . ." She waved a hand dismissively over the scattered bottles. "It was just a slip. Like cheating on a diet." She flashed puppy dog eyes at me. "Can't we write it off as a moment of weakness on a special night?"

My hand lay flaccid in hers. She squeezed harder. "I'm going to be Mrs. Benjamin Dafoe soon. The mother of your kids. I wouldn't let any chemical in the world screw that up."

She leaned forward and planted her lips on mine. In spite of my passiveness, she kissed harder, her soft tongue caressing my lips and tongue. Her hand reached under my shirt and skittered over my chest before tucking into the waistband of my jeans. Her hand crept lower until it found the perfect spot. When she rolled on top of me and dug the warmth of her groin into my leg, the last of my resistance drained. I yanked off her skirt as I wriggled free of my jeans.

The angry sex we had was as intense as it had ever been. She fell asleep with me still inside her. I clung to her warm sweaty body, wanting to believe *everything she said but sensing that we'd just rounded another curve in a downward spiral.*

Three hours after I'd set out on the mountain-bike ride that was supposed to help me forget Emily, I returned home missing her even more, almost disappointed to have remained in one piece. By early evening, despite my exhaustion, I still wasn't any closer to sleep.

At a loss for what to do, I showered and headed back to the hospital. There, I went directly to Lara Maxwell's ICU room. Despite the typical mess of machines and IV lines surrounding the sleeping patient, I was relieved to see the endotracheal tube gone from her mouth, meaning Lara was free of the ventilator.

Eyes closed, her sister Isabelle lay curled up in the chair beside the bed. With her face clear of all the tears and mascara, Isabelle looked like a normal teenager; a far sight from the drag princess of the morning. Compared to all that I'd seen this day, the two sisters were a wholesome and welcome sight. I turned to leave. Halfway to the door, I was stopped by a soft croaky voice. "Who are you?"

I looked behind me. Lara sat up in her bed.

"I'm Dr. Dafoe. I saw you in the Emergency Room."

Isabelle roused at the sound of my voice. She stretched in the seat beside her. "Remember, Lara?" She yawned. "He's the guy I told you about."

Lara looked away. "Oh."

Isabelle rose and stood at Lara's bedside. "Mom and Dad will be here in the morning." She sounded far more defiant than earlier. "And I already told them everything," she said, as if stripping me of a weapon.

I nodded. "It's none of my business."

Arms crossed, Isabelle glared at me in full agreement.

"I just dropped by to see how Lara was doing."

"My throat hurts." Lara coughed harshly. "And it's still not too easy to breathe." She adjusted the nasal prongs running under her nose, but her eyes were fixed on the bedsheet. "I guess it could've been a lot worse though."

"Much."

She looked up at me tentatively. "The nurses said you saved my life."

"There were lots of people who took care of you." I shrugged. "What I do know is that Ecstasy and cocaine just about ended your life."

She nodded solemnly. "I'm not going near that stuff again."

"And I'm not going to let her," Isabelle added with a huff. "If that's what you're wondering."

I walked closer to the bedside. "Isabelle, I had no right to lay into you the way I did this morning."

Isabelle held the icy stare a few moments longer, but then her resolve broke, and her eyes misted over. She looked at me pitifully. "No, what you said was true. I did almost kill my sister," she wept. "Lara, I'm so sorry."

Lara turned to her sister, confused.

I wavered, knowing I'd already blurred the line of professional conduct and was on the verge of stepping right over it. *Screw it!* I thought. "Listen, Isabelle, you don't know why I was so upset this morning."

Her throat bobbed. "Yes, I do."

"It's not what you think. When I was your age, I took my brother to a party. I gave him drugs. Encouraged him to take them."

"What happened?" Isabelle choked out.

On the brink of tears myself, I looked away from the girls. "Once he got that first taste, Aaron was never the same. It ruined his life. . . ."

Isabelle threw her arms around her sister's neck, sending Lara into another paroxysm of coughs. When Isabelle looked up, tears streamed down her cheeks, but her jaw was clenched and her eyes burned with determination. "That's not going to happen to Lara. I swear it!"

I forced a smile. "I believe it."

I quickly said my good-byes and then headed for the elevator.

Stepping out, I almost slammed into my colleague and close friend, Dr. Alex Lindquist. At barely five feet, Alex was more than a head shorter than me, though her diminutive size was no reflection of her fiery personality. Most of the staff loved her. The few who crossed her inevitably regretted it.

Her hair pinned back, Alex wore a white lab coat draped over blue scrubs. I tried to ignore the impact of those expressive brown eyes, luscious lips, and high Slavic cheeks but failed as usual, and her proximity brought the expected stirrings.

"Ben!" she practically shrieked. "You look awful!"

I shrugged. "I told the lady not to cut my bangs so short."

She grabbed me by the arm. "Coffee!" she commanded.

We sat in the corner of the hospital's nearly deserted cafeteria with large cups of coffee in front of us. "Was your night shift that bad?" she asked.

I shook my head. "Remember Emily Kenmore?"

"Sure." Her eyes narrowed, and I wondered if I spotted a flicker of jealousy. "The only serious ex I know of."

"She was killed last night."

Alex slammed down her cup on the table. "No!"

"Someone carved her up, Alex."

Alex sat still, cradling the cup that looked massive in her small hand while I recounted what I'd seen at the crime scene.

"God, Ben, I am so sorry." She reached over and squeezed my hand just once before withdrawing.

I nodded. "We hadn't been together for a long time."

"Doesn't matter. To see that happen to someone you loved . . ."

We stared at our coffees in silence for a few moments. "I don't get it, Ben. Why would the cops drag you down there?"

"To ID her, I suppose."

She shook her head. "Don't buy that for a second. That falls to the family. Besides, it's done in the morgue when they're tidied up. Not smack dab in the middle of the bloodshed."

"Alex, I know the Homicide detectives involved. Helen Riddell and Rick Sutcliffe worked Aaron's case. I've consulted for them on a number of poisonings and overdose deaths. I consider Helen a friend."

Alex kept shaking her head. "Even more reason not to put you through that."

"Plus, they wanted me to help identify the John Doe."

"Did you?"

I paused. "No."

"But you knew him?"

I'd forgotten how uncanny Alex's intuition was. "I'd met him once, briefly. With Emily."

Alex tilted her head expecting more, but I wasn't forthcoming. "What now?" she asked.

"They investigate." I sighed. "I should probably call Emily's parents. God, she put them through a lot. Now this . . ."

"Give it a few days, okay?" she said softly. "It's only fair to them. And you."

"Alex, I lied to the detectives."

She grimaced. "About?"

"I didn't tell them Emily and I were engaged."

Alex bit her lip. "I had no idea."

"No one did," I said. "We were going to elope. Only Aaron knew. And then, when it fell apart, we never told anyone else."

Alex squeezed my hand a second time. When she pulled away, I felt the coolness of her wedding band slide over the back of my hand. "You okay?"

I tilted my hand side to side in a so-so gesture.

Her face lit up in a radiant smile. "Why don't you let me take you out for dinner tomorrow?"

"What about Marcus?"

"Business. He's back east again for a week."

"And Talie?"

"Dad can watch her."

"Very tempting . . ." Her understanding face lifted a bit of the load off my mind. But reason prevailed over emotion. "I'm not sure dinner is such a good idea," I said, remembering the last fateful time we had gone out for dinner and drinks, a year earlier at a conference in San Francisco, and nearly wound up in bed together.

She took a final sip of her coffee and then put the empty cup down. "Good friends go out for dinner, you know."

"I know."

She smiled. "There's no harm in a phone call, though, right?"

"None."

She jabbed a finger at me. "You call me, Benjamin Dafoe. Day or night! Understand?"

I nodded. "Thanks, Alex."

"I better get back to the pit." She pointed in the direction of the ER as she rose to her feet. She crossed over to my side of the table and gave me a quick peck on the cheek. "Day or night," she repeated.

She made it three steps from the table before she stopped and turned back. "Why?"

I frowned. "Why what?"

Her eyes bored into mine. "Why was Emily carved up?"

I broke off our eye contact and spoke to the table. "I don't know, but something tells me it has to do with what happened to Aaron."

At first, I incorporated the ringing phone into my dream. But the second set of rings dragged me back into consciousness. I stared bleary-eyed at the clock radio whose fat red numbers read 5:35 A.M.

I groped for the phone. "Hello," I muttered.

Nothing.

I'd barely crammed the receiver back into the base when it rang again. I picked it up. "Yes?"

Another pause, then "Benjamin?" spoken in a whisper.

"Who is this?" I asked, feeling a sudden cool rush.

"I was there."

My skin crawled. "What are you talking about?"

"The fight. I saw it."

My heart rate sped up. "What fight?"

"The fight, Benjamin," the whisperer repeated. "You and Emily. And J.D. Let's not forget J.D."

I sat up in my bed. "J.D.?"

There was a soft chortle on the line. "It's going to work out, Benjamin."

"Listen!" My voice rose, in spite of myself. "You're not making any sense."

"I think we both know that I am."

"Who the hell are you?"

"A friend."

"Friend," I growled, "You're getting me confused with someone else!"

Another laugh. "Not if you're the Dr. Benjamin Dafoe who I saw fighting with Emily and J.D. before they died. The one who—"

I clicked the END button and threw the cordless receiver across the room. When it rang again, I just stared at it. My hands trembled—part fear, part fury.

A good minute after it stopped ringing, I climbed out of bed and picked up the receiver. I scrolled through the call display with a still-shaky thumb. The readout read: CANADA.

Canada? And how the hell did he find my number? Like most physicians', my home number was unlisted.

Confused and edgy, I changed into shorts and a drip-dry shirt. Grabbing my shoes, I headed out of the house through the basement to the attached garage. I unlocked the racing bike, which had cost almost as much as my car, and carefully pulled it off the ceiling rack. I saddled it up and locked my feet into the pedals.

I needed to go very fast this morning.

I rode out past Lake Washington, then turned back and headed for the airport. Unmoved by the striking view of the snow-capped Mt. Rainier jutting into the blue morning sky, I raced through downtown Seattle's quiet dawn. I screamed past my usual turn-back point and just kept cycling. Twenty-five miles later, and my agitation finally calmed. I turned around and headed home at a more leisurely pace.

Riding home, Aaron's assessment of my cycling came back to me. Three years after he spoke the words, I could still hear them.

Out in front of his townhouse in the trendy and pricey Queen Anne neighborhood, I straddled my bike while Aaron stood beside me swaying slightly on the pavement, as if carried by the light spring breeze. The pupils in his faraway eyes were constricted, his voice slurred.

"What's going on, Aaron?"

"Not much," he said. "Taking in the breeze. Chatting with my twin bro . . ."

"You're high."

Aaron shrugged and almost stumbled.

I shook my head. "Seems like you're always high."

Aaron didn't respond.

"This what you want for your future?"

"It will do for now."

"Listen to me, Aaron. You need help."

At first, I didn't think he'd heard me, but after a few moments, he said, "I've had help. Doesn't work."

"I know a new treatment facility. Experimental, but promising. The guy who runs it is a friend—"

Eyes glazed, he stared beyond me. "Save your breath, Ben."

I slammed my front tire in frustration. "Aaron, you're a fucking addict!"

With that, he snapped into focus. He pointed a finger at me. "Of course I am! Don't you get it, twin? It's genetic. In our blood. Remember Dad and the booze?" His finger shook. "We got no choice. We're both addicts."

"Oh? And what's my addiction?"

His finger indicated my riding getup and then settled on my bike. "You're sitting on it. That bike of yours is your bottle, bro. Your pipe and needle, too. . . ."

I had little doubt Aaron was right. But I also knew that as stupid and reckless as I might be on the bike, it was less risky than *his* alternative. Besides, unlike the drugs, cycling usually cleared my head. I did my best thinking on the bike. Not today, though. As I pulled back into my driveway, I hadn't sorted out any of this mess.

I stepped into my living room to the sound of the ringing phone. I was relieved to see that this time the call display offered a local name: SEATTLE POLICE.

Half an hour later, I arrived in Helen's office. Her royal blue blouse was a relatively subdued choice for her. I took a seat across from Helen and beside Rick Sutcliffe, who sported another thousand-dollar trendy jacket-pant ensemble. As usual, I sensed a degree of contempt in his smiley welcome.

"Get some sleep?" Helen gave me the once-over and grinned, as if to suggest I didn't look quite as shitty as yesterday.

I nodded. "Couple hours."

"We were at Emily's autopsy this morning," Helen said.

"And?"

"No big *Quincy*-like surprises, if that's what you're wondering."

I swallowed. "Any evidence of sexual assault?"

"None."

I nodded my relief. "I was thinking, there was so much blood in her bedroom . . ."

"Which happens from time to time at double homicides," Rick said.

I ignored him. "You need a beating heart to spray blood like that. Emily must have been alive for a while."

Helen leaned back heavily in her chair. "Yeah."

"And judging from the surface area covered," I said, "she must have been moving around after she was already stabbed but before the blow to her neck."

"Your point?" Helen asked.

I offered a disclaimer. "Maybe Emily just struggled hard. I don't know. But it seems to me someone took his sweet time. You ever heard that expression 'death by a thousand cuts'?"

Rick and Helen shared a glance, possibly even impressed. "It looks that way on autopsy," Helen said. "Whoever was responsible wanted her to bleed. Pathologist figures the cut to the neck was the final blow. She had little left to give by that point."

"All that blood . . ." I tasted the acid in the back of my mouth. "Someone wanted her to suffer."

Helen nodded slightly.

"Anything else on autopsy?"

"The tox screens are still pending. But under the second victim's fingernails, they found traces of Methylen . . ." Helen's voice trailed off and she threw up her hands in defeat. She laughed. "I don't even know why I tried. I didn't stand a chance of coughing out that hairball."

"Methylene dioxymethamphetamine?" I said.

Helen nodded and chuckled. "You make it sound like butter."

I sighed. "Easier to just call it Ecstasy, like the users do."

Rick eyed me with a grin that had acquired a fingernails-on-chalkboard quality for me. "My guess is that Emily wasn't quite as clean as she made out to you."

Prudently, I just turned back to Helen. "What else about the John Doe?"

"More like Jason Doe," she said. "Or more precisely, Jason DiAngelo from Redmond. Twenty-nine years old. Went by 'J.D.'"

J.D.! I fought off a shudder at the memory of the name being whispered by the predawn caller. "What do you know about him?"

"For starters, he wasn't a complete stranger to the King County criminal justice system." Helen patted around her desk until she found a piece of paper, a copy of his criminal record. "A bunch of charges for theft, assault, and small-time drug trafficking. J.D. did about three years in total. Then, two years ago, he was arrested for narcotics possession. A kilo of coke in his trunk."

"And?"

"J.D. switched attorneys. Michael Prince." She waited for a sign of recognition but I shook my head; the name meant nothing to me. "Of Pratt, Prince, and Higney. Known affectionately around these parts as the Prince of Darkness." Still didn't ring any bells for me. "Anyway, Prince convinced the judge to rule the search of J.D.'s car illegal. For all I know, Prince got the Seattle P.D. to pay for the cleaning and detailing on poor old J.D.'s violated vehicle."

Rick grunted a chuckle. "Curious how a small-time dealer from the bottom of the Public Defender's barrel rose to a five-hundred-dollar-an-hour lawyer in a few short years."

"Maybe J.D. found a better employer?" I offered.

Rick nodded, but then sighed as if it pained him to agree with me. "Maybe the kind of employer with a brutal termination policy."

"Even the Prince of Darkness can't get poor old J.D. out of this scrape." Helen stretched her long arms out wide and yawned. "Autopsy showed that J.D. died from the same knife used on Emily Kenmore."

"But not quite the same M.O.," I pointed out.

Rick shot me another unreadable glance, while Helen nodded. "J.D. didn't have a single defensive wound," she said.

"He never saw the knife coming," I said.

"More than that," Rick said. "He let the perp get very close without defending himself. No question, he trusted his killer."

Helen's eyes sparkled playfully. "Which loses him IQ points on my scorecard."

"Maybe J.D. was at the wrong place at the wrong time," I said. "Like the guy with O.J.'s wife?"

Rick folded his arms across his chest. "Or maybe he played an active role in the torture of Emily Kenmore, never realizing he was going to be the encore victim."

"Jesus . . . ," I muttered.

Helen cleared papers off her desk and looked at me with uncharacteristic solemnity. "From the lack of forced entry right down to the M.O., all evidence suggests Emily Kenmore knew her killer." She paused. "Ben, we're hoping you can help us navigate her circle of friends."

My stomach tightened. "Long time since I ran with that crowd, if I ever did. But I'll do what I can."

"Thanks." Helen lifted a photo off her desk and passed it to me. "We did get one unexpected break at the crime scene."

Expecting another snapshot of Emily, I hesitated in taking it. I knew it would only elicit another wave of unwanted memories. But Emily wasn't in the photograph. No one was. Confused, I stared at a color photo of Emily's gruesome bedroom wall. One of the arcs of blood was marked with a black arrow and a caption that read AB–.

I shrugged at Helen, though I already had an inkling of what it meant.

Rick was quick to explain. "Emily's blood type was O-positive. And most all of the blood at the scene was of that type." He tapped the photo in my hand over the arrow. "But this streak was AB-negative."

"And J.D.?"

Rick's grin widened. "B-positive."

"So this streak of blood came from the killer?" I said.

"Emily or J.D. might have got in one shot before the end," Helen said. "Or just as likely, the killer accidentally nicked himself with his own blade."

I said nothing.

AB-negative is the rarest of blood types, found in fewer than one in two hundred people.

It also happens to be mine.

CHAPTER

5

Lights off, I sat in my living room. The room was lit by only the dim glow from the solitary streetlight and the flash from the occasional passing headlights. A slight autumn chill drifted in through the open window. The beer bottle dangled in my hand like a dead weight, never nearing my lips. A revved engine or braking tires disrupted the silence from time to time, but I didn't turn on the stereo; I'd learned last time around that music only intensified the sense of loss.

In the weak light, I could barely make out the eerily beautiful black-and-white sketch, *Bather with Her Back Turned*, over the mantle. Drawn by an "up-and-comer" in the Seattle art scene—or so I was told—I thought Emily could have just as easily sketched the desolate figure. Maybe that's why it resonated so strongly with me.

The numbing shock of Emily's murder had receded. Sorrow welled in its place. No surprise. I knew the memories would be skewed and unbalanced—summer weekends at "our" bed-and-breakfast in Ana-cortes, mornings frittered away at Pike Place Market, meals playfully improvised in the kitchen, those long showers together . . . I'd expected to relive all of that usual romantic bullshit and none of the misery—the volatility, the missteps, the betrayals. What caught me off guard was how many memories of Emily also included Aaron.

With or without one of a string of transient girlfriends, Aaron's presence was a constant in our relationship. But my closeness to my identical twin never threatened my sense of identity. We were very different people. And despite his weaknesses, I always looked up to Aaron. After all, born four minutes before me, he was my big brother.

Staring at the sketch, I realized that not only had I lost Emily but that her death made me relive the loss of my brother.

The ringing phone startled me. I bobbled my bottle, spilling a few drops of beer on the cloth sofa Mom had helped me select. I glanced at my watch: 10:11 P.M. I steadied the bottle on the coffee table and picked up the cordless receiver.

"You okay?"

The question threw me. For a moment, I wondered if the whisperer had called to torment me again, but then I found my bearings. "Alex," I said. "I'm fine."

"Hmmm," Dr. Lindquist sounded unconvinced. "What are you up to now?"

"Nursing a beer." Then I added the truth: "In the dark while I reminisce about Emily and Aaron."

"You call that fine?"

"What can I say?" I said. "I have boundless capacity for self-pity."

Hearing Alex's soft staccato laugh lifted my mood. "You sure you don't need company?" she asked.

"Yeah."

"Dad's staying over with Talie and me. She's asleep. And he's too proud to get a hearing aid, so the TV is cranked up to rocket-launch decibels." That explained the distorted echo in the background. "I could use a change of scenery."

I wanted nothing more than for Alex to come over, if only for a break from the cascade of memories, but I knew it risked a complication I couldn't face at this point. "Alex, it's a sweet offer, but I think I'm better off alone right now."

"Okay," she said breezily. "Let me know if you change your mind."

Hanging up the phone, my own words—*"better off alone"*—sunk in. Having grown up with a twin, I'd never before thought of myself as much of a loner, but I had to concede that during the last few years, since my engagement crumbled and Aaron disappeared, the description had begun to fit. I had my work, a few intermittent relationships, and a small circle of friends, most of whom had either moved afield or had become understandably preoccupied with their growing families. Alex Lindquist was the closest I had to a best friend. And we had almost capsized the friendship that drunken night in San Francisco.

Through the rumor mill at St. Jude's, I'd heard how rocky Alex's marriage was. Her husband's business travel had proven too tempting for a guy with an incurable wandering eye. His affairs grew habitual; I'd even once caught him trying to prey on Emily. Marcus and Alex were already separated when she discovered she was pregnant with Talie. The pregnancy led to a revival of their marriage, but word was that if anything, Marcus's philandering only worsened.

Alex had too much dignity to share the details. But as she sat on the bed in my hotel room with a glass of red wine precariously tilted in her small hand, I knew exactly what she meant when she said, "Marcus's latest business venture has kept him in New York for weeks on end."

I sat down beside her on the bed, straightening her wineglass. Then I rested a hand on her shoulder. "I wish things had worked out better for you."

She viewed me with a smile, then tilted her head and nuzzled my hand with her face. I understood that the contact was more than friendly, but I left my hand where it was.

Alex looked up at me with her almond-shaped brown eyes and then leaned her face closer to mine. Her breath warmed my lips. I got a whiff of wine. "I should go back to my room," she said.

"Yeah." I nodded. "You should."

She stared at me a moment. Then she inched her lips to mine. She touched my lips so slightly with hers that the pressure barely registered. I kissed back, harder. I squeezed her shoulder. She wrapped a hand behind my back and pulled me to her. I felt the wetness of her lips part and her tongue on mine. I guided her back on the bed, our bodies side by side, pressing into each other.

Alex dropped her hands to her waist and slid off her top. Then her fingers reached for my shirt buttons. She moaned into my mouth. Our kisses grew more urgent as her small hands moved steadily down my shirt front. She slid her hand over my shoulders and peeled off my shirt, the smooth steady pressure electric on my skin.

I broke off the kisses just long enough to pull off my shirt. I hesitated, only for a moment, but when I moved for Alex, she turned her face away from mine. She sat up on the bed. "I should go," she said, subdued. She groped the bed for her top, snatched it up, and pulled it over her head.

Instead of bolting, she sat where she was and stared at her feet. She was so silent that it took me a moment to notice the tears running down her cheeks. I sat up beside her and wrapped my bare arm around her. "Alex?"

"This wouldn't be fair," she said hoarsely.

"To Marcus?"

"Talie."

"And you?"

She shook her head. "She's only five. She needs a stable home. I can't do this to her. Not now. Not with the way her father flies in and out of her life."

"It will be okay."

She buried her head in my shoulder. "Ben, I am so sorry."

"Don't be." I said and stroked her lustrous hair, the eroticism of my contact replaced by concern. "We're both a little mixed up." I paused. "Actually, I'm a lot mixed up. But we stopped in time."

"I wonder," she said into my shoulder.

Time had sanitized that evening for me, so I could recall it without guilt; it had become almost an innocent pleasure, like my first sixth-grade kiss. But since that night in San Francisco, things had changed for us. We stopped going out for dinners or movies after shifts. Our restraint wasn't born from awkwardness or regret, but rather the mutual realization that next time temptation would prove too strong.

A soft rapping from my front door drew my attention back to the moment. I stood up and headed for the door.

More than his late-night presence, I was shocked by the appearance of my cousin, Kyle. Wearing a T-shirt and jeans, Kyle looked even more gaunt and pale than when I'd last seen him three months earlier. He used to be the incarnation of health and vigor. Even when my brother and he were heavily into drugs, Kyle carefully maintained his cut physique and bad-boy good looks. I knew Kyle was lucky to have survived the aggressive leukemia, but I had yet to adjust to his chronically sickly appearance since his bone marrow transplant more than

two years before. Pale and balding, not only had he lost his natural rud-
diness but his once smooth complexion now always seemed to scale
or erupt with various rashes—today's variation was a line of dried,
encrusted sores over his right eyebrow.

"Ben." He threw his arms around me and squeezed his bony frame
against my body. "Damn, Ben, I'm so sorry about Emily."

I nodded. "Beer?"

"Don't do beer, not anymore." He grinned. His eyes lit up, shaving
years off his face. "But if you have some Coke lying around . . ."

With a sigh, I turned for the kitchen. I knew he meant the soda, not
the powder. Kyle had been clean since his bone marrow transplant, but
neither beating cancer nor finding God had claimed his irreverent
sense of humor.

After I dug out a can of Coke from the back of my fridge, I flicked
on the lights and we headed into the living room. We sat across from
each other on the couches in silence. For appearance's sake, I sipped
my beer, indifferent to its warm flat taste.

"How long?" Kyle asked.

"Wasn't it at Uncle Len's seventieth birthday in June—"

"No, jackass." Kyle sighed and then flashed one of his contagious
half-mocking smiles. "Not us! I mean, when did you last see Emily?"

"Last week."

Kyle cocked his head. "You two stayed in touch, huh?"

"In fits and spurts," I said.

"Yeah. You and Emily were together for what . . ." Kyle squinted up
at the ceiling, doing the math. "Four years?"

"Five."

"She was so beautiful, wasn't she?" He brought the can to his lip
thoughtfully. "Inside and out. One of those people who could turn on a
room."

I swallowed away the small knot in my throat. "But way too often
she needed chemical help."

"Or thought she did." Kyle nodded. "I used to be like that, too, Ben.
Always wanted that edge I got from the blow, the crystal, or the E."

I sighed heavily. "Emily and Aaron never really managed to kick the
junk. You were the only one."

"And I was the biggest lost cause of the bunch." Kyle folded his arms over his chest, but there was nothing defensive in the gesture. "What can I say?" He shrugged. "Leukemia saved my life." And I knew he was serious, too.

I leaned forward in my seat and pointed to Kyle with the neck of my bottle. "The other guy killed at Emily's place. I think it might have been her dealer. His name was J.D. Ring any bells?"

Kyle unfolded his arms. He nodded. "Porn star looks? In his twenties?"

I nodded.

"Yeah. I used to know him."

"And?"

"J.D. was never the sharpest knife in the drawer. But he was a smooth talker and knew some of the right people." He cleared his throat. "Kind of established himself as a supplier for the downtown coke-and-martini set."

"He was Emily's dealer, wasn't he?"

Kyle nodded.

A breeze blew in from the window. I glanced out to a passing car on the street. I had a sudden urge for a long night bike ride. I turned back to Kyle. "The Homicide detectives wonder if J.D. was involved in Emily's murder."

A fleeting glint passed his eyes. "If so, J.D. hit upon the alibi of *all* alibis."

I smiled in spite of myself. They wonder whether the murderer double-crossed him after killing Emily."

"J.D. always struck me as a kind of harmless, but . . ."

I waited for him to finish the sentence, but he didn't. "You ever heard of a lawyer named Michael Prince?" I asked.

Kyle nodded. "A big hitter criminal defense attorney here in Seattle."

I arched an eyebrow.

"When you've been on the wrong side of the law as much I have, you get to know the names." He fingered the writing on the can. "Why do you ask?"

I described J.D.'s ascension in the world of legal representation and then asked, "You wouldn't happen to know who J.D. was working for?"

Kyle only shrugged.

"Any guesses?"

Kyle's face creased into a frown. "Ben, the people who employ the J.D.s of the world tend to prize their privacy. Why don't you leave those questions to the cops?"

"J.D.'s boss may somehow be directly connected to Emily's death."

"That's not your problem."

I slammed my hand on the coffee table, upending my empty beer bottle. I took a breath and fought to keep the emotion out of my voice. "I loved her." I held up a palm. "Kyle, you wouldn't have wanted to see what they did to her!"

Kyle viewed me with a sympathetic nod.

"The same person or persons might be responsible for what happened to Aaron."

"We don't know what happened to Aaron," he said softly.

I just stared at my cousin.

He held my eyes for a moment and then dropped his chin and sighed. "Back when I was in the racket, J.D. was working for a guy named Philip Maglio."

"Is this Maglio still around?"

"Oh, yeah." Kyle nodded. "He owns some real estate and a few legit businesses, too. Like all the successful ones, he knows how to squeeze a dime from the wrong *and* right side of the law."

Kyle read my expression. "Ben, don't even think about it. Philip and his kind can be very dangerous. Say—for the sake of argument—he was involved in what happened to Emily or Aaron, and you show up poking around . . ."

"I'm not going ultra-vigilante here. I just want to pass along anything that might help the cops."

"Okay," Kyle said, but his frown was rich with skepticism.

We sat quietly for several moments. "It wasn't that long ago that the four of us were all celebrating Em's MBA," I said. "Now, look how we've all ended up."

"Life is one twisted road," Kyle said.

"Yeah." I looked down at my tapping foot. "I don't know what more I could have done for Emily, but Aaron . . ."

Kyle leaned forward in his seat. "You're not still beating yourself up over that?"

"Of course I am," I snapped and then forced the edge from my tone. "Kyle, I gave him his very first taste of coke."

"I was there, too, remember? Besides, if not then, Aaron would've been introduced to it somewhere else."

"Maybe."

Kyle brought a hand to his chest. "And how about me, Ben? I kept your brother in a healthy supply of all that junk. Then I pulled him into the business. How about that for culpability?"

I hadn't forgiven Kyle either. "We're no angels," I said quietly.

"No," he said, dropping his hand and sinking deeper into his seat. "But it's not all black-and-white. Look at you. You help people every day with the work you do in the hospital. And even I like to think I've turned over a new leaf in the past few years."

"Since you found God?"

"Don't make it sound like some kind of jailhouse conversion." He laughed. "I got a second chance, like Scrooge in *A Christmas Carol*." He nodded to himself. "I did some very bad stuff in my day, including trading in human misery. But God or no God, I caught a big break after my diagnosis. I just want to share a little of my luck."

Though Kyle hadn't ever told me, I'd heard how much time, money, and sweat he had poured back into the city's frontline battle against drug addiction. His efforts had reclaimed some of my respect.

Kyle rose to his feet, grabbing the armrest for momentary support. Then he began for the door. He stopped before reaching it and turned back to me. "Ben, can I help you?"

I stood up and met him at the door. "I don't know. We'll see."

Kyle wrapped his pencil-like arms around me and gave me another hug. "You deserve better."

I hugged him back without comment. *So did Aaron and Emily*.

CHAPTER

6

I woke with a start. Disoriented, I grappled for the ringing phone, concerned that the anonymous whisperer was calling again. The cobwebs cleared and I realized with relief that the ringing came from my alarm clock, not the phone. Climbing out of bed, I shivered slightly in my boxers; I resolved to turn my house's heat back on for the fall.

Slipping into my riding gear, I vacillated between the mountain and the road bike, opting in the end for the inherent risk of the mountain bike.

Seattle was still dark at 6:30 A.M. And for the first time since the spring, my breath froze in the moist air. I was glad for my Lycra jacket, but I attributed the chill I felt to more than only the changing of seasons. I cycled hard for the park, trying to outpace my morbid thoughts.

I reached the parkland in record time, but the slippery trails were particularly punishing in the drizzly morning. About a mile in, I lost control of my bike when trying to jump a log and slammed shoulder-first into a tree. The awkward collision ended up bruising my ego worse than my shoulder. With its new three-hundred-dollar front wheel bent beyond repair, I had to walk the bike out of the trail carrying the frame, along with the shame of my wipeout, past my fellow mountain bikers.

By the time I returned home with my crippled bike, I was too late to catch the Grand Rounds lecture at the hospital. I wasn't heartbroken about missing the lecture, but I was sorry that I would miss seeing Alex. Coffee following rounds was one of our few sanctioned get-togethers. *Probably for the best*, I thought, as I had a mental flashback of Alex with her hair up and wearing a form-fitting black business suit with pumps and an open-collar blouse. It dawned on me that even a morning coffee wasn't nearly as safe as we assumed.

Leaving my road bike in the garage, I climbed into my black Smart Car. Since the prices of gas had soared, I'd faced far less teasing from friends and colleagues about my highly fuel-efficient, compact vehicle. Rarely was I asked anymore when I was going to upgrade my toy car, or what happened to its training wheels. Most of the medical staff's ridicule was now saved for the two surgeons who drove gas-guzzling Hummers. Much as I would have liked to plead eco-friendliness for my choice in cars, truth was the boxy little car struck me from the first. The convenience of its miserly fuel tank, combined with a body that could be tucked into nonexistent parking spots, turned me into a full Smart Car convert.

I pulled up to the Seattle P.D. headquarters on Fifth Avenue, sliding my car with great satisfaction between two cars in metered spots. I was willing, almost eager, to face the prospect of challenging a parking ticket for my improvised spot.

With nods to a few familiar faces, I wended my way through the building to Homicide. I walked through the open door into Helen Riddell's office. She wasn't there, but mug in hand, Rick Sutcliffe stood staring out the window into the Seattle fog. In another of his seemingly endless supply of expensive suits (gray this morning), Rick turned slowly to me. His face broke into an automatic but unwelcoming smile. "Morning, Ben. Were we expecting you today?"

"Rick." I nodded, laboring to match his smile. "Where's Helen?"

"She'll be here soon."

Rick's steaming cup reminded me that I'd missed my coffee after my bike crash. Like any self-respecting coffee-deprived Seattleite, my mouth watered for a java, but Rick didn't offer and I wasn't about to ask. After a few more seconds of awkward silence, I said, "I have a potential lead for your investigation."

"Into your fiancée's murder?"

I inhaled slowly. "Emily hasn't been my fiancée for five years."

"How would I know?" Rick said with a helpless shrug. "You've been so secretive about it."

I kept my mouth shut and dug my thumb into my palm.

"So what's this lead?" he asked.

"Philip Maglio."

Rick's face showed no recognition, but he didn't ask for clarification. "And he's connected to the murders how?"

"J.D. used to work for him."

"As a dealer?"

I nodded.

"How do you know?"

I hesitated, unsure whether I had the right to drag Kyle into the mess. But I felt cornered. "My cousin used to be in the business. He knew J.D."

Rick's smile grew. "This whole murder investigation is one big old Dafoe family affair."

I dug my thumb harder into my palm. "What's your point, Rick?"

"My point, Ben," he said, articulating each syllable as if explaining to an intellectually challenged seven-year-old, "is that you are far too closely tied into all of this to be anywhere near this homicide investigation."

I took a long slow breath. "Don't know if you remember, but Helen called me."

"I remember," he said pleasantly. "But I'm telling you that it's time for you to disengage yourself from the process."

"My pleasure," I grunted. "If you see Helen, mention the Philip Maglio connection to her."

As I was about to turn, Helen's voice boomed from behind me. "What about Philip Maglio?"

I spun to see Helen gliding into the room and caught the lavender scent of her overpowering perfume. I was struck again by the incongruence of how lightly she moved for someone of her bulk and larger-than-life presence. She glanced from Rick to me. I suspect she either had heard or intuited the crux of our confrontation but she didn't comment. "You were saying about Philip Maglio . . ."

I relayed what Kyle had told me about J.D.'s association with Maglio.

"Interesting." Helen smiled, flashing the gap between her front teeth. "I would hate to miss an opportunity to visit an upstanding pillar of our community like Mr. Maglio."

"So you know him?"

"Phil and I go way back." Her smile faded. "Markets himself as the local poor-boy-made-good entrepreneur, but we know Maglio is a key figure in the city's drug trade. Unfortunately, he's our West Coast Teflon Don. Nothing ever sticks to him."

"Because he's smart and careful," Rick said with a hint of admiration. "He doesn't go gutting people like a couple of fishes in their own apartment. That's not his style."

I fought off a shudder at the cruel but accurate description of Emily's murder.

"People change." Helen's gray eyes twinkled. "Maybe Philip has expanded his horizons."

"Doesn't fit," Rick said.

"And what about Michael Prince?" I asked.

Helen squinted at me. "What about him?"

"Has he defended Philip Maglio before?"

"Far as I know, Maglio hasn't needed Prince's services."

"But he could have hired Prince to defend J.D. or one of his subordinates," I said.

"And how do we find that out? Ask Prince?" Rick asked.

"Worth a try," I said quietly, ignoring the mockery in his tone.

"Wouldn't be worth the cost of gasoline to go see Prince."

"Rick's right. Prince couldn't tell us even if he wanted to." She chuckled sympathetically. "And trust me, helping the S.P.D. would be right up there with a colonoscopy on the Prince of Darkness's wish list."

I nodded my defeat. "Well, now that I've done my civic duty and reported what I heard, I'm going to get back to being a doctor."

"Fair enough." Helen glanced at Rick with an unreadable expression before turning to me. "We still may need your help down the line."

"You know how to find me." I turned for the door.

"Ben," Rick called out. "That right hand of yours still looks pretty raw."

I glanced down at the gash over my knuckles. The sight caused it to ache anew. I'd scraped my hand again during my crash on the trails. The scab had peeled off and my knuckles were freshly crusted with dried blood. "From my bike chain," I said with a shrug, wondering why I suddenly felt defensive.

I hurried out of Helen's office and through the S.P.D.'s headquarters. I pulled out of the parking space in front of the building determined to distance myself from this investigation. While the urge to punch Rick still simmered, I had to admit he was right: I had no business being anywhere near the investigation. I was once wildly in love with one of the victims. In some ways, I still was. And less than a week before, I had threatened the other victim. Unsolicited and unwelcome, the scene from Emily's apartment seeped back into my head.

When I reached Emily's apartment, the door was already ajar. I rapped softly. Nothing. Taking the open door as an invitation, I pushed it open wider and walked in.

They stood in the middle of the living room. J.D.—whose name I was to learn only after his death—had his back turned to me. But I had him pegged the instant I saw him. Emily looked over to me in embarrassed surprise. J.D. spun to face me, a stack of greenbacks still in his hand. Emily had one bill left in hers.

Suddenly the whole scene registered. "What the hell, Emily?" I snapped.

Her eyes widened. "No, it's not that, Ben."

I strode straight for them, the fury rising with each step. "Do I look that stupid to you?"

A sneer contorted J.D.'s square face and he shot out a finger at me. "Who the fuck are you?"

"He's a friend." Emily grabbed J.D.'s wrist.

J.D. scowled. "Doesn't look like much of a friend."

Ignoring the drug dealer's comment, I stormed up to within two feet of them. "This is what you do with the money I give you?" I growled at Emily. "You're buying drugs with it?!?"

The skin around her eyes wrinkled with distress. "Ben, if you'll just hear me out—"

The familiar urge to protect her welled, but it was no match for my anger.

"No! I'm not listening to your bullshit anymore." I pumped my fist. "I can't be-lieve that after all these years you duped me into funding your habit again!"

J.D. made a move toward me, but Emily held him back with a grip on his wrist. "Ben . . ." She shook her head, her eyes misting.

J.D.'s eyes darkened menacingly. "Why don't you get the fuck out of here, ass-hole?"

Adrenaline coursing through me, I leaned my face nearer to his. "Why don't you?"

J.D. snorted.

"If I see you here again . . ."

A vicious smile crossed his lips. He pulled back his jacket, revealing the han-dle of the gun tucked into his waist. He blew out his lips. "You won't do jack."

Reckless with rage, my voice rose to a shout. "Trust me, asshole. You come back here, and I'll kill you!"

CHAPTER

7

Two days passed without word from Helen or Rick. My life returned to a semblance of normal, but the pain of Emily's death burned deeper. *Closure. That stupid cliché!* Just as with Aaron's loss, closure eluded me again. The need to know what had happened to Emily was an unrelenting hunger. Even a hundred miles logged on my bike couldn't quell it. Especially since I kept seeing similarities and imagining connections to Aaron's mysterious and violent end.

Only two frantic back-to-back shifts at St. Jude's ER prevented me from trying to contact Michael Prince or Philip Maglio myself. And now, as I stood in St. Jude's ER Trauma Room waiting for the ambulance with the rest of the team, I knew I wouldn't be making any investigative queries any time soon.

I took the call. The receiver froze in my hand when the gravelly-voiced dispatcher told me, "I got a crew on its way with a neck stabbing. A drug dealer. Twenty-year-old male Hispanic . . ."

I swallowed away the dryness. "Status?"

"He lost a liter of blood at the scene. He's begun to compromise his airway."

"ETA?"

"Three minutes."

I looked at the clock. 11:40 A.M. "Who stabs anyone before lunch?"

The dispatcher chuckled. "No such rules in the drug trade."

"Okay, got it," I said, but my mind was already elsewhere. *Could this stabbing be related to Emily's?*

I'd barely hung up the phone when I heard the faint *wa-wa-wa* of the siren. Overhead the page of "Trauma—two minutes!" bellowed from the speakers. I raced down the hallway to the Trauma Room. The siren's wail grew steadily. As I stepped into the room, one of the nurses handed me a yellow waterproof gown, gloves, and the clear face shield we always wear when facing the risk of spraying blood or body fluids. I had just slipped on the second set of gloves when the siren's noise abruptly stopped.

There was a moment of quiet—the calm before the storm—and then shouts echoed down the hallway. Seconds later, the stretcher burst into the room. One paramedic propelled the stretcher; the other had his hand clamped against the patient's neck, no doubt trying to plug a leaking dyke.

The Hispanic boy lay remarkably still on the stretcher. His color was dusky, his eyes bulging. He breathed in panicky short bursts, producing the kind of high-pitched gasps that brought an instinctive cringe. Thoughts of Emily evaporated as I hurried over to the critically ill patient.

The able paramedic—who I knew only as Juan—had his hand stapled to the boy's neck. Without looking up, Juan said, "Kid's name is Enrique Martinez." Then he muttered something in Spanish to his patient.

"No English?" I stood on the other side of the hospital stretcher waiting for Juan and his partner to swing the boy over from the ambulance gurney.

"He does." Juan nodded. "Just trying to reassure him. I told him that everything is okay. The doctor is here."

I wondered.

Enrique had barely touched the stretcher when the nurse had the rest of his shirt (already cut open by the paramedics) off completely. The spaces between the ribs of his skinny gray chest sucked in with each small grunting breath. Out of the corner of my eye, I noticed that Juan's hand pulsed back and forth against Enrique's neck. I didn't need to lay a hand on the patient to know he had an expanding traumatic aneurysm of his carotid artery. Untreated, the only question was whether the wound would cause him to suffocate or bleed to death first. My money was on suffocation.

"We're intubating. Now!" I said to the charge nurse, Grace. "Tell ENT and Vascular Surgery. He's going to the OR stat as soon as we've tubed him."

"Which drugs, Ben?" Grace asked.

"None." My heart pounded and my mouth dried. I elbowed my way to the patient's neck. "No time for drugs. And we can't risk paralyzing him. His vocal cords might be totally obscured by the aneurysm."

With monitors now attached to Enrique, alarms blared their concern that his pulse was too fast, his blood pressure too low, and his blood critically deprived of oxygen. All the while, Enrique lay wide-eyed and still on the stretcher, his nostrils flaring with each high-pitched gasp.

I leaned closer to him. "Enrique, we need to pass a tube into your lungs to help you breathe. You're going to feel discomfort in your throat. You might even gag. But it will help. Trust me."

Enrique either nodded or his head just bobbed in sync with his desperate breathing. I had no time to sort out which.

I took the laryngoscope from the respiratory tech's outstretched hand, aware of its sobering weight. Enrique didn't fight as I eased his head back into the "sniffing position" on the stretcher. I opened his mouth and slid in the laryngoscope's blade. When I pulled his tongue forward with the device's handle, the sight of a pulsing red glob of tissue met my eyes. As I'd feared, the expanding aneurysm had pushed his normal structures out of the way. All I could see was the relentless pinkish mass.

Sweat beaded on my brow. I repositioned the blade to my left and pulled harder. Enrique groaned in response but his head held still. I caught a glimpse of white—not the usual "pair of white running shoes" view of the vocal cords, but enough to orient me.

Afraid the streak of white might disappear like a ship in dense fog, I barked to the respiratory tech: "Tube!" She slapped the clear snorkel-like device into my right hand. Without waiting, I snaked it into the mouth and aimed it for the white patches. I had to rock the tube slightly before I felt the reassuring thuds of the tracheal rings as it glided down his windpipe.

Enrique coughed, and the sound whistled from the tube, confirming that it was in the right location. Even before the tube was attached to the ventilator, his breathing quieted and his chest relaxed because he finally had an unobstructed passage to breathe through.

While the respiratory tech taped and stabilized the tube and attachments, I turned to Juan. "I want to have a look at his neck wound."

Juan frowned. "You sure?"

I nodded.

He hesitated and then slowly peeled his hand off Enrique's neck. A few inches below the angle of his jaw, the skin swelled out like a baseball cut in half. In the center, a tidy incision, no more than a half an inch, cut horizontally across his neck. A drop of blood oozed from the base of the laceration as the wound throbbed in rhythm with the baseball below it.

I glanced at Juan. "Okay, you can put your hand back. Meantime, Grace, let's get a pressure dressing on the wound while we transfer him up to the OR."

Before either could respond, a geyser of blood erupted from Enrique's neck. I stumbled back as it hit me square in my upper chest and splattered my face mask.

"Resume pressure!" I yelled.

Juan's hand slapped noisily against the patient's neck. But even with the aid of his other hand, he had trouble holding his grip. The blood swelled between his fingers and cascaded over the top of them, making the skin of his neck as slippery as ice.

"Blood pressure is falling!" Grace said.

Enrique's eyes rolled back in his head. I knew he didn't have enough blood reaching his brain to maintain consciousness. "To the OR now!" I shouted. "Let's go!"

Someone unclamped the brakes to the stretcher. As soon as I heard the click, I shoved the stretcher and hurtled it toward the door. The staff fell into a well-choreographed routine, moving IV poles, bags of blood, and the ventilator in step with the stretcher. We sprinted as a group for the end of the hallway.

At the doors of the surgical suite, Juan shouted, "I've lost the pulse!" Like a pole-vaulter, he hopped onto the stretcher. Knees straddling Enrique's chest, Juan knelt over the patient and began urgent chest compressions.

The surgical team met us at the door. "Okay, we've got it from here," the anesthetist said as he moved into my spot and assumed control of the stretcher. He tapped me once on the shoulder to let me know my job was done. He turned to his OR nurses. "Let's get him in the room!"

Nodding, I took a step back and watched as the stretcher was wheeled away. With Juan still riding Enrique's chest, the procession soon disappeared behind the operating room's closing doors, but I knew they were fighting a battle that was already lost.

I sat at the desk scribbling my notes in the ER's disheveled and stretcherless Trauma Room. I'd washed my face and neck, but I still had stains on my scrubs from the blood that had leaked around the neck of my gown. The room's floor had been hurriedly mopped but was still awaiting a proper decontamination. I could see splatters of missed blood. They reminded me of Emily's apartment, and that solitary arc of AB-negative blood on her wall. *Her killer's blood.*

Grace poked her friendly round face through the curtains covering the entry of the room. "Enrique didn't make it," she announced softly.

"Yeah."

"We did all we could," Grace said soothingly.

"You figure?"

"You secured his airway. There was nothing else you could do, Ben."

"I should have never told Juan to release his grip on the boy's neck. He should have gone to the OR with that hand in place."

"He wasn't bleeding at that moment." Grace's voice wavered before regaining its conviction. "The artery could've erupted at any time. You can't plug a burst pipe with the palm of your hand. You know that."

"True." I mustered a smile, grateful for her support but wishing I believed her more. "Thanks, Grace."

"It's not your fault, Ben." She withdrew her head from the gap in the curtains.

I turned back to the chart. Grace had a point. Regardless of my decision to expose his neck, Enrique was unlikely to have survived. The odds had been stacked against him. And long before the knife pierced his neck, too. Enrique wasn't so much a victim of my medical mismanagement as he was of his unsavory and lethal trade. *Fucking junk!*

"Dr. Dafoe?" The small voice grabbed my attention through the curtain. It sounded familiar, but I had trouble placing it. "It's Lara Maxwell. I'm on my way home. The nurse out front said I could find you here."

"Of course, Lara," I said, genuinely pleased to hear her. I stood up and pulled back the curtains.

In a T-shirt and sweats, with her hair tied in a ponytail and a mouth full of gum, Lara could have passed for even younger than fourteen. After having seen her suffer through some very adult afflictions, both an overdose and associated heart attack, I was tickled to see the childlike innocence back on her face.

Lara's jaw fell open as her wide eyes took in the messy surroundings. "Is this where I was . . . when . . . after the ambulance?"

"Only for a couple of hours." I smiled and folded my arms across my chest, conscious of the bloodstains on my scrubs. "A long tense couple of hours, mind you."

She appeared dumfounded.

"How are you?"

"Good." She chomped on her gum, unable to take her eyes off the floor. "I'm going home today."

"I'm glad."

She looked up at me shyly. "Dr. Dafoe, I just wanted to say thanks again for . . ." She cleared her throat. "You know . . ."

"I know." I nodded. "You're welcome, Lara. Cases like yours make this job feel worthwhile."

"That's good," she said vaguely. Her eyes fell to the ground again, and her feet shuffled in place.

"Lara? Is there something else?"

"You know what you told me and Isabelle about . . . um . . . your brother?"

I tensed at the mention of Aaron. "Yes?"

"Did that one time using drugs . . ." She cleared her throat again and looked up at me plaintively. "Did it really ruin his life?"

I inhaled slowly. I studied the spatters on the floor. Now they reminded me more of Aaron's burned and bloodstained car. "I was exaggerating, Lara."

She squinted at me in confusion. "The drugs didn't ruin his life?"

"It was more complicated than that," I said, struggling to explain. "It wasn't just one time with him. Aaron got heavily into drugs. And if not me, someone else probably would have introduced him to the junk. But it's still hard not to feel responsible."

"Okay," she said, but her eyes begged for more reassurance.

"Lara, you don't need to worry," I said. "You dodged a bullet—granted, a big and pointy one—but you're going home healthy. I suspect you'll never look at those 'harmless' rave drugs the same way."

"I'm not going to look at them at all!" Lara spat. Her eyes moistened and her voice cracked. "I'm going to warn my friends, too. No one tells us that this stuff can kill you."

"You'll make a good spokesperson."

She flung her arms around me and gave me a quick hug. Embarrassed, she turned away without making eye contact. "I'm sorry about your brother, Dr. Dafoe," she mumbled. "But thanks for saving me." Without waiting for a reply, she hurried out of the room.

I tallied the week's ER scorecard in my head: one win, one loss. Batting five hundred might be a good stat in baseball, but it wasn't very impressive in an Emergency Department. Still, Lara's visit lifted my spirits after Enrique's demise.

I felt even better when I stepped out of the Trauma Room and bumped into Alex heading the other way. She stood close enough that the floral scent of her shampoo drifted to me. She pointed to the collar of my scrubs. "What the hell, Ben?"

"Neck stabbing."

"Oh." She nodded. For a fellow ER physician, that was explanation enough.

"You got time for a coffee?"

"Depends." She grinned. "You got a new shirt?"

"You're so damn superficial." I chuckled. "But yeah, I'll go slip into something less conspicuous. I think I've got another one in my locker with only urine and vomit stains."

Alex rolled her eyes. "You're all class, Benjamin Dafoe."

I grabbed a T-shirt from my locker and slipped it on. Heading out of the hospital in the steady rain, I regretted not taking my jacket. The late afternoon was even colder than the morning. I was shivering by the time we stepped into the coffee shop across the street and grabbed a booth.

Sitting with coffees in front of us, I asked, "How's kindergarten working out for Talie?"

Alex's eyes lit up. "Much better than preschool!"

"How so?"

"She's called a truce with Ella, her archenemy from preschool."

"I didn't know you can have an archenemy in preschool."

"Me neither." Alex laughed. "But those two were oil and water. Until a couple of weeks ago when they discovered a mutual love of those tiny Polly Pocket dolls. Now they're the bestest of friends."

"Ah, if only Disney and Mattel ran the world . . ."

"I think they already do," she groaned.

I had a sip of my coffee. "And Marcus? What's he up to?"

At the mention of her husband, the joy drained from her face. "He'll be tied up in New York for a while longer," she said with an evasive shrug.

"That blood bank business of his is really taking off."

"I guess," she said distantly. "Seems like all new parents want to store their children's umbilical cord blood."

I knew that umbilical cord blood contains stem cells that, if stored at birth, can be used later to repopulate the bone marrow with healthy cells in the event a bone marrow transplant is ever required. It represented another form of insurance for parents, and I understood the demand for it. If I ever had a child, I would probably want the same.

"So let's hear about your trauma patient," Alex said, clearly trying to divert the conversation away from the topic of her husband.

I told Alex about Enrique Martinez's stabbing. She said all the right things—the same things I would have said, but not necessarily believed, if our roles had been reversed. Still, I felt better for having vented to her.

She reached out and squeezed my hand supportively. "So, how are you?"

I looked away and bought some time with a long sip of coffee. "Okay, thanks. Better, really."

"Hmmm." She let go of my hand. "The cops still don't have any leads?"

"I pulled myself or I was pulled—I'm not sure which, actually— from the case. I haven't heard in a couple of days."

Alex studied me intently. "And that's killing you, isn't it?"

I smiled. "You have me pegged for a control freak, huh?"

"No," Alex said, stone-faced. "I know how much Emily meant to you. If I were in your shoes, I would be desperate to know who did that to her."

"You're not far off," I said. "I'm half tempted to start my own investigation."

A smile broke through Alex's tight lips. "What with all your training and expertise."

"Alex, I can't shake this sense that somehow Emily's death and Aaron's—" I stopped the moment I saw Rick step through the door.

Alex turned to look over her shoulder, and we silently watched as Rick and Helen approached.

I introduced Alex to the detectives. She glanced at her watch. "Oh, darn. My shift started five minutes ago." She reached over and tapped my hand. "Ben, call me later, okay?" She snatched up her coffee and hurried for the door.

Helen stood and fingered her chunky necklace that had so many big colorful stones it looked as if it would strain her neck just to hold it up. "A nurse in the ER told us we'd find you here. May we join you?"

"Sure."

Helen eased herself into the booth. Rick dropped into the spot beside her.

"You already heard about Enrique Martinez?" I said.

Helen grimaced. "Enrique *who*?"

"The neck-stabbing victim. Killed the same way J.D. was." I glanced from one blank face to the other. Suddenly, I felt on edge. "Isn't that why you're here?"

Looking particularly subdued, Helen simply shook her head. Even more unsettling, Rick hadn't yet smiled.

"What is it, then?" I asked.

"We wanted to follow up on a few loose ends," Rick said.

My sense of alarm rose another notch. "Like what?"

As if overpowering his restraint, Rick's lips curled into a slight smile. "For starters, Ben, do you happen to know your blood type?"

"I'm a suspect?" I struggled to keep my tone under control.

"We're dotting 'i's and crossing 't's, Ben," Helen said sheepishly, but her reassurance brought me no comfort.

This can't be happening.

Rick scratched his chin, unperturbed. "Do you have any idea what percentage of murders are committed by the significant other or the ex?"

"Five years after the fact?" I said.

"Any time."

"This is crazy," I muttered.

Rick shrugged. "About your blood type—"

"You know my blood type," I snapped. "It's the same as Aaron's."

"AB-negative."

"Yes."

Helen looked up at me, her big gray eyes devoid of their usual humor but not their kindness. Clearly, she was finding this interrogation as awkward I was. "Ben, at the crime scene you told us that you didn't know J.D.," she said.

I held up my hands. "I didn't. Not even his name."

"But you had met him?"

"Once."

"The day you threatened him, right?" Rick added.

I gaped at him.

"It's true then?" Rick said.

Idiot! Why didn't I tell them before? "I wanted him to stay away from Emily," I said quietly.

"Which he obviously didn't do." Rick's tone dripped with insinuation.

"You're blowing this out of proportion."

"Not from where we stand," Rick said agreeably.

Helen fingered the charms on her necklace. Without looking up at me, she said, "Ben, tell us what happened the evening you threatened J.D."

"I went to see Emily about ten days ago," I said and then hurried to add, "We had arranged to meet, but she must have forgotten because when I got there her door was already open. I walked in and saw her paying J.D. with hundred-dollar bills." I cleared my throat. "I assumed it was a drug transaction."

As I carefully recounted my visit to Emily's apartment for the detectives, I relived the scene in my mind. I remembered standing nose-to-nose with J.D., hearing him breathe and smelling his garlicky breath.

J.D.'s hand drifted down to the gun in his belt. "You got some kind of death wish?" he said as he gripped the weapon's handle.

Emily stepped between us. She physically pushed us apart and then turned to me, her embarrassment giving way to anger. "Stop it, Ben! You're jumping to the wrong conclusion."

I turned on her. "How many times have I heard that from you?"

"Well, this time you are. It's always shoot first and ask questions later with you, isn't it?" She turned to face J.D. and handed him the last bill in her hand. "There. That's all of it. Now go."

J.D.'s grip eased on his gun. But he looked past Emily and straight into my eyes. "I don't appreciate being treated like dog crap. Especially by a loose fucking cannon like you."

"It's okay," Emily cooed as she reached up and laid a hand on J.D.'s shoulder. I couldn't see her face, but I could imagine her flirtatious smile.

J.D. shrugged and broke off eye contact. He took another step away from me and turned his attention to the bills in his hand. He counted the money slowly.

When finished, he grunted: "We're good, Emily." Then he turned and sauntered toward the door. With a hand on the doorknob, he looked over his shoulder at me. "You only get one free pass, cannon." Then he left.

Hands on my hips, I stared at Emily in disbelief. She flicked back her bangs, as she often did when frustrated, and then folded her arms across her chest. A moment of cool silence passed. "You want to hear what that was about or would you rather just assume you know?"

"Remember?" I said, unmoved. "I think you've worn out your quota of 'benefits of the doubt' from me."

"That was a lifetime ago," she said quietly.

Her comment stung. "Not for me."

"Not for me either," Emily said in a gentler tone. "I meant that I've changed, Ben. I'm in the program. I've been clean for months now."

Staring into those vulnerable blue eyes, I wanted to believe her. But I didn't. "So what were you paying a drug dealer in cash for?"

"My medicine," she said.

"I thought I was paying for that."

She took a step closer and touched me softly on the cheek. "You are, Ben. Thank you."

"So you don't use a pharmacy?" I grimaced. "You buy them from a drug dealer?"

"Not always." She pulled her hand from my cheek. "A month's worth of the prescription costs almost three thousand dollars."

"But I give you—"

"I know. Some months, with the rent and everything else, I can't afford to pay it all." She looked away, humiliated. "I don't have many other sources of income right now."

My jaw fell open. "Are you telling me that drug dealers are selling HIV medications now?"

"This one does. At two-thirds their face value." She sighed. "Some of his other clients get their HIV meds covered by Medicaid."

I chuckled, partly in relief and partly in disgust. "And they trade them in for the junk?"

Emily nodded.

"Jesus, Emily." I stepped forward and wrapped my arms around her tightly. "This is what it's come to. I'm so sorry."

Emily was quiet in response. I felt the warmth of her face as she buried her head deeper in my shoulder. I heard her sniff once, and I realized she was crying.

Helen and Rick listened to my entire account without interrupting.

"So you were giving Emily money to pay for her HIV treatment?" Rick said, though his tone was anything but admiring.

"For the past five or six months, I'd been supporting her. An interest-free loan, of sorts. My only stipulation was that she had to stay clean."

Rick's expression was sheer skepticism. "You're telling us J.D. was selling Emily black-market HIV drugs he got from other users?"

I nodded.

"Well, doesn't that just make you proud to be human?" Helen said, flashing a glimpse of her usual self. "What I don't understand, Ben, is why you didn't tell us all of this that night."

"I don't know. Maybe shock." I shook my head. "Emily was so private about the illness. She hid her HIV from everyone, family included, for years. Then she started to get sick, spiraling toward AIDS. She needed an antiviral cocktail of drugs, as we call it. She only told me because she needed financial support and medical advice. Even now, it feels like I'm betraying her confidence . . . her memory."

"That's right," Rick said. "You're betraying a ghost."

The anger stirred. I wet my lips, and took a slow breath. "What was there to tell you? I didn't know anything about J.D. other than that he was a drug dealer. You were going to find that out anyway. How does the rest of it help you?"

"Might help establish motive." Rick smiled. "You would've been plenty pissed if your hard-earned donations were being funneled into coke and crystal meth."

I picked up my empty cup and twirled it in my hand, resisting the urge to crush it. "Did her autopsy drug screen ever come back?"

Rick looked at Helen. She shook her head. "Her blood was clean."

Vindication soothed me, but it wasn't to last.

"And what about your engagement?" Rick asked. "Why did you hide it from us?"

"Habit, I guess," I said. "We kept it quiet for months after we were engaged. We'd planned to elope and surprise our friends. Then, after it all fell apart, I think we were both a little ashamed. Aside from my brother Aaron, no one ever knew."

Helen smiled sympathetically. "Ben, you make it tough for us when you conceal this kind of info."

I nodded without comment, but I wanted to slap myself for the pointless omission.

Rick shifted in his seat. "Just a couple of other things, Benjamin."

"Okay," I said, uneasy with his crocodile smile.

"Last Friday night, where were you between eight and ten P.M.?"

"I got up from my nap around seven-thirty."

"Your *nap*?"

"I was working overnight, starting at eleven. Most of us sleep before night shifts," I explained, "but I like to take long rides before the shift starts. It energizes me."

"As in a motorcycle?"

"A racing bike . . . bicycle." I thought for a moment. "That evening, I did about fifty miles out to SeaTac and back."

"Alone?"

"There's only one seat on my bike."

He nodded, as if appeased.

"Anything else?" I asked.

The two detectives shared a glance. "Listen, Ben, we can clear this misunderstanding up very quickly," Helen said.

"Oh?" I felt the knot tightening in my belly. "How's that?"

Rick reached into his jacket pocket and pulled out a clear plastic biohazard bag that held a Q-Tip-like swab and a yellow-top bottle. He held up the biological specimen container, drawing out the moment. "We just need a sample of your DNA."

CHAPTER

Dazed, I drove home from my interview with Helen and Rick, grappling with the realization that I'd become the prime suspect in Emily's murder.

Emily. The woman who had broken my heart too many times to count. The woman I had loved so deeply that at times I might have killed *for* her. I remembered the closest I'd come to doing so was at the very end of our engagement. And had I followed through, the murder would have been biblical in nature, along the lines of Cain and Abel. That unpleasant incident represented the climax of a love story with too many unpleasant chapters.

Nine months into our clandestine engagement, Emily and I had finally set a date for our elopement that looked as though it might stick. We intended to fly to Hawaii and get married on the same beach on Kauai where we'd spent such a blissful week with Aaron.

We had already had a few false starts on the wedding front. After I caught her snorting coke with Aaron and Kyle, it took five months of sobriety for Emily to regain my trust enough for us to proceed with the planning. Mexico in April had fallen through because of a staffing crisis at my hospital. And we'd called off our Las Vegas plans for July when, in a fit of hysterics, we realized we were about to elope to Vegas and we might have to explain that to our children and grandchildren one day.

Perhaps the pregnancy cemented our intentions, but I'd never been more in love with Emily than that September. With the glow of early pregnancy, she had risen in my eyes from gorgeous to heartachingly beautiful. At times, I became choked up just looking at her untamable crystal blue eyes and perfect flushed features. More than husband and wife, soon we were going to be a family. And male hormones or not, the realization had turned me into a blubbering but happy mess; or as Aaron, the only other person privy to our latest secret, had dubbed me, "the Alan Alda of expectant fathers."

That evening I was scheduled to work an ER shift, but I'd cajoled a colleague into covering for me. I wanted to surprise Emily with a romantic dinner and the tangible proof (in the form of our plane tickets to Hawaii) that we were actually about to wed. I had an ulterior motive, too: I wanted to bolster her mood. In the past days, she had slipped into a deep funk. Withdrawn and uncharacteristically irritable, Emily wrestled demons I couldn't see. I wrote it off to a case of combined prewedding jitters and early pregnancy blues.

Unlocking the door to our third-floor condo, I bounded inside, tickets in one hand and roses in the other. "Em," I called out. "I have our tickets. We can't back out now!"

No reply. I checked the bedroom and living room, but Emily was nowhere to be seen. Giving up, I headed for the kitchen and grabbed a vase. The perfumed scent of the fresh roses wafted up to me. My mood bordered on euphoric as I cut away the wrapping and balled up the crinkly plastic. I opened the cupboard under the sink and tossed it in the trashcan. I was about to close the door when something caught my eye—a green band hooked onto the inner edge of the trashcan. I recognized it instantly as a patient identification wristband. I reached down, pulled it out, and read the printing on the label.

My euphoria evaporated.

I read the date on the label again, confused and betrayed by its implication. Emily had been an ER patient the previous day at Swedish Hospital when she was supposed to have been visiting her parents on the Olympic Peninsula.

I tried Emily on her cell, but the call went to voicemail. With growing worry, I decided to run the situation by Aaron. Despite his questionable personal choices, he'd always managed to keep a brotherly perspective on the highs and lows in my relationship with Emily.

I didn't want to have this conversation over the phone, so I headed down to the parking garage and grabbed my road bike from the locker. I cycled the three miles up to Aaron's townhouse, trying to figure what would have sent Emily to the Emergency Room and forced her to hide it from me. But I was stumped. If it were pregnancy-related, surely she would have told me.

Pulling up to Aaron's trendy townhouse on Twenty-fifth Street (the mortgage on which would have taxed my professional income to the hilt) I was too preoccupied to care if Aaron's vague Internet ventures were what really supported his lavish lifestyle.

I locked my bike out front. Not bothering to ring the buzzer, I dug in my pocket for the key to his place and opened the door. The moment I stepped inside, I smelt the slightly acrid smoke. The scent grew stronger with each step up the half flight of stairs to the carpeted living room. I stopped dead at the top of the staircase.

Kneeling in front of the coffee table, Aaron gaped at me, a tiny silver pipe wedged between his lips. Whether from surprise or the crystal meth he was smoking, his eyes were dilated so widely that they appeared entirely black.

"What's wrong with you?" Emily giggled, her back still to me. She reached to take the pipe from his mouth.

Aaron pulled away from Emily's hand.

"What's your problem?" she said impatiently.

Aaron nodded his chin toward me. Emily turned and looked over her shoulder. "Oh, God. Ben!" She jumped to her feet, knocking over the beer bottle on the table, and rushed toward me. She tried to throw her arms around me, but I pushed her away by her chest.

"Ben, it's just this one time . . ."

I sidestepped her and marched over to where Aaron sat. He dropped the pipe on the coffee table and rose to his feet to meet me. Our eyes locked; his expression was a mix of shame and defiance.

Without a word, I punched him as hard as I could, my fist smashing into his mouth and throbbing on contact. He stumbled back two steps. Blood erupted from his split lip. I punched him again with my left hand, hitting him in the cheek. This time, he stood his ground but his head whipped to the side and back, spraying me. I had a bitter taste of his blood—my blood—on my tongue.

Aaron stared at me, eyes as obstinate as ever, but he made no effort to fight back. He didn't even raise his hands to fend off my blows. I cocked my arm to hit him again, when I felt Emily's fingers wrap around my elbow. I shook my arm loose and spun savagely to face her, my fist poised to hit her.

"I wouldn't blame you if you did, Ben," Emily said. She pointed at the

miserable, still-smoking crack pipe on the table. "Don't pin this on Aaron. I wanted this. God, I needed it."

I dropped my arm. "What the fuck are you thinking?"

"I'm not thinking, Ben," she whimpered. "I'm not."

"The baby, Em," I said. "What about our baby?"

She shook her head and sniffed. "I miscarried yesterday. We lost our baby." Em covered her face with her palms and wept silently. "I was afraid if you found out you would call off the wedding," she sobbed. "Ben, we lost our baby."

We stood inches apart without touching, but I knew that the gulf between us was no longer crossable. My tears dripped down my cheek onto my shirt. "Em," I said hoarsely. "We've lost so much more than that."

I shook off the melancholy memory as soon I reached home. I stepped into my kitchen and headed for the refrigerator, hoping there was at least one cold beer left inside. I foraged through the shelves, but all I found was a bottle of lemon cooler left over from the last time I'd entertained, months earlier.

I sipped the flavorless drink at the countertop, debating whom to turn to after my run-in with the detectives. I ached for reassurance. I wished Mom were still alive. She had been such a supportive confidante to Aaron and me.

Mom had died four years earlier. The official cause of death was listed as ovarian cancer, but I think the ceaseless stress of nursing Dad through his alcohol-related dementia while having to watch Aaron march down the same path (albeit with a different poison) finally caught up to her. Diagnosed in May, she was dead by July. Though she was only sixty-one, I don't think she had any fight left in her. In a way, I was relieved Mom didn't live to suffer through the death of one son and now the incrimination of the other.

With nowhere else to turn, I phoned St. Jude's and asked for Alex. She agreed to meet after her shift without questioning why I needed to see her again so soon.

After hanging up, I headed out for my second ride of the day, though neither the cycle nor the long bath following it did much to relax my brittle nerves.

I met Alex half an hour before midnight at the Hudson Room on

Fourth Avenue, the spot we used to frequent before the San Francisco "incident." The funky overpriced bar was at best a third full. We chose a booth in the corner, as far away as possible from the hip-hop music echoing across the nearly deserted dance floor.

Alex drank an herb tea. I needed something with more kick, but by the bottom of my second scotch, I felt no more settled. When the ice cubes grazed my lips and I tasted only water, I put down the glass. Then I unloaded the entire story on her, beginning with the day I agreed to financially support Emily's anti-HIV drugs and ending with a recap of my recent police interview.

Alex appraised me for several seconds before saying a word. Finally, she shook her head slowly. "Why didn't you give them a DNA sample?"

"My head was swimming by that point." I waved to our waitress and pointed to my empty glass. "I was already guilty in Rick's eyes. And Helen was leaning that way, too."

She held up her palm. "Even more reason to give the sample."

"Maybe, but something feels very wrong."

"How so?"

"I never told anyone about the night I confronted J.D. and Emily. So how did Rick and Helen find out?"

Alex sipped her tea before answering. "Maybe a neighbor overheard you?"

"Right. The same neighbor who called me at the crack of dawn to taunt me about it in a whisper."

Alex viewed me with more patience than I deserved. "You're getting too keyed up, Ben. Why don't you just give them the sample and be done with it?"

I tore at a cocktail napkin. "The blood on Emily's wall was AB-negative."

Alex lips tightened, and a flicker of doubt crossed her eyes. "It's not your blood, is it, Ben?"

I swallowed. "Alex, I wasn't there that night."

Her face creased into a slight frown. She put her tea down slowly. "Are you saying you bled on her wall some other time?"

I shook my head. "I never bled on her wall. Not that night. Not ever."

She nodded. The skin at the edges of her lips and eyes relaxed. A smile fluttered across her lips. "Then what's there to worry about, Ben?"

More than her words, her relaxed body language brought me some comfort. I dredged up my first smile of the evening. "I don't know. I guess I'm getting paranoid. There seem to be so many coincidences. And then the blood of Emily's alleged killer turns out to be my rare blood type. . . ."

"So what's your next step?"

"I think I should talk to a lawyer."

She shook her head in surprise. "A criminal defense attorney?"

"Yeah."

She eyed me skeptically but didn't argue. She checked her watch. "Ben, I better get home to Talie. Sometimes she wakes up in the middle of the night and crawls into my bed. She'll wonder where I am." She chuckled. "And Dad won't hear her if she gets up. He snores like a jackhammer on overdrive."

"You go," I said. Emboldened by the scotch, I reached out and clutched her hand, squeezing a bit too long and tenderly. "Thank you, Alex. For everything."

She smiled and gently freed her hand from my grip. She stood up and hurried off without another word.

Sitting alone, I drained another scotch before I asked for the bill. The cute redheaded waitress with the sprinkling of freckles and a diamond nose stud strutted up to the table carrying the bill. Wearing a tight black T-shirt, she leaned a little closer than necessary when she deposited the bill on the table. "Did you lose your friend?" She flashed me an open-mouthed smile.

I wasn't sure whether she was hitting on me or this was an attempt beef up her tip. Regardless, I had little energy to respond. I forced a grin. "She had to go home. So do I, now."

A little tipsy, I wandered outside and flagged down a cab. I was thankful the older driver with the downcast eyes didn't attempt to engage me in conversation. I was too tired to carry on a superficial chat about the ungodly price of gas or the Sonics' latest woes.

Opening my door, I heard the electronic machine-gun blast of beeps from my ringing phone. The hallway clock read 1:15 A.M. My pulse quickened. The ringing stopped by the time I reached the phone. Hesitantly, I scrolled back through the call display, which read CANADA for the most recent call.

I was still holding the receiver in my hand when I felt it vibrate even before I heard the ring. CANADA flashed on the call display. I hesitated a moment and then brought the receiver to my ear.

"Benjamin."

The single whispered word set my heart sprinting. "What do you want?"

"To warn you."

"Warn me about what?"

"The blood."

My throat turned to sand. I knew exactly what he meant. "What blood?"

"On Emily's wall."

I froze in place; a statue couldn't have been stiller.

"It's your blood, Benjamin."

CHAPTER

10

A fitful sleep later, I climbed out of bed the next morning at 4:35 A.M. I expected another call from the whisperer, but by 5:30 A.M. none had come. Not planning to hang around for one, I changed into my riding gear. I strode down to the basement and into the attached garage. As my mountain bike was still in the shop, I reached for the road bike and pulled it down from its ceiling hook. Clicking my feet into the pedals, I longed for speed.

I headed out onto the dark and dangerously slick roads, intending to outrace my worries. With sparse traffic, I flew up and down the hills of downtown Seattle. I pumped every ounce of muscle into the steep climbs, sprinting up the hills. The lactic acid build-up in my muscles seared my thighs, and when I glanced at the heart monitor, my heart rate occasionally broke the two-hundred barrier. And yet, I couldn't reach the "high" or find the release that normally accompanied the endorphins that now coursed through my veins.

I returned home soaked from sweat and tasting salt in my dry mouth. My legs felt wobbly as I wheeled my bike back into the garage. But my mood was bleaker than ever. I couldn't shake the uncanny sense that none of the events of the past week had been coincidence.

Even before I climbed into the shower, I put in a call to Michael Prince's office. Expecting to get his voicemail at 7:50 A.M., I was surprised to hear his receptionist answer.

"This is Dr. Benjamin Dafoe." Stressing my title, I seized the opportunity to trade on my M.D. to emphasize the urgency. "It's vital that I see Mr. Prince as soon as possible."

"Of course, Dr. Dafoe," the receptionist said in her pleasant, soft Southern drawl. "I'll just have to check with Mr. Prince."

After holding for less than two minutes, I was asked to come to the office at nine.

I changed into my only suit, navy blue. Struggling with the tie, I marveled at how unnatural I looked in the mirror. I remembered Helen once teasing me that people who owned only one suit and tie generally heard the question "And how does the defendant plead?" whenever they wore it. At the time, I'd laughed, but I wasn't laughing now.

I headed down to my garage and hopped into my car. Ten minutes later, I pulled up to Prince's boxy glass high-rise office building on Fifth Avenue. I squeezed into the gap between two cars, but I almost reparked elsewhere; I was reluctant to chance anything that might bring me nearer to Seattle's legal system.

I rode the elevator to the thirty-second floor and stepped out into the sleek metal-and-wood elegance of the law offices of Pratt, Prince, and Higney.

In less than five minutes, I had a coffee in hand as I sat in Michael Prince's spacious office. The floor-to-ceiling windows looked out onto the Space Needle and beyond to the expanse of Puget Sound. The office was exactly as I'd imagined, right down to the crushed leather furniture and giant oil canvases (though I expected more splashy, Jackson Pollock–style abstracts rather than simple landscapes). As I sank into the brown chair across from Prince's desk, I wondered how many murderers and drug traffickers had sat there before me. Despite the new leather smell, I had an urge to wipe it down with an alcohol swab.

I don't belong here.

The oak door swung open and Michael Prince strode inside. In an olive suit and textured green tie, Prince wasn't far off from what I'd pictured, either. I didn't count on the long silver-gray hair that swept down to his collar nor his compact size (he was at most five-eight and couldn't have weighed more than 140 pounds), but his strong handsome features, manicured hands, and easy smile fit my preconceived notion for his line of work.

He walked up to me and pumped my hand forcefully. "Dr. Dafoe, I'm Michael Prince. Thanks so much for coming in," he said, as if he'd requested the meeting.

"It's Ben," I said. "And thank you for the taking the time."

He waved me back into the murderer's chair as he sidled around the desk and dipped into his seat. "Not at all. Janelle tells me the matter is urgent." He spoke in a smooth, clear voice, articulating every syllable as if a court stenographer were transcribing our conversation.

"Or just one giant misunderstanding," I said, clearing my throat self-consciously. "I might have reacted prematurely."

Prince leaned back in his seat and touched his palms together. "I wish all my clients reacted the same way. It would make my job so much easier in the long run."

I was tempted to ask him if he was referring to before or after they'd committed the crime, but I decided to keep my prejudgments under wraps for the time being.

"What can I do for you, Ben?"

"Did you hear about Emily Kenmore's murder?"

He nodded. "Double homicide. Stabbing in the female victim's apartment. Possible drug connection." The story had brought some mild media interest, but Prince fired off the facts as if he'd kept an eye on developments and expected to become professionally involved. "Occupational hazard, Ben. I have a habit of recounting local news items as though they were police reports."

"I was once engaged to the female victim."

Prince separated his hands for a moment and flashed his palms. "I'm sorry."

"That was five years ago," I said. "But I'd seen Emily and the other victim a few days before their murder. In fact, there was an . . . altercation."

Prince tilted his head and his frown lines deepened, but he didn't comment.

"When the detectives first approached me I didn't tell them the whole story."

Prince nodded, his face placid. "Which is?"

I took a sip of my coffee, mainly to wet my lips. Then I told Prince about the confrontation with J.D. and Emily and how I'd withheld re-counting the incident along with the details of my engagement and re-cent financial support for Emily. Recapping the week—including my lies of omission to the police, my lack of alibi, the cut across my knuck-les, and my refusal to supply a DNA sample—I was struck by what a guilty light the events cast on me. Morbidly, I wondered whether Prince ever believed his clients' version of events. Deciding I must have already stretched my credibility to the breaking point, I opted not to mention the anonymous whisperer with the Canadian phone number.

Prince sat up straighter in his chair. "And the detectives haven't con-tacted you since last night?"

"No."

"I need to ask you something, Ben."

"Okay."

Prince stared past me out to the gray drizzle falling on Puget Sound. "Is there a strong likelihood that the blood found at the scene will match yours?"

"It's not mine, but the way this week has been unfolding"—I swallowed—"I'm concerned about that possibility." Even to me, the words sounded as if they came from the mouth of an indicted politi-cian trying to put a new spin on the truth.

Prince nodded distantly, but his voice was businesslike. "The detec-tives can't request a DNA sample without cause."

"Which they might have, but it's a moot point anyway. They don't need me to get a sample."

Prince's eyes leapt from the window and locked onto mine. "How is that possible, Ben?"

"They already have my DNA."

"From a previous investigation?"

"Sort of. Two years ago, I gave the S.P.D. a saliva sample to compare the DNA to the blood they found in the trunk of my brother's aban-doned car. It was an exact match."

Prince's eyes lit with understanding. "You two are identical twins."

"Were," I said. "Aaron died in the trunk of his car on the way to wherever his killer or killers dumped the body."

Prince tapped his chin. "Did you see the car?"

I still see it in my dreams. "Yes," I said. I had a flashback to the warehouse parking lot where two years earlier Aaron's scorched BMW 330 stood outlined by yellow crime-scene tape.

It was a spectacular Seattle morning. The city glistened in the sunshine and the greenery engendered by weeks of nutritive rain. The air was still slightly crisp from a northerly breeze that carried with it the scent of the spring blossoms. Nature's perfection was wasted on me as I rode halfheartedly through my downtown circuit. I was already worried about my brother. Though our face-to-face contact had been sporadic since Aaron had moved to Vancouver (a mere 150 miles north of Seattle) the year before, normally I could always track him down by phone. Ten days had passed without my brother returning any of my messages.

People often asked us whether we thought that as identical twins we shared some kind of telepathic connection, like the characters in The Corsican Brothers. *We used to laugh at the idea. But that morning of Helen's call, I'd woken up sensing that something was very wrong. I tried phoning Aaron twice. I had just hung up the second time when Helen called. After stiff pleasantries, she said, "Ben, we've found a car in an industrial park in Fife. It's a black BMW." She paused. "Registered under your brother's name."*

"Where's Aaron?" I asked, my heart in my throat.

"Don't know. But his car has been vandalized."

"Vandalized how?"

"Someone looks to have tried to torch it, but the car didn't burn."

"Where are you?"

"I don't think there's any point in you coming out here now. We can do this over the phone."

"Where, Helen?" I insisted, the feeling of doom welling up in me.

She gave me the address. I resisted the urge to ask her why a Homicide cop was calling about my brother's abandoned vehicle. I suppose I didn't want to hear the obvious. I threw on a pair of jeans and a T-shirt and tore out to my car.

I drove the twenty miles in fifteen minutes. Tires screeching, I skidded into the warehouse parking lot. Four or five Seattle P.D. vehicles were scattered around the otherwise empty lot. When I saw the CSI van, I tasted bile. There was no more doubt.

I pulled up beside Aaron's BMW, parked in the corner and cordoned off by yellow tape. The black paint on the roof had bubbled and peeled off in spots. Smoke stains blackened the windows. The trunk was popped wide open.

I hopped out of my car. Standing by the CSI van and speaking on her cell phone, Helen tried to flag me down, but I raced past her. Dodging the CSI tech, I jumped the crime-scene tape and stopped directly in front of the trunk of the car.

Congealed and partially cooked, there was no mistaking the puddles that saturated the bottom of the trunk. Blood. It coated the surface so thoroughly that I could barely spot any sections of the gray lining that hadn't turned hemorrhagic brown.

It could have been anyone's blood. Or even the blood of a slaughtered dog or farm animal. But staring into the trunk of that smoked-out BMW, I knew it was Aaron's; which, after all, was my blood, too.

Prince scratched his chin and stared out the window for a several moments after I finished the story. "They never found his body?" He directed his question at Puget Sound.

"No."

"So he might still be alive?"

I shook my head and sighed. I'd faced the same assertion many times before. "There was too much blood in the trunk. He had to have bled out."

Prince looked over to me, eyeing me doubtfully. "That's your expert opinion beyond a doubt?" he asked as if jousting with a prosecution witness.

"I'm not a pathologist but—"

"Exactly." Prince cut me off with a snap of his fingers. "And even if you were, how could you know for certain from the trunk of a burned-out car that your brother had really died inside it?"

"What's your point, Michael?"

Prince broke into a self-congratulatory smile. "For the sake of argument, let's say the blood at the victim's apartment matches your DNA."

I knew where he was heading, but I said nothing.

His smile grew. "Who's to say it's not your brother's blood?"

CHAPTER

11

I headed from Prince's office back to the ER in a fog. Neither his $75,000 retainer nor his $500-per-hour fees fazed me. Beyond the necessities and my relatively expensive bike habit, I had minimal use for money. Even after my mortgage, the cycling, and half a year's worth of Emily's medications, I had enough saved to cover the costs. But the realization that I now shared one of Seattle's top defense attorneys with the city's most hardened criminals rattled the hell out of me.

I sleepwalked my way through my afternoon ER shift. Fortunately, none of my patients that afternoon required my "A game." Unless of course I missed something, which is always *the* great fear among emergency doctors.

Most of my nonmedical friends assume that critically ill or traumatized patients cause ER docs the most stress. Not so. Resuscitating patients is for the most part cookbook medicine. Challenging and stressful at times, to be sure, but like a pilot landing under emergency conditions, we simulate situations and practice protocols to handle those critical moments. Sometimes, as with Enrique Martinez's neck stabbing, our protocols fail us; but in those cases death is inevitable, not a mistake. What haunts most ER physicians are the ambiguous cases: the *mimickers* that most of us have faced, wrongly diagnosed, and sent home to bad outcomes. Such time bombs—which nourish the malpractice lawyers but cause the rest of us sleepless nights—include the patient's "indigestion" that turns out to be a massive heart attack, the "bronchitis" that is proven on autopsy to have been a huge blood clot, or the "migraine" in the patient who went home and died of a brain aneurysm, to name a few.

As I shuffled out of the ER at the end of my shift, I hoped there had been no mimickers hiding in the day's mix. Reviewing the mental checklist of patients I'd seen and diagnoses I'd made, I was reminded that, despite its risks, I loved my job. With all the turmoil in my personal life, emergency medicine was the one constant factor. The team at St. Jude's was my extended family. The variety and bizarreness of the problems and people I faced kept me constantly challenged and stimulated (and provided me an endless supply of cocktail party anecdotes). Once in a while, I even had the chance to touch people's lives in a positive way, and I never tired of that rush.

But now even my livelihood was threatened.

I'd originally planned to drive straight home from work—maybe even indulge in the unopened bottle of scotch tucked away in the cabinet—but I found myself heading toward a neighborhood in the Capitol Hill district that backed onto Lake Washington.

I had been in Helen's modern one-bedroom apartment once before. She'd promised to feed me a dinner that she billed as being "whipped together with leftovers and crap," and which turned out to be a five-course feast that included the best salmon I had ever tasted. Aside from discovering her culinary talents, I learned that Helen was "happily" divorced for years and that her nineteen-year-old daughter was studying drama at UCLA. Consequently, much of the year she had the place to herself, and she liked it that way.

Parking in front of her building, I realized I would likely be far less welcome on this occasion. With little to lose, I trudged up to her door anyway. Her intercom rang twice and then Helen's voice boomed over the speaker. "Don't remember ordering pizza or Chinese tonight."

I cleared my throat. "Helen, it's Ben Dafoe."

There was a pause. "Ben, this isn't a good idea."

"Please, Helen. It's important."

She didn't reply, but the door buzzed and my hand shot out for it, concerned she might change her mind at any moment.

In a bulky sweatshirt and matching pants, Helen waited for me by the door to her fourth-floor apartment. She wore a simple bead neck-lace that looked out of place with her bulky sweats. With hair down, no makeup, and an expression that lacked its trademark smile, she looked much older. No doubt, her assessment of my condition wasn't any more complimentary, but like me she kept it to herself.

Silently, I followed her into her apartment. I was struck again by the uncluttered layout of her living room: two cloth sofas, a stereo in the corner, a few standing plants, and two white orchids on either side of her mantle. The only crowded feature was the bookshelf in the corner filled with a diverse range of titles and genres.

We sat down across from each other. I was disappointed Helen didn't offer me a drink. I craved something to ease the tense awkward-ness that ran between us like electricity. "Thanks for seeing me."

She sighed. "Nothing personal, Ben, but this kind of contact isn't exactly kosher."

I nodded. "I had to see you, though. So I could be up-front about everything."

"Oh?"

I cleared my throat. "I got another call this morning."

"From your whisperer?"

I nodded.

"What did old Deep Throat tell you this time?"

I broke off our eye contact. "That the blood at Emily's place is mine."

She didn't say anything, but her blank face showed no surprise. Feel-ing my heart thump against my ribcage, I wondered if it meant the de-tectives had already gotten a positive match from the sample I'd given them two years earlier.

Helen was too good a poker player to reveal her hand. "Is that why you refused to give us a DNA specimen?"

"God, no!" I snapped. I stopped to breathe while I reined in my emotions. "Look. Things are so upside-down right now that I wouldn't be surprised if my DNA was a match for the blood at the scene."

Helen viewed me coolly without comment.

"Helen, I think someone is setting me up."

She folded her arms over her chest. When she spoke, her tone was even more detached. "Ben, we hear that a lot in our line of work. And yet in my sixteen years with Homicide I can count with one finger the number of times it's turned out be the case."

"It did happen, though!"

"Yeah, but it involved one stupid drug dealer planting a murder weapon on another stupid drug dealer." She sighed. "No one borrowed anyone else's DNA." She grunted a humorless chuckle. "That only happens to O.J."

"It's different with me. I am one of a pair of identical twins."

"But your brother died two years ago," she said, still measuring me with her eyes. "And unless you have a long-lost evil triplet lurking around, I don't see how it makes a difference."

She was right. And now I'd just exposed my attorney's defense strategy, but I didn't care. At that moment, all I wanted was to see a flicker of belief from Helen. "Why, Helen?"

She reached out and picked off a brownish leaf the plant beside her. "Why what?"

"Why would I kill Emily and some drug dealer I don't even know?"

"I do know this: The vast majority of my business boils down to two motives." She held up two fingers as if flashing the peace sign. "Money and sex." She wiggled each finger in turn. "I'm pretty sure that at one point you were sexually involved with the victim. And you've told us you were giving her money up until she died."

I gripped the armrest, digging my fingers into the fabric so hard that they pressed against the wood frame. "Helen, I was giving her money to help prolong her life, not end it."

"Problem is, Ben, there's no easy way to prove that you provided the money voluntarily."

I gritted my teeth. "You can't be serious!"

"We have to consider the possibility that Emily was blackmailing you."

"Blackmailing me? Over what?"

"I have no idea, Ben," Helen said, showing a hint of her own impatience. "Drugs? Financial indiscretions? Sexual proclivities? Or maybe over your brother's disappearance. We never did figure out exactly what happened to him."

My heart thumped harder as I tried to tame my rising fury. "So now I killed my brother, too?" I spat. "Jesus, I think I would have got a better reception at Rick's house!"

"I just threw that out there," Helen said. "I think you better step back and consider how all of this looks to us." Again, her fingers came up with each point. "You were once engaged to the victim. You paid her off in cash every month. You threatened to kill the second victim. You have no alibi. You initially lied to us about your association with the victims." She moved to the fingers on her other hand. "There's a good chance your blood is at the murder scene. And you refused to give us a DNA sample."

Steadying my breathing, I held Helen's stare.

"You tell me, Ben. What the hell are we supposed to think?" she asked, but her tone was compassionate, as if seeking some way to escape the inevitable conclusion associated with all the evidence.

The sense of defeat was so strong that I felt the rest of my emotions slip away. My chest quieted. My hands steadied. "How long have you known me, Helen? Five years?"

She looked away. "Sounds right."

"Do you really think I'm capable of butchering two people?"

Helen sighed. "Ben, you wouldn't believe what I've seen people to be capable of."

"Not people, Helen. Me."

She reached down and touched the beads hanging around her neck. She fingered them like they were rosary beads. "In some ways, I miss the old Wild West." She showed a fleeting smile. "It was easier then. The bad guys all wore black hats. There was no confusion."

"I don't own a hat."

"That's the problem. Not all murders are committed by people we recognize as bad guys. Sometimes it's just a reckless, desperate spur-of-the-moment act."

"But what happened to Emily wasn't a spur-of-the-moment crime. Someone tortured her."

For a moment, I saw agreement in Helen's eyes. But then she shook her head and looked at me with genuine sorrow. "Can I tell you about the toughest bust I ever made, Ben?"

I nodded.

"Mark Bellon. Remember the name?"

"Vaguely."

"It was big news about eight or nine years ago. Mark was a twenty-two-year-old seminary student," she said. "A shy skinny kid. A real wallflower. He volunteered at a downtown parish with a priest by the name of Father Kevin McDougall. The man was a living saint who worked with addicted street kids and the homeless. Ran a support system for half of the downtown's disenfranchised out of his small church. And young Mark, a priest-in-training, worshipped Father Kevin.

"Then this sixteen-year-old kid, Dale Einarson, showed up claiming that Father Kevin had molested him. Dale was a born con artist. Could've sold the tainted apple a second time to Adam. Dale demanded hush money for not running to the media with his all-too-common story of sexual victimization at the hands of a priest. In far more saintly terms, Father Kevin told Dale to go screw himself. He was prepared to defend himself in public."

"But Mark Bellon wasn't going to let that happen."

"Exactly." Helen nodded. "For a while Mark even paid Dale off out of his own pocket. But Dale kept wanting more, and seminary students don't have deep pockets."

I dropped my eyes to the floor, knowing where the story was headed.

"The irony was that the bribes Mark paid only served to make Father Kevin look even guiltier," Helen said. "Mark was so desperate, he honestly believed he had no options left except murder. But he didn't have a gun. Not even a knife. So Mark took a hammer from the church's tool room and used it to crush Dale's skull in." She cleared her throat. "Mark's now doing life in the state pen. Just a skinny awkward kid who wanted to be a priest. God knows how many times he's been beaten and raped since he went in."

"I didn't kill Emily," I said softly.

Helen didn't seem to hear me. "Mark didn't kill Dale out of hatred, greed, or any self-interest. The only reason he killed him was because he thought he was protecting someone he loved. Mark was—I bet you still is—essentially a good person. But it was one god-awful crime he committed."

"I didn't kill Emily," I said more forcefully.

Helen worked the beads around her neck. She answered without looking at me. "Ben, I think you better tell that to your lawyer, not me."

12

I headed out on my road bike the next morning at five for another dark ride. I cycled at a leisurely pace because my head ached and my stomach flip-flopped from the remainder of the bottle of scotch I'd polished off on returning home from Helen's. Fighting back the nausea, it dawned on me that I'd consumed more alcohol in the past week than in the past year. Memories drifted to my mind of Dad waking Aaron and me up in the middle of the night with his missteps and stumbles on the staircase from yet another night of boozing. How he managed to function in the daytime and sustain his accounting practice amazed me even then. And having witnessed my identical twin battling drugs, I didn't need a blood test to know I possessed the same predisposition toward addiction.

Blood. It suffocated me. I could still see the disappointed certainty in Helen's brown eyes. With each turn of the pedal, I grew more convinced that she already knew what the whisperer had predicted—that the blood on the wall did match mine.

But how? Had someone stolen a sample of my blood? I scoured my memory for my last blood test. Three years earlier I'd had baseline testing done at the hospital lab to check my hepatitis immune status, but there was no way the lab would have hung on to the blood for more than a few weeks.

My stomach churned again, but not from alcohol. If the blood wasn't mine, then the only alternate explanation was Prince's farfetched suggestion that it came from my brother. And unless the killer had access to highly sophisticated blood-freezing equipment, it would have to have been produced by Aaron's bone marrow in the last few months. But I wasn't ready to accept the implication that Aaron survived the slaughterhouse of his trunk and was somehow involved in Emily's death.

Pumping hard to climb the last steep hill on my cycle home, a moment of clarity overcame me. No one was going to rescue me. I'd become the sole focus of the investigation, and after hearing Helen's long list of circumstantial evidence, I understood why. I had no time left for mourning or self-pity. I had to act.

They would come for me soon.

At 8:05 A.M., I sat in Michael Prince's office staring out at the fog that hid much of Puget Sound and sipping a coffee as bitter as the last one. Across the desk, Prince leaned back in his chair, his hands behind his neck interlocked over his flowing silver hair.

"Ben, I think it probably was not the most prudent step," Prince summed up my visit to Helen's house with pained understatement.

"I consider Helen a friend," I said. "I thought without her partner around, she might see my side."

Prince pulled his hands from his head and snapped forward in his chair. "Listen to me, Ben. You have no friends left inside the Seattle P.D. From now on, you do not talk to *any* of them. That's my job."

"Meanwhile I sit back and wait?"

His expression softened. "I know it's frustrating, but that's exactly what you have to do. Go back to your regular life. Maybe this won't lead to the doom and gloom you're expecting."

I shook my head. "They think I killed Emily. They're not going to drop this."

"But they need evidence."

"I think someone is supplying them with all the evidence they need."

Prince tilted his head. "Oh?"

I told him about the two anonymous whispered phone calls. When

I finished, Prince viewed me poker-faced. "And you're certain the calls originated in Canada?"

"According to my call display," I said.

"Why Canada?"

"There could be a connection. Aaron had moved to Vancouver about a year before he died."

Prince's lips broke into a slight smile. "You mean before he disappeared."

"I keep forgetting."

His smile faded. "I won't let you."

"Michael, I don't think I can sit back and wait. The cops aren't looking for any other suspects. They're building the case against *me.*"

"Which may or may not be enough to lead to charges," Prince said, relaxing back in his seat. "We can't stop them from investigating you. What we need to do is to focus on preparing your defense should it become necessary."

I wasn't ready to let it go. "Michael, didn't you once defend the second victim, Jason DiAngelo, on charges of drug possession?"

The skin around his eyes tightened slightly. "And how is that relevant to you?"

"I'm not sure it is, but I'd heard that Philip Maglio hired you."

"Which of course I can't comment on," Prince said dismissively. "Where are you going with this, Ben?"

"J.D. was a drug dealer who sold Emily black-market HIV drugs. He worked for a supposed Seattle mob boss. A few days ago, I saw another drug dealer die in the Emergency Room of the same kind of knife wound that killed J.D. Maybe it's all tied in somehow."

Prince smiled reassuringly, but warning lurked behind the benign countenance. "Ben, we don't have to produce alternate suspects. We don't even have to prove your innocence. All we have to establish is reasonable doubt. And I think your missing brother will offer us that."

An hour after leaving Prince's office, I sat at the computer in my small home office. Trying to follow my attorney's advice, I surfed the familiar cycling Web sites looking for distraction. I logged onto the Pacific

Northwest Cyclist's discussion forum. (Having sworn never to get involved in online chatting, I'd skeptically signed on to the forum a year earlier and after following the intelligent conversation threads for a while I soon became a frequent contributor.) The online members were holding another "did he or didn't he?" discussion of Lance Armstrong's alleged blood doping in his early Tour de France wins. I'd sat through the same discussion too many times before. Besides, I couldn't stomach the topic of incriminating blood tests.

Exiting the forum, I wandered off into cyberspace. At the Google home page, I typed in "Emily Kenmore AND Philip Maglio" but came up with no hits. I tried the same with various combinations, including "Jason DiAngelo AND Aaron Dafoe." All misses. Then I searched for "Philip Maglio." I stumbled upon a few old newspaper articles that insinuated links to organized crime, before finding the official Web site of his company, NorWesPac Properties, a Seattle-based real estate development company. I clicked on the CEO's biography. Predictably, the blurb focused on his rise from humble working-class roots in nearby Redmond to become founder and chairman of the multimillion-dollar NorWesPac Properties.

I enlarged the small photo inset in the corner of the screen. Fiftyish, with thinning black hair and acne-scarred skin, Philip Maglio smiled back at me, though his face was anything but welcoming. Strong jaw clenched, his gray eyes challenged the camera. Though not handsome, his face exuded power. From the photo alone, I would've recognized in an instant that Maglio was not someone to be screwed with.

I read as much as I could find on his company, learning that Nor-WesPac primarily developed condo projects. I know little about real estate, but I was impressed by the list of their current developments, which stretched from Portland, Oregon, to as far north as British Columbia, Canada.

On a hunch, I Googled "Emily Kenmore AND NorWesPac Properties." I sat up straighter when the list of twenty-five hits popped up on my screen. My heart rate sped up as I scanned the list, including one from the official NorWesPac Web site. I clicked on that link to discover that Emily was listed as the Seattle sales director for NorWesPac's very upscale condo development called SnowView at the world-renowned Canadian ski resort of Whistler, seventy miles north of Vancouver.

Canada! There it was again. Another link to our northern neighbors.

Fingers racing and mouse clicking frantically, I pieced together the story of the SnowView development. Intended to cater to the Seattle "dot-commers" with loads of disposable income and a taste for the slopes, the development never got off the ground. Problems with zoning permits, the rising Canadian dollar, and cost overruns eventually sidelined the project. None of the sites mentioned how Emily came to part ways with NorWesPac Properties, though I knew from our own interactions that NorWesPac hadn't employed her for more than six months.

I pushed away from the computer and stared at the screen saver, a cyclist sprinting up the picturesque but grueling Peyresourde leg of the Tour de France's time trials. I empathized with the rider, but I also felt my first glimmer of hope. I'd just unearthed a connection between the two victims and Philip Maglio. Emily and J.D. had both worked for Philip Maglio—a very dangerous man, according to my cousin. I realized the link might simply be coincidence, but as far as I was concerned, in the past week I'd already chewed through a lifetime's worth of coincidences.

I wheeled my chair back toward the desk and reached for the computer mouse. I clicked my way through the NorWesPac Web site until I found the CONTACT US section. Secure in the knowledge that my home phone number was unlisted, I reached for the phone and dialed the company's main office number.

"NorWesPac Properties." The upbeat voice answered on the second ring. "This is Megan. How can I help you?"

"I'd like to speak to Mr. Maglio, please."

"Who may I say is calling?"

I hesitated a moment and then an idea struck me. "My name is J.D. Emily."

"*Amilley?*" she asked.

"No, Emily. As in the poet, Emily Dickinson."

I wondered if the reference was wasted on the young-sounding receptionist, but she simply said, "Please hold a moment, Mr. Emily."

I only had to suffer through thirty seconds of canned hold music, before the line clicked. "Phil Maglio," growled the cigarette-and-whisky-ravaged voice.

"Mr. Maglio, I'm a friend of Emily Kenmore's."

The line went quiet. "Emily Kenmore doesn't work for NorWesPac any longer."

"Emily doesn't breathe any longer," I said provocatively. "What about Jason DiAngelo, AKA J.D.?"

He cleared his throat loudly. "Doesn't ring any bells."

I glanced at the monitor where Maglio's photo still appeared. I could picture his jaw clenching even tighter and his gray eyes steaming. "He used to work for you."

"Not at NorWesPac."

"No, not at NorWesPac. I think he worked for you in a sector other than real estate."

Another pause. "Who is this?"

"Doesn't matter."

Maglio grunted his disdain.

I took a slow breath. "Phil, I want to know what happened to Emily and J.D."

"Me, too!"

The line clicked dead.

I cradled the receiver in my hand for several seconds. I considered phoning him back to try to set up a meeting, but aside from getting myself killed, I couldn't see what it would accomplish. Still, a vague buzz enveloped me. For the first time in days, I didn't feel like I was careening downhill in the backseat of a car without brakes.

I put down the receiver and glanced at the computer's clock: 5:45 P.M. I'd been snooping online for more than four hours. My stomach growled, reminding me I hadn't eaten yet today. I stood up and stretched, then decided it was time to head downstairs and reward my-self with a massive turkey breast sandwich and an icy beer. I was glad I had restocked my fridge and liquor cabinet earlier.

As I walked past the curtained window, movement from the street caught my eye. I moved closer and peered out through the gap be-tween the curtains.

I jerked back instantly, as if shot at. My chest slammed. My palms dampened.

The doorbell rang, and I shuddered.

I stole another furtive glance between the curtains. I could see two police cruisers parked on the street, one of them blocking the driveway. Two uniformed policemen stood in front of Helen's sedan.

The doorbell rang again. I knew Helen and Rick were standing at my front door.

For them to have arrived accompanied by backup meant only one thing: The blood on Emily's wall officially matched my DNA.

CHAPTER

13

I forced saliva down my tightening throat. I took several slow breaths, willing the panic to subside. Drawing on years of Emergency Room experience in facing critical situations, I focused my thoughts away from the anxiety and onto the immediate next steps.

If I go with them now, I thought, *I might lose my only chance to clear my name.*

I peeked out the window again. Even if I could squeeze my Smart Car past the cruiser blocking the driveway, I couldn't outrun the cops with an engine the size of a moped's. Suddenly the allure of the car's fuel efficiency evaporated.

The doorbell rang a third, fourth, and fifth time in rapid succession. I knew that I didn't have long before they broke through the door.

Frantically stuffing my wallet and cell phone in my jeans, I threw on a sweatshirt. I grabbed my cycling shoes and hopped into each of them on my way out of the bedroom. I tore down the stairs. Without stopping at the main floor, I rounded the corner and ran to the basement.

I opened the door to the attached garage. Stepping carefully on the concrete, I willed my bike cleats to silence. More out of reflex than reason, I slipped on my helmet, and then lifted my road bike off the rack. The gentle thud the tires made on contact with concrete sounded to me like a brick hitting the ground. I wheeled the bike to a strategic spot five feet from the garage door. I mounted the bike and clicked a foot into the pedal.

I allowed myself three long breaths then reached for the garage door opener. Heart pounding, I pressed the button.

The garage door clunked its way open. As soon as I judged the opening near bike level, I jumped onto the pedal. Ducking my head, I flew through the gap and gained speed with each pedal up the driveway. Reaching the top, I caught the bewildered expressions of the uniformed policemen as they scrambled to react.

"Stop!" the female cop yelled.

But stopping wasn't an option. I didn't even look back as I rode past. Instead, I stood on the pedals and pumped like I was sprinting for the finish line in the race of my life.

At the T-intersection at the bottom of my street, I veered hard right and was almost clipped by a car cruising past with the right of way. The horn sounded angrily, but like a bike courier with a death wish, I cut across the street and rode into the oncoming lane half a block until my next left turn. Leaning into the corner, the wind whistled by my ears, and I heard the wail of sirens behind me.

Adrenaline flooded into my system. My lungs burned as I raced along Woodlawn Avenue North, knowing my only hope of escape was Woodland Park. I hit the T-intersection at Woodlawn and Fifty-fifth, swerving to my right. I could see the park ahead of me, but the sirens were gaining. With a quick check over my shoulder, I saw the cruiser less than half a block behind.

I reached the main thoroughfare of Green Lake Way. Ignoring the stop sign and the oncoming traffic, I raced across the intersection. Brakes screeched as I veered to avoid a speeding car. I almost toppled off my bike, but I managed to regain my balance just as I hopped the curb.

I roared down the sidewalk against the pedestrian traffic. A couple walking in the opposite direction had to release hands and dive out of my way as I rode between them. I heard the man's fading shout of "Watch it, asshole!" but I didn't dare look back.

I reached the entrance to the park and cut in. I screamed along the path beside the soccer pitch, heading desperately for the park's thicker trees and paths that I hoped would offer some protection. I reached the parking lot in front of the tennis courts. Gasping for breath, more from anxiety than exhaustion, I raced on past the tennis players and around the courts until I arrived at the first footpath.

As I rode deep into the park under the cover of the dense trees, I no longer heard the sirens, but the adrenaline wouldn't let me slow down. I reached Aurora Avenue, the thoroughfare that divides the park, and I doubled back into the thicker woods.

Slowing the bike, I checked behind me again. No one.

I brought my bike to a stop by a tall maple tree. Pausing under its branches, I weighed my options. Police all over the city would be looking for a cyclist in jeans on a red bike. Reluctantly, I realized I had no choice but to ditch the bike. I tucked it away in the most concealed spot I could find behind another tree, though I knew the effort was futile. If the bike weren't stolen, the police would confiscate it. Either way, I would never see it again. After dropping my helmet behind the bike, I twisted the headlight off the handlebar and pocketed it. I took one last glance, as if saying good-bye to an old friend, and then hurried off on foot.

Feeling the pressure of the bicycle cleats digging into the soles of my feet, I jogged through the woods, darting between trails on my way out to North Fiftieth Street. I stopped a hundred feet from the road, certain I would hear sirens or see flashing lights the moment I emerged from the cover of the foliage.

I inched closer to the street until I had a glimpse of the road on either side that ran along the perimeter of the park.

Nothing.

I ducked back into the trail and wrestled with another choice: Either I could call a cab on my cell phone (and risk being traced by some high-tech GPS system), or I could stand on the busy street in bike cleats while trying to inconspicuously hail a passing cab. I decided to take my chances on the phone. I pulled it out of my jeans and dialed the number for the taxi company. I gave the dispatcher exact instructions on which side of the street to pick me up.

Heart still hammering despite the rest, I moved close enough to the street to watch for the approaching cab. In the five-minute wait, which felt like five days, I second-guessed my decision to run from the police. If Helen had any doubt left as to my guilt, I suspected I had dispelled it by fleeing.

The streak of yellow slowed to a stop at the side of the road. My cleats clicked like horses' hooves as I ran along the pavement to the cab. I grabbed for the door handle and resisted the urge to dive into the backseat. I climbed in and slumped down in the seat as low as possible without looking overly suspicious.

The young African-American driver eyed me indifferently in the mirror. "Where to?"

"Emerson and Thirty-third, please," I said, conjuring an address in the Magnolia Bluff neighborhood that was at least six blocks from Alex's home.

We drove in silence. Fighting the impulse to scan every window, I focused on the floor of the taxi where a tourist map of Seattle lay in a wadded ball. It struck me as metaphoric; to sort out this mess, I had to discard Seattle, too. I had an inkling of where I had to go, but I'd no idea how to get there.

The driver dropped me off at the designated intersection. I wandered down Emerson but turned back as soon as his cab was out of sight. Hands in my pocket and head down, I struggled to slow my pace as I strode the three blocks to Discovery Park.

Daylight had begun to dwindle by the time I reached the trails. Through my light sweatshirt, I felt a chill in the cooler evening air, but I wasn't willing to venture out until dusk had fully given way to darkness.

I found a bench in the woods and sat down. Now that the adrenaline had finally washed out of my system, I was able to consider the scope of my predicament. The whisperer's prediction had panned out—my two-year-old DNA sample must have unequivocally matched the blood on Emily's wall.

It's not my blood! I wanted to scream at the trees. *Somebody is framing me.* Someone with access to a perfect facsimile of my blood. And without any other plausible explanation, a belief began to take root that was as jarring to me as anything that had happened during the past week.

Aaron is alive.

CHAPTER

14

Shivering, I switched on the portable bike headlight and checked my watch: 9:05 P.M. Night had fallen. I navigated my way out of Discovery Park with the light held low to the ground and turned on only when necessary.

I emerged onto Emerson Street and hurried across the busy road, seeking the shelter of a quieter side street. Conscious of every street-lamp I walked under, I wove the nine blocks through the streets until I reached Alex's green cedar-sided house on Thirty-fifth Avenue.

I was relieved to see no sign of her husband Marcus's black Mercedes in the long driveway. I circled the block twice to ensure that no one was watching. With one more confirmatory glance, I rushed up the stone walkway, rang the doorbell, but then ducked around the corner and hid behind a hedge. Peeking around the edge, I watched as the door opened. Hair loose around her shoulders and wearing jeans and a T-shirt, Alex stood at the doorstep, glancing irritably from side to side.

"Kenny and Davy Paris!" she called out. "Don't you make me call your parents again!"

Before I could grab her attention, the door slammed shut. I slid out from behind the bush and walked up to the door. I rang the bell and stayed put this time.

The door whooshed open. Hands on her hips, Alex's scowl gave way to surprise. "Ben?"

"Is Marcus home?"

She shook her head.

"Your dad?"

"He's gone back to Spokane. It's just Talie and me, and she's asleep."

I nodded my relief. "Can I come in?"

"Of course." She stepped out of the way to let me pass.

As soon as I walked into the spacious foyer, I bent down and untied my shoes. It was too late. Alex spotted the cycling shoes. "Did you ride over?"

Shoes off, I stood up. "Not exactly."

Alex leaned close enough to give me a whiff of mint-flavored toothpaste. "What's going on, Ben?"

"Can I trouble you for a beer?"

Alex turned and headed for the kitchen. I followed her into the huge open kitchen with combined great room. She opened the Sub-Zero fridge and dug out a bottle of Dutch beer. "Marcus only drinks the imported stuff. Need a glass?"

"This is fine." I took the bottle from her, twisted off its cap, and took one long icy gulp.

Concern darkened Alex's brown eyes. "What's going on?"

I had another sip before putting the bottle down. "They came for me."

"The police?"

"Yes."

Alex's color drained. Her jaw dropped. "And you . . . *ran?*"

I nodded, reaching for the bottle again.

"Ben, have you lost your mind?" she said in a half whisper.

"Maybe," I said. "But I didn't know what else to do. They must've matched my DNA to the blood on Emily's wall." I met her stare. "Alex, I didn't do it."

"I thought you had a defense attorney to handle this."

"I'm not ready to trust my life to him yet."

Her mouth closed and her lips formed a stoic smile. "So what are you going to do?"

"I have to get out of Seattle," I sighed.

"And then?"

"Find Aaron."

"Aaron?" she gasped. "You think his body was dumped in Vancouver?"

I sucked the last drop of beer from the bottle. "I've been over it a thousand times, Alex. If it's not my blood on the wall, it has to be Aaron's."

Alex sat down on a barstool. "Are you saying that your missing-and-presumed-dead brother murdered Emily?" she asked in a monotone.

"No!" I shook my head vehemently. "Aaron wouldn't have done that. He had—has—no violence in him," I said, remembering the day he absorbed my punches without even trying to protect himself.

"What then?"

"I think someone either coerced his involvement or, possibly, got a hold of a sample of his blood and sprayed it on the wall."

"Blood that was over two years old?" Alex asked skeptically.

"We both know you can't keep blood that long without incredibly sophisticated equipment."

"Do you honestly think Aaron is still alive?"

"Or he was up until very close to the night of Emily's murder."

Alex's eyes fell to the countertop. "What about the burned-out car with all his blood in the trunk. How do you explain that?"

"Not easily," I said. "The trunk was saturated in blood. Well over four liters, according to the CSI guys."

"Which would have been three quarters of Aaron's total blood supply. That's not compatible with life."

"I know, but the trunk was burned with gasoline. There's no way to know how much of that fluid was blood."

She arched an eyebrow in disbelief.

"Alex, you know those old men that come into the ER bleeding from their prostate? Their urine is so red it could pass for blood, but we both know there's usually not much blood in the pee. A couple of tablespoons are enough to turn the pee blood color."

She sighed. "You think someone deliberately diluted the blood found in that trunk?"

"It might work."

"*Work?* To accomplish what?" She shook her head. "Fake his death?"

I nodded.

"Who would want do that?"

"Maybe Aaron."

"Why?"

"From what my cousin Kyle tells me, Aaron was involved with some scary people. Maybe faking his death was his only escape." I pulled back the barstool beside Alex and plunked into the seat. "God, I know how this all must sound."

"It's a bit of a stretch." Then her face filled with resolve. "But I know you didn't kill Emily. So there has to be another explanation."

Affection welled inside me, and the pressure eased off my chest. I smiled. "Thank you."

She snapped her fingers. "Maybe Aaron didn't need to dilute his blood. He could have collected it a little at a time over months, if he'd frozen it!"

"That would work, too." Despite his lack of medical training, I knew Aaron would be capable of pulling off a ploy like that.

Her expression turned businesslike. "So where do we go from here?"

"*We?*" I shook my head. "I had no right to involve you even this far. I was just hoping to just buy a few hours here to regroup. And then I'm getting the hell out of your hair."

"And going where?"

"Vancouver," I said. "That's where Aaron was living when he disappeared. I'm guessing that's where the whispered Canadian phone calls originate. Somehow, it's all tied in."

Alex viewed me with a trace of impatience. "And how do you plan to get across the border as a fugitive?"

Fugitive. The word stung like a slap. "I haven't figured that out yet."

"Let's say you make it across, how will you support yourself in Canada?" Her voice rose slightly. "Surely they'll freeze your accounts. What will you do for food and clothing?"

"I am going to go see my cousin Kyle."

"Can you trust him?"

"I don't have much choice." I hadn't considered the question before. "But I think I can."

Alex pushed herself up from the counter. "I'm changing the plans."

"What do you mean?" For a panicky moment, I thought Alex might turn me in for what she deemed to be my own good.

Alex stood across from me with her arms folded across her chest. "You're going to stay here in my basement until we've figured out a more concrete strategy," she said definitively.

I reached out and gently gripped her bare elbow. "That's crazier than my plan."

"Why?"

"For starters, what about your dad?"

"He's staying in Spokane until at least the end of the month."

"And Marcus?"

Alex hesitated. She looked away and cleared her throat. "He's stuck back east for a while longer."

Her evasiveness was uncharacteristic. I squeezed her elbow. "Alex?"

She stared at the countertop. "Marcus moved out a few weeks ago. I was going to tell you, but you've had so much on your plate, it didn't seem fair."

"Fair?" I let go of my grip. Wrapping an arm around her, I pulled her into a hug. "You've listened to my problems nonstop for the last few weeks and all this time—"

"All this time what, Uncle Benjamin?" a small voice asked from behind us.

Alex broke free of the hug. I hopped off the stool to face Talie. "Hi, sweetie," I said, trying to recover my mental balance. "How's the third-tallest Talie I know?"

"Oh, Ben," she said, sounding just like her mother. "You don't know any other Talies!" She giggled and wrapped her arms around me.

"I know fourteen of them, and you're the third-tallest." I hoisted Talie in the air. I took a step or two away from the kitchen's island and swung her airplane-style in my arms.

Alex pulled Talie out of my arms. "Come on, babe. Bedtime was yesterday."

Wrapped in Alex's small arms, Talie seemed bigger than I remembered. She looked over her mother's shoulder at me with an impish grin and brown eyes that matched Alex's. "Are you staying tonight, Uncle Benjamin?"

"No, sweetie, Ben was just about to leave," Alex said.

I sat on the bed in the comfortable basement room where Alex's father lived much of the year. A few of his heavy wool suits ("from the old country") hung in the open closet. A photo of Alex's mother stood on the dresser beside a black-and-white wedding shot of both parents. Her mom had died young, and Alex rarely spoke of her. They shared a strong likeness—not so much in the features (Alex had more of her father's dark coloring and angular face) as in the same playful expression and clear willfulness that communicated through the camera's lens.

I stood up and walked over to the small pile of Marcus's clothes that Alex had brought down to me. I lifted the navy blue long-sleeved Hugo Boss shirt from the top of the pile and slipped it on over my head. As Alex had predicted, it was a perfect fit.

I wandered over to the bathroom mirror. The silky shirt wouldn't have been my choice. I thought I looked oily in it. I know Marcus did. I remembered he'd worn the same shirt to one of the ER group's winter social functions. Our exchange that evening was still vivid in my mind.

I was talking to one of the young wide-eyed residents in our department when a hand clapped my shoulder. Even before I saw or heard him, I recognized Marcus Lindquist from the firm gesture and the smell of his expensive cologne. Excusing myself from my conversation, I turned to face him.

With brown hair gelled as perfectly as ever, blue eyes, straight nose, and a cleft in the chin, Marcus wore his usual movie-star-in-search-of-a-camera smile. "What's my second-favorite ER doc drinking?" he asked warmly.

I held up my clear glass. "Sprite."

"Sprite?" He laughed. "Are you out of your mind, Ben? Have you noticed how boring this party is?"

"I'm enjoying myself. Besides, I'm squeezing in an early-morning ride before work."

Marcus rolled his eyes. "Come at least watch someone drink a real drink."

With an arm still around my shoulder, he guided me to the self-serve bar set up in the corner of the room. He poured three fingers of scotch into his empty tumbler and took a generous sip. "Emasculating, always being the dumb spouse at these functions," he said.

"You were smart enough to get out of medicine," I said, referring to his career jump from hematologist to vice president of a company involved in umbilical cord blood storage.

"Don't kid yourself," Marcus said with a rare hint of self-parody. "Selling your soul isn't always more rewarding than saving lives."

I grinned. "Still, you got yourself a nice car in trade."

"Yeah, I do love my toys," he said. "I've got my eyes on a red convertible 911 for the spring."

"A Porsche? You getting a head start on your midlife crisis?"

"No head start required. I'm forty-four already."

With his life-of-the-party attitude, I tended to forget that he was ten years older than Alex and me.

Marcus pointed his empty tumbler across the room at his wife. Locked in a conversation with two older male colleagues, Alex threw her head back in a fit of laughter. "She's painfully beautiful, isn't she?"

In a simple black dress with her hair tied back, she was. "Hmmm," I had to agree.

Marcus reached for the scotch bottle and refilled his tumbler. "Must make it very difficult for you."

I turned to him with a frown. "Difficult?"

"The chemistry between you two isn't exactly subtle."

I stiffened. "We've worked together for over six years. We've been good friends almost as long."

"I know," he said affably. On the way to his lips, his full glass gave me the once-over. "But look at you. A handsome, available ER doc. The women should be hanging off you. Ben, it's almost weird that I haven't seen you with another woman since . . ." He paused. "Emily, was it?"

Anger rising, I simply nodded.

"She was gorgeous, that one." Marcus sighed a laugh. "I wouldn't have kicked her out of bed for leaving crumbs the size of toaster ovens."

"Maybe you should slow down on the scotch, Marcus."

"Hell, I know what it's like," Marcus said, ignoring my remark. "I'm on the road a lot. I get my share of attention from women."

"And you're just restraint personified, aren't you, Marcus?" I said quietly.

He laughed, spilling his drink. "Unfortunately for Alex, restraint is not in my nature."

"Too bad. Alex deserves better." I turned away from him.

Marcus grabbed me by the shoulder. I shook free of the grip and spun to face him again.

"No question, I'm no saint." His eyes burned. "But at least I don't try to fuck my friends' wives," he spat.

"What the hell makes you think you're my friend?" I snapped. Without waiting for his answer, I strode off.

"Hands off, Ben!" His voice followed me out of the room.

Looking back on that occasion, I realized that despite his alcohol-accentuated belligerence, everything Marcus had said was true. It didn't make it any easier to like him, even now when I was beholden to him for the clothes on my back.

What did it matter? The petty personal drama paled in comparison to my current crisis. With time to think, the hopelessness of my situation sank in; my whole strategy now struck me as a series of long shots.

I trudged out of the bathroom and back to the bed. I sat and stared at the phone on the nightstand. I decided that the only sensible next step was for me to call Michael Prince and to arrange my surrender.

I was about to reach for the phone when Alex, carrying a thick manila envelope, burst into the room. She sat down beside me on the bed. "My brother, Peter, still has six more months left in his contract with a private hospital in Taipei."

I always liked Pete, an easygoing internist, but I was bewildered as to the relevance. Then she slipped her hand in the envelope and withdrew a copy of his medical license.

Suddenly I understood.

"After Pete finished his internal medicine residency in Toronto, he qualified for a Canadian license," she said. "He's done some fill-in coverage in Victoria, and he's kept his registration up to date in British Columbia, because he hasn't decided on which side of the border he plans to settle."

"Alex . . ."

"Pete gave up his condo when he moved to Taipei," Alex continued.

"He left a bunch of stuff in storage with me here, including the originals of all his certificates and licenses."

"You're going to lend me your brother's identity?"

"Believe me, Pete would understand," she said. "And you have to admit there's more than a passing resemblance between you two."

The idea struck me as surreal, but at the same time I felt a glimmer of excitement. "You really think it's alright?"

"No." She grinned. "But it's the best harebrained scheme I can come up with on short notice."

The spark of hope was dampened by my next thought. "Of course, you don't have his passport or birth certificate, do you?"

"No." She dug in the bag and pulled out a card. "Only his Washington state driver's license."

I took the card from her hand and studied it. Peter Horvath's license photo was the typical nondescript mug shot that most of us end up with. Peter and I shared brown hair, the same hazel eye color, and strong jaw. I held it closer. "Maybe with a baseball cap and beard, on a quick glance I could pass for your brother."

"Why not?" She winked. "After all, you and I are practically twins."

"Without a passport, this won't get me across the border."

She stroked the back of my hand reassuringly. "We'll think of something."

I slipped the license back in the envelope and closed its flap. I viewed Alex with a heartfelt smile. "You've gone way above and beyond for me, but I think I better go now."

She shook her head. "You're staying put until things are better sorted out."

"If the police found out, you could be charged with aiding and abetting a felon."

Her resolve didn't waver. "They won't find out."

"What about Talie?"

"She thinks you've already left," she said. "Thanks to Marcus, we've got a huge house here. And again, thanks to Marcus, it's just Talie and me now. So you can safely stay down here for as long you need to."

I wanted to kiss her. "A day or two, maximum."

"However long it takes."

Our knees touching, we sat on the bed in silence for a few moments. When I looked over at her, her eyes had reddened. "Alex?"

"It's all so fucked up," she said.

"I know." I reached over and squeezed her hand.

She cleared her throat. "I don't want to lose you, too, Ben," she said softly.

I'd never seen Alex look as vulnerable. Or as beautiful. I wanted to kiss her so badly that it was a physical ache, but I stopped my head from moving to hers. I couldn't think of a more selfish act. She was already far more wrapped up in my personal disaster than was reasonable or safe for her to be.

I rose from the bed. "Alex, I don't think I've ever felt as greasy in my life. If it's okay with you, I'm going to hit the shower. And then try to sleep while I can."

She nodded. "I'll bring you down coffee and a bite of breakfast in the morning."

I leaned close and brushed my lips against her cheek. "Alex, you're wonderful."

Her face lit with a sad smile. "You're very complimentary when you're cornered."

"I'll see you in the morning," I said, though I had no intention of seeing her in the morning, or anytime soon.

CHAPTER

15

I tossed and turned the night through, resisting the impulse to sneak upstairs and get at the beer in the fridge or whatever else lurked in Alex's liquor cabinet. Only the risk of waking Talie stopped me.

I don't know if I slept at all, but if I did, my prayers weren't answered by morning. Still a wanted man, I had no better plan than the feeble one I'd taken to bed.

At 4:45 A.M. I got up and headed to the bathroom. I brushed my teeth, feeling dejected by the sight of the haggard face staring back in the mirror. The shadow on my chin and neck had begun to thicken but didn't yet offer any kind of camouflage. Neither did the heavy bags under my eyes.

I hurried back into the bedroom, where I chose a pair of Marcus's jeans and a casual shirt. They fit well enough, but his running shoes were a full size too snug. However, unless I wanted to make my escape on foot in cycling shoes, I had no choice except to ignore the viselike grip around my toes.

I dug behind the suits in the closet until I found a dusty old knapsack that smelled musty, as if gym clothes had been left inside too long. I sorted through the rest of Marcus's clothes, choosing two pairs of casual pants, four shirts, and a bunch of socks and boxer shorts. I stuffed them in the bag. Its zipper resisted the load but eventually relented.

I picked up the manila envelope and gently poured the contents out on the bed. An ATM card fell out beside the driver's license. I picked up the card and studied it. Registered under Alex's name, not her brother's, its PIN number was scribbled on an attached Post-It.

Alex, where would I be without you?

I stuffed both pieces of plastic in my wallet and removed out all the other cards that bore my name. I considered leaving my cards in the basement suite but realized they might incriminate Alex if the police came looking for me. Instead, I stuck them inside a plastic bag I found in the closet. I tucked the bag inside my inner jacket pocket, intending to dump them at the first opportunity. It occurred to me that I'd already begun to think like a fugitive; that sudden insight colored my dark mood even blacker.

I grabbed my cell phone from the nightstand. Having read an article on how satellites can track cell phones via the Global Positioning System, I knew it was more of a liability than an aid. Ensuring it was shut off, I stuck it in my outer pocket; another remnant of my life I was going to have to ditch on my way out of Seattle.

Suddenly, an idea dawned on me, and I pulled the phone out of my jacket. I found a pad on the nightstand and scrawled Alex a note with specific instructions. I scanned the note, barely able to read my own writing. I carefully reprinted my warning—"Hide it!"—at the bottom of the note and underlined it three times. Then I placed the phone on the nightstand with the note.

I picked up the receiver of Alex's land line, dialed the cab company's number, and gave the dispatcher an address two blocks away. Throwing the knapsack over my shoulder, I tightened the worn straps and headed for the door. I stopped and listened carefully for any indication of Alex or Talie stirring above me. Hearing none, I eased the door open and slipped out.

I took a tentative step out into the wet, predawn darkness. I hesitated a moment, half expecting to hear a bullhorn shout my name or feel the heat of laser cross hairs burn into my forehead. But after ten silent seconds, I hurried up the cement staircase to the backyard. Following the path around the side of the house, I jammed my hands in my pockets, dropped my eyes to the ground, and strode for the side street. There wasn't a soul around, but I'd never felt more exposed or vulnerable. With each step away from Alex's house, I felt like a soldier walking deeper behind enemy lines.

The cab arrived at the intersection right after I did. Slipping into the backseat, I nodded to the driver as I slid low in the seat.

"Where to?" the chubby middle-aged driver asked.

"Pike Place Market."

He eyed me warily in his rearview mirror. "It's not open yet."

I felt my chest tighten slightly, wondering if he was on to me. "If I'm not behind the counter when it does, I'm looking for new work," I blurted the first lie that popped into my head.

He chuckled and his shoulders relaxed. "Morning shifts. Don't they just suck?"

"Better than graveyard," I said, thinking of those dreaded overnight shifts at the ER. But I would have gladly done a year's worth of back-to-back nights without pay to escape my current predicament.

I deflected the driver's further attempts at conversation by pretending not to know who the Seattle Seahawks were. The tactic worked. He viewed me in the mirror as if looking at a Martian.

He dropped me off across from Pike Market. I checked my watch. It was still too early. I doubled back down Union Street and stopped in front of a Starbucks, but when I saw customers inside, my unease surged. Aching for caffeine, I dropped my gaze to the ground and trudged on.

Two blocks away, I found a small coffee shop. Aside from the young woman manning the counter, I saw no one else inside, so I went in. Without making eye contact with the girl, I mumbled my order for a large dark roast coffee. As soon as it was in my hand, I headed straight out the door.

Stepping back onto the sidewalk, I noticed the city's downtown had begun to stir. More people emerged on the street. I had a yearning to grab the first bike I saw and ride it as far as my legs would carry me. I glanced at my watch: 5:43 A.M. I couldn't wait any longer.

I hurried up Union Street until I reached the twelve-story modern condo complex. I typed the number into the intercom's keypad and listened to it ring. Kyle answered on the second ring, and his voice carried no trace of drowsiness. "Morning."

"Kyle, it's Ben," I said.

"Ben?" he said. "Holy crap! Come on up."

The alarm in Kyle's voice ratcheted up my blood pressure. As soon as the door buzzed, I yanked it open and ran to the elevator. I stepped out onto the twelfth floor and raced down the corridor to Kyle's suite. His door was ajar. Pushing it open, I walked inside and followed the hall into the expansive living room. The floor-to-ceiling windows offered a panoramic view of the lights from the boats and ferries chugging through the darkness of Puget Sound, but it barely registered with me.

Looking washed out and skinny in his oversized brown bathrobe, Kyle emerged from the kitchen with a cup of coffee in each hand. "Ben." He held out one of the cups for me. "What the hell?"

"I guess I made the news this morning."

He grunted a laugh. "You *are* the news this morning." He put the coffee down on the counter and lifted up a copy of the *Seattle Post-Intelligencer*. In a lab coat and stethoscope, my hospital ID photo had made the front page.

I slammed my cup down beside his and snatched the paper from his hand. I scanned the article. The S.P.D. had labeled me a "person of interest." The reporter described me as a former boyfriend of the female victim, but there was no mention of my blood at her apartment.

I looked up from the paper to see Kyle eyeing me impassively. "What gives, Ben?"

I took a long sip of coffee, scalding my tongue in the process. "The police came for me yesterday. . . ." Without minimizing the evidence against me, I went on to tell him of the mounting suspicion I'd fallen under.

Kyle nodded noncommittally. "So if it's not your blood, whose is it?"

"Aaron's, I think."

Kyle's eyes widened. "Seriously?"

"Nothing else makes any sense."

His expression held steadfast. "Are you telling me that with all their high-tech gadgetry, they couldn't tell your blood apart from Aaron's?"

"Being identical twins, we have the same bone marrows," I said, aware that I'd automatically begun to refer to Aaron again in the present tense.

"That means we produce identical blood right down to the corpuscle or blood cell. Indistinguishable on DNA testing."

He fought back an amused grin. "That's borderline creepy."

I stared hard at my cousin. "Kyle, do you think Aaron could be alive?"

Kyle shook his head. "That trunk of his car . . ."

"They never found his body."

Kyle rubbed the back of his neck. "Ben, no one has seen Aaron in over two years."

"Which makes sense if he wants people to think he is dead."

Kyle stopped rubbing. "Why would he do that?"

"I don't know," I sighed. "You knew more about Aaron's life in the last few years than anyone. As his business partner, can you think of any reason he might have wanted to fake his own death?"

Kyle sipped his coffee slowly. When the cup left his lip, I noticed a new lesion that looked like an early cold sore above the edge of his upper lip. "Let's go to the living room."

Taking our coffees, we headed into his living room and sat down in the soft leather chairs. Dawn was beginning to break. Behind Kyle, I could make out the shadowy forms of the vessels churning through Puget Sound.

Kyle viewed me with a look that bordered on apologetic. "Right before I was diagnosed, I had a falling-out with Aaron."

I folded my arms over my chest. "Over?"

"B.C. bud."

"The marijuana?"

"The purest, most potent stuff in the world," Kyle sighed. "They grow it like wheat in spots in British Columbia. Nowadays the bikers and other nasty big hitters control the business, but a few years ago, Aaron and I were two pioneers of the B.C. bud import business in Seattle."

Aaron's involvement in the drug trade wasn't news to me, but it didn't make it any easier to listen to Kyle describe the specifics. "You paid cash for the pot?" I asked.

"Cash or coke," he said. "A dead easy trade. We had a foolproof transport system. We bought the B.C. bud in bulk in Vancouver.

Hundreds of kilos. And we were making five hundred percent markup on the product flipping it in Seattle."

I swept the apartment with a wave of my hand. "Helped pay for this, huh?"

"Yes." Kyle shrugged sheepishly. "Paid for anything we wanted, including our own drugs. We funneled much of the profit into aboveboard investments. Aaron managed our portfolio. He was a financial wizard, too. Soon we had a steady stream of income from our legitimate investments."

I shook my head impatiently. "So what led to your falling-out?"

"Aaron wanted out of the drug business," Kyle said. "He always felt guiltier than I did. I argued it was only marijuana, but that didn't make it sit any easier with him. He figured we didn't need to rely on the trafficking for our income or even to support our own"—he cleared his throat—"costly habits."

"You disagreed?"

"I was so greedy, it's sickening." Kyle chuckled a sigh that evolved into a harsh cough. He caught his breath. "There was more to it. We'd become a vital link in the supply chain. Neither of our trading partners on either side of the border wanted the middleman to drop out of the picture."

I snapped my fingers. "Philip Maglio?"

"Phil was one of them, but he wasn't alone. The East Indian gang members who supplied much of our B.C. bud were no happier." Kyle pulled an imaginary gun from his bathrobe's belt. "And those guys are notoriously quick on the draw."

I was beginning to piece it together. "So you didn't want to give up the money *or* get yourself killed by leaving the drug running business."

"You've got it." Kyle blew out his lips. "But Aaron didn't see it that way. He'd changed. He called us 'grief merchants.'" Then he added admiringly, "And unlike me he didn't need a second chance at life to see the light."

"Maybe he did," I thought aloud. "Would your partners have let Aaron just walk away from the business?"

"I doubt it."

"Why did they let you?"

"I got sick. Even those morons couldn't expect me to run a business out of a bone marrow transplant ward."

I mulled over the chronology in my mind. "Aaron disappeared shortly after you started treatment,right?"

"Three or four months." Kyle looked away. "I always assumed one of our partners killed Aaron for leaving them high and dry in terms of the supply chain."

"But you don't have proof?"

"No."

"Sounds like Aaron had good reason to get the hell out of town," I said. "Especially if he could make it look as if he didn't get out alive."

"I guess." Kyle played with the spears of his thinning hair. "The irony is, I was allowed to walk away from it all scot-free simply because I had cancer."

"I'm glad."

"I take it you mean about the scot-free stuff, not the cancer." Kyle's smile faded quickly. "Look, Ben, say Aaron really is alive. How do you know he's not involved in everything?"

"As in, setting me up?"

He shrugged.

I wavered a fraction of a second. "No way. He wouldn't do that to me. And certainly not to Emily. Someone either coaxed the blood from him or stole it. Simple as that."

Kyle nodded.

I reached out and touched my cousin's bony shoulder. "Kyle, I have to find Aaron."

"And just how do you plan to do that?"

"I'm going to start my search in Vancouver."

His frown gave way to a sympathetic smile, the kind reserved for someone you know is heading out on a wild-goose chase. "I guess it's as good a place as any to start."

"But I don't know how to cross the border."

He flashed a grin that was vintage bad-boy Kyle. "I can get you across."

CHAPTER

16

After the sun rose, the blinds in Kyle's condo were all drawn, hiding me from the view of people in the nearby buildings, and Puget Sound from me. I paced the living room waiting for Kyle to return. He had left clutching a bag of hypodermic syringes, declaring it was his morning to pass out clean needles to the addicts in the neighborhood behind Pioneer Square. With a laugh, he said that his life wouldn't be worth living if he screwed up the weekly distribution schedule set by the ex-addict who coordinated the volunteers for the needle-exchange program.

He promised to return within two hours and take me to Vancouver. I asked again how he planned to get me across the border, but he simply flashed a mischievous smile and told me I would have to wait and see. Though frustrated by Kyle's amused evasiveness, I found his confidence reassuring. I even relaxed enough to focus on something other than self-preservation.

My stomach was still too unsettled to eat, but I craved more coffee, so I walked into the kitchen to refill my cup. Standing by the carafe, I found myself wondering in which of the many pale cabinets was Kyle's stash of liquor. Remembering that Kyle had forsaken alcohol, I didn't bother opening them. I topped up my coffee cup and headed back for the living room.

I stopped on the way to leaf through a stack of pamphlets on the countertop. Entitled "Faith Will Make You Clean," the brochure was surprisingly well written and only minimally preachy. Presenting a firsthand account that bordered on inspirational, it described how a hardcore addict found God after an intentional heroin overdose.

I wondered if a single user would ever bother to read the pamphlet. I'd learned from experience that it's impossible to coax anyone into sobriety. Our family butted heads against that wall with my father and Aaron too many times to count.

But when it came to Aaron and me, blood turned out to be even thicker than cocaine or crystal meth. Despite his chronic drug use, our bond persevered. Even our blowout (three years before his disappearance, when I'd pummeled him for sharing a crack pipe with Emily) didn't drive the same permanent wedge between us as it had between Emily and me. Though I didn't speak to Aaron for months after I'd called off the engagement, I eventually accepted his version of events. Emily had come to him seeking drugs. If he hadn't supplied them then, by her own admission, she would've gone elsewhere. Within half a year of the fight, Aaron and I were as tight as ever.

Many of our friends and family had trouble understanding how an addict and a doctor could maintain such closeness despite monumental differences in their life choices. Even I didn't understand it. The fact that we shared the same DNA down to the last gene must have played a role, but there was more to it. We complemented each other. We were usually there for one another in times of need. And more often than not, Aaron (as high-functioning an addict as I've ever met) ended up in the supporting role.

In the year before his disappearance, after he'd relocated to Vancouver, Aaron would still surprise my parents and me with unannounced appearances. I remembered his final visit vividly, and not only because it was the last time I ever saw him.

After a tiring afternoon shift in the ER, I walked into my house just before midnight to find Aaron sitting in my kitchen with the newspaper spread open on the table in front of him.

I was shocked by how much weight he'd lost in the four months since I'd last seen him. He'd never been overweight, but because of my cycling, I'd always been a few pounds lighter and a waist size smaller. Now the opposite was true, though I hadn't gained an ounce. The rest of Aaron's appearance alarmed me as much as his skinniness. His hair was long and unkempt. With a patchy beard, his face's pallor highlighted the dark bags beneath his eyes. Even when he looked up from the newspaper and smiled, deep frown lines cut across his forehead and wrinkled his eyes. Rather than four minutes older, he suddenly looked ten years older than me.

He hopped up from the table and walked over to greet me with a hug, the grip of which was as forceful as ever. "Ben, you look as if you just saw a ghost."

"Not far off. What the hell happened to you?"

"Jenny Craig," he said with a tired smile.

I wasn't laughing. "Come on, Aaron."

"The last six months have been up and down for me."

I stepped back and studied him. It was like looking in a funhouse mirror that distorted my own image. "Are you sick?"

"Not really." He shrugged. "I'm a bit off my food and stuff. Call it career stress. Maybe even life stress."

"What exactly is your career?"

"We've been over this." He sighed a laugh. "I'm a day trader."

"As in stocks?"

He shrugged again. "Yeah, stocks. Bonds and real estate, too." Then, for the first time ever, he added, "But mostly I dabble in human misery."

"You mean you sell drugs," I said, having suspected it for years.

He nodded. "Indirectly," he said with a sniff.

Aware of his bloodshot eyes and frequent sniffles, I said, "You're coked up now, aren't you?"

He stared blankly at me.

"Is the junk what's making you look so ill?"

He shook his head and walked past me into the living room. "I told you, Ben. I haven't eaten well lately. Speaking of, why don't we order in? Not Chinese, though. I get my fill of that in Vancouver. You can't beat the Chinese food up there."

Despite his evasiveness, I sensed that the time wasn't right to press him. "Do you need a place to crash for a while?" I asked.

"No thanks. I held on to my condo here in Seattle. It's sitting empty now."

"So you're going to move back home?" I asked hopefully.

"Eventually, maybe." He plunked himself down on the couch. "I have to go back up to Vancouver soon. Lots of loose ends to tie up."

I followed him into the living room. "Aaron, if it's money you need—"

He waved his hand to interrupt. His grin was a blend of amusement and gratitude. "I've got plenty, but thanks, bro."

"Then what?"

"Some of my colleagues"*—he emphasized the last word with disdain— "aren't so easy . . ." His voice trailed off.*

"Aren't so easy to what?"

"It's complicated. And messy." He shook his head. "Like the last ten years of my life." He bit his lip and then changed subjects again. "You know I saw Emily in Vancouver a few weeks ago."

I stiffened, feeling both butterflies and knots in my stomach. I hadn't heard Aaron mention Emily's name in the three years since our blowout. "What was she doing in Vancouver?"

"We were busy catching up on old times. Something to do with a ski resort at Whistler."

"Good for her," I grunted.

"It might be." Aaron sighed and his eyes drifted away. "But she's still as messed up as I am. She gave me this whole song and dance about kicking her habit, but you don't fool a fellow junkie that easily."

"Why are you telling me this, Aaron?"

His eyes focused on the floor. "When she took off her jacket, her sleeve accidentally pulled up. In the moment it took her to push it back down, I saw the marks."

"Track marks?"

He nodded. "She's mainlining now. Even I am not that stupid."

I knew Aaron never injected his drugs. Frankly, I thought his pride in that one act of "restraint" was misplaced. Aside from the risk of communicable diseases, I didn't see much of a distinction between smoking cocaine and crystal meth and injecting them. Though I understood his point; intravenous drug use represented an even further tumble down the slippery slope for Emily. "What do you expect me to do about that?" I asked.

"Expect?" He chuckled. "I don't expect you to do anything, except maybe rejoice at how smart you were to have called off the engagement." He paused and his voice quieted. "I thought you should know."

"Thank you," I said, though I didn't know exactly what I was thanking him for.

Aaron's chin hung on his chest and his shoulders slumped. I began to wonder whether my brother was suffering from depression, which so often accompanies addictions. "Hey, how about we get that chow?" I asked, trying to lift the mood.

Aaron shook his head. He leaned forward and grabbed the edge of the table. "I'm so sick of this, Ben."

I didn't know what to say.

"Remember that treatment facility you mentioned a few months back?"

"Sure," I said, filling with unexpected hope. Aaron had never shown the slightest interest in treatment before. "My friend who runs it is a psychiatrist specializing in addictions. I can call him tonight, if you want."

"Not tonight, but soon." He looked up at me, his face flushed with uncharacteristic fierceness. "Ben, I am going to do whatever it takes to escape what my life has become."

I rested a hand on his shoulder. "Hey, Aaron, that's great!"

"Whatever it takes," he repeated as if steeling his resolve.

The door to the condo opened and the memory slid from my mind.

Kyle walked in without the bag of syringes he'd left with. He viewed me with a puckish grin. "Dr. Horvath, you ready to blow this Popsicle stand that we call America?"

I nodded.

"Grab your bag," he said, turning back to the door.

I picked up the musty knapsack, double-checked that I still had Peter Horvath's ID, and then followed Kyle out to the elevator. We rode in silence to the underground parking below his building. We stopped by a gray Lincoln sedan parked not far from the elevator. Kyle raised his hand and clicked a fob, making the lights on the sedan flash twice.

Kyle must have noticed my surprise. "What? Were you expecting us to sneak into a Canada in a Ferrari or on the back of a Harley?"

I smiled. "Not sure, but I'll tell you this: I wasn't expecting to see you drive around in Grandpa Jack's car." Jack was our paternal grandfather, who always drove a huge Cadillac or Lincoln, up until his second stroke, after which someone from the Department of Motor Vehicles finally wrestled the keys out of his hand.

Kyle laughed. "It's the new me. Come winter, I'll probably move down to Florida where I'll eat dinner at four o'clock and then spend the rest of the day at shuffleboard or canasta."

We loaded into the car and Kyle shot out of the parking lot. Despite his change in style and ride, Kyle still drove with the same reckless edge that almost got us killed a few times during our teen years. He darted through the morning traffic as he headed onto the I-5 expressway.

Once we'd driven twenty miles north of Seattle, Kyle ran out of traffic to weave through. We spent much of the remaining two-hour drive to the border reminiscing about Emily and Aaron. We swapped stories of my brother's legendary lateness. Kyle reminded me about the time we were short one pallbearer at our grandmother's funeral until Aaron caught up with us at the church doors. I told Kyle of how our high school graduation almost passed without a valedictory address because Aaron's pre-ceremony nap had run long. "Maybe Aaron never disappeared," Kyle said with a sad smile. "Maybe he's just running *really* late this time."

As the road signs began to indicate the approaching Canadian border, my anxiety resurfaced. "Kyle, how am I going to get across the border without a passport or a birth certificate?"

"Wouldn't help if you had one, anyway. The border guards must have your photo. They'll be watching for you."

"So how am I going to get across?"

He pointed to a road sign that read LYNDEN, NEXT EXIT. "Not through any official border crossing."

"What are you talking about?" I said impatiently.

He veered off the freeway onto the exit ramp. "In one year alone, Aaron and I did ten million dollars in international trade. Not one penny of that passed through an official border crossing."

I shook my head in disbelief. "You're going to smuggle me through the border like a seventy-kilo bag of B.C. bud?"

Kyle's smile grew wider. "Not through, Ben. Under."

"Under?"

"You'll see."

He turned off the quasi-main drag we were following, and the country opened around us. Fields and farmhouses dotted either side of the street, which wasn't much more than a glorified dirt road. At the end of the road, a low fence guarded the highway running perpendicular to our street. Beyond that, I saw a red-and-white flag waving in the distance. I couldn't make out the emblem, but I knew it had to be the Canadian maple leaf.

My mouth went Mojave dry.

Kyle turned right onto an even smaller road running parallel to the fence. With my heart in my throat, we drove about a quarter of a mile further before Kyle turned off into the driveway of one of the farms. He pulled up to the chain-link fence in front of the yard and switched off the ignition. He turned to me slowly. "Ben, are you sure you want to do this?"

"*Want to?*" I couldn't keep the indignation from my tone. "What choice do I have?"

"You have one of the best defense attorneys in Seattle." There was no playfulness in his expression now. "We could go back and see Michael Prince. Do all of this on the level."

"The 'level' is not going to work, Kyle."

"Okay. So what can I do in the meantime?"

I smiled gratefully. "*If* you get me across the border, that will be more than enough."

"Give me a chance, Ben. I want to make amends."

"For what?"

"What I did to your brother."

I was definitely not the one who deserved retribution for that, but I nodded my understanding. "I need to know more about NorWesPac's Whistler project and how Philip Maglio ties into all of this."

He nodded. "And if I figure that out, how will I reach you?"

"I'll call you," I said. "But Kyle, remember your warning to me. Be careful with Maglio."

"I will." He reached into his jacket pocket and pulled out a wad of multicolored bills, green, pink, and brown. He passed me the stack of Canadian money. "You'll need some of this for your new home."

I didn't try to play coy. "Thanks." I took the cash from his hand and stuffed it into my wallet. "Kyle, I wanted to apologize to you."

He tilted his head, confused. "What for?"

"When you were diagnosed . . ." I cleared my throat. "And you asked me to get my blood tested to see if I was a potential donor. I shouldn't have waited. I should have come back straight away from that course I was taking in Boston."

He waved away the suggestion. "You were busy learning how to save more lives. Besides, it would've made no difference. We found a better match. Five out of six alleles."

I knew that bone marrow donors were selected based on the compatibility of six alleles — or gene pairs — in the blood; four or better was enough to try the donor marrow in a transplant. "Still, I should've gone in for the testing sooner."

Kyle sighed. "One benefit of my whole Bible-thumping shtick is that I've learned to let go of blame. For others and myself. It's a toxic wasted emotion." He smiled reassuringly at me. "Come on, Dr. Horvath, let's go to Canada."

Kyle reached under his dashboard and dug out a flashlight before climbing out of the car. I threw the knapsack over my shoulders and followed him to the padlocked gate in front of the house. He dug in his pocket and brought out a key chain. He chose one of the smaller keys, inserted it into the padlock, and twisted. The lock popped open with a loud click. "Let's hope nobody's home," he said with a half-smile.

We hurried up the pathway to the farmhouse, weaving through a garden of overgrown vegetation. As I followed Kyle past one small tree, a branch snapped back and scratched my cheek. I suspected the denseness of the shrubberies had nothing to do with neglect and everything to do with camouflage.

We reached the house's steel door. Kyle chose a different key, turned the lock, and opened the door. A high-pitched buzz greeted us. Kyle walked calmly across the stained linoleum floor to the alarm control panel. He typed in a five-digit number. The buzz held steady. He typed it again. No change.

Kyle turned to me, his face shrouded with concern. "They've changed the code."

I swallowed. "Who?"

"No time," he barked. "Come on."

Kyle sprinted down a short hallway that smelled of mothballs. He yanked open a flimsy-looking door and raced down the concrete steps, flicking on his flashlight in the sudden darkness of the unfinished basement. As soon as we reached the cement floor, the house's alarm erupted like a foghorn. "The cops will come," I shouted at Kyle over the throbbing noise.

He glanced over his shoulder at me. "It's not the cops we have to worry about."

Before I could ask whom I had to fear more than the cops, he turned and scurried down the corridor. Rushing after, I almost ran into him when he stopped abruptly in front of an old refrigerator against the wall. "Now what?" I shouted.

He moved to the left side of the fridge, stretched out both arms, and began pushing the fridge to the right. "Help me!"

Frantic, I leaped beside him and shoved my shoulder into the cool metal. The fridge scraped against the floor as it reluctantly wobbled a few feet to the right. Behind the spot where it had stood, a five-by-three-foot passageway appeared. With the flashlight's beam held in front of him, Kyle ducked down and angled his shoulders into the hole. I followed after.

The tunnel opened up a little wider and taller, but I still had to crouch to avoid hitting the wooden beams overhead. I fought to stave off inklings of claustrophobia in the dank, confined space that smelled of mold. A few steps deeper into the tunnel, and the jerky beam of Kyle's flashlight barely lit the way ahead.

He ran the beam along the wall until it found a switch. He reached out, flicked the switch, and suddenly the tunnel was illuminated by a chain of overhead bulbs. Suddenly able to see ahead of me, I now appreciated the extent of the channel. Bolstered by a series of wooden supports and rebar, the tunnel ran as far as I could see, the length of at least two football fields.

Abruptly, the alarm went dead. Kyle froze. He glanced at me with an expression that was anything but relieved. Above us, we heard creaking noises. Kyle pointed upward. "They're here," he whispered. "Let's go."

Head tucked forward, Kyle sprinted along the uneven surface leading deeper into the earth. I raced along, clipping my shoulder against the occasional beam. After running about fifty yards, Kyle's pace petered to a trot. By a hundred yards, he had stopped altogether. He was panting and wheezing loudly.

"You okay?" I asked.

He turned back to me and nodded. "You go ahead . . . ," he gasped. "I can't . . . I need to catch my breath . . . I'm gonna go back."

I pointed behind me. "What about them?"

"I know them," he huffed. "It will be okay."

"You sure?"

Kyle began to reply but a harsh wet cough stopped him. When the spasm of coughs finally broke, he spat up a large wad of mucus. The chain of drool on his lip was bloody. He wiped it away with a hand. "I can talk my way out of this." He panted rapidly and then cleared his throat. "The tunnel will take you to a farm outside of Aldergrove on the other side of the border. From there you can catch a bus into Vancouver."

"What if they're waiting at the other end?" I asked.

As Kyle was about to answer, we heard an unintelligible shout rumbling down the tunnel behind us. He turned sideways and leaned against the side of the wall to make space for me to pass.

I hesitated.

"Go!" he barked.

"Thanks," I said as I squeezed past. Automatically, I broke into a run.

"If you see Aaron, say hi for me." Kyle's voice echoed behind me.

CHAPTER

17

Without looking back, I sprinted the final hundred feet of the tunnel. I hit the end where a lopsided wood ladder clung to the wall in front of me. My chest thudded from more than exertion as I grasped a rung of the ladder and began to climb. Six feet above me, I saw light leaking through the edge of the wooden plank that covered the exit.

When my palm touched the splintering wood, I hesitated, wondering whether someone on the Washington side of the tunnel had called ahead to arrange for their Canadian colleagues to meet me. Turning back wasn't an option, so I pushed up against the plank and met no resistance. Sliding the board further out of the way, I heard a hissing noise. I froze.

Even before I noticed the green glass panels, I could tell from the tinted light flooding the hole that I'd emerged inside a greenhouse. Listening intently, I recognized the noise as coming from an automatic watering system. I waited but heard no other sounds.

Tentatively, I stuck my head up and out and glanced around. The greenhouse was crowded with rows of plants and vegetables. Swiveling my head in either direction, I saw no sign of anything except plant life. I scampered out of the opening and slid the plank across the hole, trying to replace it as I'd found it.

Tiptoeing down a row of peppers toward the greenhouse door, I stopped to gain my bearings. The structure was located behind the farmhouse and in front of a row of crops. I saw a tractor parked outside the barn and a new silver pickup in the driveway, but there was still no indication of company.

I tightened the shoulder straps of my knapsack and took a couple of deep breaths. Then I pulled open the door and dashed for the driveway running beside the farmhouse. Though free of the claustrophobic confinement of the tunnel, I felt like an escaping prisoner hit by floodlights as my feet crunched on the dirt of the driveway. Without slowing, I raced by the house and toward the eight-foot fence guarding the house from the street.

Behind me, I heard the storm door whoosh open. "Hey, what the fuck?" an angry voice shouted.

I sprinted for the gate. Skidding to a stop, I yanked at the gate's handle, but the latch didn't budge.

"Where do you think you're going, asshole?" the voice called out, moving closer.

I jumped up, grabbed for the top of the gate, and hoisted myself up, pulling with all my might. I vaulted over the top of the fence and landed awkwardly on the gravel. As soon as I regained my balance, I sprinted out into the open street.

"Wait!" But the voice was already fading behind me.

Running down the street, I heard the pickup truck's engine fire up. I ran as fast as I could, but I was certain to lose this race in a hurry. I veered across the street, heading for the neighboring farmhouse. Grunting and gasping, I scrambled up the driveway.

The same people who had built the tunnel might have owned this farm as well, but I had no other option. I rushed to the front door and rang the bell. Glancing over my shoulder, I saw the silver pickup from next door idling menacingly in the middle of the road. In a baseball cap, a young muscular East Indian man sat behind the wheel of the truck. He glared at me through the open driver's window.

Bobbing from foot to foot, I rang the bell again. The driver revved his engine.

The door opened. An older man in a denim shirt and jeans stood in front of me with arms crossed over his chest. He could have stepped out of a Norman Rockwell rural scene, except he wasn't nearly as welcoming as a Rockwell character. "I told you people a thousand times, damn it!" He scowled. "No soliciting."

"No, no," I said, searching for a passable lie but coming up empty. I pointed behind me to the truck on the street. "That man is trying to kill me."

He waved his palm, agitated. "I don't want none of your troubles!"

The old man began to slam the door in my face, but I wedged my foot into the gap between the door and the jamb. The door crushed the blisters that had formed on my toes inside my poorly fitting shoes, but I ignored the pain shooting up my legs. Though I knew I was getting nowhere with the old man, I pointed dramatically behind me to the man in the pickup.

The gesture had the desired effect. The pickup revved its engine, squealed its tires, and then fired off down the road.

I freed my foot from the door and it slammed shut with enough of a breeze to rustle my hair. "I'm going," I called to him, hoping the old man wasn't on the phone to the police.

My right foot throbbing, I hobbled back out to the street and along it as fast as I could. I followed the side street for two blocks until it gave into a busier road. Keeping an eye out for the silver pickup, I met the sporadic but growing traffic with ambivalence. One part of me felt safe amid the protection of potential witnesses, the other part overly exposed.

A rusty red Honda slowed down and rolled to a stop beside me on the road's shoulder. A bearded young guy with pierced ears and a friendly face rolled down his window. "Hey, buddy, you need a ride?" he called out. "I'm heading into town."

Unkempt with a battered knapsack, I imagined I must have looked like a down-on-my-luck hitchhiker. I was tempted to climb in the man's car, but I realized that his was the kind of attention I was desperate not to draw. "Thanks. I'm okay." I smiled without making eye contact. "I feel like walking."

"Okay. Happy travels, man."

As he began to roll up his window, I yelled, "Hey, how far is it into town?"

He pointed ahead of him. "Seven or eight blocks down the road."

I dropped my head to the ground and waved him away. Miserably, I wondered whether the old farmer or the young driver, if they saw the reports of me on CNN (or its Canadian counterpart), would remember the desperate-looking man who fit the fugitive's profile.

I trudged on, eventually reaching "downtown" Aldergrove. I almost smiled when I saw the green Starbucks emblem among the fast-food joints and gas stations that dotted the main strip. I headed inside. I dug out the Canadian money Kyle had given me and ordered a coffee from the flighty young clerk whose attempts to engage me in chatter were in vain.

Passing by a woman in the line behind me who held a cycling helmet, I had a longing that bordered on hunger for a punishing bike ride. I found a stool in the back corner and wedged myself at the countertop. Maybe it was coincidence but as I drained the large coffee, the fog began to lift inside my skull.

I picked up copies of two Vancouver dailies, *The Vancouver Sun* and *The Province*. Scanning them from cover to cover, I found no mention of my story. The newfound sense of anonymity allowed me to relax slightly.

I dug inside the knapsack and found a pencil and paper. I scratched a few notes for myself and then stood up and headed to the bathroom in the back of the coffee shop. I hadn't planned to make contact with Michael Prince yet, but the deserted pay phone in the hallway beckoned. I had two options: I could make the call collect or I could leave an indelible impression with the woman at the counter by asking for twenty dollars' worth of coins. Reaching for the phone, I opted to the dump the charge on my attorney. I dialed the number from memory, and Prince's hospitable assistant, Janelle, accepted the charges without hesitation. Fifteen seconds later, I heard Prince's calm voice. "Benjamin, I have been searching high and low for you."

"You're not alone," I said, keeping a furtive eye out on the coffee shop.

"For the record, fleeing isn't what I would have counseled," he said with veteran understatement.

"Duly noted. Have you spoken to Helen Riddell or anyone with the S.P.D.?"

"The S.P.D. is unaware that we have a professional relationship. I can't think of any helpful reason to inform them yet that we do."

The wisdom of his logic sunk in. "I imagine they're looking pretty hard for me."

"You might say that. How did you cross the border? At Aldergrove?"

I knew my collect call was bound to have tipped him off to my whereabouts, but it still jarred how quickly he was able to pinpoint me with technology as a basic as call display. "Michael, no one can—"

He cut me off. "Of course, they can't. Our discussions are entirely privileged."

My grip on the receiver relaxed.

"Ben, why don't I arrange to meet you somewhere?"

"In Canada?"

"If you prefer," he said. "I can bring you to the U.S. Consulate, and we can negotiate the terms of your . . . delivery . . . to the S.P.D."

"No, Michael! They've got a strong case against me that I just made a hell of a lot stronger. I'm not going back without answers."

He was silent a moment. "And if you can't find your brother, or you discover that he really is dead?"

"Then I'll find another explanation," I said with an absolute confidence that I didn't necessarily feel. "Something is going on in Vancouver. The anonymous phone calls. The drug smuggling. NorWesPac's aborted condo development at Whistler—"

"What about Whistler?" he snapped. He cleared his throat. "You never mentioned anything about a Whistler development before."

"I only learned about it after we last spoke."

"Oh," he said. I could picture him leaning back in his chair, his hands locked behind his silvery mane, patiently waiting for an explanation.

I gave him the rundown on what I knew of the ill-fated NorWesPac development at Whistler and Emily's involvement. "Hmmm," he said. "If I was a juror listening to that, I'm not certain I would see any relevance to the question of your guilt."

"There's more to it. I'm certain. I just need time to sort it out."

"All right," Prince said with slight disappointment in his tone. "Ben, how do I reach you if I need to?"

"I'm going into Vancouver but I don't even know where I'll end up."

"Are you using an alias?"

I hesitated.

"You're right," he said. "It's probably for the best that you don't tell anyone."

A woman approached the bathroom across from me. I turned inward, cradling the phone more tightly against my ear as if using a seashell to listen to the ocean. "Why can't I tell anyone?"

"Ben, let's assume you are being framed. The conspirator would have to know so many intimate details about you to pull it off convincingly."

I leaned tighter into the wall. "Are you suggesting I shouldn't trust my friends and family?"

"I'm saying you should be *very* careful whom you trust."

"Even you?"

"Well, technically, my membership in the state Bar depends on me maintaining a confidential relationship with you." He sighed. "Hell, Ben. I'm not even sure you should trust me with your whereabouts."

I wondered if he was joking, but I didn't have time to ask. Suddenly, a tall man with a professorial demeanor hovered over me, his body language demanding the phone. "Okay, Michael, I'll be in touch."

I hung up, brushed past the professor, and headed for the door. Stepping out into the cool fall breeze, I tucked my hands in my pocket and walked toward the bus station that I'd noticed earlier.

Inside, I approached the desk and bought a ticket for the first bus to downtown Vancouver, leaving in forty-five minutes. I asked the disinterested fat man behind the counter for change for the phone, and he reluctantly broke a two-dollar coin into eight quarters. From a vending machine, I bought two chocolate bars I didn't want in order to get another six quarters in change. After locating the nearest pay phone, I dialed a Seattle number and deposited eight quarters as instructed by the automated operator.

"St. Jude's Emergency," Anne barked.

Recognizing the veteran nurse's voice, I almost hung up, worried that she might pick up on mine as easily as I did hers. Instead, I roughened my voice as if suffering from laryngitis. "It's Dr. Horvath calling. May I please speak to Dr. Lindquist?"

"Hang on," Anne said, and the phone clicked.

After thirty seconds, the phone clicked again. "Ben?" Alex whispered.

At the welcome sound of her voice, I relaxed a little. "Yes."

"Where the hell did you disappear to?" she snapped.

"I'm sorry, Alex. I didn't feel it was safe." I paused. "For either of us."

When she spoke again, her tone was more tender. "Are you okay?"

"Kyle helped me. I'm fine."

"Where are you?"

I hesitated, remembering Prince's warning, but then I dismissed the thought. "I'm in Canada. I should be in Vancouver soon."

"Good."

"Alex, did you find my cell phone?"

"Yeah."

"It's traceable with the power on, so make sure you leave it turned off until we need it."

"When will that be?"

I wavered. "I was hoping tomorrow morning. Would that work for you?"

"No problem. Tacoma, right?"

My feet began to cool. "Alex, maybe you should drop the phone off with Kyle. He would do this for me, too. And the risk—"

"No," she cut in. "Your plan will work better with a woman."

"Okay. Thanks."

An automated operator's voice broke onto our line to demand more money. I deposited the last of my quarters.

"Ben, Marcus called me earlier." She sounded apologetic.

"Oh?" I said, confused as to the relevance.

"He was asking a lot of questions about you." She cleared her throat. "You see, he took Talie to school today . . ."

Suddenly, I understood. "And Talie told him I was there last night."

"Yes," she said quietly. "I'm sorry, Ben."

I wanted to hug her. "I had no business showing up without warning last night. Of course Talie would tell her dad! She's only five."

"Going on fifteen."

"Do you think Talie will tell anyone else?"

"She hasn't heard the news reports. She doesn't know that the police are looking for you. But I'll have another talk with her."

A dark thought dawned on me. "What about Marcus?"

"I don't know." She paused. "He was very interested. Asking a lot of questions."

"Questions?"

"Like what shape you were in, where you were going, did you kill Emily, and so on," she sighed. "I told him you were innocent and the rest was none of his business, but I don't know if he was satisfied."

"Okay. Thanks, Alex." Promising to be in touch soon, I hung up.

Why would Marcus be so interested in me?

My thoughts drifted back to what Emily had told me about him the very last time I saw her. My blood still boiled thinking of the history Marcus and Emily had shared. And it occurred to me that I had been present the first time they ever met.

Six years earlier, Emily and I were at one of the hospital's social functions I'd attended since signing on as a staff member at St. Jude's. I felt compelled to work the crowd, pumping hands and paying my respects to the more senior physicians. Among the throng of doctors and their spouses, I became separated from Emily and I didn't make it back to her for almost half an hour.

I spotted her across the crowded floor. Gorgeous in a black knee-length cocktail dress with a slit running up the side, Emily beckoned me over with a small two-fingered wave—our signal that she needed rescuing.

As I closed the gap across the floor, I saw Emily chatting with Alex's husband, Dr. Marcus Lindquist. Alex had joined St. Jude's three months after I did, but I'd already met her husband, as he was one of the staff hematologists. He was pleasant enough when he came down to the ER for consults, but his manner always struck me as slightly condescending and just a little too slick.

As soon as I reached them, Emily tucked her arm in mine and nestled her head into my shoulder. The whiff of her Calvin Klein perfume as her lips brushed warmly over my cheek sent a small erotic tingle through me, but I knew the show of affection was more than just for my benefit; she was establishing her status to Marcus as taken.

Emily pointed her water glass at Marcus. "Dr. Lindquist was just trying to find out what I am like in bed," she said. "Maybe you can answer that better for him."

Unfazed, Marcus offered me a confident smile. "Your lovely girlfriend's account isn't wholly accurate."

I fought off the surge of jealousy. "Maybe, then, you can set the record straight, Marcus?"

"Surely." He toasted me with his sloshing scotch glass before taking a long sip. "I told Emily that she carried herself like a dancer."

"And?" Emily prodded with a small laugh.

His eyes widened playfully. "And I told her that every woman I'd ever met who danced well, fucked even better." He chuckled. "So, I was trying to establish if she is as good a dancer as I think she might be."

I smiled through gritted teeth. "You'll have to take my word for it, Marcus. She's a mind-blowing dancer."

Marcus raised his glass in another toast.

"Here comes your wife," I pointed out, as a visibly pregnant Alex approached. "Maybe you would like to tell her how good a dancer you think Emily is?"

CHAPTER
18

I sat in the very last row of the bus, staring out the window as we crossed north over the Granville Street Bridge. The clouds had cleared and Vancouver's downtown skyline sparkled in front of me, framed by the dramatic backdrop of snow-dusted mountains. Nestled between the ocean and the mountains, Vancouver, with its world-class natural beauty, could legitimately compete with my beloved Seattle. I remembered how Aaron once described his relocation from Seattle to Vancouver as having moved from Eden to paradise. But he'd always planned to return to Seattle. He had said as much to me two years earlier—the last time we spoke.

A few days after his final visit to Seattle, Aaron left a message on my machine reiterating his intent to follow through with the rehab program I'd offered to arrange. We played phone tag for days, but we finally hooked up two weeks after our initial conversation. When I saw VANCOUVER, CANADA *appear on my caller ID, I answered the phone on the first ring. "Hey, little bro," Aaron said, using our long-standing inside joke.*

"You doing okay?"

"Yeah, fine," he said. "Sorry about the melodramatics at your house a couple weeks ago."

"No one does melodrama better than the Dafoes." I laughed, relieved by how upbeat he sounded. "And that problem you mentioned with your 'colleagues'?"

"Pretty much all sorted out."

"You're still going ahead with rehab, right?"

"No ifs, ands, or buts," Aaron said. "For what it's worth, I haven't touched anything for the past two weeks. Of course, that won't last unless I get some professional help. Is your friend still willing to have me?"

"Absolutely. Gary loves lost causes."

Aaron laughed. "Oh, he's going to love me plenty."

"When should I line it up for?"

"Can you give me another two weeks or so?"

"Done."

Aaron cleared his throat. "Ben, um, do you think there would be room for two at this clinic?"

"You mean Kyle?"

"No, he's still recovering from his bone marrow transplant. I mean my girl-friend."

"Girlfriend?" I laughed. "You don't have girlfriends. You have dates. Some of them don't even last long enough to qualify as that."

"Funny," he grunted. "It's different now. I've met someone."

"Who also has a drug habit?"

"No worse than mine," he said distantly.

"Come on, let's have it," I said, trying to ease the sudden tension on the line. "Tell me about her."

"She's a sweetheart, Ben. Smart and beautiful. And she's even more deter-mined than I am to get clean. We want to start over again in Seattle. Together."

"What's her name?"

"Jenny."

"Hmmm, Jenny. I like the name."

"Ben, you'll love her. She reminds me a lot of Emily. Same passion, same weakness."

After avoiding Emily's name for three years, he'd now mentioned Emily in consecutive conversations. And the comparison brought a pang of melancholy. "It won't be a problem," I said. "I'll talk to Gary. We'll make sure there are spaces for you and Jenny. In two weeks, right?"

"Two weeks." He laughed. "Thanks, Ben. I wouldn't want to have anyone else for an identical twin."

The bus pulled into the downtown depot, and the memory of Aaron's last words faded. I disembarked with the others, working as hard to avoid eye contact as I had during the ride.

I'd discreetly counted the bills Kyle gave me. His generosity (in the form of twelve hundred Canadian dollars) would make life easier in the short term, but with only two changes of clothes, no food, no transport, and no roof over my head, his donation would be stopgap at best. I was determined not to risk blowing my cover or bringing attention to Alex by dipping into her ATM accounts, except in the case of a dire emergency.

Walking out of the station, I spotted a Royal Bank across the street. I decided that my first order of business was to establish my existence—or Peter Horvath's, anyway—in Vancouver. I would start with a bank account.

I stepped into the branch and walked over to the customer service counter, where a perky young Asian clerk named Cindy Lo greeted me. Her blue blazer and navy skirt ensemble seemed out of place on her, making her look like a girl who had dressed up in her grandmother's suit.

Cindy led me from the counter to a little office. Put at ease by her naïve eagerness to please, I breezed through the steps of setting up a checking account. Until she asked to see my identification. Resisting the familiar fight-or-flight impulse, I dug Peter's license out of my wallet and passed it over to her. I hoped my face didn't betray my sudden panic.

Cindy studied the driver's license then looked up at me quizzically. I was just about to launch into a spontaneous cover story about the photo, when Cindy asked me, "Dr. Horvath, do you still live in Seattle?"

"Oh, no," I said, feeling my pulse slow. "I'm in the process of relocating here. I just don't have a permanent address yet."

She pointed at the license with a happy smile. "Okay if we use this one?"

"Perfect."

Cindy passed me back the license. She typed at her computer for a minute or two, printed out two sheets of paper, and had me sign the forms in three places. Fortunately, my signature was so illegible that it amounted to not much more than a Rorschach inkblot test for the reader. Still, I tried to make the opening B look more like a P for Peter Horvath. The process reminded me of the many pitfalls I would face as an impostor, even in the most mundane little tasks.

Cindy took the forms from me. She pulled a new bankbook from her desk drawer and had me sign it with the invisible ink pen. Her grin widened. "And now, Dr. Horvath, can I interest you in a Royal Bank Visa or line of credit?"

Yes, you can! I wanted to shout, but I knew that an application would trigger background credit checks I couldn't chance. I shook my head. "That's too much like moving in together after the second date. Let's try the checking account and see how the relationship works out from there."

She giggled and handed me the bankbook along with a temporary ATM card and a few blank checks.

"Cindy, do you happen to know where the nearest YMCA is?" I hurried to add, "I was hoping to squeeze in a workout."

"It's only about four blocks from here." She insisted on escorting me to the door and pointing out the street that would lead to the YMCA. I thanked her and headed off in the warm autumn day, satisfied I'd passed my first public test as Dr. Peter Horvath.

As soon as I turned onto Burrard Street, I found my bearings. At the top of the hill stood a familiar complex of red brick buildings, St. Paul's Hospital. Eight years earlier, during my ER residency, I had done a six-week elective at the hospital, renowned for its HIV and inner-city medicine program. Living up to its billing, the hospital serviced a disproportionate number of intravenous drug users and alcoholics who offered some of the most bizarre medical conditions I had ever encountered. Like the gang at St. Jude's in Seattle, the staff at St. Paul's managed to maintain their compassion and sense of humor, which made the working environment surprisingly tolerable.

Burying my nostalgia, I ducked into the YMCA two blocks shy of the hospital. I registered at the front desk, disappointed to learn that the room was going to set back me about fifty dollars a night. My stay here would have to be short.

I followed the stairs to the fourth floor. The narrow room smelled of cleaning products with a trace of lingering cigarettes, though smoking wasn't permitted. The room was barren aside from the twin bed, tight closet, and a small translucent window. The nearest bathroom was at the other end of the hallway. As I dropped onto the bed, exhaustion swept over me. Though it was only five in the afternoon, I stripped off my clothes and slipped under the sheets. I fell asleep almost as soon as I pulled the blanket over me.

At 9:15 P.M., I woke up and ventured out for a twelve-inch vegetarian sub, an impulse born not out of principle but economics, as the meatless choice saved me a few dollars. I returned to the room and fell back into bed.

With my body clock thoroughly upended, I woke up a few minutes before four in the morning. unable to get back to sleep. I tiptoed down the hallway, relieved to find the bathroom empty. I had a long hot shower, working to scrub away the last three days of my life.

I changed into my alternate outfit, a pair of jeans and a navy long-sleeved T-shirt. I sat on the bed, reviewing my situation. Doubts began to creep to mind. Maybe Aaron *was* dead. I remembered reading an article on how blood products could be freeze-dried indefinitely. Maybe someone had frozen Aaron's blood, or mine. But even if the conspirator had access to such high-level technology, who would plan a murder two years in advance? And if Aaron were still alive, was he more involved than I was willing to accept? Perhaps desperation, drugs, or whatever motives had kept him underground all this time also drove him to participate in Emily's murder.

No! Not Aaron.

I wanted to punch walls. I wanted to cycle up a never-ending incline. I wanted out of this nightmare.

I hopped off the bed and paced the room like a caged rat wired on amphetamines. Time crawled by. Finally, light began to seep through the windows. At 7:30, I again ventured out onto the street. I walked past the hospital to the gas station on the corner. I knew from the time of my elective that the station served passable cheap coffee and had a selection of newspapers. I downed two cups as I scoured the local papers, relieved to see I had not hit their radar screens yet.

Outside, I found a phone booth tucked behind the gas station. I checked my watch, which read 8:50. I waited five minutes, guarding the phone, and then I dialed my own cell number, collect.

Alex accepted the charges. "Ben?"

The sound of her voice grounded me. Affection welled. With longing, I pictured her reassuring smile and her warm almond-brown eyes. I fought off the emotion. "Alex, where are you?" I asked, businesslike.

"A mall, in downtown Tacoma."

"Perfect. You know the drill?"

"Yes," she said impatiently. "I put you on hold, call the precinct, and then link you up to Helen using the conference call function on your phone."

"And at the first sight of anyone official, you press the number sign three times, then hang up and get the hell out of there. Right?"

"Yeah, yeah."

"Alex, are you sure you want to do this?"

"I didn't drive an hour to this mall to buy iron-on-photo T-shirts," she grumbled. "Hang on. I'm going to get her."

Twenty seconds later, the line buzzed and I heard Helen's voice. "Hello?"

"Helen."

Silence.

"Helen?"

"Benjamin?" she said slowly. "Where are you?"

"I can't say."

"You can and you should, Ben," she sighed. "You really should."

"So you can arrest me?"

"Yes," she said. "And maybe also help you."

"Help me?"

She was quiet again. I pictured Helen covering the receiver with a hand, as she barked out orders at her subordinates to start tracing the call. "Yes, help. Or at least try to help prove you didn't do it." She grunted a laugh. "God knows, you're doing a piss-poor job of convincing anyone of that."

"But you're already convinced I did do it."

"Never said I was convinced," she said. "Everything I know about you tells me you don't have those two murders in you. Problem is, all the evidence points to you."

"So what do you do?"

"Roll up our sleeves and get down to some old-fashioned detective work. Like Baretta, before he offed his wife." Her tone turned dead serious. "But I can't do any of that while we're spending all our time and energy searching for you."

Her logic began to sway me. "How do I know you'll keep looking for anyone else once you have me in custody?"

"Ben, have you ever known me to do a half-assed job with an investigation?"

I smiled at the phone. "No."

"So trust me on this one, okay?"

"What about Mark Bellon?" I said, remembering the young seminary student she had told me about.

"Forget Mark. Life's not that cruel. A detective doesn't get two Bellons in one lifetime." She paused. When she spoke again her voice filled with empathy. "Ben, you have to know how badly I don't want you to turn out to be our guy."

"But in your heart, you think I am."

"Listen, Ben, I promise you: If you come in on your own accord, I will do everything in my power to get to the bottom of this. *Everything.*"

I wavered a moment. Then I heard three rapid beeps in succession—Alex's warning—and I snapped back into focus. "Helen, I didn't kill anyone."

Alex hung up the line before Helen could reply. I listened to the dial tone, hoping Alex escaped safely and that our little stunt might keep the S.P.D. off my trail for a while longer.

With the receiver still dangling in my hand, I realized I had never felt so lost in my life.

CHAPTER
19

After checking into the YMCA, I spent the next two days adapting to the fugitive life, watching my five-o'clock shadow grow into the beginnings of a beard, and casing my new neighborhood. I found a local optician, where I bought colored contacts that tinted my hazel eyes brown. At a nearby liquor store, I learned that alcohol in Canada is taxed to the hilt and is almost twice the price compared to the States. I went as far as to walk a forty-ounce bottle of scotch to the checkout counter, but I wasn't willing to dip that deep into my reserves.

I unearthed some local eateries, including a tasty Singapore noodle joint that fit my five-dollar-maximum meal budget. Too many times I walked past the local bike shop, pining at the window like a kid who got sensible shoes instead of his dream ten-speed for Christmas. And I spent much of my time at a coffee shop I found, where for the cost of a three-dollar coffee I could surf the Internet for up to an hour on one of their terminals before being chased out of the shop by the impatient stares of the employees or other patrons.

I followed the S.P.D.'s manhunt for me through online newspapers, though I was quick to close the sites if my photo ever popped up on the screen. I read that S.P.D. was actively looking for me in the Tacoma area, and I inferred that my call-forwarding ruse with Alex had paid off, at least temporarily. When not following the news stories on my escape, I researched NorWesPac developments and their failed Whistler property. My hunch kept growing that the development, which bound many of the people involved in my crisis, somehow played a role in what had happened to Emily.

I also exchanged e-mails with Alex. Once we got past her concerns for my welfare, she shared more of the details of her marital implosion. Marcus had raised the subject of child custody. My heart ached for Alex. Talie was her Achilles' heel. I had no doubt that was why Marcus, who had never struck me as a particularly committed father, pursued custody. *Bastard*. My dislike for him grew by the moment, but all I could do was offer Alex empty reassurances.

Despite my frugality, Kyle's money was thinning at an alarming rate. I knew that I needed to find a source of income. I was tempted to wander into St. Paul's Hospital and offer my services as a replacement physician. While Ben Dafoe might have been a qualified Emergency physician, Peter Horvath, an internist, was not. But within the scope of either of my disjointed identities, I was qualified to work at a walk-in clinic.

I scoured the yellow pages, focusing my search on the least desirable neighborhoods of Vancouver. There was nothing altruistic in my choice; I understood that the more itinerant and down-and-out the clientele, the less likely a patient was to recognize me from CNN or any other network that still covered my disappearance.

I stumbled upon the East Hastings Clinic by accident while I was out looking for thrift shops to expand my limited wardrobe. Two storefronts down from a pawnshop and on a block beside a pharmacy with metal bars on the window, the clinic felt right to me even before I stepped in.

Inside, the waiting room was jammed with patients, male and female, several of whom slumped in their seats. The intermixed smells of stale cigarettes, unwashed clothes, and body odor brought back memories of weekend overnight shifts at St. Jude's. I wove past the outstretched legs and up to the desk.

The tiny gray-haired receptionist eyed me with the look of someone who had stared down people twice my size. "Yes?" she snapped.

"I'm Dr. Peter Horvath."

"So?"

"I'm an internist from the States, but I have my Canadian license."

"And?" She held up her hand and a cluster of silver bracelets slid noisily down her arm.

"I'm interested in, um . . . ," I said, faltering under her piercing gaze. "Finding part-time work."

Her expression shifted from disdain to shock. "You mean *here?*"

I nodded.

The wrinkles at the corners of her mouth deepened and then her bright red lips parted widely; I wasn't sure if she was smiling or laughing. She hopped up from her chair, gaining little height. "Let's go see Dr. Janacek."

She emerged from a small door in the hallway behind the waiting room. I followed her along the shabby and stained carpets to a closed door at the end of the hallway. She rapped on it like a woodpecker working overtime. "Dr. Janacek," she shouted, "I got someone you have to meet."

"Let me eat my lunch, woman!" the deep voice barked back in a European accent.

Ignoring the command, the receptionist curled her small hand around the door handle and opened it. "Go on in," she said to me and then turned and walked away.

I stepped into the small office with walls papered by degrees and certificates. I cleared my throat. "Sorry to interrupt."

In a crisp white lab coat that matched the color of his short-cropped hair, a distinguished-looking man with prominent cheeks and eyebrows and intense gray eyes stared at me from behind a worn oak desk. Dr. Jozef Janacek stopped in midbite and then slowly lowered his sandwich onto the wax paper in front of him. He reached for a napkin and wiped his fingers with it. "And you are?"

"Dr. Peter Horvath. I am—"

"Horvath? Hungarian, correct?" Janacek interrupted. "Never had much time for Hungarians. A very fatalistic group as a rule."

"And I'm not wild about the Czechs," I said. "Always too blunt."

Janacek eyes narrowed and then he broke into a deep belly laugh. "Come, have a seat, Dr. Horvath."

"Peter," I said and extended my hand, which he met with a crushing handshake.

"Joe," he said. "So what brings you to my world-famous clinic?"

I sat down in the chair across from him. "I'm looking for work."

"Here?" His surprise wasn't much less than his receptionist's.

"I am interested in inner-city medicine."

The humor drained from his face. "And your credentials?"

"University of Washington med school, but I did internal medicine at the University of Toronto."

"I don't mean to insult you," he said, and I knew he was about to. "But to me you look more like the man who digs through the Dumpster behind us for soda pop cans than an academic physician."

I laughed. "How could I possibly take offense at that?" I lifted my knapsack and dug inside, pulling out copies of Peter Horvath's medical licenses along with the two generic reference letters Alex had included in the package.

Janacek glanced at the degrees and scanned the letters. He shook his large head. "All that academic training and now you want to work at a walk-in clinic on skid row?"

Glancing at all the degrees on his walls, I wondered the same of him, but I didn't ask. "I find inner-city medicine challenging," I said, trying not to sound over the top. "Besides, I've just got back from the Far East. I'm trying to get a feel for the lay of land. Keep my options open."

"Ah, you're still in that delusional stage where you think you actually have options in life." He sighed. "Youth."

I was beginning to like Joe. "I do know that if I don't pay off some of my student loans and credit card bills, bankruptcy might be my only option."

"We'll split your billings sixty-forty," he said without mentioning who got the sixty. "I'll need you five mornings a week, but you can pick and choose your afternoons." Then he flashed large white teeth that complemented his hair and coat. "Of course, on my schedule, mornings end at six P.M." He rose from his chair. "Stay with me today, and I'll show you the lay of our very arid land."

After borrowing a lab coat and an old stethoscope, I spent the rest of the afternoon shadowing Dr. Jozef Janacek. The experience was surreal, as if I'd been sent back in time to medical school. However, I hadn't observed office-based medicine in years, so the refresher was helpful, even enjoyable. Despite Joe's irreverent style, he treated his patients with dignity. And in turn, they worshiped him.

The majority of his patients appeared to be intravenous drug users. Almost all of them had acquired hepatitis C, and the majority suffered from HIV. Pain was their most common complaint. Joe appeared to have a talent for distinguishing patients with a genuine need for painkillers from those who were simply seeking drugs. Between patients, I asked Joe, "How can you be so confident in deciding which patients truly need narcotics?"

"Some doctors give people new hips or new hearts," he said with a self-deprecating shrug. "I spend my days trying to sort the drug addicts with legitimate pain from the drug seekers." He tapped his chest. "It's my calling. Besides, I know my patients. But if I am unsure, I always give people the benefit of the doubt." He paused and eyed me steadily. *"Once."*

We moved rapidly between the three examining rooms in the clinic. Joe never appeared to rush, but I realized that we still churned through a large number of patients. And yet, the number of people in the waiting room continued to steadily grow until it was standing room only and the grimy smell drifted to Joe's back office.

Halfway through the afternoon, Joe turned to me. "Is the little Hungarian ready to venture out from the nest on his own?"

"I'll take a shot." I grinned. "I always know where to turn if things go wrong."

"Sure," Joe deadpanned. "We call it the front door."

From the wall holder, I grabbed the chart that Edith—the diminutive tiger who manned Janacek's front desk—had left out. I glanced at the name on the chart, Ian Roland. I walked into the examining room to find an emaciated young man with greasy hair and pimply skin huddled in the corner, twitching on the examining table. I didn't need to ask a question to recognize the diagnosis: heroin withdrawal.

He looked up at me suspiciously. "Where's Doc Janacek?"

"I'm his new associate, Dr. Horvath." I nodded to the patient. "You're heroin sick, huh, Ian?"

Ian nodded vehemently. "I couldn't afford any fixes for two days.

I've been puking and shitting myself." He held out a hand to me. "You got to help me, Doc. It's bad."

"Let me have a look." I palpated the racing pulse at his wrist. Then I checked his blood pressure, which ran low. After a quick physical exam, I knew he was suffering from severe narcotic withdrawal. Unlike alcohol, no one dies from heroin withdrawal, but the experience can be so unpleasant that many addicts, once they've gone through it, are unwilling to face it again, making it even harder to help them get off drugs.

I pulled out from my coat pocket the prescription pad Joe had given me, scribbled out a prescription, and passed it to him. Reading the prescription, Ian's face creased into a scowl. "What's this?"

"A combination of mild sedatives and clonidine. It should take the edge off the sickness."

He crumpled the prescription into a ball. "No, man! I need methadone."

"I don't have a license to prescribe that."

"Okay." He said nodding in rapid motion. "Then morphine or Demerol would do the trick."

"I'm not going to substitute one narcotic for another."

"It's what Doc Janacek would do!"

"Maybe so, but you're seeing me today. And this is how I practice."

"Well, fuck you!" Ian threw the balled up prescription at my head. I dodged to the left, as it sailed past my ear. He hopped off the bed and stormed out of the room.

Some start to my new job, I thought glumly.

I was standing in the same spot when Ian came flying back in. He dropped to his knees and scoured the floor until he found the crumpled prescription. He smoothed out the paper and tucked it into his pocket. He looked at me with a sheepish grin. "Sorry, Doc. It's the junk. Can't even think straight no more." Then he was gone.

The patients who followed Ian were less dramatic. Eventually, I found my familiar ER groove of plowing through the volume, while still practicing satisfying medicine. For a while, the patients' illnesses and crises even pushed my own troubles out of my thoughts. Not all of Joe's patients had drug-related issues. And several had overcome their addiction, only to suffer from the complications of HIV or other ill-nesses related to their long-standing drug use.

At 6:55 P.M., the waiting room had finally cleared. Pleasantly tired, I walked into the examining room to see my last patient: Malcolm Davies. Clean-cut and wearing a button-down shirt with a sleek silver watch, Malcolm struck me as different from the others the moment I saw him. When he looked up at me, his eyes widened and I thought he might do a double take.

The anxiety seeped into my system. I assumed he recognized me from the media reports, but I decided to try to bluff my way out. "Malcolm, I'm Dr. Horvath." I extended my arm and shook his hand, staring him straight in the eye. "You look as if you recognize me."

Malcolm shook his head. "Guess not. You remind me of a guy, that's all."

"Who's that?"

"A guy I used to know who disappeared a while back," Malcolm said. "Just a coincidence, I guess."

"People tell me I have one of those faces."

"Guess so," he said noncommittally and then nodded at the chart in my hand. "You can see Dr. Janacek usually refills my prescription every couple of weeks."

I flipped open his chart. Deciphering Joe's scrawl, which wasn't any more legible than mine, I saw that Malcolm did get his prescriptions refilled roughly twice a month. In the flap of the chart, I struggled to make out the list of Malcolm's medications.

"I'm a bipolar," he said, referring to his manic-depressive illness. "Dr. J.'s got me on at least four meds."

Sure enough, I saw two antidepressants, lithium, a sedative, and another strong sleeping pill. Malcolm took more pills than most people three times his age.

"And I need more painkillers."

Of course. "What for?"

"I've been on them for over two years. You know," he said as if I was being deliberately obtuse, "after the explosion."

Without prompting, he unbuttoned his shirt to expose his chest. Ragged scars and patches of skin graft covered most of his chest. I noticed that the scars extended to the base of his neck. "The pain just keeps getting worse, you know. I'm going to need a bunch more of those oxycodone pills."

I was so desperate to distract Malcolm I would have prescribed anything he asked for, but staring at the road map that was his chest, I had little doubt his pain was genuine. As I was filling out his prescription list, I asked, "What caused the explosion?"

"My meth lab blew up," he said nonchalantly, as if an exploding crystal meth lab was as common a nuisance as being rear-ended at a stop sign.

I was so relieved at his apparent lack of interest in my identity that I just nodded and said, "Bummer."

Malcolm buttoned up his shirt. I handed him the prescription. He nodded and turned for the door.

I focused on the patient's chart and jotted a brief note about the visit. I was halfway through listing all the refills I had included in the prescription for the crystal meth chemist, when I recalled his words— "a guy I used to know who disappeared a while back." It suddenly clicked. Malcolm didn't recognize me from the newspaper.

He thought I was Aaron!

CHAPTER

20

Stopping by his office on my way out the door, I saw that Joe Janacek was almost buried behind the mound of charts on his desk. He looked up from the chart he was scribbling in and appraised me with a long stare. "Dr. Horvath, you're leaving early today?"

I glanced at my watch: 8:15 P.M. "I'm more of a morning person."

Janacek ran a hand through his thick white hair. "You will be back tomorrow then?"

"Am I welcome back?"

"Sadly, I am not Donald Trump," Joe said with a sigh. "I don't have the luxury of choice. Anyone with a pulse and a less than extensive criminal record will do."

I stiffened at the term "criminal record." I forced a grin. "You know how to make the new guy feel welcome."

"It's a gift." He pointed around the room. "What do you think of my practice?"

"I've seen worse," I said.

Joe raised an eyebrow.

"I've worked in some American inner city practices," I said. "At least in Canada, there's more of a social safety net for the addicts."

"I suppose." He sighed again. "Though our disenfranchised have become wards of the state. That's expensive for us, humiliating for them."

I cleared my throat. "Joe, um, when will I be paid?"

He eyed me steadily. "We will be paid for your billings at the end of next week. I intend to pay you then. Do you need money sooner?"

I need a roof over my head! I need food! I need a bike! "Should be okay. I wish I did a better job of saving a little while overseas. Too much travel."

"Let me know if you change your mind, Peter." Joe flashed his pearly whites. "I enjoy having people beholden to me."

I said good night and headed for the door. At the reception desk, I was disappointed to see that Edith still manned her station like a guard dog. I'd hoped to unearth Malcolm Davies's records and to steal his address and phone number, but I didn't stand a chance now.

She looked up at me with no more warmth than earlier. "If you want to survive here, you're going to need to keep up."

I nodded. "Thanks for your help today."

She shrugged her skinny shoulders. "You know we open tomorrow morning at eight."

It was a command, not a question. "See you then."

I walked into the cool drizzly night. Though it was early evening, the darkness had brought out a different element to Hastings Street. With the few shops boarded or gated, the people milling on the street looked to be the same aimless down-and-outers I'd spent the afternoon seeing as patients. Several people pushed shopping carts full of their possessions. Some staggered up and down the block, drunk, high, or both. A few men and women approached, requesting or demanding smokes or pocket change.

And yet I felt safer than I had in days. I knew none of the people I passed would blow my cover with the S.P.D.

Heading west a few blocks, the low-rent district suddenly gave way to the highly touristy cobbled streets of Vancouver's historic Gastown. High-end shops, restaurants, and studios filled the reclaimed brownstones. BMWs replaced the shopping carts.

My guard rose.

I spotted a phone booth near the landmark gas clock, and I headed for it. Turning my back to the bustle of the streets, I dialed Kyle's cell phone number and reversed the charges.

"Ben, you made it out of the tunnel!" he said joyfully.

"Yeah, it was a bit touch and go for a while," I said, brushing over the incident with the silver pickup truck. "How about you?"

"You know me. I could talk my way out of a lion's den."

"Kyle, you were coughing pretty heavily in that tunnel."

"My lungs were weakened by the radiation during the bone marrow transplant. I don't do well in dank places anymore. No big deal." He dismissed it as if explaining away a cold. "How are you coping?"

"I'm settling into life in Vancouver as a wanted man."

"Probably best you didn't hang around here. The search for you is pretty intense. They even came to see me."

"When?"

"Two days ago."

"Rick and Helen?"

"Yup."

"What did you tell them?"

"Ever since I found my faith, I've been saddled with these annoying guidelines on honesty."

My stomach churned. "What did you say, Kyle?"

"What I knew."

I squeezed the receiver tighter. "Meaning?"

"Truth was, at the time I didn't know if you were still on the American side lying dead in the tunnel or if you had hightailed it off to the Arctic or Newfoundland." He chuckled. "I told them I didn't have a clue where you were."

"And they believed you?"

"Haven't seen them since."

"Thanks, Kyle." I exhaled with relief. "You don't happen to know a guy named Malcolm Davies?"

"Why does that name sound so familiar?"

"A crystal meth chemist."

"Of course!" Kyle's voice filled with recognition. "He was badly burned in a meth lab explosion a while back. How did you run into Malcolm?"

"I saw him at a clinic I'm working in. I think he recognized me. Or at least Aaron."

"Yeah, he would."

"Why?"

"Aaron and I used to get our supply directly off of Malcolm," he said. "Cheaper than buying retail, you know."

"Do you know where he lives now?"

"Not since his lab, which was also his home, blew up."

"Kyle, I am not sure he bought my cover story. You think he's the kind of guy that might go to the police—"

His laugh stopped me. "*Malcolm*?" he said. "You could rob his grandmother at gunpoint in front of him, and Malcolm wouldn't go near the cops."

Reassured, I changed subjects. "Kyle, the last time I spoke to Aaron he told me about a woman."

"Jenny, right?"

"Did you know her?"

"They hooked up right around the time of my illness." He cleared his throat. "We'd already had a falling out. I never met Jenny, but Aaron told me about her when he visited." He paused. "The way he talked . . . it wasn't like with other girlfriends."

"You mean long term?"

He laughed. "Exactly."

A car slowed down beside the curb. *Had they traced me to Gastown?* Worry penetrated my calm. I tucked deeper into the phone booth, feeling too vulnerable. "No chance Aaron ever mentioned Jenny's last name, huh?"

"If he did, it's long gone."

The car moved away, but I was eager to move again. "Thanks, Kyle. You've been a big help," I said, trying to wrap up the call.

"Ben, I've done some digging into Maglio and that NorWesPac development in Whistler."

My grip tensed on the receiver again. "And?"

"My information is all secondhand," Kyle said. "But that development was going to be a *huge* deal. NorWesPac would've been in for a couple of hundred million dollars when it was all said and done."

"Does Maglio have that kind of money?"

"Maybe yes, maybe no. He needed about twenty million up front to get it off the ground. But he wasn't alone. He had silent partners."

"Like who?"

"Well . . . me, for starters," Kyle said.

I was too surprised to say a word.

"Remember I told you that Aaron turned our drug money into an impressive legit portfolio?"

"Yeah."

"From what I heard, Aaron was planning to put up three million as seed money for Maglio's development. But I didn't know he was going to. At that point, I was already in hospital, too sick to care about anything but staying alive."

My mind raced and my temples pounded. "You said, 'was planning to'?"

"Aaron didn't end up putting up a dime."

"Why not?"

"Turns out, the deal was more than about only real estate," Kyle said slowly, drawing out his revelation. "The development was going to be an opportunity to launder drug money. And it provided a perfect cover for Maglio to expand his cross-border drug trade."

"So Maglio gets three wins in one! A promising real estate venture. A place to clean tainted drug money. And a new supply route of cross-border drugs."

"Sounds right," Kyle said.

"But Aaron walked away from it?"

"He had turned over a new leaf by then. He desperately wanted to get clean. And this development would've put him in even deeper."

"Is that why the deal fell through?"

"One of the reasons. NorWesPac also ran into a big problem with the zoning application." He chuckled. "Which only got a lot worse after the raid and arrests."

"Kyle!" I knew he was deliberately prolonging the suspense.

"NorWesPac threw a high-end party at Whistler for several local VIPs and city council members," Kyle said. "The RCMP raided it. They found pretty healthy quantities of coke, E, crystal meth . . . you name it."

"Was Maglio there?"

"No." He clicked his tongue. "But it was hosted by the development's sales director."

"*Emily!*"

"Hmmm." I could picture Kyle's mischievous smile. "Emily was busted along with a few others. It was all hushed up and glossed over. Though it sounds like it a got a lot colder in Whistler for NorWesPac right afterward."

I turned my back on the phone and stared at the cobblestones beside me, my sense of exposure replaced by the rush of a fresh lead. "Aaron pulled out his money, while Emily's drug bust at the party led to a loss of zoning permits. Inadvertently or otherwise, they both screwed over NorWesPac."

"And Maglio."

"The potential loss of a few hundred million sounds to me like a reasonable motive for murder."

"It's practically justifiable homicide," Kyle grunted.

"Who is your source?"

"Sorry," he said genuinely. "I gave my word. I can't say."

"Guess I should be all for you protecting your sources."

"Ben, there is someone who might know more about all this."

"Who?"

"His name is Drew Isaacs. Used to be kind of our right-hand man in Vancouver. He ran the show before Aaron moved up. Not much happened north of the border without Drew knowing about it."

"Drew Isaacs," I said to myself. "You wouldn't have a number or an address for him?"

"I have a two-year-old cell number."

"I'll take it."

Kyle reeled it off. Always good with numbers, I committed it to memory.

"If you find him," Kyle warned, "I'm not sure Drew would want to relive the old days with you, you know?"

"I'll be careful. Thanks, Kyle."

My head was spinning by the time I hung up. The buzz from the new leads gave me a lift. Someone had a plausible motive for killing Emily. Someone with a history compatible with violent crime.

Maybe it would be enough to convince Helen.

I bounded down the streets, feeling glimmers of a sensation that seemed almost foreign to me. Optimism.

CHAPTER

21

I woke up from the deepest night's sleep I'd had in weeks burning with determination. Glancing around the meager room that had become home over the past four days, I knew I couldn't stay much longer at the YMCA. Cost aside, the unwanted attention of my well-meaning fellow residents—especially my lonely next-door neighbor, Ray, who smoked so much that he smelled like an ashtray—was beginning to wear on me. The colored contact lenses and my growing hair and beard afforded only a certain degree of anonymity. I knew the American news coverage of my disappearance hadn't let up; and I didn't want to be around if and when my face popped up on the TV that played twenty-four hours a day in the common room.

I stood up and stretched away the tightness in my lower back, which I attributed to having not been on a bike for days on end—my longest dry spell in fifteen years. Like any addiction, it was fitting that a physical ache accompanied my cycling withdrawal. I missed the whistle of the wind, the warm burn in my thighs, and especially that rush of speed, but like an alcoholic or a heroin junkie, what I really missed was the high that a hard ride brought me.

Knowing I would see a paycheck in the not-too-distant future, I resolved to dip deep enough into my savings to buy a secondhand bike. Nothing fancy like the carbon fiber frame and alloy component bikes I had built in my garage. Anything with wheels and a saddle would do.

I headed down the hallway to the showers, relieved that at 6:45 A.M.

I still had the floor to myself. I showered, changed, and walked down to the lobby. My luck was holding. The phone booth was open, and the floor deserted.

I called Alex collect, and she accepted the charges. "Ben, how are you?"

"Under the circumstances, not bad," I said, warming at the sound of her voice. "How about you?"

"Hard to complain to you."

More than through her words, I picked upon on the forlorn quality in her voice. "Is it Marcus?"

"He wants to alternate full weeks." Alex stopped and swallowed. "Ben, I can't imagine going every second week without Talie."

That heartless bastard. "Can he do that?"

"According to my attorney."

"I'm sorry," I said miserably. "I wish I was there to help."

"I know you would if you could, Ben." She cleared her throat. "Speaking of Marcus . . ."

I stiffened, sensing trouble. "What about him?"

"He knows you're in Vancouver."

My voice dropped. "How?"

"He was in the house yesterday, waiting to gloat about custody. When I got home, I found him scrolling through the phone's call display. After seeing the calls from Vancouver and Aldergrove, he put it together. He brushed off my attempts to deny it." She paused. "Maybe I should have erased those numbers—"

"Alex, it's not your fault," I reassured, though my pulse hammered in my temples. "What is he going to do about it?"

"I don't know. He's been so interested in you ever since the news broke. On the other hand, he never reported you to the detectives after Talie told him you were in our house."

"That's true." *So why the interest in me?*

"Ben, are you any closer to finding Aaron?"

"Some promising leads." I glanced at my watch, conscious of the time, and decided not to expand on Emily and Aaron's connection to NorWesPac and Philip Maglio.

"You know, if Talie really does go with Marcus for a week, then I'll have some time on my hands . . ."

She left the offer unfinished, but I knew what she was implying. I would have loved nothing better than for her to join me in Vancouver. Help aside, I ached for company, especially hers, but I bit my tongue as reason prevailed over emotion. "No, Alex. I need you where you are. In fact, I need to contact Helen Riddell again."

"From Tacoma again?" she said quietly.

I forced a laugh. "Maybe I've moved to Mercer Island or Bellevue now?"

Alex said little more aside from good-bye. I wasn't sure if her reticence was a reaction to my rejection of her offer or the prospect of facing every second week without her daughter, but either way, I hung up the phone feeling as though I'd disappointed my best friend.

Digging my hand in my pocket, I found a quarter. I took a quick scan of the lobby before picking up the phone. I dialed the number of Drew Isaacs's cell from memory. Hearing it ring twice, I was relieved that the phone was still in service. After the fifth ring, a curt message, presumably in Isaacs's voice, said, "You've got Drew's cell. Leave a message."

Realizing I couldn't explain myself on voicemail, I hung up without leaving a message.

Between the phone calls and the lineup at the local Starbucks, I was late arriving at the East Hastings Clinic. By the time I stepped into the clinic, the waiting room was already half full. The stagnant smell of unwashed clothes and people wafted to my nose as strong as the day before. I glanced at the clock reading 8:17. Then my eyes fell on Edith. With her gray hair pulled back tight, she sat behind her desk, barely clearing the desktop. She scowled at me as if I'd shown up late for our wedding.

I approached the desk, donning my most disarming smile. "Good morning, Edith."

It didn't work. "Dr. Janacek won't be in for a couple of hours," she grumbled. "As you can see, we're already behind. You best get started."

I decided it probably wasn't the right time to beg Edith for Malcolm Davies's chart. I turned and walked down the hallway into the office I used. I hung up my Salvation Army thrift store jacket and reached for the white coat. Unconsciously, my hand drifted to the stethoscope in the pocket, the contact with which gave me a comforting sense of grounding; my adult equivalent of a security blanket.

I picked up the chart outside the first examining room. I was momentarily confused by the label reading PATRICK "PATRICIA" HOLMES, but the mystery was solved the minute I glimpsed him. Tall and reedy, Patricia sat on the examining table with his chin hanging on his chest. In a cardigan and short black leather miniskirt, his legs were well sculpted but bruised and scraped. Below his thick brunet wig, he wore sunglasses, but the lenses weren't quite big enough to hide the navy welts that extended out beyond the chunky frames. Despite a generous application of lipstick, I saw that his upper lip was swollen and split down the middle.

He didn't look up at me when I walked in the room. "Where's Dr. J?" he asked in a frail falsetto voice.

"I'm covering this morning." I grinned as I held my hand out for him. "I'm Dr. Horvath, Patricia."

He shook my hand tentatively, but his grip was strong.

"What brings you in, Patricia?"

Without lifting his head, Patricia reached up and slowly pulled off his glasses. The bruising was worse than I'd imagined. His right eye was bloodshot, and his left swollen completely shut. "It's always the same," he said in whisper. "It's not like they don't know what they're getting beforehand."

"They?"

"The johns. They know what I am. But they still do this to me."

I felt a pang of sympathy for the transgendered patient. "Did he use his fists?"

"Boots, mainly."

I surveyed the damage to Patricia's face more closely. His left cheek looked asymmetrical and flattened. His cheekbone had to be broken. When I reached out to touch it, he winced in pain but held still. The fractured zygoma bone creaked under my thumb like a loose floorboard. "Any injuries aside from your face?" I asked.

Patricia shrugged. "Nothing I can't live with. Of course, he raped me, too," he said as if it was a commonplace occurrence, and I realized that for Patricia that probably wasn't far from the truth.

"Can I examine you there?"

"No, no. It's okay," he said, embarrassed. "My face got the worst of it."

I rested a hand on his shoulder. "Patricia, we're going to need to get a plastic surgeon to stabilize that cheek bone."

He frowned at the floor. "Will that leave a scar?"

"No, they'll make the incision above your hairline and then lift up the cheekbone," I reassured. "I'll arrange it with the hospital. Meanwhile, I'll give you a shot of morphine for the pain."

For the first time in our interaction, Patricia made eye contact with me. He nodded gratefully. "I knew Dr. J. would only hire someone with compassion."

By the time Edith and I finished arranging Patricia's transfer to hospital, I was even further behind. The waiting room was again standing room only. The patients who followed Patricia had more run-of-the-mill medical issues, so I was able to make up for lost time. Along the way, I filled several prescriptions for HIV medications. With their expensive drug habits, many of those patients looked as if they could barely afford to feed or house themselves, let alone cover the monthly three-thousand-dollar prescription cost. However, I soon learned that in the Canadian system, the government pays for the exorbitantly priced drugs.

I thought of Emily. Had she lived in Canada, she would never have had to turn to a pusher like Jason "J.D." DiAngelo for black-market HIV medications. I wondered whether that would have saved her from her violent death. I decided that probably even Canada couldn't have protected her from Philip Maglio's wrath.

By the time I took my first breather of the day, it was already noon. Heading past Edith's workstation on my way out for a coffee, I noticed for the first time that her desk was unattended. I looked over at the patients watching me from the waiting room. As casually as possible, I turned back and sauntered through the door into the enclosed reception area.

I looked at the row upon row of charts filling every inch of wall space, staggered by the sheer number of patients Joe Janacek cared for. I scanned the *D* section looking for Malcolm Davies's chart. With the charts packed so snugly, it took me a couple of passes before I located his file. After a quick over-the-shoulder check, I yanked the chart out of the pack. I hurried it over to the desk and opened the cover page. Palms sweating, I grabbed a pencil and jotted down the address and phone number. I closed up the chart and rushed it back into place.

I had just tucked it back into its slot when I heard Joe Janacek's voice behind me. "I thought I hired you to work in the *back* office," he said in his lyrical Czech accent. "Besides, Edith is not fond of competition."

I turned to face him. With his white hair combed perfectly back and his white lab coat crisp as ever, I had a mental picture of Marcus Welby. "I needed contact information for a patient for, um, a prescription refill," I stammered.

"We don't refill prescriptions over the phone. It's bad medicine." He broke into a smile. "Besides, we can only charge for refills if we see the patient in person."

"Very charitable policy," I said. "I'm just heading out for coffee. You want one?"

He nodded. "But I can't trust a Hungarian with my coffee. It will probably come back with two scoops of sugar and a half cup of cream. I'll come with you."

Without taking off his lab coat, Joe walked with me across the street to the small coffee shop. He ordered a dark roast coffee while I decided to splurge on a latté, but it was a moot decision as Joe insisted on paying.

We sat at a table in the corner. Joe studied me over the rim of his cup. "Are you surviving day two, Peter?"

"So far," I said. "Though I saw a sad case this morning. Patricia Holmes."

"Was Patricia beaten again?"

"His zygoma was crushed in. I had to send him for surgery."

"Oh, Patricia," Joe heaved a sigh. "Life hasn't been fair to her since the day she was born in the wrong body." He put his cup down and stared hard at me. "And you, Peter?"

"I make do with the body I was born in."

He chuckled, but his eyes held their intensity. "You asked about money yesterday."

I waved the idea away. "I can wait until payday."

Joe dug in his pocket, pulled out an envelope, and slid it across the table to me. "We'll sort out the paperwork later."

I picked up the envelope. Through the open flap, I glimpsed the brown tint of at least one Canadian hundred-dollar bill. "It's not necessary, Joe."

"Don't make a big deal. Just put it away." He shrugged. "In this neighborhood, you don't want a reputation for carrying cash."

"Thanks." I tucked the money in my pocket, envisioning the bike I was going to buy.

"Tell me, Peter." Joe scratched his chin. "Will you still be around come payday?"

"What do you mean?"

He leaned back in his seat. "In August 1968, when the Russian tanks rolled into Prague, I joined the student uprising. I wasn't much for politics, mind you, but I had a soft spot for a very pretty activist. Eliska Brabanek." He sighed her name. "Eliska. Deepest, most beautiful green eyes I'd ever seen. They could make a man do anything."

My guard rose, though I didn't know what he was getting at. "Joe—"

"I even learned how to make Molotov cocktails. Can you imagine?" He grunted a chuckle. "Needless to say, the authorities were not pleased with me after I blew up one of their precious tanks."

"Joe, I don't see what—"

"For six weeks I was in hiding in Prague, before I managed to procure phony papers to escape the country. I'll never forget those days as a fugitive." He sighed knowingly. "Always checking over my shoulder. Always wondering whether I was recognized. Never certain whom I could trust." He viewed me for a long moment. "I see those exact same signs in you, Peter."

I rose from my seat. "You're way off the mark, Joe."

"I called the British Columbia Medical Association this morning," Joe said, freezing me in my tracks. "According to their records, Peter, you're still working in Taipei."

CHAPTER

22

The panic welled in my chest like an expanding balloon. I eyed the door, with a view to bolting. Then Joe reached out and gently laid a hand on my wrist. "Sit, Peter, please."

Slowly I turned and sat back down in the chair. "Joe, I can explain the mix-up."

"I also spoke to the College of Physicians and Surgeons," he went on calmly. "According to them, your papers are in order and you are legally licensed to practice in the province."

I gaped at him, sensing silence was my only option.

He broke into a half-smile. "If nothing else, I pride myself on being a decent judge of character. I am going to assume the Medical Association's information is out of date, and that you left Taipei without bothering to tell them that you had come back. Is that right?"

The balloon in my chest deflated. I nodded my gratitude. "It's complicated."

Joe arched one of his bushy eyebrows.

Though I barely knew Joe, I already trusted him. I would have liked to come clean, but aside from the enormous risk of exposure, I realized that the truth would place Joe in a difficult dilemma: If he didn't call the police, technically he would be guilty of aiding and abetting a felon. I'd already asked that of Alex and Kyle; I wasn't about to throw Joe into the same quandary.

I met his stare. "I didn't do anything wrong or illegal, but I had to leave in a hurry," I said, deliberately vague. "I'm working on clearing my name, but it could take a few more weeks."

Joe's eyebrow fell. "As I told you earlier, I always give people the benefit of the doubt." Then, as before, he added: "Once."

"Thank you."

Joe picked up his coffee cup and rose from the table. "Come. We're not going to get rich wasting the whole day at a café." Before turning for the door, he flashed his very white teeth. "Maybe someday you'll tell me about your Eliska, and how she led you into your troubles?"

I assumed he was speaking figuratively and didn't actually know anything about Emily, but by this point, I wasn't sure what to believe. "Someday," I mumbled, heading for the door.

I worked through the afternoon on autopilot. Joe's acceptance of my bogus cover story brought with it a degree of relief, like unloading a dark secret on a friend, but it also heightened my sense of exposure. If Joe could work through my cover that easily, others could, too. And now that Marcus knew where I was, I wondered how long it would take him to figure out my alias.

Much as I tried to concentrate on the steady stream of patients, my thoughts kept drifting to the tasks that preoccupied me. The clock ticked louder. My existence in Vancouver as Peter Horvath came with a rapidly approaching expiration date. I had to speak with Drew Isaacs and/or Malcolm Davies. Maybe one of them could lead me to the truth about my brother or NorWesPac's Whistler development.

Halfway through the afternoon, I headed out of the clinic, claiming I needed another coffee. My offer on the way out the door to buy one for Edith was met with a cold shake of her head. "I don't drink coffee in the afternoon," she snapped, as if I should have known all along.

I went straight to the pay phone at the street corner. I dug Malcolm Davies's number out of my pocket, deposited a quarter, and dialed the number. I heard a series of escalating beeps and was then informed by an electronic operator that the number was out of service. Frustrated, I dropped in another quarter and tried Drew Isaacs's cell number again.

"Yeah?" a gravelly voice answered.

"Drew?" I said. "Drew Isaacs?"

"Who is this?"

I froze, uncertain as to the right answer. The line clicked and I heard the dial tone.

I kicked the base of the phone booth so hard that my blistered toe ached. I wanted to rip the receiver off the phone and smash the window with it. *What an idiot!*

I willed myself calmer. I wondered how I was going to convince Drew Isaacs to discuss his criminal issues with a complete stranger. I decided that a variant on the truth was my best approach. After all, how could Drew know that Kyle didn't have another cousin in the drug business?

I deposited my last quarter and dialed again. "Yeah?" the voice answered warily.

"Drew, I'm sorry we were cut off."

"Who are you?" he barked.

"I'm Kyle Dafoe's cousin."

"Aaron?" He laughed. "Aaron, you son of a bitch, are you back in town?"

It never occurred to me he would assume I was Aaron. Even more shocking was the complete lack of surprise in his voice.

"You still there, Aaron?"

"Yeah," I said. "How are you, Drew?

"Same old, same old. Christ, it's been almost a year. How goes it?"

Almost a year! My heart was pounding so fast that I felt lightheaded. "You know what it's like being dead," I said, controlling my breathing.

He laughed. "Still keeping a very *low* profile, huh?"

"Exactly."

"Can't blame you. Have you heard about all the shit your brother is mixed up in back in Seattle?"

"That's why I came back," I blurted. "To help him out."

"How can you help him?"

"Not sure yet. Hey, Drew, I wanted to ask you about Whistler—"

He cut me off. "Listen, Aaron, I'm running late. Very late. Let's grab a drink tonight. We'll catch up then."

"No, that's not going to work," I said, struggling to sound calm. "I just wanted to pick your brain on a couple of small points."

"Tonight," Isaacs said. "Don't sweat it. We'll go someplace quiet. Let's say Vertical at eleven?"

"Vertical?"

"Remember? On Richards. Where we went there last time you were in town. See you at eleven."

He was gone before I could squeeze in another word.

I held the phone to my ear and listened to the dial tone. My head swam. *"It's been almost a year."* His words echoed in my brain. For days I'd been assuming, against reason, that Aaron somehow survived the blood-soaked trunk of his burned-out car two years earlier, but Isaacs's offhanded remark was the first scrap of evidence I'd come across to support the belief.

As my pulse slowed and I began to touch down, my thoughts again turned to a subject I'd avoided: Aaron's blood on Emily's wall. The idea of someone stealing his blood or coercing his involvement struck me now as far-fetched. And yet, I still wasn't willing to believe that Aaron could have been involved in her brutal murder. My stomach flip-flopped as I went over it again and again.

Despite having my best lead yet, I wandered back to the East Hastings Clinic more unsettled than when I'd left. Distracted earlier in the day, I bordered on oblivious as I churned through the rest of my list, watching the clock and obsessing over my looming rendezvous with Drew Isaacs. If a mimicker had crept into the mix of patients, the poor bastard wouldn't have stood a chance.

We finally emptied the waiting room at 6:35 P.M. Leaving my charting for the morning, I said a quick good-bye to Joe and Edith and hurried out the door.

I'd intended to head straight back to my room at the YMCA, but the walk home took me past the bike store window. Aware of Joe's cash burning a hole in my pocket, I ducked into the store. Brushing off the redheaded salesman whose chin looked like it had yet to feel a razor, I chose a sturdy secondhand road bike from the rack and bought it, along with the cheapest lock, headlight, and helmet the store offered.

After adjusting the seat, I knelt beside the bike on the street and tucked my pant leg into my sock. The chain's grease smell drifted to me, as welcome as the aroma of Mom's cooking. I had a flashback of

Aaron and me sitting happily at the kitchen counter and joking with Mom as she cooked up a meatloaf, our favorite. Dad wasn't around much for those family meals; or if he was home, he was usually well into his fourth or fifth cocktail and quietly embarrassed about the many times he fumbled his drink or spilled his food.

Shaking off the memory, I strapped on my helmet, stood up, and hopped onto the seat. Comparing this bike to the one at home was like putting a Yugo up against a Cadillac, but the grip of the handlebars' hard rubber and the tension of the toe straps around my feet soothed my nerves like three fingers of scotch.

I tightened my knapsack's shoulder straps and began to peddle. Though heavier than the bike I was used to, the pedals were responsive and the gearshift smooth. I slipped into the traffic on Robson Street. Already dusk, I planned on only a short ride around downtown to get the feel of the bike, but half an hour later, I found myself on the other side of the Burrard Street Bridge peddling up the steep climb toward the University of British Columbia. Sprinting up a hill in work clothes, I didn't care that the drivers around me eyed me as if I'd lost my mind. I welcomed the warm ache in my thighs and the burn in my lungs.

By eight o'clock dusk had given way to night. The bike's weak headlight illuminated only a few feet in front of me, and I relied more on the streetlamps and the cars' headlights. I rode directly back to the YMCA, arriving pleasantly spent. Ignoring the inquisitive glances from the people in the lobby, I carried the bike over my shoulder into the stairwell. Maneuvering it up the tight stairwell, I wished for the first time the building had an elevator.

I'd planned to spend the evening searching for new housing, but instead I focused my thoughts on Aaron as I prepared to impersonate him. As kids, we'd swapped roles a few times to play pranks on our parents, who never fell for it for very long. I would have to do better with Drew Isaacs. I tried to recall Aaron's little nuances and tics, like the way he peeled the labels off all his beer bottles or how he tapped his teeth together when agitated. I remembered how his focus sometimes drifted away in the middle of a conversation, as if he suddenly heard a favorite song in his head, though this usually meant he was high. Drugs changed Aaron in so many subtle ways. And the familiar twinges of guilt resurfaced, as I remembered the first time I saw his floating gaze.

One night, three months before our high school graduation, Kyle, Aaron, and I were at Jeff Nolan's house. Jeff lived down the block from us, and his parents never seemed to be home on weekends. Consequently, Jeff's house became the default destination if we didn't have another party to go to.

Always the wildest of our bunch, Kyle had brought over some cocaine that his college buddies had sold him. A few weeks earlier, Kyle had introduced me to coke by teaching me how to snort it through a straw. He'd convulsed with laughter as I sneezed for about five minutes after my first snort. The high that followed was almost too intense—the colors too bright and the sounds too exquisite. But maybe because of the drug's inherent taboo, I was keen to give it another try.

And I lobbied Aaron to join me.

Kyle led the rest of us over to the coffee table in the living room. He pulled a foil packet out of his pocket and laid it on the table in front of him. Sitting down cross-legged on the carpet, he unwrapped the edges to show us the bleached white powder inside. Eyes burning, Kyle flashed us a wicked grin. "You boys up for a sniff?"

Aaron, who barely drank in high school, viewed me warily. "I don't know." His eyes searched mine for backup. "This is pretty serious shit, isn't it?"

"It's just coke," I said, assuming a worldliness I didn't possess. "What's the big deal?"

"None, I guess," Aaron said. "Come on, Ben, let's get a couple of beers to chase it with."

I followed him into the kitchen. With the fridge door open, he looked over to me. "Ben, I don't know about this."

I shrugged. "Aaron, if you don't want to, don't do it. No one is going to care. But you're not stopping me from taking a toot."

I turned and headed back to the living room. By the time I reached the entryway, Aaron was on my heels. "I want to try it," he said. He brushed past me into the living room and knelt down beside Kyle.

Like a flight attendant sharing airplane safety instructions, Kyle gave a brief tutorial on how to snort coke. He pointed at me with a laugh. "And don't try to inhale the whole pile in one shot like Keith Richards over there."

Aaron insisted on going first. He snorted a whole line of coke. He sat back and twitched and sniffed for a moment, suppressing a cough. "Wow," he said, though I knew it was too early for him to feel anything. "Jesus."

After Jeff, I dutifully did my line, managing to avoid a sneezing fit. Feeling my nose congest on contact, I never would have guessed it would turn out to be the last time I touched coke or any illicit drug again. After a few minutes, the same warmth overcame me, but it was even deeper than last time. The euphoria bordered on discomfort. Every sense was so heightened that I wanted to crawl into a dark quiet corner until it passed.

Kyle and Jeff were overcome by the giggles. I looked over to Aaron. He sat with his back against a couch gazing at the ceiling. His lips were fixed in a dreamy smile. His glassy eyes focused on nothing.

My high turned into a sense of dread verging on panic. Maybe the coke had made me paranoid, but I was convinced something had happened to my brother. The guilt sobered me up like a bucket of ice water.

Somehow, I knew I had just led my twin into a very dangerous world.

I forced the memory away and focused on my rapidly upcoming meeting. With no idea what Drew Isaacs looked like, I vacillated on whether I should be at a table, so he could spot me, or walk in late and pretend not to see him so he would have to flag me down. Neither option seemed ideal, but I decided there was less risk in getting there first.

I arrived on foot at Club Vertical just before 10:30. A tired nightclub, the place reminded me of the Hudson Room where Alex and I sometimes met. Like its Seattle counterpart, Club Vertical had several booths and a small uninhabited dance floor. The feature I appreciated most was its dimness; I had to squint to adjust to the weak light.

I claimed a corner booth. When the waiter approached, I resisted the urge to order a double scotch, and instead chose a bottle of Canadian beer. Its cool, sweet taste on my lips was medicinal, and I polished it off in a minute. Realizing I needed every ounce of my focus, I forced myself to nurse the second beer. I was still working on it at a quarter after eleven when I spotted a man walk in. He stopped near the front to hug a lonely-looking waitress, and they shared a laugh at one of his comments. He handed her his coat and then scanned the bar. I offered a slight wave from the booth. The moment he spotted me, he rushed over.

Of average height and with a slight paunch, Drew Isaacs wore jeans and an untucked floral shirt with the top two buttons undone and sleeves rolled up. He had flowing, shoulder-length brown hair peppered with gray and a beard, but unlike mine his was kept trimmed short and limited to the front of his chin. To me, he looked like an aging rock star.

I rose from my seat and extended a hand to him. Ignoring it, Isaacs threw his arms around me and drew me into a tight hug. "Good to see you, man," he said warmly, as he released me from his grip with a slap to my back. "Been too long."

"You, too, Drew," I said, willing the acid to stay in my stomach. "I like your hair."

He ran a hand back through his thick mane. "It's how the women like it these days."

I mustered a laugh. "On them, or you?"

His expression hardened a moment. I wondered if I'd pushed my old boy routine too far, but then he broke into a smile that turned into a laugh. "Shit, Aaron. I've missed you."

He dropped down across from me in the booth. He hailed the waiter, who greeted him by name, and ordered a Stoli vodka on the rocks. I ordered another beer.

"So where are you living now?" Isaacs asked.

"You know . . ." I shrugged, searching for the most plausible answer. "Probably better if I don't say."

He bit his lip and nodded. "I guess that's right."

I sipped my beer while I searched Isaacs's face for a hint of suspicion or recognition, but I saw none. "Drew, am I still as unpopular around here as ever?"

"Oh, yeah," He stretched out the words. "These guys don't forget five million dollars easily. But I think they're convinced you really are dead now." He raised an eyebrow. "If I were you? I wouldn't give them a chance to think otherwise."

"Maglio?" I said, taking a stab.

"Among others."

"That Whistler deal really went to shit, huh?" I said with a sigh, as if reminiscing on the old days.

"Maglio took a bath."

"He blames me, doesn't he?"

Isaac's head seesawed from side to side. "Not just you."

"Emily, too?"

"Emily broke the golden rule." Isaacs pointed his glass at me. "You have to keep your nose clean when doing business. Bringing coke and E and all that crap to a launch party . . ." He shook his head. "A rookie mistake. And it pretty much sunk the development."

"Maglio was really pissed, huh?" I played along as if dissecting a ball game my home team had lost. "Don't get me wrong, I loved Emily. She was basically my sister-in-law, but it seems to me she got a bit of a free pass out of the whole mess."

"Of course."

"What do you mean 'of course'?"

Isaacs held up his palms. "No disrespect to your brother, but how do you think she got the job in the first place?"

"They weren't . . ."

"Emily was fucking the boss."

Suppressing a wince, I nodded. "I should have figured."

"Maglio even brought that big hitter attorney of his up here to get Emily out of jail after she was busted."

The remark hit me like a punch. "Michael Prince?" I blurted a little too quickly.

Isaacs squinted in surprise. "Yeah, he's the guy."

"I had no idea he was involved," I said as much to myself as Isaacs.

"Very involved. I heard Prince was even one of the investors in Whistler."

That son of a bitch! But I nodded as if I knew it all along. "Drew, do you think Maglio might have killed Emily?"

Isaacs smiled knowingly. "That's what you've come back to Vancouver to find out, huh?"

"Among other things." I shrugged. "I just thought if Emily lost Maglio tens of millions at Whistler—"

Isaacs shook his head with certainty. "But that's not what sent him over the edge!"

"No? What did?"

"Word was that Maglio went ballistic when Emily was diagnosed."

"*Diagnosed?*"

"AIDS."

It was all I could do to keep my jaw off the floor. "Are you saying Emily gave Maglio HIV?"

CHAPTER
23

I stumbled back to the YMCA still reeling from my meeting with Isaacs. Overwhelmed by his disclosure that Emily exposed Maglio to HIV, I completely forgot to use the lines and gestures I'd rehearsed beforehand, but Isaacs never once seemed to doubt that I was anyone but Aaron.

Lying in bed, my head spun as I sorted through Isaacs's revelations: Aaron absconding with five million dollars of drug money, Prince's involvement in Whistler, and Emily sleeping with Maglio and perhaps infecting him with HIV.

After a fitful sleep, punctuated by nightmares about missed exams and missed diagnoses in the ER, I woke up at 5:15, impatient for dawn to break. By six o'clock, I deemed it light enough for a ride. I grabbed the bike and lugged it down the stairs and out to the street. As I stepped onto the street, my breath froze in the air. Without my Lycra riding jacket and pants, the coldness of the morning seeped through to my bones, but the chill invigorated me. I jumped on the bike. A couple of hills later, I'd already begun to warm up.

Pumping the pedals hard, I rode out around the University and along the southern border of the city beside the Fraser River. I rode past the column of rush-hour cars and trucks, their brakes and tires squeaking in a staccato of stop-and-go noises and their exhaust fumes misting the air, as I headed south over the river on the Oak Street Bridge and into the suburb of Richmond. I would have continued cycling to the American border had I not a full morning's work awaiting me. Reluctantly, I stopped and turned back for home.

I locked the bike out front of the YMCA and ran up the stairs to my room. After a quick shower and change, I returned to the lobby, but I no longer had the floor to myself. At the phone booth, a guy with a ponytail leaned against the wall with his jacket off, obviously settled in for a long call. Across the room, I saw my bald neighbor waving and trying to hail me over. I pointed at my watch and yelled, "Sorry, Ray, I'm late." I jogged for the door.

I unlocked my bike and rode to the clinic. Arriving at 7:45, I found the door open and Edith already seated behind her desk, but the waiting room was empty. I summoned my best top-of-the-morning smile. "I kind of assumed the patients began lining up at four A.M.," I said.

"They'll come at eight," she grumbled without looking up from her computer. "They always do."

"Okay, well, I'm going to grab a coffee," I said. "Do you want—"

"No," she cut me off. She flashed her catlike green eyes at me, her lips fighting back a scowl. "And Dr. Horvath, if you want a chart, ask me for it next time."

"Will do," I chirped. I wondered if Joe had told Edith that I'd been nosing around her space for charts, but I decided that she probably had hidden cameras, tripwires, body heat sensors, or more likely some kind of witch's crystal ball that let her know.

I walked out to the pay phone on the street corner, dialed Alex's cell number, and again reversed the charges.

"Ben?"

Her one syllable conjured a mix of relief and melancholy in me. "Alex, where are you?"

"A gas station in Renton," she said, referring to the suburb southeast of Seattle. "What's the latest?"

"Don't know you'd believe me if I told you."

"Try me."

I gave her the lowdown on my meeting with Drew Isaacs.

"Oh my God," she said slowly. "Maybe Aaron *is* still alive!"

"Maybe." Without thinking, I touched the side of the cold sticky pay phone. "But with or without Maglio, I still have no clue how Aaron's blood got onto Emily's wall."

"You're making progress," she soothed, but then her tone hardened. "Listen, Ben, last night Detective Sutcliffe came by the ER to see me again."

I straightened up and glanced over either shoulder, as if suddenly watched. "Just Rick? No Helen?"

"He was alone."

I tasted acid. "What did he want?"

"To know if you had contacted me."

"And?"

"What do you think?" Alex said with a trace of indignation. "I told him I hadn't seen or heard from you since that day at the coffee shop."

"Did he believe you?"

"Think so. He asked me some questions about your parents, and whether you had relatives outside of King County. He wanted to know if you had any favorite getaways or escapes." She uttered a soft-pitched laugh. "I was singularly unhelpful."

"I bet he never shed that hundred-kilowatt smile of his," I grumbled, irrationally resentful at the thought of Rick spending time alone with Alex.

"Not once."

I changed hands on the receiver and took another scan around the phone booth. "You don't think Marcus tipped him off, do you?"

She hesitated. "If he did, then why would Rick come to see me? Wouldn't he already be looking for you up there?"

"I guess," I said, unconvinced.

"Oh, Ben," she said with a sigh, and the intimacy in her voice tugged at my heart. "Marcus has always been a bit jealous of our relationship, but I can't see him turning you in."

I could, but I kept the thought to myself. Eager to change subjects, I asked, "How's Talie?"

She was quiet a moment. "Marcus is taking her on Saturday for her first full week with him."

"It's going to work out, Alex." I suppressed a groan at the hollowness of my reassurance.

"I know," she said, sounding more like her old self. "Talie will cope. I'll cope. It'll even give me a chance to tackle the list of the hundred things I've meant to do around the house."

"There you go."

"We need to get moving, Ben," she said, suddenly all business. "I'm turning your cell on now. Call me right back."

With a quick glance, I ensured no one was waiting for the pay phone and then I called my number collect. Alex accepted the charges. "Okay. Hang on, I'll get her." The line clicked once. When it clicked a second time, I heard the phone ringing.

Helen answered on the next ring. "Sergeant Riddell."

"Helen, it's Ben."

"Oh, we're playing this game again, are we?"

"This is no game."

"My thoughts exactly. So what the hell is the point of these hide-and-go-seek phone calls?"

"To try to convince you that I'm innocent."

"If you want to do that, Benjamin, come sit down in my office and convince me."

"Can't."

"Because you're not?"

"Because you refuse to believe it's possible I am," I snapped. I took a big breath, swallowing the rest of my anger. "I need to tell you something."

"I'm all ears."

"Did you know that Philip Maglio and Emily used to be an item?"

There was a slight pause. "Go on."

"Emily was the sales director on a big NorWesPac resort development. It all fell apart and cost Maglio a fortune, in large part because of Emily's drug habit." I gave her the details without mentioning Whistler specifically, as I didn't want to point her in my vicinity. "Apparently, Maglio took it a lot harder when he found out later that Emily had exposed him to HIV."

She didn't comment. I imagined she was busy scrambling the troops to trace my call.

"His money *and* his health!" I stressed. "How's that for motive, Helen?"

"I'll give you this, it's quite a yarn."

"But not worth looking into?"

"Of course it is!" Helen said. "I would investigate Philip Maglio for an outstanding parking meter violation if I thought there was a chance of nailing him."

"So you'll follow it up?"

"What makes you think I haven't been looking into other suspects all along?" Helen sounded disappointed in me.

"I assumed you'd focused exclusively on me."

"You assumed wrong, Benjamin. Problem is that the search for you is consuming so much of our time and resources that it's hard to concentrate on anything else. Understand?"

"Yeah," I said, feeling apologetic.

"Granted, you've turned into a regular Sam Spade." She couldn't resist a chuckle. "I never realized fugitives had so much leisure time. I pictured you holed up in a cave with Osama bin Laden."

"Yeah, it's nothing but caviar and champagne. You ought to give it a whirl."

"You can't have investigated this all on your own." Her tone stiffened. "You're getting help, aren't you?"

I didn't reply.

"Please listen to me, Benjamin. If you piss off people like Maglio, and they get to you before we do, a bum murder rap will suddenly seem like a minor inconvenience by comparison."

"I know," I said, aware that Helen's remark came from protectiveness, not manipulation.

The line beeped three times with Alex's warning signal.

"Aaron is alive, Helen."

"You've seen him?"

"No, but I spoke to someone who had drinks with him a full year after you found his burned-out BMW."

"Who?"

"I can't say tell—"

The line clicked and the connection was gone.

Pacing back and forth by the phone booth, I gave Alex five minutes to clear out of the gas station before I called her back on her own cell number. "Did you get out okay?"

"No problem," she said. "I took off the moment I saw the first flashing light. I drove right by the cruisers heading the other way."

"Good. Do you have call number blocking on your cell phone?"

"Yes."

"Perfect. Can we use your phone to relay one more call?"

"To?" she asked suspiciously.

"Philip Maglio."

"Maglio? You heard what Helen said about him. You think this is wise?"

"Let's find out."

I gave her the number and a quick tutorial on how to record calls on her cell phone. She put me on hold. A moment later, Maglio's receptionist Megan answered in her singsong voice. When I introduced myself again as "J. D. Emily," she laughed and said, "As in the poet, right? Please hold a moment, Mr. Emily."

More than a minute passed before the line clicked. "Phil Maglio," he growled in his gravelly baritone.

"Phil, we spoke last week."

"No shit."

I pictured the tight jaw and fuming gray eyes from his photo. "I wanted to ask you about Whistler," I said.

The cool silence that followed was broken by his wet cough. "What about it?"

"I heard that you got shafted and ended up losing a lot of money on SnowView."

"So?" he grumbled. "That's the development business for you. Rarely a day goes by when somebody doesn't screw me, or vice versa."

"Yeah, but in this case we're talking about Emily Kenmore," I said. "Somebody you were screwing *outside* the office."

"You don't have a clue what you're talking about."

"No?" I said. "I'm talking about the woman who upended your

dream development with her careless drug habit." I paused. "The same woman who exposed you to HIV."

The line went dead quiet. The receiver could have frozen in my hands.

"Phil?" I said after a moment.

"Do you have any idea how dangerous I can be?" he hissed.

"Oh, I think I do," I said with feigned indifference, though my heart was hammering. "I saw the photos of Emily's bedroom in the paper. I saw what you did to them."

He coughed into the receiver and then loudly cleared his throat. "Haven't you heard? The cops already know who killed those two."

"But I know better. And so do you."

"You don't know your ass from your elbow," he grunted. "I'm not sure who is feeding you this line of bullshit, but I do know this: It's not good for your health."

"Phil, we both know—"

"Listen to me." He cut me off. "You're as big a pain in the ass as your brother was."

I felt winded.

"Next time you want to talk to me, *Ben*"—the use of my name shot a chill through me—"we'll do it face to face."

CHAPTER
24

I had little time to consider Maglio's threat, because Edith's guarantee proved prophetic. By the time I returned to the clinic, patients filled the waiting room. And the rest of the morning passed in a blur as I raced to keep up with the unending stream of clients.

Joe Janacek didn't materialize until noon. In a black sports jacket and gray tie, he stood in my office's doorway, munching a chocolate chip cookie and studying the huge pile of charts on my desk with a look of gleeful amusement.

"You don't work mornings anymore?" I closed the chart and put it on the smaller pile of completed ones.

He finished chewing a mouthful of cookie. "Do you know when I last had help around here?"

"Six months ago?" I guessed, based on the evidence I'd seen of another physician's writing in the charts.

"Seven," he said. "So I hope you are not too terribly put out if this sixty-five-year-old physician takes one or two mornings off to catch up on a half year's worth of his personal banking and accounting."

"I'll manage somehow."

"Ah, such stoicism." He approached, holding out the bag of cookies. "Do you want one?"

My stomach growled; I hadn't eaten a bite since waking. I reached inside, pulled out a cookie, and took a bite. My hunger aside, it was delicious. "Do you bake, Joe?"

"*Pusinky.*"

"Pardon?"

"A Czech meringue pastry. Mouth-watering." He shrugged. "But my wife was the baker in my house. *Vanilkové rohlícky, orechove pracny, pusinky.*" The Czech names rolled off his tongue longingly, though they meant nothing to me. "Nothing she couldn't bake."

"I'm sorry, Joe," I said. "I didn't know."

"*Didn't know?*" he said, bewildered. Then his eyes filled with understanding, and he shook his head. "My wife's not dead." He laughed. "Between the rheumatoid arthritis in her hands and my elevated cholesterol, Eliska doesn't bake anymore."

"Eliska!" I laughed. "You *married* her!"

His forehead creased into a frown, and he patted his chest. "You think I'd blow up a tank for just anybody? You'll meet Eliska at dinner on Saturday. Six o'clock."

I wasn't keen to socialize while on the run, but I felt deeply indebted to Joe, and I had no excuse for not accepting the invitation. Besides, I was intrigued to meet the woman who converted Joe into a revolutionary. "What can I bring?"

"A bottle of wine would be nice." He turned for the door. "But for God's sake, *not* Hungarian!"

I chuckled. "Where did you get these cookies?"

"Patricia Holmes dropped them off for me."

"For *you?*" I said, remembering the transgendered patient with the fractured cheek. "I spent an hour getting her sorted out."

"I think she mentioned you could have one, too." He pointed to the remaining half of a cookie in my hand.

"How did the surgery go?"

"Well. She's decided to move back to her mother's house on Vancouver Island. A wise move on her part, I think." Joe nodded. "You did all right by her, Peter."

After he left the room, I sat at the desk, enjoying Patricia's cookie. My troubles still shrouded me like a dense fog, but for a few moments I brightened with the satisfaction of a well-managed case that ended in a positive outcome.

Finishing the last crumb, I rose from the chair and headed out to the examining rooms with a renewed sense of purpose. I reached for the first chart on the wall: Jennifer Ayott, age thirty. In the margin below the date, a note read PRESCRIPTION REFILL. Flipping back through the thick chart, I saw several blood test results for CD4 counts and viral loads. I'd already seen the same test on many of the clinic's patients, and I knew that the lower the CD4 count and the higher the viral load, the more advanced the HIV illness. Jennifer Ayott's numbers for both tests were on the wrong side of the curve, but going back over her previous results, I noticed they had improved since she had started treatment.

With a light knock, I opened the door and walked into the examining room. In jeans and layered white-on-pink long-sleeved shirts, Jennifer sat on the examining table with legs crossed. Her head was buried in the book on her lap. Though thin and slightly pale, she had a flawless complexion and striking cheekbones. I couldn't help but think of Emily.

Jennifer looked up at me and fumbled with the book before catching it with both hands. Her full lips parted and her green eyes dilated in astonishment. "Aaron?" she sputtered.

I fought off the sudden constriction in my throat. "I'm Dr. Peter Horvath," I said, hoping I didn't sound too adamant. "But you're talking about Aaron Dafoe, right?"

Dumbfounded, she nodded, as she clutched the paperback to her chest as if it were a Bible.

"People make that mistake all the time." I mustered a big grin, then strode up to her and extended my hand. "Aaron's my first cousin."

"I see." She shook my hand tentatively. "I'm Jenny Ayott."

Jenny! I buried my surprise in a cough. "Nice to meet you, Jenny."

Her eyes fell to her book. "You look an awful lot like your cousin."

"Tell me about it." I forced a laugh. "Growing up, some people thought we were twins."

She looked up with her head tilted and lips pursed. "Doesn't Aaron already have a twin?"

"Yeah, he does . . . um, Benjamin," I stammered. "But Ben put on a bunch of weight, so I've ended up looking more like Aaron than his own twin."

Her face relaxed, and her eyes softened. "That's ironic."

She seemed to be accepting my explanation, and the knots in my stomach loosened. "How do you know Aaron?"

She ran a hand through her hair, reddening slightly. "We dated for a while."

"When?"

"A couple years ago." Her voice cracked.

"You haven't seen him recently?"

"Not since our breakup." Her face flushed, and she looked at the wall. "How is he?"

I hesitated, considering my response. I opted to go with the official version. "He disappeared two years ago. It's presumed that he, um . . . died."

She was on her feet in a heartbeat. "Died?" The tears were already rolling down her cheeks. "How?"

"Well . . . they think he was murdered."

She wiped her tears away with a sleeve and then dropped back down on the examining table. "Who? Why?" Her shaky voice was barely above a whisper.

I sat down on the stool in front of her. "Jenny, his body was never found." I went on to tell her about the blood in the trunk of his car. "Some people think Aaron set it all up."

She tilted her head and bit her lip. More than her features, her expression reminded me so much of Emily that it hurt. I couldn't imagine the impact my resemblance to Aaron was having on her. "Set up his own murder?" she asked.

I shook my head. "No. I mean, faked it."

"But why?"

From the bewilderment in her wide eyes, I knew that whatever happened to Aaron, Jenny hadn't been included in the plans. "Did you know Aaron was mixed up in the drug trade?"

"He was trying to get out." She swallowed. "We both were."

"You were in the business?"

Jenny shrugged and looked down at her feet again. "Not really. Before Aaron and I . . . hooked up, I used to help an ex-boyfriend move some of the crystal meth he cooked." Her eyes drifted tentatively up to mine. "In fact, that was how I met Aaron."

I remembered Kyle telling me how Aaron and he used to get their crystal meth at a discount price from Malcolm Davies. I suspected Malcolm was the ex Jenny referred to, but I knew I would only draw suspicion by asking.

Jenny rubbed her eyes and let her hand drift through her hair again. "We were going to start over. I was going to go to Seattle with Aaron. We planned to get clean together. His brother had arranged rehab for us both."

I acted surprised as I nodded along to the story that I knew as well as she did. "What about the drug trade?"

"His cousin, who was also his partner, was already sick from cancer." She held out a hand to clarify. "Another cousin, Kyle. I don't know if he's on your side of the family or not."

"He is," I said without explaining how.

"Your cousins didn't see eye to eye, but Aaron wanted to get out of the business. With Kyle in hospital, Aaron thought the timing was perfect for him to make a clean break."

"Jenny, did you two ever make it to the rehab in Seattle?" I asked, already knowing the answer.

"No."

"What happened?"

She sniffed a couple of times. Her chin dropped to her chest. She dug in her jean pocket and pulled out three empty pill bottles of HIV medications. She held them up without looking at me. "This did."

"HIV?"

Jenny nodded. The tears welled up again and flooded over the rims of her eyes. She wiped at them with her forearm.

"What did it have to do with you and Aaron?"

"Nothing, I thought." She looked at me with plaintive eyes. "He knew about my disease early on in our relationship. He told me it was okay."

"But it wasn't?"

She shook her head slowly. "A couple of days before we were supposed to go to Seattle, he showed up at my place acting strange." She sniffled. "He said we had no future together. He blamed it on my illness." She stopped to get her voice under control. "He said he didn't want to risk having 'mutant' kids with AIDS."

I shook my head, stunned by the anecdote. "Aaron told you that?"

She swallowed. "Yeah."

"Unbelievable," I mumbled. The heartless words sounded nothing like my brother. Despite his fatal weaknesses for drugs, Aaron was a gentle person. I'd never seen or heard him be deliberately cruel to anyone. Or was I wrong? *Could I have my misjudged my own flesh and blood that badly?* I wondered. *No. Not Aaron.*

"I was sure something was wrong with him. Drugs or whatever." Jenny spoke to the wall. "He'd never acted like that before."

"And later?"

Her head bobbed slightly, and I knew she was crying again. "I never saw him again. He just . . . disappeared."

CHAPTER

25

Embarrassed, Jenny Ayott tucked the prescription in her pocket and made a hasty exit with only a quiet thank-you spoken to the door. I sat at the desk, wondering whether she'd truly believed my cover story. My fingers trembled as I flipped open her chart and copied her address and phone number onto a piece of scrap paper that I hurriedly stuffed into my pocket.

I was still staring at her chart when Joe poked his head into my office. "Tell me, please," he said, his tone dripping with sarcasm. "How are you enjoying your retirement?"

I closed Jenny's chart, rose to my feet, and followed Joe out to the examining rooms. With my mind miles and years away from the clinic, I grabbed the first chart on the door and walked in to face a skinny, skittish heroin addict. He claimed his addiction was a direct by-product of cold-hearted physicians unwilling to prescribe sufficient quantities of the painkillers he needed for his chronic back pain. I didn't even bother to put up a fight. I simply reached for my prescription pad.

I coasted through the rest of the afternoon in a similar vein, repeatedly choosing the path of least resistance. My thoughts kept wandering back to Jenny's account of how cruelly Aaron had stomped on her heart on his way out of her life. I couldn't correlate the anecdote with the brother I knew, especially thinking back on our last conversation and what a promising future together he had painted for them.

I wondered why he would go to the trouble of asking me to arrange rehab for both of them if he never planned to follow through with it. Such a pointless step. Unless Aaron suddenly needed to fake his death in a hurry! Was the frigid breakup Aaron's way of protecting Jenny from the people he was running from?

But everything indicated that if Aaron had staged his own death, he had planned it meticulously. As Alex pointed out, the blood in the trunk alone would have taken months to collect.

My head pounded as I dwelled on the possibilities. My anxiety receded and frustration bubbled up in its place. The fragments of history I'd painstakingly collected had begun to contradict one another. *None of this makes any damn sense!*

As I ground my way through the afternoon, one person crystallized in my mind as the focus of my anger, confusion, and sense of betrayal: Michael Prince. Though I doubted it would serve any purpose, by the day's end I couldn't resist the urge to contact him. With the last of the patients gone, I pushed my stack of charts out of the way and reached for the desk phone. I typed in the code used to obscure the caller identification and then dialed his office number.

Janelle patched me straight through. "Hello, Benjamin," Prince said in a formal but warm tone. "I was hoping you would call."

"Why?" I snapped. "You need to mislead me about something else?"

"Excuse me," Prince said calmly.

"Oh, I'm terribly sorry." I gripped the receiver like a pair of pliers I couldn't squeeze tightly enough. "Was I not being clear? How selfish of me, after all the trust and forthrightness you've poured into our relationship."

"Ben, would you like to tell me what is bothering you?"

"Not what. Who!"

"And by that, you mean me."

"Exactly, you lying son of a bitch," I spat.

He was the epitome of patience. "Lying about what?"

"For starters, pretending you didn't know Emily when you were involved in diffusing the legal charges at Whistler!"

He didn't reply.

"Or acting as though you knew nothing about Philip Maglio and his Whistler scam when in fact you were one of the principal investors."

"No, I wasn't," he said softly.

"You were going to be, if the thing was ever built!"

"I never committed to it."

"But you knew about it, inside and out," I growled. "Some service you're providing to me at five hundred bucks an hour!"

"This is exactly the reason why I get paid as well as I do."

I threw my free hand up, flabbergasted. "For selling out your clients?"

"The contrary," Prince said with a slight sigh. "Let's assume what you've said is true, and the others you mentioned are also clients of mine. Did it ever occur to you that I might be protecting *their* attorney-client privilege by not discussing them with you?"

"Emily is dead," I said, faltering.

"That doesn't alter the law. Think about it, Ben. How could you trust me to protect your sensitive information with them, if I were to discuss theirs with you?"

His logic was twisting me in knots, but I found it hard to argue. I relaxed my grip. My tone steadied. "Sounds like you have an inherent conflict of interest in all this."

"Not at all," Prince said. "When it comes to trial, I will represent you against the state of Washington, not any of my other clients."

When it comes to trial. My stomach sank digesting the inference. "What if the information I uncover implicates one of your clients?" I asked.

He was a silent for a long moment. I picked up a pen and began to doodle on the prescription pad in front of me. Without thinking, I sketched a gravestone. "Can you be a little more specific?" Prince finally asked.

Prince hadn't won back my trust, but as I'd already confronted Maglio over the phone, I had little to lose by elaborating. "Philip Maglio had very good reason to kill Emily," I said.

"Namely?"

Though I suspected Prince knew more about the doomed Whistler development than I did, I still summarized what I'd pieced together.

As I spoke, I wrote the letters R.I.P. inside the gravestone and shadowed them in black ink. I saved the biggest revelation for last. "But that was just money. The kicker came when Emily risked Maglio's life."

"Oh?"

"Emily exposed him to HIV."

Prince exhaled slowly. "As for Whistler, I can tell you unequivocally that factors far beyond Emily's ill-conceived cocktail party led to its collapse." He cleared his throat. "And as for the more personal motive, you'll have to trust me when I tell you that it is simply not true."

I dropped my pen. "Are you saying Emily and Maglio didn't have a relationship?"

"I'm saying that Emily never exposed Philip to HIV."

"How can you know that?"

"I am not at liberty to say."

"Client-attorney privilege."

"Something like that."

"Very helpful, Michael."

"I can tell you this, Ben," he said adopting the tone of a concerned father. "It is a big mistake to antagonize someone like Philip Maglio."

I'd grown numb to the threat of Maglio's retaliation. "Let me ask you, Michael. What if it comes to the point where you have to choose between clients?"

"That won't happen."

"No?" I decided to take a stab in the dark. "Didn't it happen to you before with Emily? And Aaron?"

For a moment, all I heard was breathing. Then he spoke quietly. "I don't play favorites."

I knew I was on to something. "You represented Aaron, didn't you, Michael? What was it about?"

"We've been over this."

"Tell me!"

"I can't, Benjamin." He sounded tired. "I have been practicing law for a long time. Believe me, it won't be necessary for me to choose between clients."

"You're damn right, it won't." I slammed the receiver into the cradle before he could answer.

I buried my head in my hands, even more confused than I was before making the call. Prince was convincing, but I knew that this was how he made his living. Still, his insistence that Emily hadn't exposed Maglio to HIV weakened my conviction. Irrationally, I wished that his version was true. I had no right to be jealous—our engagement had ended three years before her alleged involvement with Maglio—but the thought of Maglio possessing Emily with those cold hungry eyes of his had gnawed at me.

How had it come to this?

I reached for the folder in front of me, intending to lose myself in the pile of unfinished charts. I was working on the fourth one when the door to my office burst open. I looked up to see Edith standing in the doorway in her customary white uniform with a pen clamped between her teeth like a cigarette. She pointed at the phone. "You have a call, Dr. Horvath."

"Oh?" I said, trying to mask my surprise. "Who is it?"

She shrugged. "Said he was an old friend."

"He didn't give you a name?"

She eyed me with undisguised scorn. "No name." She turned away from me. "Line three."

I picked up the phone and hit the button to activate line three. "Dr. Horvath," I said in a tone far more relaxed than how I felt.

"Benjamin."

The single whispered word froze me in mid-breath. I glanced at the call display on the phone that read PRIVATE NUMBER.

"Benjamin?" the whisperer repeated, singing the syllables.

I spun my chair away from the door and cupped the phone's mouthpiece, replying in a whisper of my own. "Who are you?"

"Oh, Ben." He uttered a throaty chuckle. "I wish I could say."

My temples throbbed, my throat tensed.

"They're closing in on you."

"They?"

"The police."

"How?"

"People talk, Ben."

I rested my elbow against the desk to quell the shaking. "Who talked?"

He laughed again. "You have to be more careful whom you trust."

"But I should trust you, right?"

"Could be worse people to trust."

"If you know so much, tell me where Aaron is!"

"Gone," he said.

"Gone where?"

But the whisperer didn't reply.

"Listen to me, you son of a bitch—" But I was talking to dead air.

CHAPTER

26

I stared helplessly at the phone as if it held a supernatural grip over me. In an instant, the whisperer's call had stripped what little sense of security and anonymity I'd cobbled together in the days since arriving in Vancouver.

Run! The impulse throbbed in my head like a siren. *But where?*

I remembered the whisperer's exact words: *They're closing in on you.* That didn't mean they knew where I was, but the caller did. I was deluding myself to think I had time left in Vancouver. But more time was exactly what I needed. I was close. I had unearthed a promising suspect, and I'd picked up the trail of my presumed dead brother. I just needed a little longer.

How did the whisperer know where I was? I went through the names of people who knew my alias or whereabouts: Kyle, Prince, Alex, and Marcus. The last name resonated with me. I trusted Marcus Lindquist even less than I trusted my lawyer, who at least had warned me not to tell anyone where I was, including him. And I realized the list included only the people from Seattle who might have tipped off the whisperer, but he'd phoned originally from Canada, presumably Vancouver. In this city Malcolm Davies, Drew Isaacs, Joe Janacek, and Jenny Ayott either knew or suspected I wasn't Peter Horvath. Any one of them might have talked.

Anxiety gave way to hopelessness. I had no idea who to trust or where to turn.

Rising from the desk, I grabbed my jacket and knapsack. I stopped in the bathroom to wet my face and wash the remnants of sweat off my forehead. Glumly, I stared at my reflection in the mirror. I knew my artificially brown eyes and full beard weren't going to help me much if the manhunt intensified and photographs of me surfaced in Vancouver as visibly as they had in Seattle.

I zipped up my jacket, tightened the straps on the knapsack, and then headed back out into the hallway, relieved to discover that Joe was busy with a patient in one of the examining rooms. I doubted I could face him. Head down, I hurried past Edith's pen. "Have a good weekend, Edith," I said without looking up at her.

"Night, Dr. Horvath,"she said coolly.

An unexpected pang of melancholy hit me as I stepped out into the rainy evening knowing I wouldn't ever be coming back. The clinic had become the closest I'd found to a haven in the middle of my personal storm. Now that I'd been exposed, I couldn't risk returning.

I unlocked my bike and hopped onto the saddle. With the wind whipping and the rain falling in horizontal sheets, the cold dampness soaked through the cheap nylon jacket down to my skin. The streets were slick, and my brakes were impaired by the weather. Stopping suddenly wasn't an option, as I discovered when I twice had to swerve to avoid cars that cut into my lane. And yet the rhythm of the pedals, along with the demand the strong headwind placed on my heart and legs, helped to settle my emotional whirlpool.

Despite the unforgiving weather and poor lighting, I cycled twenty-five miles out through the suburb of Richmond. Along the way, I decided I would steal as much time as I could in Vancouver to intensify my search for Aaron and dig up more on Maglio. Then I would head back to the lion's den that Seattle had become. If Helen weren't willing to believe me, I would confront Philip Maglio face to face, as he'd suggested, regardless of the risk. I was sick of life on the run.

Back downtown, I stopped at an ATM and emptied out Peter Horvath's bank account. A block from the YMCA, I stopped and debated whether it was safe to return to my room. I scanned my memory, but I didn't remember telling anyone where I was staying. Still, I circled the block twice before I convinced myself there wasn't a SWAT team waiting to ambush me outside the hostel. Satisfied, I pulled up to the steps and dismounted. Carrying the bike over my shoulder, I rushed past the front desk and up the steps to my room, planning to hunker down for one last night's stay.

Sleep came surprisingly easy, but the nightmares were vivid. I dreamed that *I* was locked in the trunk of Aaron's burning BMW. With smoke seeping in around me, there was enough light from the flames for me to see my own blood beginning to pool in the nooks and crevices of the trunk. That image was enough to jerk me out of bed for the night.

I waited for the first light of dawn before I gathered my belongings, paid my bill, and headed out into the sopping Saturday morning. I walked my bike to a nearby donut shop that served passable coffee. Leaving my helmet on for camouflage, I sat at the countertop while I sipped my coffee and half-heartedly chewed on a glazed donut. Flipping through the pages of *The Vancouver Sun,* I scanned it for any reference to my case. With relief, I reached the last page without finding any mention of me.

I walked outside to the pay phone by a sheltered bus stop. I tried Drew Isaacs's cell number but heard only his voicemail greeting. I opted not to leave a message.

Hopping on my bike, I rode several aimless miles through picturesque Stanley Park—an oasis of forests, ponds, and paths in the midst of urban sprawl. Then I crossed over Burrard Inlet via the landmark Lion's Gate Bridge to the stunningly mountainous North Shore. With much steeper hills to climb, I was panting hard when I finished the ascent that took me to the foot of Grouse Mountain. At the concession stand there, I bought another coffee and a tasteless muffin that at least replenished my blood sugar. As soon as I'd downed them, I found a pay phone by the rest rooms and tried Drew Isaacs again, only to reach his voicemail again.

As I rode back toward downtown, I mulled over how the anonymous caller might have tracked me down to Joe's clinic. I thought of Alex's comments about Marcus's unusual level of interest in my whereabouts. Increasingly, he stood out in my thoughts as the most likely candidate to have blown my cover. I began to wonder whether Marcus might even be the whisperer.

It occurred to me that Marcus was far from an impartial bystander in Emily's homicide. After all, he had once been intimate with the victim, too. I'd only learned about their relationship the last time I saw Emily alive.

After J.D. tucked his gun back in his belt and stormed out of her apartment, I cradled Emily in my arms for several minutes. Neither of us spoke a word during that silent slow dance. Finally, Emily ran her hand across her eyes and gently slipped out of my embrace. Staring at me, she broke into an amused smile.

"What?" I asked.

She pointed at herself and then to me. "Who would have thought that we could have ended up like this?"

I shook my head.

She bit her lip. "What did you picture back then? Happily ever after and all that jazz?"

"I imagined that all the time, Em."

"But you didn't expect it, did you?" She swallowed hard, but her tone was free of accusation.

"Not really," I said.

Her smile withered.

"Em, remember how I grew up. My parents didn't exactly wind up happily ever after."

"Because of your dad's drinking?"

"I guess. There were so many fights. So many hurtful comments," I said. "And yet, there was still warmth there, maybe even love. Remember that night we all went out to celebrate after I finished my residency? Dad's brain had already started to pickle from the booze, but he didn't drink that night."

Emily nodded warmly. "Your mom and dad ended up blowing us all off the dance floor."

"I didn't even know they danced," I said. "Later, Mom told me that they used to go dancing all the time. Then Dad's drinking got so out of hand that he usually couldn't walk straight after dinner. And the dancing stopped."

"Your mom was a saint to stay with him," Emily said. "I wouldn't have."

"Me neither."

She reached out and touched my hand. "You stuck with me through an awful lot."

"Maybe not enough."

"No, Ben." She caressed my hand softly. "I used up all nine of my lives."

I didn't know what to say, so I kept quiet.

She let go of my hand. "You deserve the real-life equivalent of happily ever after."

"I don't know, Em. I've never found anyone else since we broke up."

"How about Dr. Lindquist?"

I frowned. "Alex?"

"Sure," Emily said. "The two of you are pretty close, aren't you?"

"She happens to be married."

"Still?" Her eyes darkened. "I can't believe she's stayed with that prick."

"You remember Marcus?" I said. "I thought you only met him at one or two hospital parties."

"I know him a lot better than that." She sighed. "He called me after you and I broke up."

"And?"

"The guy has a silver tongue to go along with his black heart. He had me convinced that his marriage was over."

I remembered Marcus's drunken comments about Emily's sexiness. I tasted bile. My surging jealousy might have been unfounded, but the thought of Marcus possessing both Emily and Alex tightened my stomach in knots. "Marcus and you were together?" I asked through clenched teeth.

"A while ago. But it didn't take me long to see through him."

"Christ, Emily, I didn't need to hear this." I turned away from her.

She grabbed me by the arm, pulled me back to her, and threw her arms around me tightly. She kissed me softly on the cheek, and her warm breath tickled my ear. "He couldn't hold a candle to you, Ben."

The sudden wail of sirens yanked me out of the memory. Instinctively, I sprang into action. I began to sprint up the hill, weaving through the traffic on the busy downtown street.

When the first fire truck screamed past me, the hammering in my chest subsided and I slowed my pace. They weren't coming for me. Yet.

My thoughts drifted back to Emily's admission. I hadn't told Alex about Marcus and Emily, or any of his other affairs that I knew of, but now I regretted more than ever how we'd restrained ourselves in that hotel room in San Francisco. *Bastard*.

Feeling the chill through my nylon jacket, I wondered how I was going to put a roof over my head come nighttime. I couldn't go back to the YMCA. Hotels were out of the question, as they would demand identification. I needed to find a cheap rooming house or apartment where I could pay in cash.

Cycling without a destination, I soon wound up in the lower-middle-class neighborhoods of East Vancouver. I slowed down on East Fourteenth Street as I passed a series of monotonously similar grayish-white two- and three-story apartment buildings that must have been built in the mid-fifties from the same set of blue prints. Several had vacancy signs on the front lawn. A few billed their one- and two-bedroom units as "fully furnished." Randomly choosing an apartment complex in the middle of the block, I locked my bike on the stand out front. I buzzed the intercom for the manager. Two minutes passed before an obese gray-haired woman in a floral muumuu hobbled up to the door. She opened the door a crack. "I'm only looking for a certain *kind* of tenant," she said, her tone and expression rich with the implication that I wasn't what she had in mind.

"I am a physician from Spokane," I said, improvising on the spot. "I'm coming up to Vancouver Hospital to do extra training in cardiology."

"Oh, you're a *doctor*!" The mention of my M.D. had a magical effect on her disposition. She threw the door open and ushered me up to the "best" apartment on the second floor. On the way, she shared her medical history with me as she solicited my opinion on the merits of knee-replacement surgery.

Dorothy Fleemand—"Dotty to you," she insisted—unlocked the door to the apartment, which smelled cleaner than I expected. The furniture, consisting of a sofa, a kitchen table, and two matching chairs, was in better shape than I would have guessed, too. Without even checking the bedroom, I agreed to rent the apartment. After I paid four hundred dollars for the damage deposit and the balance of the month's rent in cash (leaving me nearly tapped out), Dotty handed over the keys and promised to return with the paperwork.

I dropped my knapsack on the bedroom floor, and I collapsed on top of the bedspread. I was half asleep when I heard Dotty's heavy fist on the door. I stumbled out of bed and signed the papers, unsure a minute later whether I'd signed as Peter Horvath or Ben Dafoe. But I was too tired to care.

Returning to the bed, I meant only to catch a catnap, but by the time I woke the fading light through the bedroom window told me it was late afternoon. I looked at my watch: 5:30 P.M. I realized Joe and Eliska would be expecting me for dinner in half an hour.

At first, I dismissed the thought of going to the Janaceks as reckless. But recognizing I was hungry and broke, I decided I had little to lose by showing up for a free meal. Despite my disequilibrium, and unsure whom I could trust, I was confident Joe posed little threat. I walked into his life long after the whisperer had begun to torment me, and my photo had yet to hit the local news.

I showered and changed into the least-crumpled clothes I dug out of my knapsack, then headed downstairs.

The rain had finally relented. And with the thick cloud cover, it was warmer outside. I realized I could have easily walked the fifteen or sixteen blocks to Joe's house if I wasn't running so late. Cycling along the thoroughfare of Broadway, I passed a liquor store and stopped to duck inside. When I found the Eastern European wines, I couldn't resist. I bought a bottle of white and headed back out to my bike.

I found Joe's house easily in the heart of the City Hall district. Wearing a jacket and tie, Joe met me at the front door of his renovated duplex. He read the label on the bottle of wine and shook his head, breaking into a belly laugh. "Hungarian! I give you one simple instruction . . ."

Joe's wife joined us at the door. As tall as he, with gray hair, deep brown eyes, and full lips that amplified her welcoming smile, she stepped in front of Joe. "Dr. Horvath?" She extended her hand, revealing the swan neck and knobby fingers that were typical of advanced rheumatoid arthritis. "I'm Eliska Janacek," she said in a much slighter accent than her husband's.

"It's Peter," Joe replied for me. "For God's sake, Eliska. He's not much older than Martin!"

I smiled at Eliska. "Pleasure to meet you."

"Come, Peter." Her eyes sparkled. "We'll go to the living room and have an aperitif."

We sat in high-back chairs in front of a wood-burning fireplace. I resisted the urge to gulp the delicious red wine in my glass, but I still made short work of it. With the melodic strings of a cello concerto filling the background, by the time of my second glass I began to relax. "What is this music?" I asked.

"Dvořák," Eliska said. "His cello concerto played by Yo-Yo Ma. Lovely, isn't it?"

"It's not just lovely, Liska," Joe piped up. "It is one of the greatest pieces of music ever composed."

I smiled. "Dvořák was Czech, right?"

"Of course!"

I turned to Eliska. "Is Martin your son?"

"Among other things," Joe answered for her.

Eliska rolled her eyes. "Our oldest. Martin keeps himself very busy."

"Oh?" I said. "Doing what?"

"He's a civil engineer," Eliska explained. "He works for a Christian charity that is active in reconstructing villages after natural or man-made disasters."

Joe stood up and refilled my glass without asking. "That's right. He goes into a village wiped out by bombs, earthquakes, or plagues . . . and he helps the poor hungry people build the biggest church they can erect to thank God for their good fortune."

"Jozef," Eliska said, "Martin is doing good work."

"He does build the odd bridge or dam, too." Joe smiled, showing a glimmer of pride in his son.

Eliska leaned closer to me and rested her bony fingers on my wrist. "Neither Jozef or I is at all religious, but the Church has been good for Martin. He had some . . . problems in college."

"Cocaine," Joe said candidly. "Very bad. He could have ended up like the others at our clinic."

"Then Martin found God," Eliska said.

"My cousin Kyle was saved the same way," I said.

"Religion is like methadone," Joe grumbled. "Replacing one crutch with a slightly more benign one."

"Excuse him," Eliska said, as if apologizing for a misbehaving child. "A dyed-in-the-wool socialist. He can't help himself." She stood up. "Come, let's feed you."

We moved to the dining room. At the long oak table, there were four table settings laid out. I pointed to the fourth setting, my apprehension rising.

Joe shrugged. "Edith sends her regrets. She's fighting a cold today."

"That's too bad," I said, hiding my relief.

While Eliska busied herself in the kitchen, Joe took the opportunity to turn the conversation to politics, and point out all the shortcomings of the current U.S. administration, as if I'd handpicked them myself. Rather than tell Joe how much I agreed with him, I sat back and let him vent.

Based on our earlier discussion of Eliska's cooking, I'd expected a traditional Czech meal. Instead, she served us a contemporary feast with butternut squash soup, followed by a pecan and blue cheese salad, and then a duck risotto that was as good as I had ever tasted.

Not until dessert did we sample our first Czech dish, *pusinky*, which Joe had baked. Served with vanilla ice cream, the pastries were as good as he'd boasted, and I had three of the light meringue crescents.

After dinner, Joe insisted I keep Eliska company while he cleared the dishes. Pleasantly tipsy from what must have been my fifth glass of wine, I said, "Joe tells me you made a militant of him?"

The skin around her eyes crinkled. "I made a militant of *him*?"

"In Prague," I said. "Joe said he became a revolutionary on your account."

She laughed. "Joe lies."

"Oh?"

"It was vice versa," she said. "I was a perfectly apolitical schoolteacher. Joe drew me into that hopeless revolution and almost got us both killed in the process."

Joe walked in from the kitchen. "I don't remember it like that."

Eliska turned to me, ignoring her husband. "For his entire life, he has been the defender of the underdog and champion of the lost cause." She shook her head. "You've seen his clinic, haven't you?"

"Don't listen to the woman." Joe grinned self-consciously. "I do it for the same reason I've always done it. The money."

I laughed. "And you've really made a killing on Hasting Street, haven't you?"

Joe shrugged. "More than enough."

Eliska stood up. "Peter, it has been delightful meeting you. With my arthritis, I get a little tired in the evening. Please excuse me."

I hopped to my feet, almost spilling my wine. "I should go, too."

"No!" Eliska waved away the idea. "Please stay. Jozef is a night owl. He would love the company."

I was genuinely sorry to see Eliska go. After thanking her for dinner, I followed Joe back into the living room where he poured me a glass of single-malt scotch without asking; not that I would've refused.

Joe wanted to hear more about my life. Aside for the borrowed name, I was otherwise accurate in describing my middle-class childhood. I told him about my father's battle with alcoholism that cost him his accounting practice and eventually his life. I even outlined Aaron's struggle with drugs, though I neglected to mention that we were identical twins. I tried to press Joe for details about his son's history, but he avoided the topic. Instead, he told me of his youngest daughter, Hannah, a concert violinist who lived in Victoria. He beamed when he announced that she and her husband were expecting "my first grandchild" in three months.

At eleven o'clock, Joe abruptly switched on the TV. "I need to know a little something of what's happening outside my window." He flipped through the channels to find the local news.

Silently, we watched the lead story about a shooting that killed two Indo-Canadians reputedly involved in the drug trade. Remembering the driver of the silver pickup truck in Aldergrove, I wondered if the victims or killers were associates of his.

The anchorman turned to a story about a threatened transit strike. Slightly drunk and stomach full, I was so relaxed by the Janacek's hospitality that it hadn't occurred to me I might make the news. But the moment I heard the anchorman say "Seattle authorities are looking north to . . ." I sat bolt upright in my chair.

"Dr. Benjamin Dafoe is the leading suspect in the double homicide," the anchorman continued. "One of the victims was Dr. Dafoe's ex-fiancée, Emily Kenmore. Seattle police believe the suspect might be hiding somewhere in the greater Vancouver area."

My fingers dug into the sides of the chair. My temples beat a drum solo. Acid filled my mouth. My eyes darted over to Joe who watched the screen impassively.

Then a picture of my face filled the TV screen. "If you see this man, please contact Vancouver police immediately."

Slowly, Joe's head turned toward me.

CHAPTER
27

Time froze while Joe silently appraised me. His face registered no signs of shock or outrage, but his cheeks tightened slightly and his eyes showed a guardedness that I'd never seen in him.

To my surprise, the expected spike of adrenaline never came. Instead, I was filled with calm resignation.

Eyes locked on me, Joe switched off the TV with the remote. "Dr. Benjamin Dafoe, I presume?"

I nodded.

"So who is Dr. Peter Horvath?"

"The brother of a good friend. As you already guessed, he's still in Taipei."

Joe rubbed his chin. "And who is Benjamin Dafoe?"

I pointed to the blank TV screen. "I'm the man accused of butchering my former fiancée along with a drug dealer named Jason DiAngelo."

"Accused?" He arched a bushy eyebrow. "Not guilty of?"

My shoulders slumped involuntarily. "You really want to hear?"

"Let's say that I'm mildly curious," he said, never taking his eyes off mine.

I raised my glass to my lips. The ice cubes cooled my lips, as I drained the last of the scotch and then put the glass down on the coffee table. "What I told you before about my life isn't that far off the truth. I had an identical twin brother . . . or I do have one."

"There's a slight distinction," Joe pointed out, as he leaned back in his chair as though he was settling in to watch a movie.

"I think Aaron may still be alive."

"*Think*?" He held out his palms. "You don't know?"

Numb with indifference, I summarized the events without trying to hide or minimize any of them. I laid out the details surrounding Emily's murder and my subsequent incrimination and finished by describing the mixed results of my amateur detective work in Vancouver.

Joe rose silently to his feet and walked into the kitchen. I reached for my tumbler and sucked on the ice cubes. The cool wetness with the trace of scotch was exactly what my parched mouth needed. Even if Joe was on the phone with the 911 operator, I had no intention of bolting. I was simply too exhausted to run again.

Joe returned five minutes later with an unopened bottle of scotch. Cracking open the cap with a snap that made my mouth water, he refilled my glass and then topped up his.

"One time, when Martin was still having troubles," Joe said, sinking back into his chair, "Eliska and I had gone out for dinner, but we missed our movie and ended up coming home early. When I walked in, I heard sounds from our bedroom. I grabbed a carving knife from the kitchen and tiptoed upstairs. The room was a mess—nightstand overturned, pictures on the floor, and the bedsheets torn. Martin sat on our bed, counting the roll of money he'd stolen from the lockbox under the bed. My own son, the cocaine addict." He grunted. "I screamed at him to get out. I told him he wasn't welcome in our house anymore."

Joe stopped to take a long sip of his drink. "Martin just laughed at me and said, 'You'll get over it, old man.' He walked toward me for the door, still gripping my money. I didn't trust myself with the knife. I dropped it on the floor." He shook his head. "But if I was still holding that knife when Martin walked by me . . ."

I understood Joe's insinuation, but I didn't bother to proclaim my innocence. We sat in silence for a minute or so, sipping our scotches. Finally, Joe looked up at me. His eyes bored into mine. "Did you kill her, Peter?"

"It's Ben," I said. "Since the moment we met, you've been telling me what a good judge of character you are."

"True."

"Emily wasn't just murdered. She was hacked slowly to death." I swallowed, fighting off the unwanted flashback of her mutilated corpse. "Do you think I'm capable of something like that?"

"I would like to hear it from you."

I held his stare. "I swear to you on my mother's grave, I did not kill Emily or anyone else."

He looked away and sighed. "Dafoe, is it? That's not even Hungarian."

"English, I'm afraid." I chuckled. "Now you know all my dirty secrets."

Joe reached for the bottle and refilled his glass. Reluctantly, I waved him away from mine. "So now what?" he asked.

"Depends," I said. "Did you call the police?"

"Not yet."

"Then I'm going to use what time I have left to try to find Aaron and assemble as much evidence as I can."

"You mean against this Maglio person?"

"And whoever else is involved," I said. "All along, I've thought the only way to convince the police of my innocence is by providing a better suspect."

Joe studied his glass before sipping it. "Do you think Malcolm Davies or Jenny Ayott can help you?"

"I'm not sure," I said. "I would like to talk to both of them again. But the contact information in the chart for Malcolm is wrong."

"I might be able to find him for you," Joe said.

I put down my glass and stood up. "Look, Joe, you've done more than enough." I forced a smile. "And despite your vow to give me the benefit of the doubt only *once*, we're well into double digits now. I don't want you or Eliska mixed up in this any more than you already are. If you'll let me go now without turning me in, that alone is a favor I probably can't ever repay."

Joe rose to his feet and walked me to the door. "We'll see. How can I reach you?"

"I don't have a phone."

"Where are you staying?"

Joe grabbed a pen and paper from the nightstand. I didn't hesitate in jotting down the address of my new apartment, and I scribbled my latest e-mail address below it.

At the front door, he dug my coat out of the closet and passed it to me. Then he reached into his wallet and pulled out several one-hundred-dollar bills.

"Joe . . ."

He shoved the money into my palm. "Believe me, Dr. Horvath's billings of last week will cover this."

I pocketed the money and shook his hand firmly. "Thank you, Joe."

It was after midnight by the time I stepped into the relatively warm evening. The fresh air sobered me. My numbness receded, replaced by the familiar survival instinct. I unlocked my bike and rode slowly back to Dotty's building, careful to keep to the side streets.

I was relieved to reach my apartment without seeing anyone in the building. I crawled under the sheets, and thankfully, the alcohol in my veins helped to drift me into a dreamless sleep.

Shortly before seven the following morning, I sprang out of bed, driven by the pressing sense of borrowed time. After brushing my teeth and reinserting my brown contact lenses, I sat at the kitchen table and scribbled notes to myself. I tried to summarize what I knew graphically with boxes and intersecting circles, but the diagram became so crowded with names and other chicken scratch that it began to resemble a large inkblot. Frustrated, I balled up the paper and threw it in the corner.

On the next page, I scrawled out a list of all the people whose paths I'd crossed, adding brief notes beside each name. I put a star and a question mark beside Marcus, Maglio, and Prince. But my eyes kept drifting back to one name: Drew Isaacs. He was the only witness I'd found to attest to Aaron's survival. Maybe he knew more than he was saying, or had forgotten to mention some detail that would lead me to Aaron.

I threw on my clothes and headed out to find a pay phone. I had my hand on the building's front door when a voice from behind stopped me. "And where do you think you're going?"

It took me an anxious moment to place the scratchy voice. "Good morning, Dotty." I spun slowly, wondering whether she might recognize me from the newscasts.

Grinning madly, she stood by the mail slots in another muumuu, a mauve and pink one today. "Well, good morning, Doctor," she said in a singsong tone, and I assumed my cover was still intact with her. "Have you had breakfast?"

Fearing an invitation, I lied. "Yes, a big one. Thanks. I've got to run to the hospital."

"Doctors," she sighed. "It's nothing but work for you."

I simply nodded and hurried out the door. I unlocked my bike and hopped on as soon as it rolled off the grass. I would have loved to work off my mounting stress with a long punishing ride, but every minute was precious now. I cycled onto Main Street and found a phone at the corner gas station. I dropped in a quarter and dialed Drew Isaacs's number. After five rings, I reached his curt voicemail. I was about to hang up, but I changed my mind. "Drew, it's Aaron. I need to talk to you urgently, but my cell is dead." I scanned the street until I spotted the Vietnamese restaurant across the way. I squinted to read the name off the sign. "How about the Saigon Palace, on the corner of Fifteenth and Main? I'll wait for you there at around one o'clock."

After hanging up, I reached for my wallet and dug through it until I found Jenny Ayott's address. I couldn't place the street, so I went inside the gas station and bought a map along with a coffee that tasted so acrid I managed to swallow only half of it before tossing the rest. I pinpointed Jenny's address on the map and then rushed out to my bike.

As I headed north, I thought more about my initial conversation with Jenny. Her description of Aaron's final cruel words to her still troubled me. His personality aside, something else didn't jibe with the comments but I couldn't articulate exactly what.

I reached Jenny's apartment building (another grayish box from the fifties) on Pandora Street. I checked my watch: 8:10 A.M. Collecting my thoughts, I buzzed her apartment from the ancient intercom by the door.

It rang three times before she came on the line. "Who is it?"

"Jenny, it's Dr. Peter Horvath."

"Dr. Horvath?"

I sensed suspicion in her tone. "Can I see you for a minute?"

She didn't respond immediately. "I could come to the office later," she finally said.

"No. I was hoping now."

"Now isn't so good, Dr. Horvath. I'll call the office and make an appointment—"

I cut her off. "Listen, Jenny, we both know my name isn't Horvath."

She didn't say a word, but I could tell from the intercom's crackle that she was still on the line.

"You're Aaron's twin, aren't you?" she said.

"Yes, Benjamin. And I need to talk to you about my brother."

"What about him?"

"I think he's alive."

The intercom deadened, and I thought I'd lost her. Then the door buzzed, and I grabbed for the handle before Jenny could change her mind. I walked along the worn carpet in a hallway that smelled much staler than the building Dotty maintained. I followed the stairs up to the second floor and found her room three doors down.

I knocked softly and Jenny opened the door. Hair pulled back, wearing a light blue T-shirt and jeans, she appeared even gaunter than when I first met her at the clinic. I had a flashback to my brother's last visit. And the inconsistency that had been rattling around my brain suddenly crystallized into a theory.

Jenny stared at me with the same wariness I'd seen in Joe. Slowly, she lifted the newspaper in her hand and held open a page of *The Province* for me. My colorless, clean-shaven face stared blankly back. The black-and-white photo sent my heart into a flutter, and sweat ran under my arms. "Can I explain?"

"You'd better," she said with an edge.

Jenny led me past the galley-style kitchen to the round table and chairs in the kitchen nook. We sat across from each other. Jenny sipped a glass of water without offering me anything. "Your explanation . . ."

I gave her an abbreviated summary, focusing on the events of the past few weeks. By the time I finished, her jaw hung open. "If what you say is true, then Aaron is alive."

"I think so."

Her eyes clouded. "And you think he was responsible for stabbing two people?" she asked hoarsely.

I shook my head adamantly. "He's not capable of that."

"So where does the blood come from?"

"I don't know." I sighed. "I think someone took it from him, maybe against his will."

Her face creased with doubt. "Why should I believe any of this?"

"I can't give you a reason." My voice was calm, but my heart slammed so fast and hard that it felt like someone was tap dancing on my chest. I pointed to the countertop. "The phone is over there. If you don't believe me, I won't stop you from calling nine-one-one."

She stared at me for a long moment while my bluff hung in the air like a grenade whose pin had been pulled. "Why can't you convince the cops?" she asked.

"They can't see beyond the fact my DNA is a perfect match for the blood at the scene."

She leaned back in her chair. "What do you want from me?"

I dried my palms on my jeans. "Jenny, in the last two years has Aaron ever tried to contact you?"

"No."

"No letters or e-mails or anything?"

"Nothing. Why?"

I shook my head. "I spoke to him days before he disappeared. And the way he spoke about you . . ."

Her eyes brightened, and she sat up straighter. "What did he say?"

"He was in love with you."

She swallowed. "Did he tell you that?"

"He didn't have to. He was planning a whole new life with you. And this would've been only a few days before he broke up with you." I paused. "Nothing else happened between you in those days in between, right?"

"No!" She folded her arms across her thin chest. "It all came out of the blue."

"And how long had he known about your HIV?"

"Long before then," she snapped.

"That's not what I meant, Jenny." I tried to soothe over her flare of anger. "Did you test positive before you met him?"

"No. It was a couple of months later." Jenny flushed with embarrassment. "But I told him right away. And we were always . . . careful . . . with protection, you know?"

"Sure." I swallowed. "But, um, before you tested positive, were you as careful?"

She shook her head. "We didn't know we needed to be."

"Of course."

She squinted at me. "What are you getting at?"

"The last few times I saw Aaron, he had lost considerable weight."

"I know," she said. "He wasn't eating much, though. He was under a ton of stress."

"Do you remember when you first became sick with HIV?"

She squinted at me. "Yes . . ."

"Did you lose weight?"

Jenny's eyes went wide as saucers. "Oh, God, you don't think . . ." Her words dissolved.

"I think it's possible."

Jenny gaped at me for a long moment. "It makes so much sense," she sputtered. Her eyes reddened and soon welled over with tears. "No wonder he stormed out on me. *I gave Aaron HIV, didn't I?*"

CHAPTER

28

I sat with Jenny for at least half an hour longer, trying to reassure her. Overcome by self-recrimination, Jenny was inconsolable. With the benefit of hindsight, she remembered Aaron's fevers and loss of appetite that she decided must have heralded the onset of HIV. Aaron had a phobia about needles and, unlike her, had never shot up in his life, so she reasoned that he must have acquired it through sexual contact. This could only mean she was the source.

I wandered out of her apartment with my head reeling. Worry, sadness, and shock stirred in a boiling pot of unease. My heart went out to Jenny. She had never overcome the loss of Aaron, and now I'd inadvertently saddled her with the guilt of having made him ill.

As I mounted my bike, my thoughts turned to the Human Immunodeficiency Virus. HIV had become so prevalent in our society and seemed to touch so many lives, especially mine. I had seen through my medical practice that with newer antivirals, most people living with HIV led full lives; however, twenty-five years after its terrifying appearance, the virus still carried a stigma like no disease since leprosy. And for those unfortunate souls who could not afford the exorbitant cost of treatment or whose disease progressed to AIDS in spite of medications, it could be as cruel a killer as any.

Aaron, HIV-positive! The thought struck me as surreal, in the same way that you know plane crashes and car accidents happen but you never expect them to touch your life directly. But if he had HIV, why would he walk out on Jenny claiming he didn't want "mutant kids with AIDS"? Again, I wondered whether Aaron might have used Jenny's illness as an excuse to end their relationship, because he needed to protect her from whatever threat had sent him on the run.

Reaching Main Street, I glanced at my watch. It was now 12:48. In my message, I'd promised to meet Drew Isaacs in twelve minutes. I rode the two blocks to the Saigon Palace, parked my bike out front, and walked in.

If not for a few scattered scenic posters with what I assumed were Vietnamese letters, the Saigon Palace could have passed for a roadside truck stop with its orange vinyl-covered booths and long counter with barstools anchored to the floor. But the exotic smells were distinctly Asian. Wafting to me, they made my mouth water.

I grabbed a corner booth with a direct view of the door but still tucked away from potential prying eyes. Unsure when or if Isaacs might turn up, I ordered some pot stickers and spring rolls. With the warm memory of the previous night's wine and scotch, I was tempted to order a beer, but knowing I wouldn't stop at one, I opted for coffee instead.

My appetizers arrived and I polished them off without taking my eye off the door. Shortly after one o'clock, the door opened and a man stood in the doorway, his face blocked by the doorframe. All I saw was a black boot, one leg of his jeans, and part of a black leather jacket. My mouth dried, and my temples pulsed. Ten seconds passed before a platinum blonde in leather pants and a tight white T-shirt walked in, followed by the man from the doorway. Even before I saw the biker's face, I knew he wasn't Isaacs.

I withstood a few more heart-skipping near-misses, but by the bottom of my fourth cup of coffee, I still hadn't seen Isaacs. An hour after I'd arrived, I gave up. I left a ten-dollar bill on the table and hurried out of the restaurant.

I rode in the general direction of my new home. Along the way, I stopped at a convenience store that advertised ninety-nine-dollar prepaid cell phones. Though cognizant of how traceable cell phones are, I decided that standing at pay phones would be even more risky after my newfound celebrity in Vancouver.

As I rushed through the registration forms, I avoided eye contact with the willowy Filipina clerk who stood beside the stack of *Province* newspapers that all bore my photo inside. I prayed she hadn't had the time or inclination to read one, but I calmed as it became increasingly obvious that she had no interest in me. Using Joe's cash, I paid for a cell phone that came with three hundred preprogrammed minutes of local airtime.

I cycled back to the complex on East Fourteenth. I rushed my new purchase up to the room with the anticipation of a boy bringing a new truck home from the toy store. Inside, I pulled the phone out of the casing and plugged it into the charger. Too impatient to wait for it to charge, I left it plugged in and punched a zero into the keypad followed by the rest of Kyle's number.

A moment later Kyle was on the line. "Ben, what is going on?" he asked with concern. "Where are you?"

"Running."

"Aren't you cycling anymore?"

I suspected he was joking, but I took his question at face value. "As in *on the run*. They know I'm in Vancouver."

"Yeah," he said without a trace of surprise.

"Is that what the Seattle papers are saying, too?"

"Pretty much," he said. "And Detective Sutcliffe came by yesterday. He was asking a lot of questions about who you might know in Vancouver."

"Rick was there without Helen?"

"Just Rick."

"Same as Alex," I mumbled. Clutching my new phone tighter, I wondered why Rick was interviewing my friends and family without his partner.

"Alex? What are you talking about?"

"Nothing. It's . . . I don't know." I sighed. "There's something about Rick."

"I hear you," Kyle said. "Never trusted that perma-grin of his. I bet he's one of those shouting-on-the-inside guys. He was the same in Narcotics."

"You knew Rick before this?"

"Oh, yeah. Aaron and I definitely made his radar screen in the old days. And once he got wind of you, he stuck on you."

"I've noticed."

"Of course, even back then there were rumors."

"Rumors?"

"What with the expensive suits and cars . . ."

"Hold on!" I hopped up from the bed. "Are you saying Rick was a dirty cop?"

"He never asked me for money, but word was he could be bought." Kyle covered the receiver, but I could still hear his harsh though muffled cough. "Ben, in that business there were so many rumors." He breathed heavily, sounding winded. "And most of them were just that, unfounded rumors."

"I guess," I said, but my chest fired like a piston engine. If Rick could be bought when he was with Narcotics then the same might be true in Homicide. And if someone needed help in framing me for Emily's murder, who better than a dirty Homicide cop?

Kyle cleared his throat. "Any luck finding Drew Isaacs?"

"Yeah. He met me for a drink. But he thought I was Aaron."

"*Aaron?*" The surprise sent him into another coughing spasm. "Drew thinks Aaron is still alive, too?"

"With good reason. They went out for drinks a year after Aaron was supposed to have died."

"Holy, Ben!" Kyle croaked. "You were right all along."

"But no one else has confirmed the sighting."

"Still." Kyle was quiet for a long moment. "Did he say where Aaron was living?"

"Aaron never told him," I said. "Don't forget I was pretending to be Aaron, so there was only so much I could ask about myself."

"I suppose." Kyle still sounded shell-shocked. "What else did he tell you?"

I gave him a rundown of my conversation with Isaacs, including his revelations about Emily's relationship with Maglio and his potential HIV exposure. "Did you know about Emily and Maglio?" I asked.

"Again, only rumors." He sighed. "I never knew what to believe about Maglio, though."

"Why?"

"Well, there's always been talk that he might be gay."

"Gay?" I massaged my aching temples with my free hand. "In which case, Emily wouldn't necessarily have exposed him to HIV."

"Unless Maglio swings both ways," Kyle said. "Besides, this is no more than just gossip. Why don't you ask Isaacs?"

"Because I can't reach him on his cell." I climbed back onto the bed, careful not to pull the cord out of the wall. "You wouldn't have any other way of finding him?"

"Hmmm." I heard Kyle's teeth tap together, and it reminded me of Aaron. "Drew used to hang out at a bar downtown. I'd meet him there from time to time."

"Club Vertical?"

"That's the place," Kyle said. "He was there at least a couple nights a week."

"Good, thanks," I said, mentally planning to go back looking for him.

"It's kind of depressing, huh?"

I chuckled. "You'll have to be *way* more specific."

"Say Aaron has been alive all this time," Kyle said. "In two years he never tried to contact either one of us, but he visits Drew Isaacs when he's in Vancouver. That stings a little."

More than a little. "Maybe Aaron was trying to protect us the same way that I think he might have been protecting Jenny."

"*Jenny*? Did you find her?"

"She found me."

"What does that mean?"

"Long story."

"What did she tell you?" He pressed me for details.

I relayed what Jenny had told me about her relationship with Aaron, including its abrupt end.

"What?" Kyle's surprise launched him into another violent cough. "Jenny was HIV-positive?"

"Yes," I said. "Did you see Aaron in the months right before he died?"

"Yeah," he mumbled, catching his breath. "He visited me a couple of times while I was still in the hospital."

"How did he look to you?"

"Fine, I guess."

"You didn't think he looked thin or pale?"

"Do you remember the bone marrow transplant ward I was on? We were a bunch of bald skeletons. Everyone else looked rosy in comparison."

"Fair enough," I said sheepishly. "But I remember how unwell Aaron seemed the last few times I saw him. He wrote it off to stress, but looking back, I don't think so."

"Even if he was HIV-positive," Kyle said, "what does that have to do with his disappearance or Emily's murder?"

"I don't know." I exhaled heavily. "I can't say why. It just feels important, you know?"

"Ben, would it help if I came up to Vancouver?"

I would have welcomed his company, but instead I said, "I don't think so, Kyle."

"Never hurts to have family around in a crisis. Besides, I could help track down Drew. Maybe even find a new lead on Aaron's trail?" He laughed. "Hey, I could even show you how this new prayer gig of mine works. It's been doing wonders for me lately."

Religion aside, his offer was tempting, but he didn't sound well enough to travel. "I think you'd better look after that chest of yours. What does your doctor say?"

"Sounds worse than it is. I get a lot of chest infections ever since the radiation. A few more days of puffers and antibiotics, and I'll be ready for a triathlon."

"Let's wait until then," I said. "Kyle, there is one thing you can do for me."

"Name it."

"All that stuff you found out about Whistler and Maglio . . ."

"What about it?"

"I need to know your source."

"Ben, I gave my word."

"I know," I said. "Do you remember my anonymous caller?"

"The whisperer?"

"He tracked me down in Vancouver. I think he's leading the police to me. I don't have much time. I need to know who's pulling the strings here."

"Ben, I don't know—"

"Please, Kyle, it could be key. Who is he?"

He was quiet for a moment. Finally, he said, "Michael Prince."

CHAPTER

29

After I hung up, I lay on the bed resting my new phone against my chest. Fragments of information swirled in my head. Sources were unreliable, leads contradicted each other: Emily exposed Philip Maglio to a lethal sexually transmitted disease; or he was gay. Rick was a dirty cop; or he was just tenacious. Drew Isaacs thought I was Aaron; or he played me for a fool. My twin brother was alive and visiting former drug-dealing colleagues while ignoring his own family; or he was dead. Prince was the most tight-lipped attorney in the world; or he had acted as my cousin's own "Deep Throat" informer.

Who was telling the truth? What information was significant? *Maybe they're all involved in a conspiracy to frame me*, I thought miserably, recognizing I was verging on paranoia. My head felt as though it might burst. Had I more energy, I might have sprung off the bed and decimated Dotty's apartment like a drunken rock star.

I wished I had accepted Alex's or Kyle's offer to join me in Vancouver. A familiar face and a sympathetic ear, someone to talk through these contradictory facts, was what I needed to hang on to my weakening sanity.

I raised the phone and tried Prince's number. Janelle's sweet voice answered, but it was only a recording. Even Prince didn't work Sundays. Then I wasted another minute of airtime trying Drew Isaacs. I hung up as soon as I heard the first words of his familiar voicemail greeting.

My stomach growled. I kicked myself for not picking up food while

235

I was buying the phone at the convenience store. Now I had to risk exposure again foraging for food.

I stepped out of the room and rushed through the lobby, thankful not to bump into Dotty or anyone else. Head down, I walked the two blocks to a supermarket on Main Street. I strode up and down the aisles filling my basket with fruit, vegetables, cheese, bread, cold cuts, and bottled water. I even found a flashlight and a baseball cap that I tossed into the basket.

Nearing the checkout counter, I heard a voice calling, "Peter!" I didn't realize that he meant me until the third call. My chest sinking, I looked over to see my balding former neighbor from the YMCA standing at the far checkout, buying two cartons of cigarettes and waving to me like he was trying to hail a cab.

Scanning my brain as he loped nearer, I dug up his name only when he reached me. "Hi, Ray."

"Peter, you've checked out of the Y," Ray announced like it was news to me. "I did, too. I found a cheap rental in this 'hood. Are we neighbors again?"

Ray smelled like an ashtray that hadn't been emptied for too long, but I forced a grin. "No. I'm on my way out of town."

He looked down at my basket doubtfully.

"Road trip." I shrugged. "I'm heading east. To Alberta. I needed to fill the car with supplies."

His inane smile widened. "I thought you rode a bike?"

"Only in the city," I said. "For longer hauls, I have an old beater of a Buick that gets me from town to town. Barely."

He nodded, looking pleased. "You're environmentally friendly, like me."

Except for the three packs of cigarettes you burn into the ozone layer every day, I wanted to say but bit my tongue. "It's good to see you, man, but I got to hit the road." I turned toward the other checkout.

"Did your friend ever find you?" he asked.

I stopped dead, but managed to stop myself from whirling around to face him. "Friend?" I asked, as casually as I could muster.

"Yeah. Some guy came by the Y asking for you. Your last name *is* Horvath, right?"

I turned slowly. "That's me."

"Thought so."

I clenched my jaw, fighting back the surge of adrenaline. "I haven't heard from any friends lately. Did he happen to give you a name?"

"Nah."

"When was this?"

"Couple of days ago. I tried to tell you that morning, but you were rushing off to work."

I nodded. "I'm not from here, so I don't have many friends in Vancouver. Maybe if you describe him, I could figure out who we're talking about."

"I'm not so good at that."

I gave him my best what-have-you-got-to-lose encouragement. "Give it a shot."

He scratched his smooth head. "Kind of short brown or black hair, I couldn't tell. Guess he was around your height. Skinny like you, too." He laughed, patting his large belly. "To me, anyway."

"Hmmm." I shook my head. "Doesn't ring a bell. Anything else stand out about him?"

"Can't think of much." He scratched his barren scalp. "Well, he was a dapper dresser. I'd bet his suit alone was worth more than I see in a couple months."

"Don't know too many rich people." I laughed and then made a point of looking at my watch. "I better get on the road. Thanks, man. Maybe I'll see you back at the Y someday."

I rushed over to the free clerk at the other checkout and dumped my groceries onto the rubber conveyor belt.

A bag in each hand, I walked back to my room mulling over the possible identity of my "friend." It had to be someone smart and determined enough to case the downtown for cheap lodgings where I might be staying. Someone my height, thin, and a "dapper dresser." I knew it could have been an undercover cop or one of Maglio's men, but two prospects loomed large in my brain. Rick Sutcliffe always dressed to the nines. I knew he'd been conducting solo interviews with my contacts in Seattle over the past few days, but Vancouver was less than a three-hour drive; he could have snuck up in between them. Still, the timing would have been tight. That left Marcus Lindquist, who, as I knew from the castoff clothes I now wore, was another snappy dresser. Emily's former lover had shown an inordinate interest in my where-abouts. If it were Marcus, why would he try to track me down by him-self like a private investigator? Not a skill set common to most hematologists.

Hematologist! I almost dropped my bags. Not only was Marcus a blood specialist, but he made his living preserving umbilical cord blood. He had the expertise *and* the facilities to keep blood cells alive indefinitely.

My heart pounded in my throat. Marcus wouldn't need Aaron alive to frame me for murder. Hypothetically, if he had a sample of either Aaron's or my blood from any time, he could have kept it fresh enough to spray on Emily's wall.

I remembered the blood tests to check my hepatitis immunization status three years earlier at St. Jude's, the same hospital lab where Mar-cus used to work. I had no idea how often and where Aaron might have given blood for testing, but as I now believed that Aaron was diag-nosed with HIV before his disappearance, he must have had at least one blood test, too. Presumably, Marcus could have got his hands on either one of our indistinguishable blood samples.

I had nothing to substantiate my hypothesis, but the idea gave me a second wind. Hands full with weighty bags, I bounded the rest of the way home and tore through the lobby and up to my room. Stuffing the groceries into the fridge, I thought more about the possibility of Mar-cus framing me for Emily's murder. Was he capable of such violence? Like most womanizers, Marcus had struck me as having a misogynist edge—as if his extramarital flings were only about possession and con-quest, nothing to do with emotion. The more I considered his cool oily personality, the more convinced I grew that murder wasn't beyond him. But I had to concede that my visceral dislike of him was clouding my judgment.

The excitement of a new lead stirred my appetite. As I walked through various scenarios in my head, I swallowed two salami sand-wiches and a bag of baby carrots. I was eager to learn more about Mar-cus's blood-preserving business, but I realized that it would have to wait. My first priority was to track down Drew Isaacs.

At ten P.M., I put on the baseball cap that I'd picked up at the store and assessed my appearance in the bathroom mirror. With a thicker beard and hair hidden under the cap, I was pleased to see that my reflection had begun to look vaguely foreign even to me.

Forgoing my helmet, I headed out the front door and grabbed my bike. I rode the two miles downtown to Club Vertical at a leisurely pace. I circled the block twice before locking up my bike a block away and approaching the nightclub on foot. A short, swarthy bouncer in tinted glasses stood at the front entrance. His nylon jacket strained to hold in his overdeveloped shoulders, and I didn't need to see the results of a urine test to know he was on anabolic steroids. The once-over he gave me was disquieting, but his expression drifted to disinterest as he nodded permission to enter.

Inside, the club was even less crowded than during my last visit. Squinting to adjust to the dimness, I scanned the bar for any sign of Isaacs's long mane, but saw none. The same blonde I'd seen flirting with Isaacs sashayed up to me and offered me a drink. If she recognized me from the last time I was there, she didn't acknowledge it. I ordered a bottle of beer and headed for a seat at a raised counter in the corner.

My beer arrived moments after me. I was developing a real taste for the Canadian beer, thanks to its higher alcohol content and extra kick, but the nine-dollar cost aside, I imposed a strict one-drink limit on myself. Sitting at the bar sipping the beer, my vigil for Drew Isaacs passed much as it had at the Saigon Palace with a few near-misses but no sighting. The prolonged exposure felt uncomfortable, though the dim lights gave me some sense of cover, like hiding in the shade. By 11:30, I gave up again on Isaacs and headed for home.

I managed to sleep much of the night but I awoke early, determined to dig deeper into Marcus's involvement.

On the road by seven, I cycled over to another coffee shop on Fraser Street with Internet access. Walking by the countertop at the window, I stopped to pick up an abandoned copy of *The Province*. My heart froze when I saw the page-three story with my photo framed underneath along with the caption DR. BENJAMIN DAFOE WHO HAS BEEN POS-ING AS DR. PETER HORVATH.

My cover is blown! Panic welled as I gleaned from the quick read that the police had confirmed I was staying at the YMCA under the alias of Horvath. Feeling as if the walls of the coffee shop were sliding toward me, I fought off my instinct to run. Instead, I pulled my cap lower on my head and headed to the counter. Speaking to my shoes, I ordered a large coffee.

Hand trembling, I paid in exact change and then took the coffee over to the corner where the free computer terminal thankfully faced the wall. Within a minute, I'd found the official Web site of Marcus's company, Hope Bank Cryogenics. I scanned the site, learning that more than 40,000 parents had already banked blood from their newborn's umbilical cord with Marcus's company. Hope Bank Cryogenics had become the leaders in the Pacific Northwest with the profits for the previous year running in the tens of millions. And the site described their storage facility as cutting-edge, secure, and massive. *Easily big enough to hide a vial of Dafoe blood for later purposes,* I thought bitterly.

Exhausting my research into Marcus, I logged on to my e-mail server and scanned my messages. Alex had sent me four e-mails that grew sequentially more insistent, demanding to know where I was and how I was coping. I responded with a quick note telling her that the pressure was mounting but the trail was getting warmer.

The last email on the list was from JJ99. With an empty subject line, I almost deleted it as spam, but I opened the note on a hunch to discover that "JJ" was Jozef Janacek. In the first paragraph, Joe provided me a contact phone number for "MD" (Malcolm Davies). The next and final paragraph intensified the shake in my hand: EXPECT COMPANY SOON. NO PROBLEM. I REMAIN A GOOD JUDGE OF CHARACTER. JJ.

Company? What the hell are you getting at? I wanted to yell at the screen. *Who did you tell, Joe?*

I took note of the e-mail's time stamp and realized that he'd sent the message about fifteen minutes earlier. Leaving the rest of my coffee on the table, I hopped to my feet and ran for the door.

I jumped on my bike and sprinted back to the apartment. Joe's e-mail aside, I presumed Dotty would see my photo along with my alias in the morning paper. I had to get out of her complex before she notified the cops. But I needed to pick up the knapsack with Horvath's identification, the rest of my clothes, and my cell phone.

Ensuring with a quick ride-by that there were no police outside, I locked my bike out front and hurried in. I rounded the corner and almost slammed into Dotty, who looked enormous in a fuzzy pink housecoat and slippers. My chest banged when I noticed the rolled-up copy of *The Province* tucked under her arm.

She gaped at me. "Dr. Horvath!"

I stared back silently, wondering anxiously if I would have to become physical with the hobbled old woman.

Then she broke into a smile. "Oh, you gave me a fright. Have you had breakfast, yet?"

"Yeah, just ate, thanks." I mumbled. "Listen, Dotty, any chance I could borrow your paper for a few minutes? I wanted to catch up on my football scores before I race back to the hospital."

She tapped the paper under her arm. "Soon. Won't take me but a half an hour to get through it and finish the crossword." She laughed. "I'll drop it off, right after."

"Okay, great." I swallowed. "I better go get ready for work."

As soon as I got into the stairwell, I dashed for my room, knowing I had little if any time to escape the building. I stuffed the clothing and toiletries haphazardly into the knapsack. Grabbing my helmet and giving the room a final scan, I slung the bag over my shoulder and rushed for the door.

I made it to within two feet, but my hand froze halfway to the doorknob. Three loud raps came from the other side.

CHAPTER
30

I stood absolutely still, afraid to breathe. Seconds passed. Nothing.

My eyes darted around the room and fixed on the small window across from me. I had no idea if the hinges would shriek or if the window would even open at all. Even if it did, I would face a ten-foot jump to the cement below.

What choice do I have? I thought.

The knuckles rapped harder on my door. The banging propelled me into action. I ran across the floor on tiptoes, sliding to a stop at the window. My hand shot out for the latch, prepared to smash the glass if need be. As I touched the cold metal, a voice from the other side of the door stopped me. "Ben."

I froze again.

"Ben, it's me."

Alex?

I ran back across the floor, unlocked the door, and threw it open. Alex Lindquist stood at the doorstep, her face creased in a look somewhere between shock and relief. "Ben, I didn't know how else to reach you—"

I cut her off with a bear hug. I'd forgotten how tiny she was. I lifted her off the ground and swung her effortlessly inside the apartment. Closing the door quickly with my foot, I lowered her to the ground and kissed her cheek, drinking in her familiar vanilla-scented perfume. "Alex, thank God!"

"That new beard tickles." She laughed. "I take it you're not mad I came."

Reluctantly, I freed her of my embrace. "I am. You shouldn't have come. What about Talie?"

She glanced away. "She's with Marcus this week," she said quietly.

"Alex, I'm not safe to be around."

She pursed her lips, and her eyes lit with amusement. "This is not news to me, Benjamin Dafoe."

"But the manhunt for me is getting hotter by the second." I grabbed her hand. "We have to leave. Now. Did you drive?"

She nodded. "I'm parked out front."

"Great."

I led Alex down the stairs and onto the main floor. Scurrying past Dotty's apartment, I brought a finger to my lips. With relief, we reached the front door without running into anyone.

Outside, I stopped where I'd chained my bike to a tree. I looked over my shoulder at Alex. "Don't suppose you have room for—"

"Plenty." She pointed the fob she was holding to the SUV parked on the street and clicked the remote to unlock it. I wheeled the bike to the back of her car and tossed it in through the hatch.

I climbed in beside Alex. As she pulled away from the curb, I sank into the heated passenger seat. Feeling the smooth quiet hum of the car's engine, my heart rate settled for the first time in hours. I looked over to Alex. "Joe told you where to find me?"

She nodded. "I had to call twenty clinics in Vancouver before I found where Dr. Peter Horvath was working. Then it took me another day to reach Dr. Janacek, but he wouldn't speak to me on the phone. We met early this morning at his office."

I smiled at Alex's ingenuity. "How did you convince Joe?"

"I said I was your best friend in the world," she said, reddening slightly. "And that you needed my help."

"Right on both counts." I reached out and squeezed the back of her hand on the steering wheel.

She glanced at me. "Ben, I get the feeling he knows you're not Peter Horvath."

"It's all over the news in Vancouver." I let go of her hand. "Besides, Joe knows the whole story."

She nodded and turned back to the road. "As I was leaving, he said something to me that I didn't understand. He wouldn't explain it, but he said you would understand."

"What's that?"

"He told me you could use an 'Eliska' of your own right now."

Giddy with relief and Alex's proximity, I burst into laughter.

Alex reached over and punched me on the shoulder. "What's an Eliska?"

"I guess you could say Eliska is Joe's muse."

Alex shook her head and sighed. "As Talie would say, *whatever*."

The reality of my situation crept back to me, as sobering as the storm clouds that now threatened the previously blue skies above us. "Alex, they all know I'm here, and who I'm pretending to be."

She nodded. "Why don't we leave?"

"Not yet," I said. "There are still questions I have to answer."

"Let's find those answers in a hurry, huh?"

I resisted the urge to kiss her. "I don't even have a place to stay."

"I've got a hotel room downtown. Great view of the city—"

"Alex . . ."

"Come on, Ben, this is no time to act prim and proper," she snapped. "What choice do you have?"

"This has nothing to do with propriety. What if the cops find me hidden in your hotel room? Or worse, what if Emily's killer finds you with me? It's too dangerous."

She dismissed the thought with a wave of her hand. "I'm all grown up, Ben. I'm willing to take my chances."

"And Talie?"

Alex hesitated, but then she shook her head. Slowing at the next red light, she turned to me with eyes afire. "Tell me you wouldn't do the same for me if our roles were reversed, Ben, and I'll drop you off right here on the corner."

I swallowed the lump from my throat. "Let's go see this supposed view of yours."

"Now you're talking."

We drove a while in comfortable silence. "What's next?" Alex finally asked.

"Not what, who."

"Okay, who?"

"Malcolm Davies or Drew Isaacs."

She tilted her head. In profile, frown lines formed at the corner of her eye. "I remember you telling me about Isaacs, but who is Malcolm Davies?"

"My brother's former crystal-meth supplier. I think he dated Jenny before Aaron." I went on to tell Alex about Jenny's HIV, and how I suspected Aaron had acquired the virus from her.

She sighed quietly. "It just keeps getting more complicated."

I nodded at the window.

Downtown, we pulled into the underground parking lot of the Sheraton hotel a few blocks from the YMCA where I stayed. Leaving my bike in the hatch, we walked into the hotel and rode the elevator in silence to the twenty-ninth floor.

Alex slid the card into the key slot in the door. The lock clicked and flashed green. She opened the door, and we stepped into the spacious bedroom. As advertised, the tinted windows offered a spectacular view of downtown Vancouver and the snowcapped mountains that stood guard over the northern border of the city. Turning from the window, I noticed the room had only one king-sized bed. Alex followed my stare. "I could ask to change for a room with two beds," she offered.

I shook my head. "That would only draw attention to the fact that you have a guest. Is this okay with you?"

She grinned. "I had a male roommate for a year in med school. I survived."

I chuckled. "Did he?"

"Barely." She looked away. "But I married his best friend."

The reference to her husband tensed my spine. "Is Marcus still asking about me?" I said, trying to sound as casual as possible.

"Didn't mention you when he picked Talie up on Saturday," she said.

"Anyway, I think he's preoccupied. He was out of town on business most of last week."

I wondered whether his business involved following me to Vancouver, but I kept the thought to myself. Anxious to change subjects, I said, "I need to make a phone call."

"Want me to leave?"

"No. You just have to stay quiet."

Alex flashed her perfect teeth in the warmest smile I'd seen in weeks. "Not my forte, but I'll give it a whirl."

I pulled the cell phone from my pocket and plopped down on the side of the bed. Still standing across from me, Alex watched as I dialed Michael Prince's number collect. Janelle transferred me through. "Benjamin, how are you?" Prince said.

"I've had better weeks," I said coolly.

"How can I help?"

"Michael, I've been mulling over your attitude toward the attorney-client privilege." I waited for some response but he didn't comment. "I thought you told me it applied uniformly to all clients."

"It does."

"Yet it didn't prevent you from discussing the details of my case freely with my cousin Kyle."

"I didn't discuss a single detail of your case with him." He sounded as unfazed as ever.

"Is that right?" My grip tightened as I felt my heat rising. "I heard you were his source for all kinds of details about Maglio and the Whistler development."

"Depends on your perspective."

"I don't have time for your goddamn legal doublespeak!" I snapped.

Alex fired me a cautionary glance.

"Listen, Ben," Prince said calmly. "Kyle and your brother were potential investors in the NorWesPac development. As, we've established, was I. Under the circumstances, Kyle has the right to know certain details about the project and its subsequent unraveling. This is very different than disclosing sensitive information about one client to another." He paused. "Are you following?"

"I get it." I exhaled heavily, involuntarily swayed by his rationale. "You're saying you found a legal loophole, through my cousin, to supply me information I needed without compromising the privilege of another client."

"You can read into it what you want." Prince's tone suggested he agreed with my assessment. "I merely gave your cousin details he was entitled to anyway, primarily by validating what he already knew to be the case."

"Is that right?" I said, unable to remember which details Kyle had known before and after his conversation with Prince.

"It is."

"Well, Michael, would you help me validate something that I've heard to be the case?"

"Depends what it concerns."

"Your client, Philip Maglio."

"You know that I, I cannot—"

"Yeah, yeah, I know," I said. "But I also know that you told me there was no way that Emily could have infected Maglio. And yet, by all accounts they were an item for almost a year."

Prince said nothing.

"In which case, there are only two possible explanations. One, Maglio already had HIV. Or two, he's gay and Emily was his beard."

"Beard?"

"The woman who provides a cover story, like when a gay Hollywood star gets married to quell rumors."

"I am not privy to Mr. Maglio's medical history," Prince said. "However, I will say that in his business, appearances can be very important."

I took the evasive comment as confirmation of Maglio's homosexuality.

"I understand the police are now looking for you in Vancouver," Prince said.

"You understand right."

"So you haven't found your brother yet?"

"No," I said quietly.

"Perhaps it's time to return to Seattle to let me deal with the charges?"

I looked away from Alex. "I don't think so."

"Why is that?"

"Because I don't trust you, Michael."

"I'm sorry to hear that. I've been as forthcoming with you as I can, under the circumstances."

"Then answer me one more question."

"If I can."

"Just exactly how involved are you in Emily's murder and the cover-up that has happened since?"

"Benjamin," he said in his father-knows-best tone. "Trust me when I tell you that I have your best interests at heart."

"Bye, Michael." I hung up the phone.

Arms folded across her chest, Alex stared at me. "Well?"

"If Maglio killed Emily, it had nothing to do with her exposing him to HIV."

"So he's not your prime suspect anymore?"

"He still ties the victims together. One dealt drugs for him, and the other helped to screw up an important business venture."

"But?" Alex demanded.

"There are others who deserve a very long look."

"Like?"

Your estranged husband, I wanted to say, but I merely shrugged in response. I didn't know how to break it to Alex that I suspected Talie's father was involved in the murders.

CHAPTER

31

Alex insisted I stay in the room while she went out to pick up food, declaring that she wasn't prepared to "live on room service from now on."

As soon as she left, I tried the number Joe had given me for Malcolm Davies. Malcolm answered on the second ring.

"Malcolm, it's . . . um . . . Dr. Horvath," I stammered, uncertain how best to approach him.

"Doctor who?" he said, seemingly oblivious.

"Dr. Peter Horvath," I said, relaxing slightly. "We met at Dr. Janacek's clinic."

"Oh, yeah. How are you doing, Doc?"

Either Malcolm was a hell of a good actor or he hadn't seen the news reports on me yet. I assumed the latter. "I'm doing well, thanks. And you?"

"My burns and scars still ache, but that's life, right?" His tone turned inquisitive. "How come you're calling me?"

"Going over your chart, I wondered if I'd prescribed you enough painkillers," I said, fabricating on the fly.

His voice brightened, as if he'd just won a door prize. "Now that you mention it, I've been going through them two or three at a time. I definitely could use more."

"No problem," I said. "Are you still living on . . ."

"Powell Street," he finished the sentence, as I'd hoped he would.

"I am not allowed to phone in prescriptions for narcotics, but Powell is basically on my way to the hospital. Why don't I drop a prescription off this afternoon?"

"Sure. Thanks."

"Give me your address and I'll come by around two-ish."

Malcolm reeled off his address, and I jotted it down. "Do you mind slipping the prescription under the door?" he asked.

"Why do I need to do that?" I said, trying to keep my frustration out of my tone.

"Because I won't be home today."

I punched the pillow beside me. "Malcolm, I make it a policy that I only give narcotic prescriptions in person." I scrambled to salvage the situation.

"Too bad," he said with a heavy sigh. "Then it's going to have to wait until Thursday. I'm out of town for the next couple days."

I don't have until Thursday. "Okay, why don't I call you Thursday morning?"

"Sounds good, Doc."

"Oh, one other thing," I said. "You used to date Jennifer Ayott, didn't you?"

"Jenny . . . yeah." His tone took on an edge. "Why do you ask?"

"Bizarre coincidence, but when I first met her, she mistook me for another person, the same as you did. She thought I looked just like an ex of hers, Aaron Dafoe."

"Aaron Dafoe," he repeated slowly.

I waited, hoping Malcolm might elaborate, but he didn't. "The irony is that Aaron is actually my cousin. We grew together up in Seattle. Small world, huh?"

"Very," he said quietly.

"I don't know if you heard, but Aaron disappeared about two years back," I said.

"I heard."

"His dad—my uncle—has never gotten over it. Just destroyed him. He spends all his time and money searching for Aaron."

"He's wasting his time."

I went cold. "What do you mean?"

"Listen, Doc, I gotta go."

"Come on, Malcolm," I said. "You can't leave it like that. All my uncle lives for now is closure on his missing son."

He hesitated. "Are you also Kyle's cousin?"

"Yeah, same side," I said impatiently. "Malcolm, what happened to Aaron?"

"I'm not sure."

"But you know something. Please, Malcolm. Anything."

He was quiet for so long that I wondered if he was still on the line. "Listen," he finally said. "My meth lab blew up the same week Aaron disappeared. Just about killed me. Right?"

"Right . . ." I remembered the roadmap on his chest and belly but I didn't see the relevance.

"In a meth lab, you have so many unstable gases. So many flammable and incendiary molecules," he said, sounding more like my old chemistry prof than someone who cooked street drugs. "I was a very, very careful chemist. I'd been doing it for almost ten years, and I never had an accident before. I didn't make mistakes."

"Wait a minute." I sat up straighter. "Are you saying someone booby-trapped your lab?"

"Bingo."

"Aaron?"

"No."

"Who?"

"Word was that the same person who rigged my lab also got to Aaron, if you know what I mean."

"*Got* to him?" I asked. "Who?"

"How does that matter to your uncle?"

I ignored the question. "Was it Philip Maglio?"

"No, closer to home than—" He stopped abruptly in midsentence. "Hey! How do you know about Maglio?"

"Okay, I admit I've done a bit of research into this—"

"No. No. No. I've already said way too much." His voice was panicky. "Forget that prescription, Doc."

I only squeezed out "Malcolm" before the line clicked dead.

I was still staring at the pad with Malcolm's address when Alex burst into the room. She closed the door with a foot and dropped her grocery bags on the floor. She rushed up and grabbed my hands in hers. "Ben, I think I'm on to something." Her cheeks glowed, and her eyes burned.

Her eagerness bumped the thoughts of Malcolm from the forefront of my mind. I squeezed her hands tighter. "What, Alex?"

"Say Aaron is HIV-positive."

"Okay."

"And say it's his blood on Emily's wall."

"Yeah . . ." My heart sped up; her excitement was contagious.

"Even in a dried blood sample, any sophisticated lab could test the sample—"

It suddenly clicked. "For the presence of HIV!" I threw my arms around her. "Alex, you're a genius!" Without thinking, I kissed her on the lips.

She kissed back, her wet lips sliding over mine, but after a moment she broke it off. She stared into my eyes. "But if you're wrong about Aaron being HIV-positive."

"Then I'm still no worse off than I was two minutes ago." I reached out and stroked her warm cheek. "But if the blood is HIV-positive, then it will clear my name."

Flooded with hope, I hopped off the bed.

"Where are you going?"

"I have to call Helen."

Alex followed after. "But if you call her from Vancouver, she'll know you're here."

"Believe me, she already knows."

Alex drove me out to Burnaby, the suburb immediately east of Vancouver, where we cased several pay phones until she chose one at a gas station with the right combination of remoteness and ease of escape.

Alex sat in the still idling car beside the phone booth where I stood. I laid out a pocketful of change on the stand and then dialed Helen's direct line. After several rings, a woman answered in a New England drawl. "Seattle Police Department, Homicide. Carol speaking."

"Can I speak to Sergeant Helen Riddell?" I asked.

"She's out of the office today," the receptionist said. "Can I take a message?"

"It's Benjamin Dafoe calling."

"Oh," she said as if she'd just swallowed something foul. "I see."

"I need you to track Helen down on her cell phone."

"Hold on a moment."

"That won't work," I said. "I'll call you back in two minutes. If you don't have Helen on the other line, I'm gone." I hung up without waiting for her response.

As soon as I phoned back, my call was immediately forwarded to Helen.

"Helen, I've got news."

"So do I," she said, sounding subdued.

"Me first," I said. "Look, I'm not sure if Emily did infect Maglio with HIV—"

"Because girls aren't Phil's bag?"

"That's right," I said without hiding my surprise.

"See, Ben, we do check leads out."

"Thank you," I said sincerely. "Now there's one more lead you better check out."

"Oh? What's that?"

"You have to test the blood on Emily's wall for HIV."

"Nobody doubts that Emily was infected."

"Not Emily's!" I said. "The blood streak that you think is mine."

"You don't have HIV, do you?"

"Exactly. But I have reason to believe that my brother Aaron might."

"That's not necessary, Ben."

"It is!" I snapped. "If that blood is HIV-positive then you'll know for sure it came from Aaron and not me."

"It's not Aaron's blood," she said with quiet certainty.

"You can't know that without testing it."

"Yes, I can."

"How?"

"We found Aaron."

I froze in midbreath. "Where? *When?*"

"A few days ago, though we only heard confirmation this morning."

My stomach fell. My hands began to tremble. "Confirmation?" I croaked.

"Off a trail at Mount Rainier, a hiker and his dog found a human bone. From there, it was easy to find the shallow grave in the woods. With DNA and dental records, the lab established beyond a doubt that the remains belong to your brother."

A wave of nausea ripped through me. I gagged back lunch. "*Aaron . . .*"

"The forensics experts say that the remains date back at least eighteen months but probably longer, which makes sense considering we found his burned-out car over two years ago."

The sky spun. I gripped the edges of the booth to support myself.

"Ben," Helen said gently. "It's time to come in."

CHAPTER
32

I have little recollection of the drive back to the hotel. Aside from telling Alex that the Seattle P.D. had found Aaron's body, I don't think I said another word.

The shock lasted less than an hour. Sitting in the chair in the corner of the hotel room, I missed the numbness as soon as it dissipated. The combined senses of loss and hopelessness were as smothering as a log across my chest. I eyed the window with a half a view to leaping from it.

Alex sat on the bed, respecting my silence. Staring into her understanding eyes, I realized I was going to miss her more than anything else once the police caught up with me. "My dad doesn't recognize me anymore," I finally said.

Alex frowned. "Pardon?"

"My mom and my brother are dead," I muttered. "The only family I have is my dad, and his brain is so pickled from alcohol abuse that he doesn't recognize me anymore."

Alex swallowed. "Ben, I'm so sorry."

"I went through this already," I said dropping my gaze to the carpet. "I mourned Aaron's death once. I had accepted it. And then after Emily died, I convinced myself that maybe it wasn't so. That somehow, Aaron had made a Houdini-like escape."

"Ben . . ."

I laughed bitterly. "Even more pathetic, I deluded myself into thinking that somehow my brother—the addict—was going to ride into town and rescue me at the very last moment. One big happy Dafoe twins' reunion."

Alex rose to her feet. "Ben!" she said more forcefully.

"Helen is right. It is time to turn myself in."

Alex stepped toward me. She knelt down and brought her head so close that our faces were only inches apart. "Did you kill Emily?"

"What does it matter?"

"Did you?" she snapped.

I shook my head. "No," I whispered.

She grabbed me by my shoulders. "Then there must be another explanation." She shook me with surprising force. "And if we don't find it soon, you're going to rot in jail and Emily's killer will just walk away, scot-free."

Her words cut through my despair. Anger pushed away the shroud of defeat. I shrugged off Alex's hands and rose to my feet. "You're right," I said.

"They haven't found you yet. There is still time to figure this out."

"You think?"

"I know."

"And what if the answer is not what you want to hear?"

She tilted her head. "What does that mean?"

"I mean, what if Marcus is involved."

Alex's jaw dropped and her eyes widened. "*Marcus?*"

"He's a hematologist who owns a company that stores blood indefinitely."

"So?" she said, her eyes still wide as quarters. "Why would he have any reason to kill Emily?"

"They had an affair."

"They did, huh?" The shock left her face. I thought I glimpsed a trace of hurt in her eyes, but it was gone in a flash. "When was this?" she asked evenly.

I laid out what I knew of the relationship between Marcus and Emily. She accepted the news with more grace than I had. "She was hardly the only one when it came to Marcus," Alex said calmly. "It still doesn't give him a motive to kill her."

"Unlike the others, he had the means to pull it off. And maybe he had the same issue with HIV exposure that I thought Maglio had." I regretted the words the second they left my lips.

Alex stared at me blankly. "You think Marcus might have picked up HIV from her?"

"No! I just pulled that out of the air. I have no reason to think—"

"It's okay, Ben," she said, reaching up and resting a hand on my shoulder. "I got poked by a discarded needle in the ER two months ago. I was tested right after. I don't have HIV." She sighed heavily. "And I'm pretty sure I haven't been intimate with Marcus since."

"Alex, I was just brainstorming," I said apologetically. "I don't know what, if any, motive Marcus might have had. He just seems like an obvious choice with his training and access to blood storage."

Alex lifted her hand from my shoulder. "Ten years I've lived with him. I've learned that he's capable of far worse than I would have ever guessed." She shook her head. "But not this."

"Then who?"

"I don't know, but it seems to me the answer is somewhere in Seattle, not Vancouver. Don't you think it's time to go back?"

"Not quite yet, Alex."

"Why?"

"Malcolm Davies knows something. He out-and-out told me this morning that Aaron was dead. He implied he was killed by the same person who rigged the explosion at his lab." I nodded to myself. "Malcolm knows who did it, too."

"Even if he does *and* he is willing to tell you, there is nothing to indicate that Aaron's killer is also Emily's."

"My gut tells me they have to be linked." I pointed to her. "And what about the whisperer?"

Alex shrugged. "I am not following."

"He knew that Aaron was 'gone.' And he knew all the details of Emily's murder. So there is a link. And remember, his calls came from Canada, not Seattle."

"Yeah." She bit her lip. "I suppose."

"It has to be connected," I said. "And there's someone else in Vancouver who definitely knows more than he told me."

Alex frowned. "Who?"

I fought off a sneer. "The same son of a bitch who apparently had drinks with my brother a year after he was murdered."

"Drew Isaacs."

We headed out just after nine o'clock. We stopped at Malcolm Davies's ground floor apartment, but his lights were off and there was no answer at the intercom. We waited for close to an hour in front of his apartment building, but he never showed up.

Alex drove us directly from there to Club Vertical. After circling the block twice, we pulled into the lane behind the nightclub.

When I saw Alex reaching for the door, I said, "What are you doing?"

"Coming with you."

"I need you to stay here."

"Look, if this is about my safety—"

"Not at all," I said. "If Isaacs shows up, I don't know how it will go down. It could be that I'll need to leave in a hurry. What good does having both of us stuck inside do?"

She squinted defiantly for a moment but then her forehead smoothed. "Whatever."

I opened the passenger door and turned around to her before getting out. "Keep the doors locked with the key in the ignition at all times, okay?"

"Got it, Dad," she said with a forced smile.

I realized there was no rear entrance, so I hurried down the alley past a couple of Dumpsters and out to the street. I took a quick glance both ways before I turned left. At the intersection halfway down the block, I turned left again onto the street that led to Vertical's entrance.

The same steroid-enhanced bouncer eyeballed me without a hint of recognition but granted me entry with another nod. I walked the short hallway into the bar, feeling my pulse rise with each step. Inside, the club was more crowded than on the previous night. Ten or twelve people were on the dance floor. But with two quick surveys, I didn't spot Isaacs. I walked to the corner of the bar and staked out the same seat I'd grabbed the night before.

I didn't recognize the tall dark-haired waitress. For appearance's sake, I ordered a beer though I sensed that I couldn't afford to risk even a single drink tonight. As soon as the server walked away, I looked over to the entrance. Drew Isaacs had suddenly materialized in a long brown leather coat. He waved to one of the staff before his gaze drifted across the dance floor.

Our eyes locked. Without breaking the eye contact, I slowly rose to my feet.

Isaacs twirled and sprinted for the entrance.

I took off after him. Halfway across the dance floor, I slammed into a young man gyrating on the dance floor. I landed on top of him and rolled off.

"What's your problem, asshole?" he growled.

"Sorry, man." I scrambled to my feet and ran for the door.

I burst onto the street just in time to catch sight of the hem of Isaacs's jacket rounding the corner to my right. Ignoring the yell of the bouncer, I sprinted after.

I turned the corner, but Isaacs had already disappeared. Paralyzed with indecision, I wondered which way he'd gone. Then I heard a series of honks from the lane.

Alex! She must have seen him.

I sprinted up the street to the lane's entrance. I didn't see Isaacs, but the headlights of Alex's car flashed at me. I ran toward them. As I passed the first Dumpster, I was suddenly hurled to the pavement. The pain shot through my shoulder like a thunderclap. I rolled over just in time to see the wooden club smash into my chest, knocking every molecule of air out of me.

Breathless, I slithered to my left and Isaacs just missed me with the next swing of his club.

Gasping for air, I shot out my hand and caught his wrist in midswing. I grabbed it with the other hand and grappled for the weapon. I'd almost freed it from his fingers when his boot slammed into the other side of my chest. I yelped and lost grip of the club as he yanked it loose from me.

Helplessly, I gaped at the hovering figure of Drew Isaacs outlined by the glow of the headlights. "You should have left it alone," he grunted.

He raised the heavy club above his head. I brought my hands up to my face, to protect my face and to shade my eyes from the blinding high beams that suddenly hit us.

Alex laid on her horn as she brought the car to a screeching halt a few feet behind Isaacs.

He hesitated a second, then dropped his arm and raced past the car in the opposite direction, heading for the far end of the lane.

I lay on the ground, fighting to breathe as Alex ran out of her car and crouched beside me. "Ben! Are you okay?"

"Isaacs!" I panted. "We have to . . . get him."

I struggled to rise, but Alex gently pushed me back to the ground. "Later! For God's sake, Ben, you're not moving until I've cleared your cervical spine and chest."

Alex's hands expertly palpated my neck. I felt no pain along my spine. When her thumb pressed into the right side of my chest, I heard the grinding sound of cracked ribs moving against each other. The pain ripped through me as if Alex had taken a swing with the same club.

"There's no time," I gasped. "Help me up, Alex. I have to find Isaacs!"

CHAPTER
33

Loading myself into the car, the searing pain in my chest almost brought tears to my eyes. Each barely perceptible gearshift change or slight bump delivered another jolt of pain, but breathing was even worse. I couldn't understand why I felt so winded minutes after taking the beating. I had to breathe in rapid, shallow gasps because anything more felt like a knife sticking out of the right side of my chest.

Alex turned to me with concern. "Ben?"

Suddenly, the symptoms clicked in my brain and I made the diagnosis. "Alex, I think a broken rib might have collapsed my lung on the right."

"A traumatic pneumothorax?" Alex said. "I'm taking you to the ER."

"No, Alex!"

"If this develops into a tension pneumothorax . . ." She didn't need to finish her warning. Without treatment, I would most likely die from a tension pneumothorax—the rarer form of collapsed lung where air leaks out of the lung with every exhalation but not back in with inhalation, forming a deadly one-way valve.

"If you take me to the ER . . . I'm as good as done."

"What choice do we have?"

"Call Joe Janacek," I panted.

"He's a family doctor," she said. "What can he do for this?"

"Get supplies from the hospital," I said in the longest sentence I could squeeze out in one breath. "You can decompress my lung."

"Me?" she said.

"Or hold a mirror up." I laughed, and regretted it immediately. "And I'll do it myself."

"This is beyond craziness," Alex said, but she reached for her cell phone in her glove box.

The operator for Joe's clinic patched her through to his house. Alex gave Joe a quick rundown on what had happened. "Joe, I need supplies from the hospital," she said. "A chest tube kit and a Heimlich valve."

He must have agreed, because her next words were: "Thanks, Joe. We're in suite 2905 at the Sheraton."

By the time we reached the parking lot, my breathing had worsened. I tried to hide it from Alex, but she was too astute not to notice my panting. Pain aside, each step toward the elevator felt the same as a sprint up the steepest of hills on my bike.

"Ben, are you sure?" she asked. "There's a hospital across the street."

"I'm okay. Just need to lie down." I reached for the wall by the elevator for support. I was seeing stars and my legs felt as if they would buckle at any moment. I knew the lightheadedness was proof of an evolving tension pneumothorax, but I kept it to myself and held on to the elevator wall.

By the time the elevator doors opened, I was so air-hungry that the pain had receded and a warm swimming feeling replaced it. I had to lean on Alex as I stumbled my way down the hallway to the room.

Alex fumbled with the key at the door while I leaned against the wall. I couldn't hold myself up and ended up sliding to the floor. The door opened, and Alex turned to me. "Come on, Ben, let's get you into the bed." Her voice echoed as if heard through a megaphone.

She knelt beside me, leaned me forward, and tucked an arm underneath each armpit. Despite our size mismatch, she was able to hoist me to my feet, while I focused every shred of energy on getting air to my lungs.

She dragged me to the bed. I collapsed on top of the covers. After rolling me onto my back, she stood over me and felt the pulse at my neck. A halo of light outlined her, as my visual field began to tunnel. Unable to speak a word, I merely stared vacantly at her angelic-looking form.

"Ben?" she pleaded in her underwater voice. "Your pulse is so thready. Your blood pressure must be collapsing. I can't wait for Joe. I have a needle and syringe in my bag. Just hang on a few more seconds."

She let go of my wrist, and I felt the world begin to drift away like a departing ship.

The room darkened.

I heard a faint ruffled, ripping noise and thought I saw her tearing my shirt with a knife. Then I had a fuzzy vision of Alex bringing a syringe to my chest. At that moment, the room went pitch black.

I have no idea how much time passed, but I felt Alex's soft fingers at my neck and heard her welcome voice before I could see her. "Ben, talk to me."

I opened my eyes to see Alex standing over me with the same focus etched on her brow. "Alex," I said, surprised I could talk.

"How's the breathing?"

"Not normal, but easier."

I heard a hissing noise nearby and looked down to see a sixteen-gauge needle buried to its hub in my right chest a few inches above my nipple. I understood immediately. Alex had stuck the needle into my chest—a procedure called needle thoracostomy—to convert the tension pneumothorax into the regular kind. I knew she hadn't fixed the air leak, but she had converted the one-way valve in my chest into a two-way valve. And by doing so, she had decompressed my lung and saved my life.

A firm knock at the door drew our attention. Alex hopped to her feet. "Who is it?" she asked at the door.

"A very tired, very old doctor," Jozef Janacek replied, and Alex opened the door.

Carrying a plastic bag in one hand and a black doctor's satchel in the other, Joe barged past Alex and hurried over to where I lay. He squinted at the needle in my chest. Without a word, he laid the bags on the floor and pulled a stethoscope out of the black one. He leaned forward and listened to my chest as he felt my pulse at the wrist. Pulling the nubs out of his ear, he turned to Alex. "Tension pneumothorax?"

"Yes," Alex said. "I decompressed him temporarily but he needs a chest tube now."

Joe lifted the white plastic bag off the floor. "This isn't cat food and toilet paper," he said, passing it to Alex.

She laid the bag on the bed and pulled the items out one at a time, sorting them beside me.

Joe turned to me with a concerned smile. "You didn't try to blow up a tank, did you?"

I laughed and winced at the same time as the sharp end of the needle dug into my lung.

"What happened?" he asked.

Despite the pain and shortness of breath, I was able to speak easily now. While Alex silently organized her equipment, I summarized the last two days for Joe. When I mentioned Marcus, Alex didn't comment or even look over at the procedural tray at my side. I finished with a description of Isaacs's ambush.

Joe shook his head. "And you still won't turn yourself in?"

I shook my head. "I'm so close. I can't let Isaacs slip away now. If I can find him again, he will lead me to Emily's killer. Might even be him."

Joe pointed at my upper body. "With a needle in your chest."

My resolve was unswerved. "Got to find him."

Alex spread open the plastic bag and put it on the floor at her feet for garbage. Then she looked at me. "Ready?"

"Absolutely."

"Roll on your left side," she instructed.

While Alex and Joe slipped their hands into sterile gloves, I rolled over and lifted my right arm over my head to allow her access to the area of my chest directly below my armpit.

With my head craned into the mattress, I could see most of what was going on, albeit sideways. I smelled the rubbing alcohol and felt the cool wetness below my arm as Alex swabbed the area with cleaning solution. She brought the syringe and needle with local anesthetic to the skin. The slight pinch and burn were nothing compared to what I'd experienced with the pneumothorax.

Curious rather than apprehensive, I studied the scalpel as the blade painlessly penetrated through my frozen skin. Then Joe passed Alex the slim plastic chest tube. She stuck a small tweezers-like clamp into my chest and spread the arms. Air whooshed out of my chest in a loud rush, as Alex seamlessly slid the tube into my chest cavity like feeding a rope into a well, and then attached the stopcock and Heimlich valve to the end of it. Joe sutured the tube in place, and Alex bandaged up the side of my chest.

As soon as they finished, I sat up. All three of us watched the plastic flapper flutter inside the Heimlich valve, proving that the tube was se-cured in the right spot and draining my chest cavity of any air accumu-lated outside the lung. Joe turned to Alex and clapped her on the shoulder. "Pretty slick technique." He grinned. "Maybe one day they'll let women become doctors, too."

My laugh reminded me that the chest tube hadn't cured the pain of my broken ribs.

Alex feigned a scowl. "Would you say that to Eliska?"

Joe chuckled. "I might be brave, but I'm not suicidal." He leaned over and dug in his bag until he found a pill bottle. He passed the bottle to me. "Here are a few hydromorphone painkillers for your chest."

Then Joe closed up his black satchel and stood to leave. "I think this glorified courier better go home now. If you have to reach me, call me directly at home." He recited his home phone number, then eyed me intently. "Do you need anything else before I go?"

I smiled. "You got any *pusinky* in that bag?"

He smiled back. "I save those for my best patients. The ones who don't bother me after hours." He turned to Alex with a fatherly nod. "I know he's an awful burden, but you take care of him, Dr. Lindquist. He might be worth the effort in the end."

She ran the back of her fingers softly along my cheek and over my beard. "I will. Thanks, Joe."

Alex walked Joe to the door and hugged him good-bye. After she closed the door, she climbed onto the left side of the bed and carefully nestled herself under my left arm. "What are we going to do, Ben?"

"I don't know," I said.

Minutes passed as we snuggled silently, lost in our own thoughts. The pain dampened, I felt myself drift toward sleep. I think I had just shut my eyes when I heard the knocks. In that void between wakefulness and sleep, I couldn't localize the source and half wondered if I was dreaming.

The next series of bangs yanked me straight into alertness. I looked over and Alex was already sitting up in the bed. She turned me to wide-eyed and mouthed the word, *Who?*

"Vancouver police," the bark came as if in response to her unspoken question. "Open the door!"

34

I sat up gingerly in the bed, amazed by my calmness. I had lost, though I suddenly realized that I'd never stood a chance. My mood verged on relief, aware the whole ordeal was finally inching to a close.

The pounding on the door grew even louder. "Vancouver police. This is your last warning."

I looked over to Alex with the most reassuring smile I could summon. "It's okay, Alex. Let them in."

She jumped off the bed and rushed to the door. "I'm coming," she called.

She opened the door. Two Vancouver policemen in body armor held their guns at eye level, trained on us. "Hands up and stand back from the door!" the taller one barked.

Alex raised her hands and back-pedaled toward the bed. Slowly, I brought my hands over my head aware of the ache in my chest as I did so. The two cops burst into the room with guns still drawn. Once they had a quick look through the hotel room and a glance into the bathroom, they lowered their weapons and the one with the moustache called over his shoulder, "We're clear."

A plainclothes officer walked into the room followed by Helen and Rick. The wiry white-haired detective, who looked otherwise not much older than me, spoke first. "Dr. Benjamin Dafoe?" He turned to Alex. "And Dr. Alex Lindquist, correct?"

"Yes," she said.

"I am Detective Scott Vance with the Vancouver Police Department," he said stiffly in his flat Canadian accent. "You may lower your arms providing you keep them where we can see them."

I lowered my hands to my lap, while Alex dropped hers to her side.

"I believe you know Sergeant Riddell and Detective Sutcliffe." Vance pointed from Helen to Rick and then turned back to us. "You are hereby under arrest, pending an extradition hearing on behalf of the United States government. Do you understand?"

We nodded in unison.

"Thanks, Detective Vance," Helen said. "Do you mind if we have a word with your prisoners?"

Vance held out a palm to us in a be-my-guest gesture.

Hands on her wide hips, Helen shook her head slowly. "Ben, it didn't have to be this difficult." She sounded like a disappointed aunt.

"How did you find us?" I asked.

Arms folded over his thousand-dollar sports jacket, Rick flashed me a smile so wide that my chest ached at the sight of his perfect teeth. He nodded to Alex. "You can thank Dr. Lindquist."

I turned to Alex who looked back at me with a bewildered shake of her head.

"She didn't know," Rick said affably. "We've suspected Dr. Lindquist was helping you for a while now. Probably relaying those calls from your cell phone, right?" When I didn't answer, Rick turned to Alex. "We've been tracing your cell phone for the past three or four days. Thank you for leading us to him."

Alex's head whipped over to face me. "Ben, I'm sorry."

I reached out and touched her arm. "You have nothing to be sorry for."

Rick clicked his tongue disapprovingly. "That remains to be seen. People who abet an accused murderer after the fact can still be charged with second-degree murder."

I felt my anger boiling, but before I could say a word Helen turned to her partner and said, "Rick, how about you dial it down a notch?"

Alex was unfazed by Rick's menacing words. "When do we get to see our lawyers?"

"As soon we have processed you at lockup," Vance replied.

Alex held out her hands, inviting handcuffs. "So process us."

Vance looked to Helen, who shrugged. Then he nodded to the uniformed officers. They approached us with their handcuffs in front of them.

I stood awkwardly from the bed, wobbly after my emergency surgery. Alex jumped beside me and slipped an arm under mine to support me. "Ben?"

"Just a little dizzy. I'm fine."

Moving closer, Helen chewed her lip and frowned. "What's wrong, Benjamin?"

I lifted up my loosely hanging shirt to expose the bandages and the tube protruding from my chest.

Helen did a double take. "What is that?"

"A chest tube," Alex said.

"What do you need that for?" she asked.

"To save his life," Alex said. "After someone shattered his ribs and collapsed his lung."

"Who?"

Alex put her hands on her hips and squinted intently at Helen. "One of the people who *was* actually involved in these murders," she snapped. "Drew Isaacs."

In handcuffs, I was taken across the street to St. Paul's Hospital. The veteran ER doctor who examined me was more than a little surprised to see me arrive with a tube already sticking out of my chest. Chest X-rays confirmed that Isaacs's blows had fractured two ribs on the right and one on the left, but with the aid of Alex's well-placed chest tube, my lung had fully reexpanded. Leaving the tube in, the physician discharged me with the same painkillers Joe had given me earlier.

In the back of the police cruiser, I rode past Joe's clinic on my way to the nearby Vancouver Pre-Trial Service Center (the city's warm and fuzzy euphemism for jail). After being registered in its computer system, I was traded Marcus's old clothes for a blue jumpsuit and then was taken to a cell in the infirmary area, where the jail's nurse could monitor me.

My compact cell had a single mattress that rested on a built-in shelf.

My chest pain had settled to a dull ache and my breathing was easier. I tried to reclaim my earlier detached calm, but as I paced the cell, my worry for Alex kept growing. Up until the moment they separated us in the hotel lobby, she had maintained her impenetrable poise, showing concern only for me. I knew, though, that she had to be racked with worry for Talie, not knowing how long they would keep her from her daughter. I felt even worse for confiding my suspicions about Marcus to her. Alone in a cell, a hundred miles and a national border away from Talie, she must have had doubts about the man looking after her child.

I was relieved to find out that I was allowed more than one phone call from lockup. After the attendant brought the phone to my cell, the first call I placed was to Joe Janacek's home. "I'm in jail," I told him.

"Alex already phoned me."

I tapped the phone, anxious for news. "How is she?"

"Fine. I like that one. She's tough." He sighed. "Listen, Ben, I have spoken to a criminal defense lawyer whom I know and trust. Murray Hlinka."

"Hlinka?" The laugh aggravated my chest pain. "Czech?"

"Of course," Joe said. "And good, too. Believe me, you can trust him."

"As long as he takes good care of Alex."

"He will."

After I hung up, I dialed my cousin. Even though it was after two A.M., Kyle sounded wide awake. "Ben, I'm sorry about Aaron," he said before I could explain my situation. "I'd started to half believe that maybe he was still alive, too. And then when I saw the news tonight, it felt kind of like losing him all over again."

"Yeah. I know."

"So where does that leave you now?"

"Prison."

"*Prison?* Where?"

I recapped the last two days, from Alex's arrival to my arrest.

"Wow," Kyle croaked. "Isaacs, that S.O.B.! He really did this to you?"

"Isaacs set me up from the get-go. He strung me along to make me think Aaron was alive, and then he ambushed me." I paused to let the flickers of rage die. "Before he took off, he said I should have 'left it alone.' Any idea what he meant by that?"

"Not really," Kyle said distantly. "But I should have warned you about Drew."

"You did."

"Not enough. I'd forgotten what a con man he was. Kind of guy who can disarm you with a smile and then stab you in the back when you turn. Aaron never trusted him. One of the reasons he moved up to Vancouver was to keep a closer eye on the operations and Drew."

"That would have been nice to know."

"I am sorry."

"Forget it. It wouldn't have changed what happened. Besides, I don't know about Aaron, but I doubt Isaacs could have killed Emily in Seattle while he set me up from Vancouver."

"He probably knows who did, though."

"If the cops even bother to look for him." I sighed. "Kyle, do you know a guy named Marcus Lindquist?"

"Can't place him."

"Alex's estranged husband. A hematologist who runs a company that stores umbilical cord blood."

"Whoa! You think this guy was storing Aaron's blood?"

"His or maybe mine." I rubbed my tired eyes. "I don't know how else to explain it."

"I'll give you this, cuz. With what you've dug up so far, you would make that woman from *Murder, She Wrote* proud." Then his tone darkened. "You're not going to crack this case from jail, though. You need to focus on getting out. Have you spoken to Michael Prince?"

"Not sure I trust him. I'm going talk to a Canadian lawyer first."

"Your choice, but Prince is the best," he said. "I'm coming up to Vancouver."

"There's no point, Kyle," I said. "I'll be back in Seattle sooner than later."

"Have it your way." He sighed. "Do you mind if I say a few prayers for you at least?"

"Mind?" I chuckled bitterly. "At this point, prayer might be all I have left."

CHAPTER

35

Despite my broken ribs and grim outlook, I slept heavily after my new lawyer, Murray Hlinka, finally left me alone at four A.M.

True to Joe's word, Hlinka seemed competent and compassionate. He explained that he could do little to prevent my extradition, though, ironically, the death penalty was my one "ace in the hole." (Not only is capital punishment banned in Canada, but apparently Canadians are loath to extradite anyone to a country where he or she might be executed.) If Washington state wasn't willing to forgo a shot at the death penalty, it might lead to a lengthy legal battle and a prolonged stay in Canada. "Here's hoping for the noose," I toasted with my Dixie cup of water.

At eleven the next morning, I was still lying on the mattress worrying about my predicament and Alex when Jane, the boyishly cute prison nurse, showed up at the cell door. "Dr. Dafoe, you have visitors."

I looked up into Jane's kind eyes. "Oh, who?"

She glanced at the clipboard in her hand. "Sergeant Riddell and Detective Sutcliffe."

Bracing my chest with a hand, I sat up and swung my legs over the side of the bed. "Can you give Sergeant Riddell a message?"

"Fire away."

"I'm only willing talk to her, alone."

She grinned. "I wonder how that's going to go over with the dapper detective."

Dapper. The word stuck in my head, reminding me how my YMCA neighbor had used the same word to describe the man who came looking for me. I wondered again if Rick's involvement went beyond his professional capacity.

Jane returned a minute later with two guards in tow. "Sergeant Riddell's okay with your stipulation." She smiled mischievously. "Detective Sutcliffe, not so much."

The two burly guards, one of whom was surprisingly soft-spoken, led me to the open visitation room where Helen was waiting on the other side of a desk in a bright blue pantsuit. There were no prisoners at any of the other desks, so aside from the guards posted at the room's corners, we were alone.

Helen smiled and dabbed at her lipstick with her little finger. "You never were too fond of Rick, huh?"

"How do you put up with him?"

"He's actually a good partner. Reliable. Affable. And one of the smartest people I've ever met." She chuckled and winked. "And a sharp dresser to boot. Even a post-menopausal old bat like me can do with a little eye candy now and again."

I nodded. "Guess you don't mind that he does a bit of investigating on his own."

Her face scrunched. "How so?"

"Apparently, he went to see both Alex Lindquist and Kyle Dafoe without you."

"He goes to the bank without me, too, sometimes." Helen heaved her shoulders in an exaggerated shrug. "It's a divide-and-conquer thing."

I thought I detected more concern than she was letting on, but I let it go. "Are you going to stay in Vancouver until they transfer me?"

She shook her head. "We're on our way back. I wanted a chance to chat before we left."

"Hoping I might confess?" I asked.

"It would sure make the paperwork easier." She sighed. "You're not going to, are you?"

I shook my head.

"I never get the open-and-shut cases."

I pointed at her. "Helen, tell me something. How did you know about my big fight with J.D. in Emily's apartment?"

She considered the question a moment and must have decided the answer was innocuous enough to share. "A tip."

"Anonymous, right?"

She nodded.

"And Aaron's"—I cleared my throat—"corpse?"

"As I told you, a hiker's dog found the, um, femur."

"No coincidence there, huh?" I said. "Two years after he died, a hiker's dog sniffs out his corpse at the same moment I'm trying to build my case."

She smiled helplessly. "I've never scheduled a random corpse discovery before."

"You know what I mean."

"I do." Helen brought her pinkie to her lip again, smoothing another granule of lipstick. "I'm having the lab run that test you suggested on the dried blood."

"A waste of money."

She grimaced. "Why?"

"I asked you to do it when I thought my brother might still be alive," I said. "I think Aaron contracted HIV shortly before he disappeared. All along I assumed the blood on Emily's wall would be his, and therefore HIV-positive. But if he's been dead all this time . . ."

Helen nodded. "My point, Ben, is that I'm keeping my word to you. I followed up on the blood streak. I followed up on Maglio and Emily. *And* I will continue to chase any lead that points to someone other than you, but so far . . ." She held up her palms. "All I've hit are dead ends."

"What about Drew Isaacs?"

"Vancouver P.D. is looking for him. For the time being, he's vanished."

"And Malcolm Davies?"

"Old Malcolm had very little to say." She rolled her eyes. "Apparently, you're not very memorable. He doesn't even recall ever meeting you."

"Everyone lies," I said despondently.

"Welcome to my world!" she chortled.

Filling with the now familiar sense of defeat, I hung my chin and stared at the desk in front of me.

"I still want to help, Ben." Helen reached over and grabbed my wrist. "But if you didn't kill Emily, please give me some plausible explanation of how your blood ended up on that wall."

"Don't know about plausible, but I do have a theory."

Helen patted her chest. "Try me."

"Umbilical cord blood storage."

"Pardon?"

I gave her the rundown on Marcus Lindquist and Hope Bank Cryogenics.

"And you're sure Emily and Marcus were getting a little on the side, huh?"

"According to Emily."

She squinted. "This facility could keep blood intact for a few years?"

"Pretty much forever. That's what the parents pay hundreds of thousands of dollars for."

Helen nodded. "Okay, I'll look into it." She rose to her feet and cocked an eyebrow. "Anything you want to tell me before I go?"

I showed a tired smile. "One, I didn't kill Emily. And two, thank you."

"We have to get you out of that jumpsuit. Blue is my color, not yours."

With that, she was gone.

I had another brief visit with my lawyer, but spent the rest of the day in my cell. Jane checked in on me every two hours. She assessed my chest tube, which continued to function well, and brought me painkillers on the one occasion I asked for them. The rest of the time I was on my own.

Even before my fugitive days, I'd grown accustomed to being alone, but perhaps because of the sense of confinement I felt lonelier now. Without the threat of capture hanging over me, I had more time to ruminate over Emily and Aaron. They had been the two most important people in my life. As I sat in my cell, their loss sank in deeper and harder than I'd expected. The grief was as raw as in the days immediately following Mom's death.

At dinnertime, I was staring uninterestedly at the barely touched macaroni on my tray when Jane showed up. "I'm going off shift, but you have another visitor."

I pushed the tray away. "I thought there was only one visiting time a day."

"He demanded to see you," she said. "Claims he's your lawyer."

"Prince?"

"That's him."

More out of curiosity than hope, I walked with the burly guards to the visitation room.

His long silver hair sweeping over the collar of his navy jacket, Michael Prince rose from the chair behind the desk. His citrus-tinged cologne reached me before his hand did. He released the handshake and sat down. "I'm sorry it's come to this, Benjamin, but at least now maybe I can start using my experience on your behalf."

I eased into my chair, wary as ever of the man across from me. "Problem is, Michael, your defense strategy was dug up by a nosy dog on Mount Rainier."

He broke into a soft laugh. "As you've been contending for quite some time, you don't need a live donor to rig a crime scene. The same killer who let Aaron bleed out in the trunk of his own car could have easily preserved a few test tubes of his blood."

"Not easily, but possibly."

"Semantics, Ben." Prince waved it away with his manicured hand. " 'Easily' sounds better than 'possibly' to a juror, but either establishes reasonable doubt."

"My local attorney tells me that it could be a long while before I'm extradited."

Prince shook his head gravely. "For an American citizen charged with a crime committed on American soil? You'll be in Seattle before the week is out. Sooner, probably."

"What about the death penalty issue?"

"Not for a respected doctor accused of a crime of passion. The state would never ask for it."

My stomach sank, but I felt somehow detached, as if watching someone else's life implode. "What am I supposed to do?"

"My advice? Do *not* fight the extradition," Prince said. "It's essentially a rubber-stamp decision. You're going to have choose your battles. This one isn't worth it." He tapped the desk with a finger, more impassioned than I'd ever seen him. "Once we get you to Seattle, I'll launch a very aggressive and *very* public campaign to have the charges dropped. If that fails, I'll push for early arraignment and a pretrial. Circumstantial evidence aside, the state's case is shaky. I want to hit them hard and sink their arguments before it even gets to trial."

I nodded along, swayed by his articulateness. "You honestly believe you can win at trial?"

He smiled. "I promise you I can."

"But will you?"

"Yes." The hesitation in his pale blue eyes lasted only a nanosecond, but was long enough to deflate my hope. "I have to go back to Seattle tonight, but you'll be seeing a lot of me once you're brought back." He stood to leave.

"Michael, you did know Aaron, didn't you?"

The question stopped him. "Yes."

"You were his lawyer, too?"

"I really shouldn't comment, Benjamin."

I held his gaze. "Please."

"Only once and for very briefly," he said. "A drug-related charge. It never went to trial."

"Why was that?"

"The evidence—marijuana and other drugs—was mishandled at the scene. The prosecution couldn't prove that it had not been tampered with."

I was going to leave it at that, but I suddenly had a glimmer of insight. "Who was the arresting officer?"

He thought a moment. "Detective Rick Sutcliffe."

CHAPTER
36

My next two days in jail crawled past. Though I didn't miss the constant sense of being hunted, the loss of autonomy wore on me. My fate was in everyone's hands but my own. And I had the growing worry that despite coming tantalizingly close to the truth, I might rot away in jail without ever knowing what happened to Emily or Aaron. The thought sickened me.

But the progress of my physical recovery surprised even me. On the third day of imprisonment, the prison doctor pulled the tube out of my chest. Afterward, I needed only aspirin to take the edge off the dull ache of the broken ribs. I could breathe and move (provided the motion wasn't impulsive) free of pain. And I knew I was well on the road to recovery when the longing for my bike resurfaced. My sense of confinement compounded my hunger to fly down a road or pound through a bike trail.

On the fourth day, the prison barber visited. With my hair trimmed short and beard shaved off, my reflection looked more familiar in the mirror, but I still shuddered at the image of me in the blue jumpsuit. The idea of growing old in that jumpsuit—or its Washington state equivalent—blackened my mood.

Shortly after the barber left, Murray Hlinka met me in the visitation room. I sat across from the middle-aged lawyer with the basset-hound eyes and mop of thick graying hair.

'Ben, there's little more I can do for you." Murray fidgeted in his seat. "The judge has signed the extradition papers."

"When do they take me?"

"Tomorrow morning."

Events had played out exactly as Prince had predicted, so I wasn't the least surprised, but that didn't lessen the crushing sense of finality.

Murray eyed me solemnly. "I am sorry, Ben."

I shrugged off my disappointment. "You did everything you could, Murray. What about Alex?"

His eyelids rose slightly. "Much better news. The state of Washington dropped the charges. She was released last night."

My mood brightened. "Good."

"There is one condition, though." He cleared his throat. "Alex is not allowed to visit you. She was very upset, but there was nothing I could do. The Canadian officials already escorted her onto her flight last night."

I'll never see her again. I rubbed my eyes, as I swallowed away the lump in my throat. "Are we allowed to e-mail or speak on the phone?"

Murray nodded. He rose to his feet and extended his hand to me. "Joe thinks you're going to come out of this okay, you know?" He smiled stiffly. "And Joe is hardly ever wrong."

I shook his hand. "Thanks, Murray."

Though I barely knew him, as I watched him go I felt like one more door had just slammed in my face.

Standing between Hank and Ali, the two likable pillars of muscle who had been my guards for the past three days, I trudged back to my cell in silence.

Inside, I lay on the mattress staring at the white ceiling. Wanting to give her time to catch up with her daughter and adjust to freedom, I tried to resist the urge to call Alex. My restraint didn't last more than an hour. Desperate to hear her voice, I asked Hank for the phone.

I reached her on her cell phone. "Ben!" Alex cried. "I wanted to come see you."

I warmed at the sound of her voice. "Murray told me."

"Are you okay?"

"You did a great job, Doctor. Chest tube is gone. Ribs are healing well."

"That's not what I mean."

"I'm okay, Alex," I said. "They're going to move me to Seattle tomorrow. Prince says it's for the best. He thinks he can poke holes in the state's case."

"Prince," she snorted. "Do you trust him?"

"Yes and no."

"What does that mean?"

"I'm sure he knows more than he's telling me. But I also believe he's the best defense attorney in King County and that he'll fight tooth and nail for me."

"He'd better!"

I chuckled. "How's Talie?"

"She's still with her father." Her voice faltered.

"What is it, Alex?"

"Marcus came to meet me at the airport last night. We went together for dinner. 'A family dinner,' he called it. He was already putting the pressure on."

The acid shot up my throat. "To win you back?"

"Yes," she said quietly. "Ben, I see Marcus for what he is, but Talie was so happy. For the first time in months, she seemed totally at ease."

I squeezed the receiver until my hand ached and my fingers went numb. *Marcus is a narcissist and a sociopath who might also be a double murderer! For God's sake don't let him near you or Talie!*

"Ben?" she prompted.

"I'm here," I said quietly.

"Say something."

I wanted to tell her that I loved her, but I couldn't imagine anything more selfish. "Listen, Alex, you have do what is right for Talie *and* you. I can't tell you what that is."

She sniffed. "God, I wish things were different . . ."

"Me, too."

I spent the rest of the day in my cell. My behavior bordered on catatonic. I didn't touch my food. And I ignored every attempt Jane and the guards made to engage me in conversation.

I felt the will to fight slipping away. And I didn't even mind seeing it go.

◎

The thoughts of Alex with Marcus tormented me into the late evening. By daybreak, I wasn't sure that I had slept a wink, but having done nothing in the past three days, I didn't feel tired. In fact, I didn't feel anything. I was numb as I sat on the bed waiting for the marshals who would come take me back to Seattle.

Hank and Ali arrived a few minutes after nine o'clock. Expecting to be loaded directly into a van or cruiser, I was surprised when they led me down the hall to the visitation room. I was equally amazed to see Helen, wearing an iridescent floral blouse, waiting for me at one of the tables.

"Are you taking me back to Seattle?" I asked even before I'd sat down.

She flashed a gaping smile. "If that's what you want."

I grunted. "I get a choice? I didn't realize the Washington state penal system was so accommodating."

Her smile stretched right across her face. "Oh, it's not accommodating at all."

"What's going on, Helen?"

"I never cancelled that test you told me was going to be a waste of money."

I was bewildered for a moment, but then I made the connection. "You're talking about the blood streak on Emily's wall?"

She nodded.

My heart leaped. "It *was* HIV-positive?"

"Apparently." She chuckled. "Providing you don't have HIV, our case against you has just crumpled like a cheap tent."

My mouth fell open. After a disoriented moment, a wave of euphoria washed over me. "I'm free, Helen?" I asked, not daring to raise my voice above a whisper.

"You will be."

CHAPTER
37

A certified lab technician drew my blood while Helen watched and two official witnesses notarized all the appropriate paperwork.

Word of my impending release spread rapidly. Minutes after the entourage left, Jane, Hank, and Ali showed up at my cell with a plate of prison-issue blueberry muffins they had converted into cupcakes with icing and candles. I laughed all the way through their out-of-tune rendition of "For He's a Jolly *Free* Fellow."

No one, myself included, doubted that my HIV test would come back negative. While I waited, I was allowed access to the phone. I decided that I would break the news to Alex in person, but I felt I owed Kyle a phone call. I tracked him down at home.

He was quiet for a moment, before uttering a soft laugh. "Remember your words, Ben? You said all you had left was prayer."

"I know." I didn't have the heart to tell him I never actually resorted to prayer.

"Sometimes things have a way of working out, huh? Even in your screwed-up family."

I laughed. "You're part of that family."

"Keep that to yourself," he said. "So what's next?"

"I'm going to come home."

"And play detective here?"

I hadn't really considered it before Kyle asked. "I don't know, Kyle, but this isn't over yet."

"You are a stubborn S.O.B., aren't you?" he said with a sigh.

"Thanks for everything, cuz."

"I didn't do much," he said. "But if you really want to thank me, maybe one day you'll come check out my church and meet the big hitter I tried to bring in on your behalf."

I hung up the phone still considering Kyle's comments. Maybe I was pathologically stubborn, but there was no way I could walk away from murders of two of the most important people in my life simply because I was cleared of suspicion.

At 3:05 P.M., I heard the official news, unofficially, through Jane. My HIV test had come back negative. A half hour later, I shook hands with the director of the jail and walked out of the modern facility onto the sunny Vancouver streets a free man.

But not an anonymous one.

A throng of reporters, held back by a line of uniformed policemen, shouted questions to me while I followed Helen to an unmarked black police sedan. "How do you feel, Dr. Dafoe?" I heard one reporter call out through the noise.

I turned and smiled at the reporters and cameraman, reveling in the freedom of not having to hide my face from each pair of eyes. "Relieved!" I ducked my head under the edge of the car's roof and slid into the seat beside Helen.

On the way to the airport, I insisted that the driver stop by the East Hastings Clinic. The others waited in the car while I walked inside and up to the reception desk. In the same white uniform as always, Edith viewed me as indifferently as ever. "Ah, Dr. Dafoe," she said, using the name without any indication I'd ever gone by anything else. "I suppose you want me to get Dr. Janacek for you."

I couldn't help smiling. I was really beginning to admire the woman. "Don't want to put you out, Edith. I'll find him myself."

I walked into his back office to find Joe in his pressed snow-white lab coat sitting behind a stack of charts. He looked up at me with a slight grin. "What did I tell you? All you needed was a good Czech lawyer."

He rose to meet me. I stepped over and gave him a hug. 'Murray was great, but what I really needed was a good Czech friend. Thank you, Joe."

Looking slightly embarrassed, he shrugged. "Eliska will be happy. Of course, she didn't have to work with you." He pursed his lips. "I don't suppose Dr. Benjamin Dafoe has a Canadian license?"

"No," I said, honored by the implication. "I might have to get one, though."

"When are you leaving?"

"Now."

"Going back to life in the ER, are you?"

I nodded.

"And to Alex?"

"I'm not so sure about that."

"Do you want my advice?" he asked, but he didn't wait for my answer. "You ought to marry her, Ben."

"She already is married."

He shook his head and chuckled. "Hungarian or not, you are surprisingly short-sighted."

I sat beside Helen on the half-hour flight from Vancouver to Seattle. I was staring out the window at the birdlike cloud formation below us when Helen tapped my shoulder. I turned to her. She raised the safety instruction pamphlet in her hand. "I've read this three times, but if we drop ten thousand feet into the water, I doubt I'll remember which string to pull or the right valve to blow into on the life jacket. So if you see me flailing in the surf, lend a hand, will you?"

I rolled my eyes.

Her smile faded. "Ben, when do you think your brother turned HIV-positive?"

"I'd guess three or four months before he died. Six at the most."

"So that streak of Aaron's blood on Emily's wall would have been collected anywhere from twenty-six to thirty-two months before she was killed?"

"Sounds right."

She grimaced. "It's not easy to store blood for that long, is it?"

"For four months, you just need a fridge. Anything longer requires sophisticated lab equipment and freezers."

"Like they have at Hope Bank Cryogenics?"

"Yeah."

Deep in thought, the skin wrinkled around her eyes. "Okay, let's say Marcus Lindquist had the means, maybe even the motive to do it."

I sat up straighter in my seat. "Yes, let's."

"Who plans two and a half years in advance to frame someone for murder?"

The same thought had gnawed at me. "Maybe he hadn't planned to when he originally stored Aaron's blood."

"Then why did he store it?"

"Maybe he stores lots of people's blood for research or other purposes. Hell, maybe he has some kind of blood fetish, like those vampire cults."

Helen arched an eyebrow at me.

I knew how lame it sounded. "You have a better idea?" I asked.

"No. And that's the problem." She looked up at the bulkhead, exasperated. "What makes me a decent Homicide detective is that most times I can appreciate the killer's inner logic. I can see the upside from the perp's point of view. Even with the sick and twisted sexual predators or serial killers, I can see what's in it for the killer. Not this time." She shook her head so hard that her bead necklace shook. "It never made sense for you to have killed Emily. And it doesn't make much more sense for Marcus Lindquist or anyone else on our list."

I wasn't ready to let Marcus slide that easily. Glancing out the window, I noticed that the clouds were closer as we began our descent. "What about your partner?"

"Rick? I don't think he has any better idea than I do."

I looked back at Helen. "Do you trust him?"

"Yeah."

"What about the investigating he was doing behind your back?"

"He was following up on hunches. One of them—tailing Dr. Alex—led us to you."

"Did you know that when Rick worked in Narcotics, he once busted my brother?"

Her expression remained placid. "Go on."

After I told her about the drug bust and tampered evidence, she simply shrugged. "I knew he had a case go bad before he switched from Narcotics to Homicide. Guess that was it."

"Awfully big coincidence, don't you think?"

She grimaced. "Are you suggesting Rick is mixed up in this?"

"It's possible."

"Anything is possible." Helen groaned. "It's not a question of what is possible. It's about what makes sense. And Rick's involvement doesn't make any sense."

"Revenge?"

"Revenge?" she echoed. I was pulling at straws, and Helen knew it. "Are you suggesting that for screwing up a drug bust, Rick got back at Aaron two years after he was already dead by killing Emily and framing you?"

"Listen, Helen." My voice was edgier than I'd intended, but a fire was building in my gut. "All I know is, someone murdered my former fiancée and deliberately left my brother's blood at the scene. Whoever it was had the resources and know-how to do it. What's more, he had reason to!"

Helen met my stare. "You leave this to the professionals, all right, Ben? I don't want you getting yourself killed or screwing up *my* investigation—not necessarily in that order—by nosing around where you don't belong. Understand?"

I nodded and turned away sullenly. Her warning was wasted on me. Despite how much I respected Helen, I knew the official investigation was no closer to nailing whoever killed Aaron and Emily.

And I wasn't about to stand back and let that person walk free.

CHAPTER

38

Any hope I had of avoiding a media zoo in Seattle was dashed as soon as I walked through the arrival gates at SeaTac Airport. As in Vancouver, the police were present to hold back the blitz of reporters and cameramen. Though Helen offered me an escape route, I decided to stay and make a statement, publicly thanking friends and family for their support and best wishes. I fielded a few questions and then turned to leave when a female reporter called out, "How do you feel now that it's all over, Dr. Dafoe?"

"It's not over." I sought her eyes out in the crowd. "Not even close."

I trooped away, catching up with Helen in front of the terminal. I got into her waiting car and she drove me home. As we turned onto my street, I was relieved to see that the press had not found my unlisted address. I was happy to arrive home without fanfare.

I dug the extra key out from under my front porch. The smell hit me even before I'd opened the door. Stepping around the piles of mail and newspaper that had accumulated in front of the mail slot, the rotting garbage stench got worse with every step nearer the kitchen. Breathing through my mouth, I pulled the trash bag full of decayed organic waste, including a few dark chicken bones, from under the sink and raced it out back. Even with windows open and air freshener generously sprayed, the stench lingered long afterward.

Ignoring the mail and my voicemail, I surveyed my house. From the rearranged furniture and stacks of paper in the office, I realized that the cops had gone through my house, but aside from the persistent smell, the place was otherwise intact. I checked the garage. Fresh from the shop, my mountain bike hung from my ceiling but the empty hook beside it reminded me of how I had had to abandon my road bike in Woodlawn Park.

I hopped into my Smart Car. I warmed the engine for a minute and then drove to Alex's house. Her car was in the driveway, but I noted that Marcus's Mercedes was nowhere to be seen. Though relieved that Marcus wasn't with Alex, I was almost disappointed to miss a chance to confront him, though the impulse was born from emotion, not reason.

Alex opened the front door. Barefoot in jeans and a pale green T-shirt, her face lit with a demure smile, she didn't seem the least surprised to see me. I stepped forward and wrapped my arms around her, squeezing her so tight that a jolt of pain ripped through my chest. She gently wriggled out of my grip. "Careful, Ben. Your chest."

"Screw my chest. Alex, I'm free!"

Her cheeks flushed with more color and her brown eyes sparkled. "I saw you on the news. It's amazing, Ben."

I leaned closer and kissed her on the mouth. Her lips met mine softly, but after a moment, she pulled her face away and stepped back.

"Alex?"

Her gazed drifted from mine. "I'm just a little overwhelmed, you know?"

"Sure." I mustered a reassuring smile to cover my confusion.

She grabbed me by the hand and pulled me to the kitchen. "Will you have tea with me?"

Cups in hand, we headed into her living room. I sat on the couch. Alex sat down beside me facing sideways, her legs bent at the knees and her bare toes touching my leg.

"Did you ever doubt I'd go free, Alex?"

"I never doubted your innocence." She swallowed. "But at times I wondered if you were ever going to clear your name."

"Me, too." I reached over and touched her foot. "Without your help, I wouldn't have."

She sipped her tea without comment.

"Alex, what I went through, when I thought I was going to lose everything . . . it made me realize what's most important in my life. And *who* is."

"Ben, maybe we shouldn't have this conversation now," she said without making eye contact.

I let go of her foot and stared into my cup. "Is it Marcus?"

"No. It's Talie."

I swallowed the lump in my throat.

"Ben, you should have seen how excited she was last night when we were all together. She told me that she doesn't want to live in two homes. She doesn't want to have to spend a week at a time away from her mom or her dad." Alex's lip quivered. "It broke my heart to see how she cried when we parted out front of the restaurant. It's not fair to put her through this."

"Is it fair to you to do otherwise?" I asked hoarsely.

"I've put up with Marcus for ten years. He may be a shitty husband at times, but he's a good father. And whatever your suspicions are, he's not a killer, Ben. I know it. The same way I knew it of you." She reached up and touched me gently on my cheek. "Can I really let my daughter be torn apart for the sake of my happiness?"

I didn't know what to say, so I just sipped my tea and stared straight ahead.

Alex put the cup down on the coffee table and sat up straighter. She leaned forward until her head touched my shoulder. I heard the sound of her soft sniffles, and I knew she was crying. "Ben, I love you," she said. "I've been in love with you for a long time."

I turned to look at her. I lifted her chin off my shoulder with a hand. Gazing into those endless brown eyes, I would have done anything for her. Even walk away.

I kissed her on the cheek and let my face linger long enough to drink in her sweet scent. Then I pulled back and stood up from the couch. "I understand, Alex."

"Really?" She chuckled, wiping her eyes. "Because I don't."

She walked me to the door. At the door, she stood on her tiptoes and pressed her warm lips into mine for one long sensual moment. "Everything has happened so quickly. Give me a little time to sort it out, okay?"

"Sounds reasonable." Though it sounded anything but.

Heavy-hearted, I trudged out to my car. The full moon above me struck me as oddly poignant as I loaded myself into the compact vehicle and pulled out into the street.

While I was stopped at the first four-way intersection, I was still ruminating on recent events when a pwair of bluish-tinted xenon headlights came skidding to a halt behind me. I drove past the intersection with little thought to the car, until it began to tailgate me.

Assuming the car was full of hopped-up teenagers, I pulled to the shoulder of the road to let it pass. The car didn't pass. It rolled up right behind me and nudged into my bumper with a slight thud.

What the hell?

I looked in the rearview mirror, but I couldn't make out much in the darkness, except for the shadowy figure of a sole occupant. I turned to look over my shoulder just as the blinding flash of the car's high beams hit me. Squinting through the brightness, I saw the car reverse a few feet and then fly forward slamming into my bumper with enough force to whip my head toward the steering wheel.

It's him!

My heart leapt into my mouth. I punched the accelerator, generating an angry whirring noise and screeching the tires into action.

Chest aching and palms sweating, I rocketed down the road as fast as the little car would accelerate. At the bottom of the street, I took a hard left and my car leaned to the right.

Realizing I couldn't outrun the car behind me, I zipped down side streets, taking as many quick turns as possible. But with each turn, the eerie blue headlights burned in my rearview mirror and lit up the interior of my car.

Temples pounding, I spun onto Thirty-ninth Street and, at the last second, took a right on West Fulton.

For the first time in minutes, I didn't see the glow of the headlights. My pursuer had missed the turn! My breathing slowed and the anxiety quelled.

Ahead of me, I suddenly saw that the road ended in a cul-de-sac.

I slammed on the brakes. I jerked the gearshift into reverse, just as the blue-tinged headlights flooded my car again, boxing me in.

Trapped, I considered hopping out and running, but with broken ribs, I knew I wouldn't get far.

Frantically, I scanned the inside of my car, looking for anything that might serve as a weapon. Then I remembered the bike chain. I reached behind the passenger seat, groping at the small space until my fingers touched a hard metal link. I grabbed the chain and stuffed as much of it as I could under my right sleeve and before I closed my fist over the remaining links.

The car idled around ten feet behind mine. I knew that he might ram me again at any moment. I suspected his car could crush my tiny Smart Car like a tin can. I took two deep breaths and then reached for the door handle. I stepped out of the car gingerly, dangling my chain-concealing right arm by my side.

For several seconds the black sedan continued to idle with its headlights fixed on me. Then the driver's door opened slowly. A foot and a leg appeared. Then the man languidly rose from behind the car door. He closed the door and turned to me.

With the headlights in my eyes, I couldn't make out his face. But as he lifted his arm up, I had no trouble recognizing the long blade in his hand.

My hand tensed involuntarily around the end of the bike chain.

"Ben, I've been looking for you," he said.

I recognized the voice immediately.

CHAPTER
39

"You son of a bitch!" I spat.

"Me?" Marcus took three steps closer, holding the knife up.

I was able to make out his dark features. His upper lip was curled, and his eyes narrowed to slits. "*Me?*" he growled again. "I warned you, didn't I?"

I stood my ground. "When?"

"At that lame party," he hissed. "I warned you to stay away from Alex!"

Fury overcame me. Despite the knife in his hand, I stepped toward him. *"Alex?"* I shouted. "This is about Alex?"

"This is about *my* family." He waved his knife menacingly. "You're not going to take them away from me. Even if I have to collapse your lungs for good."

I squeezed the chain so hard that the links dug into the skin of my palm. "You are one sick twisted bastard!" At that moment, I wanted to hurt him in any way possible. "Alex can't stand you. She has hung in there *only* because of Talie." I broke into a malicious grin. "She loves me."

He moved so quickly that I was taken by surprise. Uttering an incoherent scream, he lunged for me. Out of reflex, I dodged to my right. The blade whisked past, ripping my left sleeve above my elbow.

Just as he spun back, I dropped the chain into my hand and swung it as hard as I could, catching him under his left arm. It rapped across his chest with a rattling slap.

He howled and stumbled to his right but held on to the knife. Still yelping, he jabbed the knife wildly at my head but missed by at least six inches. I whipped the chain down on his outstretched arm. The blade clattered to the ground as his arm dropped to his side like a demolition ball.

He fell sideways, yanking the chain out of my hand. While he was still off balance, I drove my shoulder into him, knocking him backward to the ground. Landing on top of him, I felt his elbow dig into my chest. The breathless pain stunned me. I could hear my ribs crackling again. The pain overcame me. I tried to pin Marcus in a hold, but I couldn't take a single breath.

From the ground, Marcus elbowed me in the side of the head, but all I felt was the fire in my chest. Immobilized by pain, I couldn't stop Marcus from squirming free. Helplessly, I watched as he rose to his knees.

If I don't move now, I'm dead.

Ignoring the pain, I grabbed for the chain beside me. Panting for air, I saw Marcus's hand pat the ground for the knife. I crawled up to my feet and dove for him. I reached him just as his fingers wrapped around the knife's handle. I kicked his wrist as hard as I could, sending the blade clacking down the street and out of his reach.

Marcus stood up and spun to face me. I cocked my arm with the chain dangling behind me, ready to slash it across his miserable head. He brought his arms to his face to protect himself. "Don't, Ben," he moaned.

"Get on your knees," I gasped, lightheaded with pain and rage. I raised the chain higher and shook it threateningly.

Marcus dropped to his knees.

"Lie facedown."

"Ben . . . ," he pleaded, his face contorted with pain and fear.

"Now."

He dropped to the ground on his belly.

"Don't you move a fucking muscle." I sidestepped his prone body and then backed up to where the knife lay. I knelt down and scooped it up. I swapped hands, so that the knife was in my right and the chain in my left.

I was breathing more easily now, so I knew my lung hadn't deflated again. But I didn't care as I stormed back to Marcus, murder on my mind.

"Roll on your back!" I spat, and he did.

Wide-eyed, he gaped at me as I knelt down closer to him. Hand trembling, I brought the blade to his throat. I wondered if I could stop myself from slashing. "You killed Emily because of Alex?"

"*Killed Emily?*" His eyes went even wider. "*What?*"

I pressed the blade firmer, agonizingly tempted to saw through his neck. "Don't you dare lie to me now," I barked.

"I always liked Emily," he blurted. "I didn't kill her."

"But you were involved, weren't you?" I pushed his head back against the ground until it hit with a thud. "Weren't you?"

"Yes," he cried. "When I found out you were in Vancouver pretending to be my brother-in-law, I went up to find you. I wanted to lead the cops to you. I wanted you in jail and out of our lives. Forever."

"And the blood?"

"What blood?"

I heard the wail of sirens as I slammed his head into the ground again. He moaned in response. "Aaron's blood on Emily's wall. You preserved it for the killer, didn't you?"

"No!" His eyes were saucers. "Where would I get your brother's blood? I never even knew you had a brother."

I released the tension on the blade. From the panic in his voice and the bewilderment on his face, I knew. Marcus hadn't killed Emily or Aaron.

Then the police cruiser's flashing lights swept over us.

The woman in the neighboring house who had alerted 911 witnessed the whole altercation. She verified my story, and I was released within a few minutes of making a statement. I got a glimmer of satisfaction seeing Marcus hauled away in handcuffs.

Though my breathing was fine when I returned home, my chest throbbed as I stepped into my kitchen. I washed down two painkillers with three tall glasses of scotch. Sitting at the table bracing my chest with a hand, my exoneration now struck me as hollow consolation. Alex was unattainable. And I had missed the mark on the killer.

With the scotch and narcotics sloshing in my system, I staggered upstairs and collapsed on top of my bedspread.

I didn't wake until 9:45 the next morning, when the ringing phone roused me. My mouth tasted like seaweed, my chest ached, and my head pounded with the beginnings of a hangover. I rose carefully from the bed and reached the phone too late to answer it. I recognized the number on the call display as Kyle's.

I decided to talk to him in person. After a quick shower, I changed and walked out to my car. I stopped to assess the damage Marcus had inflicted. Except for a few deep grooves into the bumper, the resilient little vehicle seemed to be okay. In better shape than I was, I noted glumly.

I found parking a block from Kyle's apartment complex and buzzed his intercom. When he met me at the doorway to his apartment, I waved off his hug. "My ribs can't take it this morning."

Sitting across from him in his living room, I recognized that despite Kyle's cheeriness he looked even frailer than the last time I saw him. His shirt and jeans hung off him like he was a coat hanger. And he had a new crop of blisters encircling his right eye, which was red and slightly weepy.

"Kyle, are you okay?"

He studied me with an amused grin. "Ben, I haven't been okay since the day I was diagnosed with leukemia. But that last chest infection really knocked the stuffing out of me. Good news is, I'm on the mend again." He dismissed his health concerns with a wave of his hand. "Let's face it. After the crap I've pulled in my day, I'm more than lucky to be here at all. All in all, I got it pretty good."

I shook my head with genuine admiration. "I don't know how you stay so upbeat."

"I know it turns your stomach to hear this, Ben, but faith can be just as uplifting as a line of coke or a hit of Ecstasy." He winked, as if sensing my hangover. "And believe me, you feel better the next morning, too."

"Hallelujah." I smiled and rubbed my temples.

Kyle leaned forward in his seat. "Marcus Lindquist didn't kill them, huh?"

"No, but he came to close to killing me." I went on to tell him about our fight.

When I'd finished, Kyle whistled. "Man, Ben, you bring new meaning to the term 'going through the wringer.'"

"Not by choice."

"We've basically ruled out Philip Maglio, Marcus Lindquist, and you. Who does that leave?"

"Well, there's your buddy, Drew Isaacs." I shook my head. "And of course, Rick Sutcliffe."

"Rick Sutcliffe," Kyle echoed softly. "With all his expensive suits."

"Maybe one or both of them are involved, but I somehow get the feeling they're just the supporting cast, you know?"

Kyle pouted his lower lip as if to indicate "maybe, maybe not." Then he pointed at my left arm. "You're bleeding, Ben."

I looked down at my arm. Over the bicep, where Marcus had slashed my shirt, the scrape had opened and I was bleeding through my long-sleeved shirt. I hopped to my feet. "Do you have any Band-Aids?"

Kyle idly pointed to the bathroom behind him.

Inside the bathroom, I took off my shirt trying not to spread the blood. The cut from Marcus's blade had spontaneously opened and the far edge beaded with fresh blood.

Blood. It had caused me no end of grief.

I wet some toilet paper and dabbed at the edge of the cut, applying pressure for a minute without stemming the trickle. I opened up Kyle's medicine cabinet and dug around for the Band-Aids. I couldn't find them on the first two shelves, but on the third shelf I came across a series of prescription bottles.

Intrigued, I pulled down the bottles and read the labels. The first was cyclosporin, a drug used on organ transplant recipients to prevent rejection. In Kyle's case, it was his new bone marrow (borrowed from a live donor) that the cyclosporin was preventing his own immune system from attacking. The next pill bottle was cefuroxime, a potent antibiotic that I assumed he was using for his lung infection. The final bottle was nelfinavir. I did a double take as I read the label a second time. Nelfinavir is an antiviral drug used exclusively for treating HIV.

Kyle is HIV-positive?

I had no idea, but it made so much sense considering his drug-use history, recurrent infections, and declining health.

I looked down at my arm. The blood continued to trickle.

A dark thought hit me.

I went cold.

CHAPTER

40

"Ben, you don't look so hot," Kyle said when I emerged from the bathroom.

I waved it away. "It's nothing."

He chuckled. "You're not one of those doctors who is afraid of your own blood, are you?"

I am getting to be. "No, but my shirt is a mess."

"You want one of mine?" he offered.

"I don't think we're the same size anymore, Kyle."

"Guess not."

"I'd better go home and change."

Kyle walked me the door. "You sure you're okay, Ben? You look kind of pale."

"I'm fine. Everything is just catching up with me." I turned for the door. "Thanks for hearing me out, Kyle."

"Any time."

After leaving his condo, I headed straight to my car. As I pulled out into the street, I couldn't shake my growing suspicion. I considered finding Alex or Helen to talk over my wild theory, but as if guided, I found myself heading north out of downtown Seattle. I saw Lake Union and turned right onto Fairview Avenue. Two blocks later I pulled into the Ed Grayston Cancer Research Center, one of the world's pioneer research and treatment centers in the field of bone marrow transplants.

I had been there as a student and a visitor, but I still had to follow the signs inside the huge complex to find the entrance to the bone marrow donor clinic.

I had no game plan as I approached the buxom African-American woman who sat behind the reception desk. The nametag on her powder-blue uniform read ROWENA. She looked up from her computer with a welcoming smile.

Knowing that my name was still making headlines in Seattle, I remembered I still had Peter's license in my wallet. "Rowena, I'm Dr. Peter Horvath."

"Morning, Doctor."

"Sorry to bother you, but a patient of mine at St. Jude's Hospital who was treated at the Grayston Clinic is not doing well." I shook my head gravely. "Not well at all."

She rested her cheek against her palm. "I'm sorry to hear that."

"The thing is, I think his condition might be related to his bone marrow transplant. I suspect he might have acquired something in the donor's blood."

Her shoulders stiffened. "Yes . . ."

"I need to know the medical background of the bone marrow donor, but I don't know who he or she is."

Her eyes narrowed. "Did you ask your patient?"

"He's in a coma." I clenched my jaw in my gravest professional frown. "This might be his last chance."

She held both palms above her head and waved them frantically. "I'd like to help you, Dr. Horvath. I really would. But you know I can't. Patient confidentiality comes first. Besides, I could lose my job for showing you privileged information like that."

I laid a hand on the counter separating us. "Rowena, I would never ask if it weren't so important. We're literally talking about a life-and-death situation here."

"I just can't." She rose from her desk. "But I'll tell you what, Dr. Horvath . . . I'll get my manager. If anyone would do it, she might."

Rowena disappeared into the back room before I could get another word in. I paced in front of the counter as five long minutes passed.

Rowena eventually returned, followed by a shorter Asian woman, whose nametag read SHIRLEY.

Shirley was grinning as she approached, but halfway to me, her jaw dropped and her smile vanished. "Is this some kind of joke?" she asked.

"Excuse me?"

Shirley put her small hands on her hips. "Are you testing us, *Mr.* Dafoe?"

My pulse sped up. "I don't understand."

"We would never hand your confidential information away to someone who came in off the street asking for it," she snapped. "And I don't appreciate you waltzing in pretending to be a doctor."

I held out my palms in mock misunderstanding. "Shirley, you're losing me," I said, though she was beginning to make perfect sense.

"You'll have to do better than that." She wagged her finger at me. "I have a good memory, Mr. Aaron Dafoe. You were here two years ago for donor blood compatibility testing. I wouldn't forget that. I took the blood myself. It was for your cousin's bone marrow transplant, isn't that right?"

The room spun. I wanted to grip the desk.

Shirley's face clouded with concern. "Are you okay, Mr. Dafoe? Maybe you ought to speak to a doctor. Are you on any . . . er . . . medications?"

I turned and stumbled for the door. Despite the ache in my chest, I sprinted down the hall. As soon as I made it outside, the hangover and shock caught up to me. I vomited in the bushes by the front door.

Aaron donated his bone marrow to Kyle. All the pieces fell into place in one awful instant. A bone marrow recipient would have indistinguishable blood from the donor. Kyle had Aaron's blood in his veins.

Emily's crime scene made sudden brutal sense. It wasn't either of the Dafoe twins' blood on her wall. The blood was Kyle's! *But why?*

With my shirt stained and the acidic taste of vomit filling my mouth, I drove the short distance home overcome by emotion. Disbelief gave way to anger. Aaron had given Kyle another chance at life with his own bone marrow. Kyle repaid the gesture by killing him and implicating me in Emily's savage murder.

I knew I should call Helen immediately, but as the anger boiled over,

I hesitated. I couldn't stomach the thought of waiting for the plodding legal system to catch up with Kyle. I wasn't sure he would live long enough to face justice. I imagined taking matters into my own hands. I wanted to stare into Kyle's treacherous eyes right before I killed him.

I pulled into my driveway with my head filled with dark fantasies of revenge. But as I headed for the front door, my emotion gave way to reason. Reluctantly, I decided I would have to leave Kyle to Helen.

I opened my front door and staggered into the kitchen, my stomach flip-flopping. Feeling like I was about to throw up again, I raced for the bathroom.

Halfway there, I froze.

I wasn't alone.

CHAPTER

41

Kyle sat and stared at me from the chair in the far corner of the living room. A gun rested in his lap. His face was as placid as ever. "You figured it out, huh?"

My throat burned. Only the certainty that I would be dead long before I got my hands on him stopped me from charging. "How did you know?"

He raised the pill bottle in his hand. From ten feet away, I could see the red smudge on the label. "You left your blood on my bottle."

I sneered at him.

He smiled. "It really is thicker than water, isn't it, cuz?"

"Not for you."

Kyle's grin widened. "Oh, it is, Ben. That's what makes my revenge so sweet."

"*Revenge?*" I stepped closer. "Revenge for saving your life?"

His hand drifted languidly to the gun. Unhurried, he raised it in my direction. "Close enough, Ben."

I stopped halfway across the floor.

"Look at me, Ben." He tapped his chest with his free hand. "Do I look like someone whose life has been saved?"

"Aaron gave you his bone marrow!"

"His *tainted* marrow." Kyle's face went bluish, and he unleashed a harsh cough as if punctuating his point. "Some fucking doctor you are. You didn't even notice I'm dying, Ben. And not from the *curable* leukemia I had before." He patted his chest harder. "That's cancer. My lungs are full of Kaposi's sarcoma, thanks to the AIDS your brother gave me."

"Aaron didn't know he had HIV before your transplant. They would have tested him before bone marrow donation."

Kyle sighed. "And yet here I am, dying of AIDS."

"When a person first gets infected, there's a six- to eight-week window when he doesn't seroconvert, and will still test negative for HIV even though it's in his blood."

"Lucky me," he sang.

I scoured my brain for an idea of how to get to him before he could shoot me. "So basically you killed Aaron for trying to save your miserable life."

"It wasn't miserable back then, Ben," Kyle said pleasantly. "Besides, it wasn't just because of AIDS that I killed Aaron."

"What else?" I muttered through gritted teeth.

"Aaron fucked up my Whistler deal."

"*Your deal?* What about Philip Maglio?"

"I own Maglio!" The remark set off another spasm of coughs. He caught his breath, waving the gun at my head. "NorWesPac was nothing before me. I built an empire with Maglio as the front man. And while I'm fighting for my life in hospital, your brother threatens to bring down that empire because of some easy lay named Jenny and a few pathetic pangs of conscience."

I fought off the rising fury, desperate to buy time.

Kyle shook his head. "Your brother was always content to be a low-level pot smuggler, even though all the real money was in designer drugs. Then, after ruining Whistler, he tried to pull out of our business while I was most vulnerable." He held up a palm as if his rationale made perfect sense. "*That* was unforgivable."

I knew the only way to distract him was to keep him talking. "And Emily?" I said, surveying the room.

"Putting aside dear Emily's role in fucking up my Whistler deal . . ." Kyle grunted. "I knew Aaron didn't use needles. Since the three of you had such a creepily close relationship, when I heard Emily was HIV-positive, I just assumed she had infected Aaron in bed."

"They were never involved," I said hoarsely.

"Who knew his other bitch, Jenny, had AIDS? What are the chances?" He shrugged and smiled as if reminiscing over a humorous misunderstanding. "I guess that's why Emily stuck to her story even while J.D. held her and I was going at her with the knife."

It took every shred of my restraint not to lunge for him. "And me?"

"You, Ben." He shook his head slowly. His features darkened. "You are the reason I'm dying."

"*Me?*"

"If you hadn't been too fucking high and mighty to give a sample of your blood, then you would've been the perfect bone marrow donor for me. I could have had your clean blood instead of Aaron's crap."

"Remember?" My hand tightened into a fist. "I was in Boston taking an ultrasound course. By the time I got back, you had already found your match."

"Don't give me your bullshit. If you gave a rat's ass, you would've come back sooner." The gun trembled in his hand.

"Christ, you're so warped!"

"Warped? I think this all makes perfect sense, Benjamin," he whispered in the exact tone and cadence of my anonymous caller.

Though I knew it had to be him, my jaw still dropped as I connected the voice to the face. "How did you make those calls from Canada?"

"I didn't. Ever since we set up shop north of the border, I've kept a separate Vancouver-based cell phone. Tricky, huh? I'm calling you from downtown Seattle, and your caller ID reads Canada!"

"All of this just to set me up?"

"I wanted you to feel *my* panic and helplessness before you went down." His face relaxed into another smile. "I even wrote you a letter. After you were convicted and my bones cremated, I was planning to have it sent to you. It was too cryptic to have been much use to your lawyers, but you would've understood. The thought of you rotting in your cell knowing that I'd set you up has kept me warm at night."

"Then why did you help me flee Seattle?"

"To string it out. Give you the same false hope I was given. I knew I could turn you in at any moment. Besides, it made you look even more guilty when you fled." His laughter turned into another cough, and his face went dusky.

Next coughing fit and I make my move.

"The joke is you kept pulling phantom suspects out of thin air." He chuckled again. "I never set out to make you think Aaron was still alive. You can thank that retard, J.D.! Maglio's right-hand man. The idiot couldn't pull off the *one* simple task of getting rid of your brother's car after we dumped his body. Instead, J.D. abandons the car half-burned with a trunk full of Aaron's blood!" He shook his head. "I'm glad I put J.D. out of his misery. The fool didn't even notice I'd turned on him until after I'd cut open his windpipe." He shrugged. "I guess I should thank J.D., because it worked out better than I could've planned, sending you on one wild-goose chase after another."

"With Drew Isaacs's help?"

"Yeah." Kyle nodded. "That was brilliant, huh? Feeding into your delusion that Aaron was still alive." His smile faded. "Then Isaacs overplayed his hand. He should've never mentioned HIV. And he had no business attacking you. I told him to leave that for me." He sighed. "If it makes you feel any better, I think my Indo-Canadian partners have already taken care of him. I let them know Drew was cheating them for the past three years on the border tunnel."

I inched forward, biding my time for a sign of an impending coughing fit. "I take it you're not as religious as you made out?"

"What the fuck has God ever done for me, except give me one illness after another?" he snapped. "I never bought that bullshit the Bible-thumpers piled on me in hospital, but I did recognize a good cover story when I saw one."

"Cover?" I said, anxious to keep him talking.

"*God* gave me a way out." His eyes glowed. "As a 'convert,' the cops left me alone while I passed out pointless pamphlets and clean needles to the junkies. The joke is, I was passing the crap out to the people who were buying *my* drugs!"

"Would've made your parents proud, wouldn't it?"

"It would have been fucking brilliant. I could've walked away with tens of millions in a couple years." He raised the gun higher. "But thanks to the Dafoe twins, it was all for nothing."

I was near enough that I needed only one more good cough to pounce, but I sensed our conversation was winding down. Desperate, I reached for clichés. "You don't think you're going to get away with this now, do you? If so, you're even sicker than I thought."

"I don't have to get away with anything. Whether in jail or here, I'm too ill to enjoy my last few months." He cleared his throat. My leg muscles tightened, ready to spring. "But at least I will get the pleasure of putting a bullet in your head before I go."

He stood to his feet and steadied the gun. His face started to tighten again, and I saw the signs of the impending coughing fit.

Just as my toes flexed to move, a voice made me freeze. "Hello, Kyle."

Kyle broke into a welcoming grin. "Rick! Good to see you, buddy."

My stomach plummeted. Rick had to be Kyle's partner. *This is how it ends*, I thought.

"Drop the gun, Kyle," Rick said, surprising me.

I glanced to my right. I could see at the edge of the doorway Rick's head from the eyes up, his arm raised and his gun targeting Kyle.

"Drop the gun!" Rick repeated.

The room stilled. Kyle stared at Rick, his gun still pointed at my head.

"Last chance, Kyle," Rick said.

Kyle nodded slowly and his hand relaxed. "Okay, Rick, okay. I'm putting it down." His hands lowered slowly. Partway to the ground, the gun barrel suddenly jerked back up to eye level. I felt the breeze rush by my ear and then I heard the gunshot.

Two crisp blasts replied from beside me. Kyle clutched his chest and toppled backward, collapsing into the chair. Eyes still open, he stared at me for a long moment with his gun dangling from his hand. Then it fell to the ground with a quiet clatter.

CHAPTER

42

Kyle was still alive when I reached him. He was barely breathing, and small bubbles of blood formed at his lips. His glassy eyes opened a crack and found mine.

His lips curled into a partial smile. He coughed. A fine mist of blood sprayed from his mouth. "You've got nothing left but ghosts, Ben," he whispered.

His eyelids drooped further and the bubbles stopped forming.

Instinctively, I shot a hand to his neck. My fingers stuck to the tacky blood as they roamed his cool and clammy skin in search of a carotid pulse. I found none. "Rot in hell, Kyle," I muttered.

From the other side of the chair, Rick frowned. "Dead?"

"Yeah."

Nodding, he tucked his gun into the holster and then reached for his cell phone.

As I headed for the kitchen, I heard Rick say, "I'm at Ben's. We've got Kyle." He paused. "No. That won't be necessary."

I was scrubbing my hands at the sink when Rick walked into kitchen. "Drink?" I asked.

"Water, please."

I poured Rick a glass of water and then grabbed a beer from the fridge.

"I'd begun to suspect you were personally involved in all this," I said, too drained to be diplomatic.

"I am."

I took a long sip of beer. "How?"

"Before I left Narcotics, I spent the better part of a year working undercover to bring down your brother and Kyle's operation." He smiled. "I kind of liked Aaron, actually. Always had the feeling he was a victim of his habit. Not your cousin, though. Kyle was rotten through and through."

"What happened?"

"I nailed them red-handed with a ton of B.C. bud and almost as much coke and crystal meth. The takedown was textbook."

"But?"

His expression hardened. "Someone got to the evidence locker. Half the coke went missing. Your buddy, Michael Prince, had a field day! The charges were tossed. Not only that, but fifty thousand dollars showed up in an account with my name on it. Suddenly, I came under suspicion. The dirty cop who got away with it."

"Kyle!"

"No doubt," he muttered.

"That's why you ended up in Homicide?"

"Helen gave me a chance for a new start." His eyes narrowed. "But I never bought your cousin's born-again act. I knew I would get another shot at him." He drained the last of his water and held the glass out for a refill. "You mind?"

Hearing the faint hum of sirens in the background, I topped up his glass. "You seemed pretty convinced I was your killer."

"Yes and no. I always suspected Kyle, but you acted so damn guilty as the evidence mounted." He toasted me with his glass. "And just kept mounting. Almost too much, you know? Like that anonymous tip about your fight with Emily and J.D. And the sudden discovery of your brother's buried corpse. The whole thing began to feel orchestrated."

"And you thought of Kyle?"

Rick nodded. "I never stopped thinking of him, but I had nothing to pin it on him. After you were cleared of the charges in Vancouver, I knew in my bones that he was going to do something. I've been on his tail ever since. Waiting." He gestured to the living room. "I followed him here. And then when you pulled up, I came in after you."

"You were here all along?" I slammed my beer down on the table. "He could have put a bullet in my brain at any moment."

"Nah. He was itching to let you know exactly how he'd screwed you over." Rick broke into one of his fashion-model smiles. "Besides, I wasn't about to interrupt a confession like that."

"A confession like what?" Helen boomed as she trooped into the kitchen.

"Kyle's." Rick turned to his partner. "You'll never believe how he pulled it off."

"Try me."

While the EMS and CSI teams swarmed my living room, Rick outlined Kyle's M.O. and motive. I didn't say a word.

Helen eyed me. "The lab couldn't tell Aaron's blood apart from Kyle's, huh?"

I shook my head. "Kyle's saliva, sweat, and so on wouldn't resemble Aaron's, but after the bone marrow transplant his blood was produced by the same stem cells that made Aaron's. From a DNA point of view, their blood was a perfect match. And of course, Aaron and I had genetically identical bone marrows. So Kyle's blood matched mine, too."

"Except for the HIV," Helen pointed out.

"Yeah," I sighed. "Aaron must have been infected with HIV within days to weeks of giving the marrow donation. When it was too early to show up on his screening blood tests."

Helen shook her head. "I dunno. Maybe it will sink in later, but right now . . . I just don't miss Kyle that much." Beaming, she turned to Rick. "That tricky bastard. Our hunch wasn't that far off, huh?"

I gaped at Helen. "You thought it was him the whole time, too!"

Helen put her hand on my shoulder. "Let's say I never thought you masterminded these murders."

"No," I grunted. "You just thought I was Kyle's henchman?"

"I was never convinced you were involved." Helen freed my shoulder. "But Lord knows your cousin went to enough effort to make it look like you were. And we needed to find you to figure it out."

I shook my head.

"Besides, you do good work when you're on the lam." She broke into a hearty laugh. "We ought to make you our prime suspect in some of our other cold cases. Maybe while on the run you can dig up the real killers for us."

I laughed in spite of myself, but I didn't share Rick and Helen's celebratory spirit. I put my bottle down on the counter. "I need a little time to myself." I headed for the hallway, sorely tempted to march straight to my garage and hop on my mountain bike despite my broken ribs.

Helen's voice stopped me. "Ben, are you going to be okay?"

I turned back and mustered a smile. "In a while."

With the bedroom door locked, I sat on my bed and stared at the wall. The commotion from the CSI guys in the living room faded to a dull white noise that barely registered in my consciousness. Remembering the past weeks, I felt the cumulative weight of my life's losses bearing down on me.

Maybe all I do have left are ghosts. And Kyle was now one of them.

A knock from the door disrupted the thoughts. "Not now, Helen," I called out.

"It's me," Alex said.

Chest thudding, I rose from the bed and opened the door.

She stared at me with eyes that looked puffy from lack of sleep. "You okay?"

"Yeah." I smiled tentatively. "How did you hear?"

She swept back her hair. "Helen called. Said you could use a friend."

I swallowed. "I think so."

Alex stepped into the room, stopping inches from me. She reached out and grazed her warm fingers over my cheek. My chest thumped harder. Alex looked away sheepishly. "I heard what Marcus did to you, too."

I didn't say anything.

"I spoke to my attorney this morning," she said softly. "That stunt he pulled might not keep him in jail forever, but she thinks it will earn me sole custody of Talie."

The sudden glow warmed me. "Sole custody?"

She broke into a shy smile. "Don't suppose you are into women with emotional baggage?"

I laughed. "I've been known to carry a bit of my own from time to time."

She leaned forward and pressed her mouth into mine. Relief flooded over me as I met her lips, kissing her back hard and tasting the mint of her toothpaste.

Alex broke off the kiss long enough to ask, "Your ribs okay?"

"Perfect." Despite the ache in my chest, I couldn't hold her tightly enough against me. I wanted to lose myself in her.

Her lips skittered over my cheek. Her warm breath tickled my ear. "Ben," she whispered. "It's finally over."

"No, Alex." I laughed. "It's finally beginning."